UNDEAD SANCTUARY

STEEL CITY APOCALYPSE
BOOK 2

A.M. GEEVER

ALSO BY A.M. GEEVER

THE UNDEAD AGE
Love in an Undead Age, Book 1
Damage in an Undead Age, Book 2
Reckoning in an Undead Age, Book 3
Undead Age: The Complete Series, Books 1 - 3

STEEL CITY APOCALYPSE
Undead Menagerie, Book 1

Available at retailers everywhere, including direct from the author. Signed paperback copies are available at live events and from the A.M. Geever website.

For Rachel,

*The best indentured wingwoman
an author could ever hope for.*

AUTHOR'S NOTE

One of the places mentioned in this book is St. Marys, Pennsylvania, which is a real place. While it might look a typo, there's no apostrophe between the 'Y' and the 'S' in Marys.

City of St. Marys website: https://stmaryspa.gov/

CHAPTER 1
IMOGEN

For hours, imaginary scenarios percolated in Imogen's mind, each more horrible than the last. She'd had to put the phone away to stop herself reading the text over and over.

See you in 10 hours.

Her stomach clenched. The sensation of falling swallowed her up. Araminta had been on a plane. On a plane after curfews had been imposed in Edinburg and Glasgow in Scotland, and the major northern cities in England. People from those places might be on the same plane as her sister. People who'd been bitten, not understanding the implications. Had they started turning into zombies on the flight?

Her sister on a plane. She could only conjure three scenarios. The first was that everything with the flight had been fine. The plane arrived in America as scheduled—in New York City, one of the most densely populated cities in the world—just as all hell broke loose.

In the second, an infected person had been on the plane, turned, and the rest of the passengers had become zombies. Perhaps one or two people had survived, locked in a bathroom, but then what? How did you get out of a plane full of zombies? Exit doors still had to be opened and Araminta might not be near one. Even if her seat was in an exit row, the plane had to *land.* To get out of the plane, the inflatable emergency slide had to be engaged, didn't it? Failing that, you could jump, but the zombies would follow you right out the door. You might get away. More likely you'd break your leg or ankle. Chances of a successful escape in that scenario didn't seem likely.

In the third scenario, only the pilots survived, perhaps with some of the cabin crew if they'd let any of them into the cockpit. The locked cockpit offered the only real protection on a plane, but then they would land with a plane full of zombies. She didn't even know if the pilots could escape. Could you break a cockpit window? Was there an escape exit in an airplane cockpit? There must be, but it wouldn't help her sister. Assuming Araminta made it to New York without incident, then what? She might be running down the street this very moment with runners in pursuit, knowing she couldn't escape. Perhaps she'd found a hiding place but was alone with no one to help her. Maybe she hadn't eaten in days and was growing weaker, or maybe she'd already—

Stop it. Just stop.

She shifted in her seat. Pins and needles prickled her bum. Dust and road grime spotted the windows of the minibus, coloring the world with a brownish haze. Not that the world needed help, since the farther north they drove, the browner the landscape became. In Pittsburgh, the autumn leaves still painted the hills and valleys in vivid scarlet, orange, yellow, and salmon pink. The blaze of autumn leaves had already peaked here. The view wouldn't be improving.

"Why are we stopping?" Sandy muttered.

As soon as Sandy said it, the deceleration of the vehicle percolated through Imogen's brain. She sat up straighter. "Is something wrong?"

"Not that I can see," Sandy said. Imogen could see her straining higher from behind the steering wheel. "Maybe someone in the lead vehicle has to pee."

Clyde groaned, stretching his arms high over his head, then

glanced at his watch. "I sure could use a quick break. We've been on the road for almost ten hours."

"How long does it usually take to get to your friend's place?" Imogen asked. She'd already asked him countless times but couldn't seem to help herself. Maybe if she asked him enough, he'd say, 'Oh, it always took ten hours. We're doing great.'

Clyde said to Betty, "Three hours?"

She nodded. "About that."

"It's about time we stopped," Amy said.

Imogen's former boss, Amy—stressed out, exhausted, and scared, like everyone else—was the only one complaining. First, she had complained about the supplies taking up the last four rows of the minibus because she wasn't able to stretch out as much as she liked. Then she was hungry, and then the snacks were not up to par. She had whined about how long it was taking and critiqued everyone's driving but didn't want to drive herself. They were all so tired they'd given up telling Amy to stop complaining a solid two hours before she gave up the ghost and stopped whining.

Imogen bristled at the sound of her former boss' voice as it wormed its way into her ear but kept her irritation to herself. She couldn't imagine not saving someone who had been in Amy's situation when they'd fled the zoo. She wanted to not regret her decision, but if she'd known the price, would she still have done it? That she was even thinking along these lines disturbed her, but she couldn't help it. Losing her lynxes, and her complete failure to protect them, cut too deep.

The door of the minibus opened with a *whish*. Through the windshield Imogen could see the driver's side door of the truck in front of them open. Zach hopped down from the cab of Clyde's truck, moving stiffly from sitting so long. Imogen couldn't see the passenger side door but imagined Mike doing the same with more grace. His taller frame made it easier for him to manage the high truck cab.

The air outside of the minibus smelled fresh. Imogen took a

deep breath, feeling the chill in her throat. A hundred miles from Pittsburgh you could almost be fooled into thinking everything was fine. The rolling hills of Pennsylvania, dotted with farms and treed hillsides, looked as they always had. Cows and horses grazed in pastures. Several times she'd seen people walking into barns and houses or standing on the hilltops to peer down at them. Only their time on the turnpike reflected the changes they faced. The same day Imogen had encountered those first zombies on the bridge, the turnpike had been closed. The reason given was a slow chemical leak from a convoy of tanker trucks that had contaminated the roadway with toxic chemicals. Now, they knew it for the lie it was.

It made a certain sort of sense. Once people knew what was happening, they'd flee and spread the infection. The highways and interstates would be jammed with vehicles that would end up abandoned, which would quickly stymie any official rescue or containment efforts. The authorities had tried to do something, that was clear. The hulking forms of tan and green Army and National Guard trucks dotted the turnpike like forlorn mushrooms. Fire trucks, state police cruisers, and SWAT vans rounded out the assortment—all abandoned. They blocked the road every few miles, which was part of why the trip was taking so long. Some of the emergency vehicles had crashed, some not. There were some civilian vehicles, too, but not as many.

Where people had forced their way onto the turnpike, zombies wandered among the stopped cars. Everyone in the minibus had let those in the trucks deal with the runners first, since the trucks had a height advantage. When it was down to the slow zombies, Imogen, Sandy, and Clyde had helped, too. Mike's ability to hot-wire cars had come in handy more than once. They'd picked up some weapons and ammunition, too.

It was very American, Imogen thought, to think of guns as the first resort. Even gentle Betty was eager to get a gun. Imogen understood, but it still puzzled her, their conviction that a gun could solve their problems. What did they think they were going to do with them? Guns were too loud to use without attracting more zombies. Maybe if you had a sniper rifle and the skill to make a shot from half a mile away, but they had neither.

Imogen decided not to dwell on her puzzlement. She liked Americans. They were friendly, ready to welcome strangers at loose ends into their homes for holidays and family gatherings. Some were racist, others not. The former were disheartening, the latter reinforced her belief in humanity's fundamental impulse toward good rather than bad. She'd never understand Americans' love affair with guns. They were a tool for a killing—a very effective one—but to Imogen's mind they were the weapon of last resort.

Mike walked toward her, raising his hand to shade his eyes from the sinking sun. The angle was just right to get in his eyes no matter what. Betty, Sandy, and Clyde clambered from the minibus, followed by Amy.

"Is everything all right?" Imogen asked him.

"Yeah," he said. She saw him try not to wince when he looked at her—at her swollen and bruising face—and failed. "We're just switching off. Zach needed a break. You might want to go to the bathroom."

Imogen looked up and down the highway, her stomach beginning to churn. As if reading her mind, Clyde said, "Don't worry, hon. We'll keep watch. Why don't you gals go on the other side of the minibus?" He grinned. "We'll keep our backs turned."

Zach joined them, stretching his arms high over his head. "Everyone okay?" he asked, scanning the group.

Imogen knew he was really asking her. She nodded. "Just going to go to the toilet."

Once on the other side of the bus, Amy, bringing to mind Old Faithful—the geyser in Yellowstone National Park that had been erupting hourly for decades—started complaining. "Does anyone have tissues? I'm not air-drying."

"Like I carry them around in my pocket just for you," Imogen heard Sandy mutter under her breath, and smothered a giggle.

"I have some," Betty said, handing a few to Amy. Amy snatched the tissues from Betty's hand, as if Betty had been trying to steal them. She didn't thank her.

"When are we going to get there?" Amy whined when Imogen rejoined the group. "If it's going to be much longer, we should stop for the night. I can't take much more of this. It's exhausting."

Sandy gave Imogen a sidelong glance. "It must be all the complaining."

"We'll turn off the highway soon. It's five miles to the lodge from there," Clyde said. Then he added, brow furrowed and eyes unfocused as he thought, "Well, no. It's five miles to the park and then another couple miles to the lodge."

Amy groaned and opened her mouth.

"How does your friend have a house in a state park?" Sandy asked, cutting her off.

"It was there before the state owned it," Clyde said. "It's grandfathered in. He owns the building with a ninety-nine-year lease on the land."

"Who built it?"

"A group of teachers, in the nineteen twenties," Betty said. "All women, of course. Someone must have donated the land, but I don't know the details."

"We should get going," Mike said. "It'll be dark soon. If we've only got ten more miles to go, hopefully we won't have to drive in the dark for long."

The group fell silent, reluctance heavy in the air. Everyone was tired. Ten miles sounded like a hundred.

"Can't we stop for the night?" Amy said, her voice verging on a whine.

Jay said, "It would be nice to get some rest."

Imogen hadn't seen Jay approach. Mike crossed his arms and stared at Jay, his expression so cold an electric shiver skittled across the back of her neck. "It doesn't make sense to stop when we're this close. We'd have to find a safe place for the night, and by the time we do, we might as well have kept going."

Kevin nodded. "I know we're in the sticks, but we're going to run into zombies sooner or later. Let's keep going. It's getting dark, and being out here gives me the creeps."

"Fine," Amy huffed. "No one paid attention to anything I had to say before. I don't know why I thought you would now." She turned on her heel and stomped onto the minibus.

As people started returning to their vehicles, Zach sidled up to Imogen. "How's your face?"

She stopped herself from frowning just in time. "It hurts. I'd kill for some ice."

"Have you taken anything for it?"

She nodded. "Some ibuprofen. I'll take more soon. Maybe there will be some ice at the lodge."

Zach pursed his lips, looking at her hard from under furrowed brows. "What's wrong?"

A sudden longing for her sister welled up. If Araminta were here, all of this would be so much easier to bear. Tears pooled in Imogen's eyes. "I'm fine. I mean, I'm no worse than anyone else." She motioned to her face. "Apart from this… I'm just tired."

She was lying since she still had told no one about the text.

"We're all tired. Something else is bothering you."

Why did he have to be so perceptive? She sighed, giving up, and the tears welled up again. "I got a signal when we split up and Peter left for Bedford. There was a text from Araminta."

Zach's eyes widened. "Oh. When did she send it? Was she okay?"

Imogen swiped at the tears on her face. "She was at Heathrow, catching a flight here to see me."

Zach stared at her for a moment, looking astonished. "Oh, Imogen."

He pulled her close. She tried not to cry harder. Failed. She could hear concerned murmurs from the others. After a minute, she broke the embrace.

"Maybe she's—" Zach began, then stopped, scrubbing his face. "I don't know what to say… I'm sorry."

Imogen sniffed and wiped her nose on her sleeve. She felt relieved to have told him and grateful that he'd pressed her, but the hopelessness that swallowed her whole felt endless. She saw Mike and Sandy hovering by Clyde's truck, casting surreptitious glances their way.

"Something's in the road ahead."

Everyone turned to where Kevin, who had spoken, stood at the front of their makeshift caravan. Imogen's heart beat faster. Her hand moved to the knife on her belt. She and Zach hurried to catch up to Mike and Sandy, who'd already joined Kevin.

"Are they zombies?"

Kevin shrugged. "I can't tell."

Two figures stood in the road about a hundred feet away. The sky's dark-blue hues were giving way to the darker purples of twilight. The figures waved their arms over their heads, flagging them down. Imogen couldn't tell if they were men or women, or an adult and a child, just that one was bigger than the other and they wore heavy packs.

"We should leave," Amy said, joining them. Her curiosity must have won out over her need to pout in the minibus.

Imogen glanced at her, sure the horror she felt showed on her face.

"They're people," Mike said, sounding shocked.

"They could be dangerous," Amy persisted.

"What's wrong with you?" Sandy said. "If you were on the road, wouldn't you want someone to help you?"

"That's… well… that's different," Amy stammered. "I'm not dangerous."

"Just annoying as crap." Sandy dismissed Amy with a disgusted sneer. "Stay here. I'll go talk to them."

"I'm coming with you," Mike said. "The rest of you, wait here."

"I'm a police officer, Mike," Sandy said. "I know what I'm doing."

"Still coming," he said.

Mike fell in step with Sandy. As they closed the distance, Imogen could see Sandy's hand rested on the gun on her hip, but otherwise her posture was relaxed.

"Come on," Imogen said, giving Zach's hand a tug and pulling him along. She wasn't sure why she was ignoring Sandy's orders; she just was. "We should have brought a torch. Do you have one?"

Zach shook his head. Sandy wasn't using her torch, Imogen noticed, perhaps to avoid drawing attention to themselves? Imogen could hear the murmur of voices as she and Zach approached. They stopped about fifteen feet behind Mike and Sandy.

"—could really use a ride if you're willing," a man's voice said.

"We have our own food," the other person—a woman—said. "You won't have to share yours. Even if you just take us a little farther down the highway…"

Imogen's brow crinkled, memory tugging at her as the woman's voice trailed away. It sounded familiar.

"Have you been on foot the whole time?" Sandy said.

"No," the man said. "We had a car for a while. A couple of our friends were with us, but…"

When his voice trailed away, the woman said, "We won't be any trouble, I promise."

"Oh my God," Imogen said, her heart soaring. She didn't realize she'd spoken aloud until Sandy glanced back at her. "Bec? Is that you?"

The woman's body stilled. "Imogen?"

"Yes, it's me!"

Bright light bathed them from behind. A detached part of

Imogen's brain noted that someone must have turned on the truck's headlights. Bec's lightly tanned and freckled face was smudged with dirt. Her hair stuck close to her head, the light blond now several shades darker and dirty. When her eyes met Imogen's, she burst into tears. Imogen darted forward before Sandy's hand, still outstretched in caution, could stop her.

"We know her," Zach said, pushing past Sandy and Mike. "Bec, it's Zach!"

Imogen hit Bec like someone had fired her from a rocket and clamped her in a hug like a vise. "I can't believe this," she said, her speech garbled from crying. "Is Doug with you?"

Bec sniffed, releasing Imogen, but keeping hold of her shoulder. She shook her head. "He left the next day, after we met you. I know he got to California okay, but I wasn't able to reach him after that."

Bec turned to Zach, who pulled her into a fierce embrace. "I'm so glad you're okay."

"I can't believe this," Zach said. "You're a sight for sore eyes."

"You know these people?" Sandy asked.

Imogen turned back to Sandy and Mike, nodding. "This is Rebecca—Bec—and…" She let the rest hang, a question in her voice.

"My friend Jeffrey," Bec said.

"Come on," Imogen said, taking Bec's hand and giving it the squeeze. "You're coming with us."

CHAPTER 2
MIKE

MIKE BLINKED, TRYING TO KEEP HIS GRITTY EYES FOCUSED ON THE road. The bright-red taillights glowed, tiny beacons to follow as Clyde led them deeper into Cady's Run State Park. They'd entered the park about twenty minutes ago. At first, they passed picnic areas, but for the last twenty minutes, forest lined either side of the road with the occasional pullout for a hiking trailhead. This last part, with trees stretching toward the star-spattered sky, felt more still and silent than the rest of their lonely journey.

"We've got to get there soon." Zach's voice sounded scratchy and filled with longing. He sounded so weary that Mike couldn't believe he hadn't fallen asleep since he wasn't driving. Mike could relate and was grateful that Zach made the effort to stay awake. He might see dangers Mike missed.

"I hope so. I hate driving on nights like this."

"Yeah. It feels like the light from the headlights is sucked away."

After leaving the turnpike, they'd traveled Route 120, a two-lane state highway, for a while. Then they'd turned onto an even narrower and windier two-lane road which had improved and worsened their journey—the better because there were no blockages on the road; the worse because the few small towns felt deserted, to the point that they could have been ghost towns. But ghost towns, in Mike's experience anyway, didn't have the soft glow of lights behind tightly closed curtains, and every face that peeked out between them pinched and frightened. People were still here, still alive, still people, but the fear that pulsed through the empty streets of the small rural communities was palpable.

There'd been some runners, too, but nearer to the turnpike. Thankfully, they hadn't been able to keep up, especially with how twisty the roads were. At times they made so many nonsensical turns and loops that Mike and Zach had decided Clyde was doing his best to make it impossible for anything undead to follow them.

The taillights on the minibus brightened. Mike's heart leaped in his chest when it slowed, then turned off the road.

"I think we're here," Zach said, his voice thick with relief.

Mike's entire body slumped. He knew this didn't mean they were in the clear, but assuming the lodge was safe, they could get some much-needed rest and food in their bellies in relative safety. By the time they caught up, Clyde was out of the minibus and standing at the side of the road, the minibus parked in a graveled parking area that would fit two or three vehicles depending on their size. Mike stopped and lowered his window.

"Just pull ahead and park alongside the road for now," Clyde said.

Mike nodded. "Thanks for getting us here, Clyde."

He eased the truck forward, pulling it partially off the road. Zach hopped out of the truck while Mike wrestled with heavy rhododendrons that seemed intent on keeping him where he was. Everyone milled around the parked vehicles, stretching their legs and talking softly. The headlights of the minibus were still on. They shone into the rhododendrons, which weren't as thick here, and over the bank of a creek. The far side of the creek was lower and littered with rocks and boulders. The rushing water almost seemed like another voice quietly welcoming them. Just beyond the parking area was a wide footbridge that spanned the creek.

Clyde said to Mike, "Will you come up with me to check things out and make sure it's safe? I left the minibus lights on so we have a little light getting up there."

"I'll get a flashlight."

Clyde rubbed his face. "I'm so tired I didn't think of it. Give me a minute. I want Sandy to come, too."

Mike couldn't suppress a wince when he saw Imogen in the backwash of the minibus headlights. She leaned against the vehicle beside Betty. She smiled, then grimaced. One of her eyes had puffed shut and the entire left side of her face was swollen. He knew she'd taken ibuprofen, but it didn't seem to have made much difference. Mike could feel the heat of an ashamed flush flooding his face. She looked like a woman whose partner had beaten the crap out of her. Amy stood near her in the minibus' open door, frowning.

Clyde returned, Sandy in tow. "I'll be surprised if anyone is up there since there are no cars, but you never know. Do we all have flashlights?"

Sandy pulled her flashlight—a heavy, full-sized Maglite—from the utility belt slung around her hips that she'd worn as a police officer. Mike reached into the small zipper pocket on the breast of his leather jacket for his mini flashlight.

"Everybody," Clyde said, raising his voice a little. "Me, Mike, and Sandy are going up first to make sure everything's okay. We'll let you know when it's safe to come up. I know we haven't seen any of those…" He hesitated. "Zombies for a while, but I'd feel better if you all waited in a vehicle."

Immediately, the group dispersed, followed by the soft *thunks* and *thumps* of doors being pulled shut. Mike and Sandy followed Clyde. Mike shined his light on the massive tree by two wide stone steps up to the bridge. He hadn't noticed the tree before, nor the sturdy gondola built on a steel frame that was suspended from a heavy cable beside the tree. Mike's light traveled the length of the cable toward the road. It was affixed to a half-sized telephone pole hidden in the rhododendrons.

Clyde's flashlight swung to the right, toward it. "That's the gondola."

Mike took a moment to look at the gondola, a three-sided contraption made of heavy wood planks about six feet long and four feet wide. The front of the gondola, which faced the creek, didn't have a side, but given its twenty-degree upward slope from the cable it hung from, it didn't need one.

"If someone was injured, you could bring them up in this," Sandy said.

"I guess," Clyde said. "I know they've moved furniture with it… the couch and chairs, the fridge, too. Usually, we load it to get our stuff up there, but I doubt there's any power. Even if there were, the winch is up by the lodge. Someone has to go up first and turn it on."

Mike followed Sandy and Clyde over the bridge, their hollow footsteps almost drowned out by the rushing water. The bridge was wide enough to accommodate three adults walking abreast. In the combined beams of Clyde and Sandy's flashlights, he could see a winding path of closely spaced rocks that made a footpath on the bridge's far end.

Clyde's bobbing flashlight beam moved with the assurance of someone familiar with the way. "Watch your step. The path stones are from the river. They're a little uneven." Ten seconds later, Clyde's flashlight climbed up a set of stone stairs. "The lodge is up there."

Through the trees, Mike caught glimpses of a building painted green and white. Clyde started up the stairs, using the old-fashioned handrail on the left made of two-inch pipe. The painted iron of the handrail chilled Mike's palm, the surface uneven in patches where paint had flaked away to be painted over again. They climbed fifteen steps of rough-hewn stone, then the stairs turned left at ninety degrees. At least twenty more steps wound up the steep hillside before the staircase turned again, this time right at ninety degrees, revealing eight more steps. Before climbing, Mike shined the puny beam of his flashlight down the way he'd come. Altogether, the elevation was about forty feet above the road where the others waited. His muscles turned to jelly, so suddenly that he had to grip the handrail tighter. There was no way a zombie was going to climb these stairs. If they rigged up some kind of alarm, they'd have a lot of warning if one tried. For the first time since this whole thing started, he felt almost safe.

"Watch your step," Clyde said, his voice disembodied. "It's a little uneven here, too."

A massive tree stood at the top of the staircase and more paving stones littered the ground around it. The ground was more uneven here, the damp stones glistening in the flashlight beams. Moss blanketed some, making the footing more slippy. Mike followed Sandy and Clyde around the tree, the dark hulk of a two-story building blocking out the shadowy woods that surrounded them. Clyde's light flashed away from the house to a small building about six feet high at the roof's peak beside the big tree at the top of the steps.

"That's the winch for the gondola," Clyde added. He didn't stop, but continued to the building.

Below, Mike could see the interior dome light of one of the trucks. It looked so small. They weren't up a hillside, but atop a bluff. The squeak of a spring pulled Mike back to the present. At the top of two steps, also made of stone, Sandy was holding a screen door open. Mike followed her onto the screened-in porch.

"Watch you don't bang into the table," Clyde said, walking alongside a long wooden table with benches on either side. The porch was at least twenty feet long. "Wait here. I'm going to get the keys."

He disappeared through another screen door at the far end of the porch. The light of his flashlight winked out when he turned around the corner of the building. The front of the clapboard-sided lodge faced the bluff, overlooking the creek. A set of green double doors were nestled at the center, with a set of double windows beyond them. On this side of the doors, where Mike stood, was a counter made from a six-inch slab of a tree, still edged with bark. Above the counter were three windows, the old-fashioned single-paned kind.

"Those windows must be five feet tall," Sandy said, the rectangular panes of glass inset in the window winking in the beam of her flashlight. She stepped closer, pressing her flashlight against the window and shading her eyes. "Looks like the kitchen's through there."

The hinges of the screen door Clyde had disappeared through squeaked again, then Clyde strode to the front doors. "Bob leaves a key outside in case guests beat them here or if they're coming up on their own." He opened the left-hand side of the double front door and ushered them inside. Mike could feel, rather than see, a large open space before Sandy panned her flashlight from side to side. "Wait here. I'll get candles."

Clyde walked through a door on the far side of the open area. As Mike shone his flashlight around, bright light illuminated the doorway Clyde had walked through. Clyde yelped, then appeared backlit in the doorway. "We've got power. I turned on the light out of habit."

"Where are the switches?" Sandy asked.

"Let me." Clyde turned off the light he'd accidentally turned on before walking toward them. "I want to use the dimmers. This place doesn't have curtains and we probably shouldn't advertise we're here."

A moment later, lights built into the ceiling on the back wall brightened, then dimmed as Clyde adjusted them. Even with the low light, what Mike saw left him a little speechless. Clyde stood midway between the front and back of the building, at the bottom of stairs leading to the second story. A support pole made from a tree trunk that still had bark attached was directly opposite Clyde to Mike's right. On the other side of the support pole was a comfy-looking couch upholstered in light-green velvet, with a shearling area rug on the floor. The couch faced a massive fireplace that sublimated everything else, but in a good way, as a focal point. Made of stones that were probably collected from the rocky creek bed nearby, the fireplace started at the floor and continued all the way to the honey-colored wood that paneled the ceiling. The same paneling was on the walls, Mike realized, which gave the room a warm feel even though the temperature was chilly. Almost floor-to-ceiling bay windows flanked the fireplace on either side. Beyond the far bay window was an archway into a small room, through which Mike could see a desk and more windows.

To Mike's right, a comfy chair that matched the couch sat below the front windows that looked over the screened-in porch, with the near bay window beside it. A recliner was near the other end of the couch. There were other chairs—rocking chairs and old-fashioned wood chairs that looked like they might once have been in a library—as well as small tables for setting down cups and books, and lamps, too.

"Will you look at this place?" Sandy said, wonder in her hushed voice.

"Jiminy Crickets," Mike said, feeling equally awed.

Sandy chuckled. "Jiminy Crickets? Who are you, my grandpa?"

Mike laughed softly. "My dad used to say it. Guess I'm turning into him."

"You didn't say this place was so luxe, Clyde," Sandy said.

Clyde grinned, looking proud on behalf of his friend. "They did a lot of work on this place."

Clyde bustled around, deciding which lights to turn on. The lodge had a mostly open floor plan that Mike's brain organized into thirds. The front door he had just walked through was in the middle third. To the left of the front door was the third devoted to a large dining table and kitchen. A wall that started about fifteen feet from the front of the lodge separated the kitchen proper from the rest of the first floor. On the other side of that wall were the stairs to the second floor. To the right of the front door was the remaining third, consisting of the 'living room' with the fireplace.

Mike trailed his fingers over the dining table with benches pushed underneath, custom-made for sure, as he walked into the kitchen. The wood slab counter below the front windows that Sandy had peeked through extended inside with a bank of cabinets below. The table was almost as long as the counter and cabinets, and big enough that everyone would fit around it.

"Damn," Mike said, whistling softly as he took in the kitchen.

A long stainless-steel counter with three integrated sinks was along the exterior wall closest to the stairs from the road, with cupboards underneath. Two more of the old-fashioned nine-pane windows were above the sinks. Across from the sinks, on the other side of the wall the staircase was built along, stood a gleaming stainless-steel refrigerator. It was sandwiched between double built-in ovens toward the back of the house and upper and lower cupboards on the front side with a butcher-block counter.

But the real stunner—the pièce de résistance—were the professional grade six-burner stovetop and grill situated against the back wall. They sat atop an oblong… Mike wasn't even sure what to call it because it wasn't a counter. It was more like an altar made of stone, with an open arch at the front below the cooktop that he could see was crammed with pots and pans. The six-burner stovetop was on the left, the grill on the right, with a sheet of stainless-steel mounted on the wall behind them both. An industrial exhaust hood that was eight feet wide and three feet deep hovered above the cooking area. Everything, from the stainless-steel counter with its integrated sinks to the appliances, were industrial grade equipment that could only be ordered from a wholesaler.

Apparently, Clyde's friend really liked to cook.

Clyde stood by the grill, fiddling with light switches above another square butcher-block counter.

"I can't believe we have power," he said, glancing at Mike. Then he frowned, looking around the kitchen. "I never thought about this place not having any curtains. It's so nice, you know, to have windows everywhere and see the woods outside, but now... Well, we'll keep the lights turned low, just until we can get everyone up here and settled. I still can't believe there's power. It'll be so much easier to get our stuff up here now."

Sandy sidled up to Mike, her expression almost dazed. "I thought this was going to be some rustic hunting camp, not a swank getaway cabin. This is nicer than most bed and breakfasts I've stayed at."

Clyde quit fussing with the lights and turned to Mike and Sandy. A soft jangle of metal was the only sound as Clyde thumbed through a hefty set of keys. They reminded Mike of the keys Mr. Wiśniewski, the janitor at Immaculate Heart of Mary, had worn clipped to his belt.

"The thermostats are in the main room," Clyde said, then he grinned, his eyes twinkling. "Radiator heat, for however long the power lasts. Turn both of them to seventy."

"Both of them?" Sandy asked.

"One for each floor," Clyde said. He pointed toward the dining table. "That first window at the end of the table is actually a door, Mike; open it up. When we get supplies to the top, someone can stay in here and we'll hand things through. It's easier than carrying stuff in by the front door. I'm gonna go out back and turn on the power to the pump."

Clyde disappeared out the back door. Mike turned around, noticing for the first time the three door-sized, multipaned windows at the end of the dining table, on the same wall as the counter and sinks. The locks stuck but he was able to work them free so he could push the window-door open. Outside, the bottom of the window-door was about three feet from the ground, with the little winch house for the gondola about twenty feet beyond the lodge. This would definitely make getting things inside easier.

A slight hum, followed by the discreet hiss of water flooding into pipes, sounded loud in the quiet house. Sandy joined Mike in the kitchen, head cocked to one side. "Sounds like we'll have hot running water, at least for a while."

Mike chuckled. "This is not what I expected when Clyde and Betty invited us to come with them."

Clyde bustled through the back door. "Ready? Let's get everyone up here."

They followed him, pausing when he flicked another switch near the front door. Exterior lighting that offered enough illumination without ruining the ambiance popped into existence, beginning just outside the screen door near the winch house. They snaked down the hillside along the stairs, path, and bridge.

"We can turn the outdoor lights off once everyone's up here," Clyde said. "You two go down and get the gondola loaded. The short end folds down; you'll see the little sliders. People should bring up just what they need for the night, and load some food, too. We can get everything else in the morning."

"Shouldn't we bring it all up now? Anyone could..." Sandy's voice trailed, then she said, "We haven't seen anybody for a good ten miles. It's probably not gonna be a problem."

Clyde followed them outside and went to the winch house. Now that there were lights, Mike could see the steel cable running from between two small doors at its front, secured with a padlock. Clyde unfastened the padlock with the seventh key he tried, opened the little doors, and flicked yet another switch. A small light turned on, illuminating the winch and cable and releasing the faint scent of machine grease.

"The gondola sticks on the tree," Clyde called after them. "You have to push it to the side; you'll see."

They descended the stairs, which felt less treacherous with the lights. Mike could hear vehicle doors opening and a low, excited babble of voices from the far side of the creek. There were more lights in the parking area and by the gondola, shielded with small cones so the lights weren't too bright—safety lighting that kept ambiance in mind.

"Okay," Sandy said when they reached the others. "Get only what you need for tonight and put it over by the gondola. Mike and I and maybe one more person will load it." When Kevin volunteered, Sandy smiled. "Then head on up and watch your step. The stairs are sound but they're not uniform. Use the handrail."

The pile of bags at the gondola grew quickly, so much so that even with three people they couldn't keep up. "We'll have to do two loads," Kevin said.

"I'm afraid to see the pile that includes nonessentials," Sandy said, but she sounded relieved.

"Can you take this, Mike?"

Mike looked up from bags he was moving closer to the gondola for the next load. Imogen held out a small bag. "Are you sure you don't need any help?"

Mike shook his head. "Tell Clyde he can bring up the gondola but to send it back down for another load. See you in a few minutes."

She nodded, exhaling her breath in a huff. Her face looked worse up close, even in the low light from the path lighting. He hoped they had some ice.

Zach joined them, dropping a bag to join the pile. He gave Imogen's shoulder a squeeze. "Ready to go up?"

She nodded, then said to Mike, "See you up there."

A mechanical whine rumbled to life on the bluff. Mike stepped away to push the gondola out from the tree. Zach and Imogen were trudging up the stairs by the time he finished, their plodding steps betraying their exhaustion. Mike's heart twisted into a knot. The group climbing the stairs was a lonesome sight.

There'd been so much heartbreak this past week, so much that it hadn't really hit them yet, and there was probably more to come.

There would be more losses to witness—to bear—but he let the gratitude reverberating in the marrow of his bones loosen the knot in his chest. Now, for a little while, they were safe.

CHAPTER 3
IMOGEN

THE SOUNDS OF THE CREEK FILLED IMOGEN'S EARS. THE WATER rushing over the rocky creek bed made so much noise that at first she thought it was raining. In the bed next to hers, Bec's breathing was deep and even, like a meditation. Imogen slept fitfully, tossing and turning in the bed. She knew she'd slept a little because she'd woken up several times. When she rolled onto her left side, she woke with what felt like a spike behind her eyes and a generalized pain from jaw to temple. Her face had swollen more. The ice she'd gone to bed with had slipped off.

If that didn't wake her, dreams that left her afraid and confused about where she was and how she had gotten here did. It only took a few moments until she remembered they were at the lodge of Clyde and Betty's friends, but those minutes felt like an eternity. She reached around the floor without success to find the ice pack, but the idea of going downstairs to get more ice felt gargantuan. So, she lay in the bed, listening to Bec's breathing, the creek, and the wind.

But now she had to pee, so she had to get up.

Her foot landed in a puddle and thin plastic.

There's my ice pack.

She crept across the room, wiping her foot on the rug and taking her time so she wouldn't stub her toe or trip. She couldn't sleep but that didn't mean Bec needed to join her. The door creaked as she slipped into the hall. She squinted, not expecting the dim, orangey light from fixtures that looked like oil lanterns. Squinting made her eye and cheek ache, but it was nice to have light to see by.

Imogen walked to the bathroom, feeling like a burglar who'd slipped into someone's home and stayed. It made no sense; she'd been invited, after all. The same dim, orangey light gave the bathroom the barest illumination, but enough. She didn't bother turning it up. She eyed the waterfall shower on her way to and from the toilet. Her grubby skin prickled, knowing hot water was just a turn of a knob away. She might as well get her shower now, before there was a line. She was pretty sure she'd seen a towel at the foot of her bed.

After relieving herself, she slid the dimmer switch a fraction brighter so she could inspect her face in the mirror over the sink. She looked like she'd run up against the wrong side of a brick wall. She ran her fingertips over her swollen skin, inspecting the damage.

"Goodness… No wonder Mike wouldn't look at me. That eye is definitely turning black."

She found Tylenol in the medicine cabinet and took two, cupping water in her hand to wash them down. I will not be the wanker forcing other people to whack me to save me from myself ever again, she vowed, taking a last look at herself in the mirror. She was almost to the bedroom door when she noticed the draft of cool air on her calves. She'd worn only her knickers and a man's tee shirt she'd found in a drawer to bed. Betty had collected anything smelling of dead zombie and started the washing machine straightaway.

She shivered and looked at the door at the end of the hall, at the front of the house. It stood ajar several inches. The door had an inset window, but she didn't think she'd see much in the dark. She hadn't paid attention to the door before but had a vague impression of Clyde or Betty saying something about another screened-in porch above the one at ground level. Now that she knew it was open, she noticed the rushing water of the creek was louder here in the hall.

The simplest explanation was someone was out there, or had been and not shut the door properly. She walked toward it, her palms sweaty and heart pounding. What if it was a zombie out there? She tried to dismiss the idea as nonsense. How would a zombie get upstairs and through a door and then stay on the porch with no one noticing? For that matter, how would it get inside in the first place? Perhaps it could come down the hillside behind the lodge but that seemed unlikely, since the hillside was heavily forested. If a zombie wandered in from the road, it would have to get up the bluff—also unlikely. Besides, there would be the stench of a decaying body, which was absent.

None of these carefully reasoned arguments made it easier to breathe. The cool metal of the doorknob slipped underneath her sweaty palm. She didn't need to turn it, but she had to grip it tighter to keep it from slipping. She pulled the door open and whispered, "Hello?"

"Hey, Imogen. Over here."

She sighed, relief rushing through her that made her sleep-deprived body feel leaden. It was Zach. She stepped through the door and squinted, following the sound of his voice. She didn't make out the outline of his body until she was a few steps away. She sat down beside him, running her hands over her goose-flesh-pebbled arms. A faint whiff of mildew wafted up from the soft *pftttt* of the glider cushions when she sat down.

"Can't sleep?" he asked.

"I keep waking up."

"Me too."

They sat in silence, the only sounds the rushing water below and the wind in the trees. Imogen pulled her feet up, bending her knees so she could pull the oversized tee shirt over her legs, wishing she'd brought a blanket. It wasn't cold enough to frost her breath, but it was close. "I suppose I should sleep with my jeans on in case we need to run."

"There's a blanket on the chair," Zach said.

He got up before she could tell him she'd just go back inside and handed her a blanket. She took it, grateful for the warmth of the woven wool that heated her hand even as she held it.

"Thanks. Do you want some?"

"Nah, I'm good." He took a deep breath as she pulled the blanket around herself. "It smells good here. I knew it stunk at the zoo, but I didn't realize how much."

"You're right," she said, inhaling the cold, moist air. "Maybe that's why we can't sleep. Like when you're used to the city and the country is too quiet. Perhaps our brains are missing the stench of rotting corpses."

Zach snorted. "I doubt that." He was quiet a moment, then said, "Look at those stars."

She aborted the smile Zach's dry commentary prompted before it hurt more. A patch of inky sky visible through a break in the trees shone with stars so thick they looked as if someone had smeared them like soft butter on bread. A ribbon of the starry sky was wedged between long bands of illuminated, star-studded clouds on either side.

"There's the Milky Way," she said on a sigh. "Too bad we aren't in a field where we can see it properly. I can't remember the last time I was anywhere dark enough to see it."

They sat in silence, looking at the stars. Even with everything that had happened, this world—this galaxy—was so beautiful Imogen's heart swelled. The warmth and solidity of Zach's body against hers and the soft pile of the blanket began to lull her toward sleep.

"How's your face?"

She blinked, trying to rouse herself from her drowsy almost slumber. "It hurts. I just took some Tylenol. I'll get some ice when I go inside."

"He shouldn't have hit you."

Her eyebrows started to rise but again, she caught herself. Facial movements involving her forehead set off a cascade of pain from her temple to her jaw. So did smiling and yawning and chewing too, she reckoned. "Zach, Mike saved my life. I was jumping out of the truck to open the lock on the lynx crate. There wasn't time to argue with me, and I wouldn't have listened. I don't like that he hit me, but I'd be dead if he hadn't."

"He could have tried something else. He could have pulled you into the cab of the truck."

"You were there… You know how many zombies there were, how chaotic it was. He didn't have time if he was going to get behind the wheel and drive because I would have fought him. We'd all be dead. Or at least he and I would be. You could have driven away with Amy—"

"I would never leave you," Zach said, interrupting her. He sounded offended, like she had accused him of kicking puppies.

"Then you'd be dead, too."

A long silence stretched between them. Finally, he said, "I'm just worried this isn't a one-off thing."

Imogen felt for his hand, then gave it a squeeze. "Mike's not like that. Believe me, I know the type, and Mike's not it."

Zach shifted and turned so that he faced her. "What do you mean, you know the type?"

"Not from personal experience. Mike's not manipulative. He's not the kind of person who comes on too strong, too fast, and then gets possessive. Besides, he feels terrible about it. He could scarcely look at me when we stopped on the way here."

"They all feel terrible afterward," he countered, the tone of his voice indicating he wasn't buying what she was selling. "That's how they suck their victims in. They beat you, then get all sorry and sad and are nice for a while. It's called a honeymoon period. And then they beat you again."

"I understand the cycle of abuse. I just don't think Mike is that kind of man. Nothing he's done since I've met him even hints at it."

"I don't like people who hit my friends." Zach shifted on his cushion as if to stand, then seemed to think better of it. He perched on the edge of the glider. "It looks like he hit you with a two-by-four."

His voice vibrated with suppressed tension. The light spilling through the glass door to the hall brightened. They both looked to the door to see who might join them, but no one did. Imogen studied the bit of Zach's face she could see in the better light. He looked stiff, his posture so rigid he seemed like a coil about to break from overwinding. She'd known he was concerned about her, but she hadn't realized he was angry.

"Do you have any idea how nice it is that you care?"

"I shouldn't have to, Imogen. That's the point."

Imogen took a deep breath and blew it out. "Not just about this, but that you care about me. Not everyone has a friend like you. You're a genuinely kind person, Zach. I can't tell you how —" She choked up, emotion welling up so fast she couldn't keep speaking through her tightened throat.

Zach slid back beside her. "Please don't cry, Imogen. You know how useless I am when women cry."

She half cried, half laughed, and one hundred percent winced. Zach was pathetically ineffectual in the face of female tears. If he hadn't come to the zoo, almost all her companions would be new to her apart from Amy and Jay, who didn't count. She and Zach had history, a well of friendship and understanding to dip into. They had all the little things that weren't so little, like inside jokes. Zach loved the outdoors and animals as much as she did. They liked the same books and bands. She loved his curiosity, and she'd never had a more compatible travel buddy. He was even better than Araminta, and she'd thought no one could top her twin in that department. She knew Zach would like Mike once they got to know one another, but that might not happen if he held this against him. She didn't know why it was so important to her that they become friends, but it was.

"I know you only want what's best for me. Please don't make a big deal of this, at least not with the wider group. I think we'll have enough on our plate with Amy and Jay."

Zach groaned. "You mean the Crybaby Cabal?"

Imogen winced as she shook with laughter. "Stop making me laugh; it hurts."

Zach sighed, sounding unhappy again, and she kicked herself for bringing up the very thing that was troubling him. She leaned against him. He put his arm around her shoulders and pulled the edge of the blanket when she tossed it over. Imogen felt her whole body relax, and a moment later, the tense muscles of Zach's arm and shoulders did, too.

"Promise me you won't have a closed mind about Mike. I'm right about him; I know I am. I think you'll like him if you give him a chance."

Zach was quiet for so long Imogen didn't think he would answer. Like a child who didn't want to admit he was tired when told to go to bed, he said, "I'll reserve judgment, but if he hits another woman, I'll kill him."

"Let's skip killing people right off the bat, shall we? Maybe give things a little time to develop?"

He chuckled under his breath. She felt him relax a little more. Imogen closed her eyes, enjoying the warmth of his body against her and the sounds of the natural world… Sounds that weren't zombies.

"I won't kill anyone right away," Zach said, sounding more tired than a moment ago. "Besides, Mike's bigger than me. If I'm going to kill him, I need time to plan."

Imogen smiled—on the inside—at his pragmatism. She was so lucky he was here that calling it luck didn't come close to describing the miracle of his presence. She knew the Tylenol had kicked in because the pain from her jaw didn't feel as sharp. If the price of having him here with her was pain a thousand times worse, she would take it, and more. Zach was worth it.

CHAPTER 4
MIKE

M**IKE'S EYES PEELED OPEN LIKE RELUCTANT SOLDIERS, THE DULL,** persistent ache making sleep impossible. For a moment, as he looked at the honey-colored wood of the ceiling, he felt displaced. Then he remembered their flight to the lodge, the late arrival, and finally sorting out who would sleep where. The base of his skull thumped like a faraway drum. Inky black filled the paned windows, which meant it was either early or late.

When he checked his watch, he groaned; it was 4:32 a.m. There was a bed for him, but he'd made the mistake of sitting on the couch and got no further. He'd woken several times but had been too tired to bother moving. Mike hadn't expected to sleep well—and he hadn't—but four in the morning? He just wanted to lie here, stay still, and do nothing. The last week and all the changes it had wrought hit him like enormous waves at the beach, the ones that hammer you when you aren't paying attention. The pounding at the base of his skull picked up, his heart raced, and his stomach twisted.

Breathe, just breathe, he told himself, willing his body to settle down. He closed his eyes, hoping for something that would make sense to occur to him. How on earth had this happened? How had dead people started to not stay dead, and how was he going to keep everyone safe? The more he considered questions that had no answers, the more his head hurt. He resolved not to think about it anymore, at least until he'd had some coffee.

Mike stretched his arms over his head, arching his back, reveling in the slight release when several of the vertebrae in his back popped. He uncurled his legs and pushed himself upright with a groan, unable to remember when he'd last been this stiff and sore. His shoulders protested when he rolled them, and his knees ached. Hitting middle age was no joke. Hitting it during the zombie apocalypse flat-out sucked.

The fire in the fireplace had burned low, brilliant ruby coals peeking out between cracks of the black and gray ash coating the remaining log. He got up and put another log on the fire as quietly as he could. Jay slept on an air mattress in the small library room on his left, beyond the recliner and bay windows by the fireplace.

He turned, taking in the homey environment of the lodge— the comfortable furniture, the warm honey-colored paneling, the plentiful windows that were beautiful, but filled him with dread because of how exposed they made him feel. It must have been nice before all of this, looking out those windows at the woods and the sunlight that dappled the ground where it found gaps between the pines and deciduous trees. Now the windows felt dangerous. They needed to make some shutters or something, especially for the ones that were almost floor-to-ceiling.

The chill of the hardwood floors seeped through his stocking feet as he walked to the kitchen. Slippers—another thing to add to the mental list. It was already longer than he could remember. He was about to open a cupboard to look for a pan to make something for breakfast when he remembered they had power, which meant they had hot water. Tiny prickles crawled over his skin like ants, making him itch. He'd had a shower just a few days ago, when he and Imogen had been at Clyde and Betty's, but so much had happened since. So much hard work and sweat and muck from killing zombies on the way here. It felt as if he hadn't been clean in a month.

He climbed the stairs, freezing for a moment on a step that squeaked. On the left at the top of the stairs was the first bedroom. It had an irregular, undersized door, the top third a pane of inset glass. Watch your head! was printed in red and black ink on a piece of white cardboard tacked to the top of the doorjamb. Mike wondered how many people had knocked their heads before the sign was tacked up, and how many after.

He could see the bathroom door at the other end of the opening for the stairs. Across the hall from the bathroom was another door. He was pretty sure that was where Amy and Sandy had bedded down for the night. The room next to it was the one with two twin-sized Murphy beds built into a shelf and wardrobe along one wall—more beautiful custom woodwork. Betty had said they were down all the time, and there was a sleeper sofa with a double mattress. That's where he, Kevin, Jeffrey, and Zach would sleep. Imogen and Bec were in the room across the hall, where there were two twin beds, and Jay on the air mattress downstairs—at his own insistence. Mike was sure that wouldn't stop him from bitching about not having an actual bed.

He entered the bathroom, pulling the door shut behind him. When he flicked on the light, he stopped in his tracks. "Whoa."

His steps were slow as he walked into the bathroom, past the sink on his right made of cemented river stone with a tree trunk base tucked against the wall by the door, to look at the shower.

It was a waterfall. Not a waterfall shower, but an actual waterfall. Glass enclosed it on two sides; the third was an exterior wall mostly inset with the same multipaned windows found everywhere else. The shower was constructed of irregularly shaped sedimentary rocks, the kind found all over Pennsylvania, stacked one upon the other along the wall for about eight feet, ending three feet shy of the tall peak of the sloped ceiling. Some rocks stuck out from the rest to make shelves for shampoo, conditioner, soap, and other soon-to-be-history First World Goop.

Mike inspected the shower for a few minutes. He'd never seen anything like it. He looked around for the toilet. What looked like a whimsical recreation of a little outhouse enclosed the corner beside the sink. He pulled the door open to find he was right; there was the toilet. There were windows on the rest of the remaining walls, more of the antique nine-pane with single glazing. There were no curtains here either, but steam from the shower would take care of that quickly enough; why lose the view? It wasn't like there'd been tons of people tromping by to see inside before; now there'd be less. Below the windows that faced the back of the house was a low window seat, but he could see that the top flipped up in two sections, where he found towels and washcloths.

He stripped away his grimy clothes, belatedly realizing he should have brought up something clean from his bag. He still could, but the idea of going back downstairs made every ache and pain from the past twenty-four hours ramp up in preemptive discomfort. Instead, he stepped inside the shower.

The cool stones and concrete mortar felt good beneath his feet, textured enough that they weren't slippy. Almost immediately after turning the knobs, water tumbled from the center of the waterfall in an uneven, heavy spatter. The lip of large stone had a slight dip in the center fashioned to look like it had been worn down by thousands of years of water rushing over it, rather than being shaped by a chisel. It was a small detail, one of many that Mike had noticed that made the lodge feel so special. This hadn't just been someone's weekend place, but a labor of love.

He adjusted the temperature, stepping under the hot water already steaming up the glass. He looked down at his feet, feeling the pull of the tight muscles responsible for the pounding at the base of his skull, and let the waterfall rush over him.

CHAPTER 5
MIKE

The scent of the cooking oatmeal filled the kitchen. Mike stirred the pot with the wooden spoon to make sure it didn't stick to the bottom. He'd never made a pot of oatmeal this big before, but he figured everyone would be hungry. There were how many people now? He counted—ten, assuming he hadn't forgotten anyone. His brow furrowed and his lips pursed as he looked at the oatmeal again. It looked like there would be enough, but ten people... Well, they could always make more. He put the lid on the pot and turned the flame down as low as it would go.

The six-burner stovetop was meant for a commercial kitchen, which meant the flames were set higher than those for home use. Restaurants had to cook dishes quickly, so in that context, it made sense. But here, for the long term, Mike thought it might be wasteful. Clyde had mentioned the cooktop was fueled by liquid propane. When he'd looked down the bluff this morning, he'd seen the tank, sheltered from the road by a discreet blind. When the gas was turned on using the valve on the side of the stone base of the cooking area, the burner pilot light had to be lit. If you didn't, the LP fumes accumulated in the kitchen. It would take some time before you'd notice, but it would happen all the same.

Betty had told him when they came up for the weekend with their friends, they left the LP on the whole time, only turning it off overnight. Now, however, they had no idea when—more likely if—there might be LP deliveries again. They needed to get into the habit of turning the LP off when they were done cooking to conserve it. For now, Mike turned the burner off and left the oatmeal over one of the pilot lights to keep it warm, reasoning that would use less fuel than the burner on low.

He'd set a stack of bowls and some spoons on the counter to save everyone the search he'd done earlier. He grabbed a bowl and a spoon and watched the steam rise and disappear when he took the lid off the oatmeal pot. He ladled himself a generous portion, returned the lid to the pot, and nestled the ladle in another of the bowls. He kept his hand on the handle until he was sure it was balanced and wouldn't tumble to the floor while splattering oatmeal everywhere. Dogs were good for such kitchen calamities, but they didn't have one.

He scooped up a few teaspoons of the walnuts he'd chopped while the oatmeal cooked, and a handful of dried cherries. Dried fruit was better when cooked in the oatmeal for a minute or two, but he wasn't sure others would like it that way. He stirred his oatmeal as he walked to the table, the scent of coffee strong in the air from the pot he'd made earlier. There had been several kinds to choose from, and a glance at the selection told him this hadn't been an all one brand household. He'd have been SOL if all they had was Starbucks. He'd quit drinking their coffee years ago on principle, but he would have made it for everyone else. It might be the end of the world as they knew it, but as long as there was coffee, it might be a little easier to bear.

Soft footsteps on the stairs caught his ear. By the time he looked up, Betty stood at the foot of the stairs, hair fuzzed out in a way that resembled a poodle. Her eyes were puffy, as if she'd been crying last night, but Mike didn't remark on it.

"Good morning," he said.

"Good morning," Betty answered, her reply distorted by a yawn.

"There's coffee on the counter by the cooktop and oatmeal in the pot. Help yourself."

"No one, and by that I mean Clyde, ever makes food for me," Betty said, walking over to the stove. "What a treat." She sat down heavily across from him a minute later and took a bite. "This is delicious. I like dried fruit and nuts in my oatmeal, too."

"They're better when they're cooked in it, but I wasn't sure if everyone would like it. The dried fruit, I mean."

They ate in companionable silence. Mike sipped his coffee while Betty plowed through her oatmeal like a twenty-year-old who'd just finished running a marathon, stopping short of licking the bowl.

"I don't suppose you or Clyde have any idea when your friend last had the propane tanks filled?"

"I do," Betty said, brightening. "Not the exact day, but sometime last month. Clyde was up here helping Bob split wood. Clyde mentioned the LP truck coming."

The tight coil of anxiety in Mike's chest unwound a little. "Any idea how big that tank is?"

Betty's brow furrowed as she thought. "I think it's three hundred gallons, but I might be wrong about that. You should check with Clyde."

Relief cascaded through Mike's body like water rushing down a drain. He didn't know how long five hundred gallons of propane would last, but they'd get through the winter, certainly. The radiators wouldn't work when the power went out, which he was sure would happen, but the cooktop would still work. "That's a break. Someone's looking out for us."

Betty nodded. "I remember Jill, that's Bob's wife, didn't want to get the bigger tank since this was just a weekend place. She said he should just get a third of the kind they had, but I guess it was cheaper to upsize to one tank when all was said and done. Bob wanted to live up here full-time after he retired." She lifted an eyebrow. "I think Jill saw the bigger tank as part of his case for moving here because she didn't want to."

Mike nodded, then yawned. "Sorry. It's not the company."

"Didn't sleep well?" Betty asked, setting her spoon in her empty bowl.

Mike took a sip of coffee and nodded. "Not very. But I got a shower. It's impressive."

Betty nodded. "It's funny—well, not ha ha funny—but Bob built it himself and he didn't think to check the floor joists first. He realized about two thirds of the way up that it was too heavy. He had to rip it out, reinforce the joist, and then rebuild it."

Mike groaned, because ripping it out meant a jackhammer for the concrete. "That must have sucked. I'm glad he redid it though. A lot of people would have given up." He looked past Betty at the kitchen and the main room of the lodge. "This place is really special. Thank you for bringing us with you."

Betty waved his words away. "Don't be silly. I can't imagine Clyde and me here rattling around on our own. Have you looked around yet?"

Mike shook his head. "A little in the kitchen, but not really. Not outside."

"There's a springhouse out back. You'll see it and hear the rushing water. It's by the back porch."

"Really?" Mike said. That was a stroke of luck. He'd thought that the creek below was where they'd get their water, but a springhouse was much better. "I think I'll pop out and take a quick look."

"Take the keys. Clyde hung them by the back door. All the outbuildings will be locked."

Mike carried his dishes to the sink, quickly rinsing the bowl before setting them in the first of the three sinks. He walked through the kitchen to the back door, where the keys hung on a large hook. Through the windowpane on the top half of the door, silvery mist hugged the ground and hazed the woods beyond the back clearing. For a second, he debated getting his jacket, then dismissed the idea. He wouldn't be outside long.

The bite of the air felt sharp on his skin but not too cold. Mike took a deep breath—the first since he'd awakened that felt like his lungs truly expanded—and reveled in air that didn't stink of rot. The stone back porch was about ten by eight feet, tucked into a corner between the kitchen and the utility room to Mike's right that jutted out from the back of the house.

The rushing water from the stone springhouse almost sounded like wind in the trees.

He rifled through the keys as he approached it, taking the three steps down to its door carefully since they were slick with condensation. After he'd found the right key and removed the padlock, he pushed the door. It opened noiselessly on well-oiled hinges. Mike ducked inside, mindful to not bang his head on the low stone lintel. The temperature dropped a good fifteen degrees as soon as he crossed the threshold. He waited a moment, giving his eyes time to adjust to the low light. There was a small window on each wall; the building was about ten feet square. Around two sides—the one to his right and straight ahead—was a deep trough of poured concrete about two feet wide and as many feet deep filled with dark, rippling water. The rest of the room was open, with some tools and shelves along the wall on his left.

His fingers prickled with pins and needles as soon as he dipped them in the freezing water. If it was this cold in early October, then they'd have no trouble with short-term refrigeration when the power went. Waiting for the other shoe to drop was the new normal. The water from the spring filling the trough splashed noisily, unaware of the disaster that had befallen the world.

The pipe must be there, he thought, squinting his eyes at the end of the L-shaped trough that pointed toward the lodge. It didn't make sense to pump water up from the creek when this spring and gravity were already doing most of the work. They'd lose most of the water pressure when the power to the pump died. The waterfall showers would end, but they'd still have running water, assuming the pipes didn't freeze. Running water into the kitchen—power or no—was nothing to sneeze at given the circumstances.

He locked up the springhouse and walked into the clearing behind the house, where a firepit was surrounded by benches made of logs. About fifty feet from the firepit on his right was an outbuilding—this one painted brown—on the same end of the lodge as the fireplace. Mike thought of the fireplace side of the lodge as the 'up' side of the building—why, he had no idea.

That had to be the toolshed because behind it were blue tarps covering the largest woodpile he'd ever seen, perhaps thirty feet long. Clyde had mentioned it last night. It looked as wide as the shed, so about fifteen feet deep. Mike walked over to get a closer look. The top of the woodpile was eye level, and he was six foot two. He didn't know how many cords that added up to, nor whether it would be enough wood to get them through the winter since they'd be using the fireplace every day. It had defi-nitely been more than enough for someone who used the lodge on weekends and the occasional week away. Either way, it was a windfall. The gratitude that welled up in Mike's chest caught him by surprise. Right now, they had radiators but even set to seventy degrees, the first floor had a slight chill without a fire and upstairs was chilly. It was the old single-paned windows and the lack of curtains, but mostly the windows. Once the power went, they'd need every scrap of this wood. They'd also have to bundle up and get used to living in a house that was colder than they were used to.

On the 'down' side of the lodge, about a hundred fifty feet from the woodpile, was another outbuilding. It was easily twice the size of the shed with a four-foot crawl space below it. One end was screened in. It must be the other building that Clyde had mentioned called 'The Branch.'

No, not branch… What had he called it?

"'The Twig,'" he said aloud.

Betty had said there were bunk beds and a swing on the screened-in porch. Mike spent a few more minutes walking around the clearing and peering into the woods on either side of the lodge. There was an outhouse about thirty feet beyond the 'up' side of the lodge. He made a mental note to inquire if it was maintained and something they could use. The woods behind the lodge climbed to a ridge Mike could barely make out through the trees, which was good. That meant they were near the top of the hill behind the bluff. With the spring and the springhouse, they shouldn't have problems with the water becoming contaminated.

He walked around the front of the lodge, surprised to realize the front of the screened-in porch was almost at the edge of the bluff. But if the building hadn't fallen over it by now, it probably never would. The water of the rushing creek below almost sounded like rain. He looked over the bluff, feeling comforted by its height from the road below. The minibus and pickup trucks were visible through the trees in the parking area and alongside the aggressive rhododendrons. They would have to do something about the parking area. It was clearly visible and its purpose well defined, making the fact that there was something here that might be worth investigating obvious. Maybe he was being paranoid, but he didn't like the idea of people they didn't know showing up on their doorstep.

When he stepped back inside, this time through the front door, the warm air wrapped around him like a lover. He shivered, conscious now that he felt the warmth of how cold it was outside. Betty still sat at the table, sipping her coffee. He rejoined her, facing the three large windows that looked over the porch.

"How long has your friend owned this place?"

"Hmm… Good question," Betty said, a thoughtful expression on her face. "He got it when his kids were small so at least thirty years. It was nothing like it is now. This was all pretty much just one big room with the stairs in the middle.

He put in that wall along the stairs to make the kitchen and the bay windows by the fireplace. There were tables with benches like the ones on the porch in the main room on either side of the fireplace. Upstairs was just two big rooms if I remember right, set up like a dormitory. The women who built it just wanted a place where they could get away—no men allowed."

"It feels remote now. It would really have been getting away back then."

Betty nodded. "Those women built this place on their own from the ground up. You see that pot rack?"

She pointed behind him at the hanging pots and pans near the stovetop. He looked at the pot rack more closely—and more caffeinated—than earlier. The semicircle of metal holding the cast-iron pots was a six-inch piece of metal, jagged on the top side and smooth on the bottom.

"That's a saw blade."

"Sure is, from a two-person saw. They cut the trees down themselves. Can you imagine?"

Mike shook his head, a grin on his face that matched Betty's. "They must have been a determined group of ladies."

They fell silent. After a minute, Betty said, "Do you think we're going to get through this thing?"

A leaden feeling settled in Mike's stomach, the lightness of their discussion vanishing as quickly as it had come. "I don't know. We'll try."

"Our girls live out of town," Betty whispered. "Janey's in Chicago, Kimberly's in San Diego. They're so much bigger than Pittsburgh. It's hard to believe they're safe." She sniffed. "I don't think they made it."

The lump in Mike's throat appeared fully formed, as hard and jagged as the saw blade pot rack. "My girlfriend, Steph, was at work. She's an ER nurse at Passavant Hospital." Betty winced. "I was on the phone with her when a commotion happened in the background. I told her to run but I don't think... She didn't understand. The last thing she said to me was that she had to go, that they needed her help."

He shut his eyes, seeing the phone, the black numbers sharp against the silver background. He could feel the desk under his sweaty grip, the complete powerlessness he'd felt in that moment.

Betty reached across the table, her plump hand settling over his. "How awful. I'm so sorry."

Mike swallowed, barely, a sheen of tears filming his eyes when he opened them. He wiped them away quickly.

"Do you have any family in the city?" Betty asked.

Mike nodded, thinking how odd it was that they were trading these stories now, rather than when they'd first met. "Two sisters, Faith and Beth. I tried, but I wasn't able to find Beth. Imogen came with me to Faith's house. Beth and Katie, Faith's youngest, weren't there. Maddy—"

His voice broke. He realized he was shaking. Small, perfect toes with blue nail polish filled his mind's eye. "She was Faith's oldest… She'd been… you know. Faith's husband, too. Someone had—" He stopped, remembering the sunken eyes, hollowed cheekbones, and the furious, angry moan that had hissed between his sister's lips. His voice dropped to a whisper. "I had to take care of Faith."

Betty's eyes swam with unshed tears. "You were a good brother."

Mike almost choked. He shook his head. "No, I wasn't."

The ache—as sharp as the jaggers on the blackberry brambles they'd wormed their way through in the summer as kids—began to spin faster and faster. Sharp talons flew out like grappling hooks, catching on his lungs, his bones, his heart.

"You took care of your sister the only way you could," Betty said softly, giving his hand a squeeze. "That makes you a good brother."

Mike studied his hands, unable to look into Betty's kind face. They were his father's hands down to the shape of his fingernails. His dad had taken good care of them. He hadn't been perfect but he'd always done his best, and most of the time, that had been pretty damn good. After his parents died, Mike had tried to do right by Faith, Beth, and Jonah, tried to do what his parents would have done. He'd thought Jonah would always be the worst, but he'd been so wrong. He'd never failed more than when he had to kill Faith. He could almost talk himself into believing that it hadn't been her. What he'd found in the basement of her house had been a horrific mirage—a distorted reflection of the sister he'd so loved. What had mattered, what had made her Faith, was long gone by the time he found her.

It wasn't that he didn't believe Betty's kind words, but that he couldn't. If he'd been a good brother, he would have tried harder, gotten there sooner, made the difference between finding what he had and finding his family. He couldn't believe what Betty was saying because it just wasn't true.

Clumpy footsteps clattered on the stairs. Bec staggered to the table like a drunk, rubbing at her eyes. "Did someone cook something?"

Mike cleared his throat, then said, "There's oatmeal on the stove. And coffee on the counter."

"Guess I better start liking oatmeal." Bec's nose wrinkled, disgruntlement twisting her pretty features into a frown. "At least there's coffee."

CHAPTER 6
MIKE

"Everybody comfortable?"

Clyde looked around expectantly as heads nodded and voices murmured yes. Mike leaned against the wall between the fireplace and one of the bay windows. Imogen sat in the comfy upholstered chair-and-a-half on his left, while Clyde stood in front of the fireplace. Everyone else gathered around on the couch and the floor in front of it or stood close enough to feel the fire's heat. Clyde rubbed his hands together, looking nervous. "I hope everyone slept well enough?"

For a beat, no answer. Then Amy said, "I barely got a wink. I'm a very light sleeper. Sharing a room isn't going to work for me."

Mike smothered a burst of laughter by pretending to cough. He glanced at Imogen, who rolled her eyes. How she had worked for this lady, Mike did not know, but she must have the patience of a saint.

"All the beds are full," Clyde said. "You could trade for a twin with Mike or Zach."

"Share a room with a bunch of men?" Amy cried.

Zach looked down at his shoes. Mike saw the corners of his mouth quirk up in an ironic grin.

Clyde shrugged. He had the grace to look apologetic. "Then

unless you want to sleep down here on an air mattress, I think you'll need to make the best of it."

Amy frowned. "An air mattress?" She sounded as if he'd suggested she sleep on a pile of stones. "That would be… totally unacceptable," she huffed. "I guess I can give where I am a try."

She sounded aggrieved, as if she were complaining to the manager of a hotel about towels that weren't folded just so. It occurred to Mike that maybe that's what she thought was going on here. Not that they were running for their lives and lucky to have a place like this, but that she was a guest to whom Clyde and Betty should be catering.

"Anything else about the sleeping arrangements?" Clyde asked, but this time there was a marked hesitance in his voice. When no one else spoke up, he continued. "I want to thank everyone for pitching in last night. Thank you, Mike, for making breakfast." Murmurs of assent and a few thank-yous rippled around the room. "So." Clyde clasped his hands in front of him. "This isn't mine and Betty's place; it belongs to our friend Bob, but I know he'll be okay with us being here."

Kevin said, "Do you think he'll be showing up?"

Clyde's slumping shoulders said it all. "He and his wife were in Virginia. I mean, there's always a chance but…"

"We need an inventory of supplies after we get the rest of our stuff up here," Mike said.

Clyde nodded. "That's a good idea."

"And a list of ways to make things safer," Jeffrey said. He sat on the floor, tucked in close beside Bec. "We need shutters for these windows. And curtains so no one sees the light at night."

Clyde nodded. "Should we draw up a list of chores?" He looked to Betty, like she was the chores expert. Mike smiled to himself because Steph would have murdered him if he'd done that.

"I can do that," Betty said.

"We should have a schedule, too," Zach said. "Thinking people will just see what needs done always leads to people being mad at each other. I know we're all adults, but things fall through the cracks with a large group."

"Are you in charge then?" Jay demanded, his comment directed at Clyde.

Clyde shifted on his feet, looking uncomfortable. "Well, this isn't really my place…"

"I think we should choose someone," Amy said. "I have extensive management experience."

She spoke as if the truth of her statement were self-evident. Mike saw rolled eyes around the room and looks of *no way in hell* on several faces.

"I think we should decide things together," Betty said, with more tact than Mike would have mustered. "Let's get all the food and supplies we brought with us up here and get everyone acquainted with what you need to know about the lodge. You know, where things are, stuff like that. We don't need to figure everything out the first day."

Clyde said, "Everyone can get a shower—" A round of cheers interrupted him. "But we need to conserve propane. It's a tank-less hot water heater, so once it gets going, it'll stay hot."

Amy jumped to her feet. "Where are the towels? Is there shampoo and soap?"

"Maybe we wait till after we get everything up here?" Sandy muttered, giving Amy an incredulous look.

Mike snorted, loud enough that several people looked his way. "I'll get the keys for the gondola," he said, hoping his annoyance wasn't too obvious. Of course Amy would claim the first shower when there was an entire group of people who felt just as grubby as she did. Except for him, but he'd also been up since four thirty. She didn't even pretend she'd chip in with the chores. As things broke up, Mike said to Imogen, "How are you?"

"I'm fine. Tired, but fine." She sounded tense, but stress and anxiety seemed to be everyone's baseline right now. "I'll be out to help in a minute."

Exactly a minute later, Imogen joined Mike, Kevin, and Bec on the porch and they made their way outside. Zach and Jay had gone out ahead of them. At the top of the steps, Jay looked up at them from the first landing and said to Imogen, "You're not going to attack me again, I hope."

Imogen froze, her entire body vibrating like a high-tension wire. Mike looked over her shoulder at Jay, incredulous. Jay's round, boyish face looked guileless, but a faint gleam of viciousness shone in his eyes. Mike had seen Jay's and Imogen's confrontation on the way here. She believed it was Jay's doing that the lynx transport crate had not been properly hitched to the pickup. She was probably right. Jay's grudge against Imogen predated that episode; Mike had seen how he'd treated her at the zoo. Despite his words, Jay was trying to provoke her.

Mike opened his mouth to intervene but Zach, a few steps ahead of Jay, cut Mike off. "Apologize. Now."

"You want me to apologize? She's the one attacking people," Jay sneered. "She—"

Zach flew up the few steps and shoved Jay, almost knocking him down onto the ascending stone stairs behind him. Jay whirled around, one hand fisted.

"Are you deaf?" Zach demanded. "Apologize, before I make you apologize. I promise you won't like it if I do."

Mike couldn't see Jay's face but saw his shoulders hike toward his ears.

"Stop it," Imogen said. "Please. It's not a big deal, Zach."

Jay turned around. He looked unnerved, but angry, too. "You're all so sensitive. Sorry, Imogen."

He had said the right words, but the sincerity wasn't there. Zach's hand curled into a fist, but instead of resorting to further violence, he pressed against the handrail and Jay sidled past him. Then he said to Imogen, "You okay?"

"I'm fine."

"He's a real jagoff," Kevin said, surprise in his voice.

"All of you, it's okay," Imogen said. "He just wants the attention. Ignore him."

"I'm going to say something to him," Kevin said.

Imogen opened her mouth, looking alarmed, but before she could object, Bec said, "No, you aren't."

Mike glanced back at her. Bec stood a step below Kevin, looking up at him with her hands on her hips. Kevin towered over her, his height accentuated by the additional foot of height advantage the step gave him. She should have looked smaller than Kevin, but somehow she didn't. Her eyes narrowed, but it seemed to Mike she wasn't annoyed so much as tired.

"Imogen is a competent individual who can stand up for herself. You're only perpetuating the patriarchy when you decide you'll stand up for her because you're a man and that's what men do."

"It's not about patri...rachy," Kevin said, looking flustered and getting tongue-tied. "He's a bully."

"And Imogen is a grown-ass woman. You can't go around robbing women of their agency." At this, she gave Zach a pointed stare that let him know what she thought of his actions a few moments ago.

"I'm not—" Kevin started, but Bec cut him off.

"You are," she countered. "Maybe you didn't grow up thinking about how to deconstruct patriarchy, but I did. Don't be part of the problem." She smiled at him, turning to include the rest of them. "How about we try to make this crapfest a little less sexist instead of helping it slide even deeper down the toilet?"

Kevin looked somewhere between stunned and confused as he looked down at Bec. Mike tried to hide smile. Zach still looked angry, though his scowl and combative posture had softened. He said to Imogen, his voice low, "You're really okay?"

"I'm fine, Zach," she said. "Really."

Zach didn't look entirely mollified, but he nodded and started down the steps. Imogen said to Mike, her voice cheerful, "Come on."

As soon as she stopped speaking, her mouth compressed into a hard line and her eyes flashed. If she was going for 'no big deal,' she was failing in a big, bad way. Then she seemed to realize her anger was showing and wiped it from her face like she might clean a window. They started down the steps and Mike said, "I'd be angry, too. That was a crappy thing to say."

"It's already forgotten," she said breezily over her shoulder.

If that was true, then Mike Wójcik wasn't a Polack from Polish Hill. An astronaut up on the space station could see she was furious. Confronting Jay when they'd caught up with the others after escaping the zoo, and when she'd made bringing her lynxes with them a 'take it or leave it' proposition, were the only times he'd seen her stand her ground regardless of the feathers it ruffled. He'd never seen her admit to being angry apart from when she'd blown up at Clyde and Betty's place. And even then, she'd attributed her behavior to the stress of their situation. Mike knew in his gut that the flashes of anger he'd seen after her antagonistic interactions with Jay, and not speaking up when she disagreed, had also been part of it.

In retrospect, Mike could see that her blowup at Clyde and Betty's house had been brewing the entire time they'd been at the zoo. Maybe denying her anger was due to what she'd told him about her family. If she'd been the good girl to manage her father's temper, then admitting how she felt wouldn't have been acceptable. It would have been necessary to hide those feelings. Mike knew if a person did that long enough, they risked becoming so detached from their emotions that they didn't know what they were feeling.

He watched Imogen descend the stairs, her posture rigid as stone. He agreed with Bec that Imogen was a competent individual. She shouldn't be robbed of her agency. But that was where his agreement ended. Based on what he'd seen so far, he wasn't sure that Imogen had developed the skills to stick up for herself. Instead, she reined herself in until she couldn't, with all the resultant fireworks of repressed anger when it was finally released.

Distracted, Mike wobbled when his foot landed on a slanting step. He gripped the handrail tighter to steady himself, a tiny ripple of trepidation bubbling in his stomach. They were a small group in a situation that was as far from low stakes as it got. If they couldn't get along, it was going to be a long apocalypse.

CHAPTER 7
IMOGEN

Imogen held her breath and gripped the shelf in one hand, holding the box under her other arm. The uncomfortable sensation of a sneeze building behind her eyes and nose almost crescendoed, then subsided. Zach hadn't wanted her up on the washing machine to reach this shelf in the first place. She'd never hear the end of it if she fell. She hoisted the box from her hip and pushed it onto the shelf, dislodging a dust bunny. She waved her hand in front of her face, feeling the tickle in her nose again.

Carefully, she turned around, her right and left feet trading places on either side of the washing machine's lid. Zach stood on the floor, his arms raised to catch her if she fell.

"All done," she said.

The tickle detonated like a bomb. She raised her hand to cover the loud *achoo*, bending forward without thinking, and teetered atop the washing machine.

"Careful," Zach said, reaching up to steady her.

She coughed, wrinkling her nose and wincing. "I hate all this dust." She held Zach's hand while she sat down, then hopped to the floor and leaned on the dryer. A low-level hum of vibration buzzed against her forearms, the metal warm to the touch. Her lips puckered as she scanned the items they had inventoried. She raised her hand to her cheek, touching it lightly. It was no doubt psychosomatic, but doing this seemed to blunt the twinges of pain her bruised face doled out for the—five? No, six, she corrected herself—days since they'd fled the zoo.

"Still smarts?"

She glanced at Zach. Her lips quirked up in a small smile. The swelling had subsided a great deal over the last two days. "Now and then. It's a lot better, believe it or not, though I'm not stopping the Tylenol yet."

She returned her attention to the list, divided into two columns: Foodstuffs and Supplies. Under Supplies, they'd dutifully recorded the cleaning supplies (lots), laundry detergent (also lots), dish soap, washing machine detergent, batteries (lots and lots), along with toilet paper, flashlights, traffic flares, and other sundry items.

They'd done well filling in the foodstuffs column, too. They were only half-finished here in the storeroom and Imogen felt encouraged, especially since the inventory of the root cellar was still in progress. Clyde and Betty's friend had been a member of the Hundred Dollar Club. There were flats upon flats of canned kidney, green, cannelloni, and black beans, corn, peaches, pumpkin puree, tomatoes, and more. Dry foodstuffs included a hundred pounds of dried beans all told, eighty pounds of rice, two unopened twenty-five-pound sacks of oatmeal besides the one they were using, a hundred pounds of all-purpose flour, and several fifty-pound sacks of white and wheat bread flour, too. Sixty pounds of granulated sugar, plus powdered sugar, a carton of vegetable shortening, several pounds of active dry yeast, quinoa, ground flax, bags of granola, and evaporated milk. Zach had suggested they use the evaporated milk to make pumpkin pie if they found some eggs.

"I think we have enough toilet paper to last a year," Zach said.

"It'll go quicker than you think," she said. "Same for the food."

"There's a lot of food, plus whatever we can grow next year."

"That won't be available until the end of the summer and into autumn. That's a long time to make all this last."

"Kevin's a hunter. That should help."

Imogen raised her eyebrows at him. "I can hunt, too, you know."

"I know that," he said. "It's just Kevin's talked about it."

She shook her head, amused at Zach's embrace of Kevin as a hunter while forgetting she'd been an excellent shot before Kevin learned how to use a rifle, since Kevin was younger than she. "The food will still disappear faster than you think with ten of us."

Zach looked at the shelves. "We haven't finished yet, Imogen. I think we're pretty lucky."

"We are very lucky, but we can't count on luck."

Zach cocked his head. "You worry too much."

"It's my superpower, thank you very much."

Zach's grin made her feel like he was indulging her. He said, "I'm surprised there's so much, to be honest. This was a weekend place."

"They must have thought of it as their bolt-hole."

They fell silent, sobered. The couple who'd prepared all the food and supplies hadn't made it here to use them—not yet, anyway. Imogen shrugged and folded the list in half. "We won't starve soon, in any event."

Zach headed for the door into the main room of the lodge. Imogen took one step before a sharp *snap* made her jump. She looked down at her feet.

"Yuck," she said, her stomach feeling the tiniest bit queasy. "There's another one."

Zach had turned back, a quizzical expression on his face until he saw the mouse trap beside Imogen's toe was sporting a freshly dead mouse. He wrinkled his nose. "How many is that?"

Imogen shrugged, stepping aside for him. "I don't know. Amy's the one keeping track."

Zach picked up the mouse trap. "Sorry little guy."

She followed him into the main room of the lodge, where Amy was folding a basket of laundry. Jay sat at the kitchen table, reading a book. Shouldn't he be doing something? Imogen thought, her lips twisting into a scowl, but only for a moment. The sight of Jay made her furious, but she tried to hide it, the momentary scowl notwithstanding. She didn't want to give him the satisfaction of seeing how much he'd hurt her when he'd sabotaged getting the Iberian lynxes out of the zoo.

Amy took one look at the mouse trap and sniffed, her features screwing up in disgust. "We're all going to end up with hantavirus."

"It not that bad," Zach said, heading for the back door.

"It is," Amy called after him, her cheeks turning pink. "You'll change your tune when you've got typhus or the plague! Or when they've ruined the food!" She snorted, resuming the laundry folding like she was trying to teach the bath towels a lesson. It was a good thing the towels were in good condition; otherwise, she might rip them to shreds.

"There are a lot of mice," Imogen admitted. "A friend from university had a weekend cottage. With no one there all the time, they had the same problem. She was always setting traps, but I think with so many of us here, they won't be as bad."

Amy looked at her for a moment, as if what Imogen had said hadn't registered, then said, "Oh— I— Thank you, Imogen. If we'd put down some poison like I suggested, instead of traps like Mike wanted, they'd be under control by now."

Imogen tried not to roll her eyes. It would be rude, but more than that, it would set off a fresh round of complaints. Mice eating poison and then crawling below the floorboards to die and rot was a terrible idea, but Amy took the rejection as a personal slight. That Mike had been the one to point this out, however kindly, didn't help matters. "Choosing to do traps was nothing personal. It's just—"

"It's just what Mike wanted," Amy said.

She sniffed again. Imogen wondered how she packed so much into such a tiny gesture. Scorn, disgust, anger, persecution… all in one tiny inhale. "Bec's been trying to coax those two cats. They would help—"

"We can't bring them inside," Amy said, looking horrified. "People think they're fastidious because of how they groom themselves, but they spread toxoplasmosis. We can't have them walking all over the tables and furniture." She shuddered and added, "Who knows where their paws have been…"

"You don't like house cats?" Imogen said, gawking at her former boss.

"It's not that I don't like them," Amy said. "They're better than dogs."

She said dogs like she might say turd, so Imogen didn't think she was paying cats much of a compliment. Talking to the woman was maddening. She could—and did—shoot down any and everything.

"I guess it depends on what's more important to you, Amy. No cats or no mice," Jay said.

Imogen jumped, he startled her so. Her blood pressure inched skyward, making her skin feel hot and tight. The last thing she wanted was for him to agree with her, but it wouldn't do the group any good if she carried on like a child. Mostly, she tried to avoid him, but that only worked to a point. There were ten of them in a house with three bedrooms. As gorgeous as the lodge was, ten people in residence full-time made for a lot of togetherness.

"Do you want help with that?" Imogen said to Amy, gesturing at the laundry. She ignored Jay.

"No," Amy said, sounding defensive. "I've got it."

"Okay," Imogen answered. "It's just— There's more in the dryer. If you change your mind when it's ready to be folded, I'll be outside." She turned to leave, then turned back, letting her anger with Jay get the better of her. "Jay, I thought you were helping Mike and Sandy with their inventory."

Jay looked up from his book, which he'd resumed reading, looking annoyed at the interruption. He snapped it shut and stood. When he reached the foot of the stairs, he said. "They didn't seem to need me."

She almost followed up with a question as he climbed the stairs, but he was already gone. It wasn't worth it anyway, though she wondered about the accuracy of his statement. Mike and Sandy were doing an inventory of the sheds. A third person would make a big difference on such a task. She didn't think they'd tell him to go, even if he complained.

Amy finished folding the towels and picked up the basket, disappearing up the stairs without a word. Imogen watched her go.

And goodbye to you, too.

CHAPTER 8
IMOGEN

WHEN IMOGEN STEPPED ONTO THE BACK PORCH, ZACH WAS nowhere in sight. She saw the locked padlock on the smaller shed, the nearer of the two to the campfire area. Mike and Sandy must be in the larger one. She walked past the log benches around the firepit. As she neared the Twig, the little outbuilding with the porch swing and bunk beds, she heard the soft murmur of voices. She walked to the far side of the Twig, which she had to pass on her way to the larger shed anyway, to find Bec and Zach crouched on their knees. "Everything all right?"

A blur of orange and yellow streaked away into the underbrush. Bec groaned. Zach stood and offered Bec a hand up. "You scared the kitties away."

"They were so close we could almost have touched them," Bec said, her voice brimming with longing.

"I'm sorry," Imogen said.

Bec shrugged, signaling her forgiveness. "I'm sure they were pets. Have you seen them?" Imogen shook her head no. "One's a fluffy orange and white tuxedo with a white blaze on her nose. She's so stinking cute! The other's all white with these gorgeous green eyes. They're scared but the tuna will win them over."

"You're giving them our food?" Imogen said, surprise making her voice squeak.

Bec squinted at her in a way that made Imogen feel thick. "What did you think I was using—charm?"

Zach laughed. "If anyone could, Bec, it'd be you."

"They're not much more than kittens. I wonder if their owners turned into zombies."

Imogen chuckled a little at this, picturing a cat dodging a zombie while it bumped from one piece of furniture to the next like a trapped moth. Bec's cats were more likely spooked by being outdoors all night, hiding from coyotes and other predators.

"What?" Bec demanded. "That would be terrifying for a pet. They're used to people taking care of them and providing laps and pets, then they turn into a snarling beast trying to eat you." She looked up at Zach. "She's supposed to love animals and she's hating on my kitties."

Zach shook his head. "You've changed, Imogen."

"I wasn't laughing at you, Bec," she said, smiling while Zach looked exceedingly pleased with himself. "It was just the image that popped into my head. Zombies don't eat animals, but I can see how it might frighten them."

"They'd help with the mice situation if I can get them to trust me."

"Yeah, good luck with that," Zach said. "Amy will pitch a fit."

Bec snorted as they moved back to the more cleared area around the campfire. "Amy pitches a fit about everything."

Imogen agreed with her. After her conversation with Amy just now, she thought the cats might become a pitched battle. "I'm going to see if Mike and Sandy need a hand."

Zach jutted his chin over Imogen's shoulder. "Looks like they're finished."

By the time Imogen turned around, Mike was locking the larger shed. Sandy walked ahead of him, closing in on the firepit. "How'd it go?" Imogen asked Sandy.

Sandy flopped on a bench. They joined her, Imogen taking

the next bench, which sat at a ninety degree angle from Sandy's, while Bec and Zach claimed the bench opposite.

Mike arrived and sat beside Sandy. "I forgot how much it sucks to stand on a ladder."

"How can you need a ladder?" Bec asked. "You're at least nine feet tall."

Mike smiled, but it didn't quite dislodge the dark smudges under his eyes. "Not quite."

Imogen looked at her friends. Despite the good spirits, they all looked exhausted. Yesterday was the first day they'd gotten down to the serious work of inventorying the contents of the lodge so they could decide where to start, though Mike had taken charge of organizing meals and making sure the dishes were done and the kitchen kept clean.

"I thought it would never end," Sandy said. She held up the piece of paper in her hand. "But there's a lot in there that we can use."

"A lot more we still need," Mike added, taking the list from her. He pulled a pencil from his back pocket, flipped the paper over, and started writing on it.

"Same for us," Imogen said. "I think we're okay for food, for now, but we need to look for more. And better storage containers as well."

"How so?" Mike asked.

"A lot of the staples, like the flour and sugar and rice, are in paper or fabric sacks. We need containers that will keep out mice and bugs, like metal." She paused, screwing up her lips. "It's like they got the food and supplies but weren't thinking about keeping it from spoiling."

"We need to bring in my cats," Bec said.

Mike smiled at Bec, then asked Imogen, "Will metal keep things fresh with the right seals?"

Imogen shrugged. "I don't know about long-term solutions. In the short term, we need metal, glass, ceramic. Even heavy plastic would be better than paper and fabric."

Mike nodded. "When Kevin and Jeffrey get back, we'll sit down with Betty and Clyde. We'll have a better idea where to forage then, I hope."

A stab of worry pierced Imogen's gut. They hadn't seen a single zombie since they'd arrived, but that didn't mean Kevin and Jeffrey might not run into some while they scouted which cabins looked worthwhile for scavenging. Today was the first anyone had ventured out. They'd all been so tired and frazzled that they'd not done more than sleep a lot and explore the lodge. It seemed to Imogen that Mike wanted to be in the thick of things. Finding supplies was important, as in the thick as it got. So was an accurate inventory of what they had, though it lacked sex appeal compared to venturing into danger. She'd been surprised that Mike hadn't joined Kevin and Jeffrey, but secretly relieved when he'd opted to stay behind. Mike was a doer, the kind that might run himself ragged when the chips were down. He needed the rest. And she felt better when he was nearby.

"Does anyone know where Jay is?" Mike asked. "It would have gone a lot quicker if he'd helped like he said he would."

Imogen's eyebrows climbed her forehead. "Jay's inside. He told me you didn't need his help."

"What?" Sandy said, sounding annoyed. "What was he doing?"

"Reading a book," Imogen answered. "Amy was doing laundry."

Sandy swore under her breath. Mike's lips pressed together in a frown, then he said, "Amy bitches non-stop but at least she'll pitch in if you tell her what to do."

"I didn't ask what the book was," Imogen said. "Maybe he was studying something that will be useful."

Zach looked at her from across the campfire ring, his expression loud and clear: why are you defending him? "I wouldn't hold my breath," he said.

"He's barely doing anything," Bec added.

Imogen shrugged. "Maybe he needs time to adjust." As soon

as the words were out of her mouth, she cringed on the inside. They were all stuck with one another, so it was vital to get along, but she was furious with Jay. Why was she taking his side?

"Imogen," Bec said. "Quit trying to smooth things over. I mean, it's clear you're a way nicer person than me. You'll be canonized someday if you say things like that because Jay's been nothing but a jackass to you."

"If Kevin and Jeffrey find nothing promising, we can eat mice," Zach said. He held up the empty mousetrap. "I sent another to the mousy graveyard."

"Yuck, get that thing away from me," Bec said, scooting away from him. "Mice are nasty."

Zach grinned. "You sound like Amy."

Bec gasped while everyone else laughed. She clutched her heart in mock horror. "That's a black mark on your permanent record."

Imogen tried not to grin and failed. She couldn't wait for normal facial expressions to not hurt. Still, it could be worse. Mike could have punched her and knocked some of her teeth loose, but she couldn't picture Mike punching a woman, even while they'd been trying to flee the zoo. He was so even-tempered that she couldn't picture him punching anyone, though she was sure he would if defending himself. Even-tempered did not equate to pushover.

"I'll just have to catch those cats," Bec said, swatting at Zach. "I don't think it'll take too much longer."

"You know who's going to complain about that, don't you?" Sandy said, trying to smother a yawn.

Everyone but Mike said, "Amy."

"But she complains about the mice non-stop," Mike said. "I've heard more about mice the last three days than the last three years."

Sandy stood up and stretched. "I think the she's got opposi-tional defiance disorder. If you agree with her, she'll tell you why you're wrong!"

Everything they'd said about Amy was true, apart from the last. Still, Imogen couldn't help but feel sorry for her. "She's just an unhappy person."

Mike stood up, dusting off his hands. "I need to add the plywood from the shed to the inventory list inside. We need more, but we can use what's here to start shutters for the windows. I bet you're handy with tools, Zach. We can do it together."

Imogen didn't know if Zach was handy with tools, but she'd never seen his face cloud over like it did now.

"I need to organize supply runs, too," Mike said, almost to himself. "And make sure Clyde and Betty have finished marking the map for which towns they think we should check out." He sighed. "And figure out something for laundry for when the power goes out."

Sandy said to him. "How about one thing at a time? Like checking in with Betty about lunch?"

"I'll help with that. I'm starving," Bec said. Then she added, a glint in her eye, "I need to wash my hands after sitting next to the mouse killer."

Zach watched Bec walk to the lodge. Imogen couldn't tell if Bec was just being friendly or something more, but she was very familiar with the way Zach's face lit up. The attraction to Bec he'd expressed when they'd first met hadn't waned. But his smile faded when he said to Imogen, "He has a lot of nerve."

"Mike?"

Zach nodded. "He just decides we're going to do things, like shutters and supply runs."

"We need shutters and supplies."

"I know we do," Zach said, a touch of defensiveness in his voice. His lower lip jutted out as he frowned. "He acts like if he doesn't do it no one will."

"You just have an attitude about him because of this," Imogen said, gesturing to her face.

He didn't answer right away. Then he shrugged and said, his voice noncommittal, "Maybe."

Imogen laughed, deep to her down to her belly, wincing the whole time but unable to stop.

"What?" Zach demanded.

"You." She giggled, wiping tears from her eyes. "You liked Mike just fine when we were still at the zoo, but now you glower at him like he stole your girlfriend. It's obvious what's bothering you."

He shot her a disgusted look, but amusement tinged its edges. "You don't have to rub in how well you know me, Shorty."

"That is low," Imogen said, ignoring the ache as she laughed at him. "Just because you're a bean pole."

He lunged for her, but Imogen was already on her feet, still laughing while he chased her inside.

CHAPTER 9
IMOGEN

"Hey," Zach called. "Hold up."

The small group—Imogen, Bec, and Jeffrey—halted. All around them on the trail that wound through the forest around the lodge, the last of the fall leaves rustled overhead with vivid splashes of color.

"I didn't realize you were going on a walk," Zach said. "Mind if I come along?"

"Of course not," Imogen said at the exact moment Jeffrey said, "Just when we thought we ditched you."

Zach grinned. "You'll have to do better than this."

Bec, a few feet farther down the path, squinted at them. "Come on, slowpoke."

Illuminated in a beam of sunshine that made the last of the colorful leaves glow, Bec looked like an elfin princess. Zach sucked in a breath.

Jeffrey elbowed Imogen, then said, "Like what you see?"

It took a second before Zach dragged his gaze from Bec. "What?"

Jeffrey grinned. "Oh, nothing." When Zach turned away, Jeffrey's flashing eyes caught Imogen's. He leaned in close. "Looks like he has it bad."

Imogen nodded.

Zach pulled ahead and caught up with Bec. They followed the path that hugged the edge of the bluff. Jeffrey sighed. "It's kind of sad that it took all this to get me up here to see the leaves."

It was only with his face upturned that Imogen noticed how pointy Jeffrey's chin was. His nose was pointy, too, giving him the aspect of a fox. He was right that it was gorgeous here in the woods. Imogen took a deep breath, relishing the fresh air. It was so unlike the city they had left behind. Imogen hadn't realized how oppressive the stench of rot and death and smoke had been until they were away from it.

"Guys!"

The urgency in Bec's voice sent a spike of anxiety through Imogen's body. When she didn't see Bec or Zach, she took off running, only to almost run into Zach as she rounded the bend.

Zach caught Imogen's arm to steady her. "Easy."

Bec smiled and waved for Imogen to join her. "Look at this waterfall!"

Below them, to the left of the path, a creek nestled in a small ravine tumbled over a sharp slab of rock jutting into the air. Imogen walked closer to the edge of the ravine. A hollow in the layered sedimentary rock under the falls was about twenty feet at its deepest point. Imogen could see herself sitting behind the rushing water on a hot day. One could enjoy being close to the water without more than the occasional cooling spray, but this was not the season for it.

"I wonder if that's the inspiration for the shower," Jeffrey said. "I mean, look at it… All those layers of stone in the shower look like the same sedimentary rock."

"Could be," Zach said.

They followed the path and half walked, half slid down to the footbridge. A sign next to the bridge read Treemont Falls. Another sign warned hikers to stay on the trail. Imogen brought up the rear of the column as they crossed the footbridge and scrabbled up a steep slope. The path on this side of the falls was paved with gravel rather than an earthen trail. All four of them could walk abreast. The path went two directions: up to the nearby crest of a ridge at a gentler grade than behind the lodge, and down, which led deeper into the forest.

"Which way?" Zach asked.

Jeffrey pointed at the downward route. "This way. Clyde said it meets up with the creek."

Imogen trailed the others and pulled a small green book from her pocket. She'd found the slender little hardback yesterday on a bookshelf in the small room they'd started calling the library. The fabric at the edges of the cover was frayed, and the gold lettering of the title on the book's cover had almost completely worn away. She flipped through the pages, then looked around. None of the jumble of weeds and wildflowers resembled the illustrations she'd studied. She caught up with the others, keeping her place in the book with her finger.

"What's that?" Zach asked. Imogen handed the book to him. *"Pennsylvania Wildflowers and Medicinal Plants,"* he murmured.

"I found it yesterday and thought it would be a good idea to learn this stuff." She shrugged. "You know, in case this goes on for a while."

Zach's brow furrowed and his mouth turned down. He flipped through the book. "This is cool," he said, but the resignation in his voice implying that things would drag on made Imogen feel the urgency of her undertaking more keenly.

Zach handed the book back to her and they caught up to Bec and Jeffrey. Through the trees on their left, so far away that she had to squint to see it, Imogen could see the thin line of the road they had taken to the lodge several days ago. A shiver prickled her neck. Once, roads had been an optimistic promise of connection with others. Now they were the path of least resistance for the undead creatures they'd fled and people they didn't know. She'd gone from not thinking about danger from other people to being paranoid and afraid in the space of less than two weeks.

The fear and paranoia that were always at the forefront of her thoughts made her crazy.

She'd always been perplexed by the obsession with personal safety that seemed woven into the DNA of her adopted home. Americans were fearful. They were afraid they'd lose what they had, and admittedly for many people, that wasn't a lot. This led to an anxiety about the future that she'd never experienced in other first world countries. Imogen had spent most of her life in the UK, where support for education and childcare was better than here, and where healthcare for everyone was a given. The anxiety that Americans lived with in these areas she understood.

But the rest of their fears made little sense to her. Some were afraid of people who didn't look like them or practice the same religion, especially as America became more multicultural. ManyAmericans were fearful of—and sometimes angry with—those whose politics weren't the same. They were fearful they'd be steamrolled by ideologies they didn't agree with, and fearful that the fabric of reality was being unraveled as opinions were bandied about as facts. She'd never met people as friendly and as fearful as Americans. Now, she was getting just as paranoid. *And it only took a couple weeks of dead people trying to eat me to do it,* she thought wryly.

Tucked in the creek's bend ahead was a small picnic area with two weathered tables, an indestructible-looking outdoor grill, and a rusty metal barrel for garbage with a hinged lid and latches to keep it closed.

"If whoever put that garbage can here thinks it's keeping out bears, they're sorely mistaken," Jeffrey said.

"Let's sit a minute," Bec said. She gestured to Imogen's book. "Have you found any plants?"

"Not yet." Imogen handed the book to Bec. "But I haven't any practice and so many need to be harvested in the spring and summer. It's going to take longer than I'd like, I think."

"I'll come with you," Bec offered. "I'd like to learn, too."

Zach perked up at that. "Me, too," he said.

Imogen gave him a baleful look. "Bec and I are strong, independent women. We don't need a man along to defend us all the time. You'd escort us to the outhouse if we were using it."

Embarrassment tinged Zach's smile. "Never hurts to have help."

"Let him tag along with you and Bec." Jeffrey tried not to smile but couldn't quite keep his lips from curling up. "You might find something heavy that needs moving." Then he sighed. "I wouldn't mind looking for some mushrooms."

Bec snorted. "Don't start that again."

"What?" Jeffrey demanded. "People have foraged for mushrooms for thousands of years."

Zach made a low noise of disagreement in his throat. Imogen said, "Or you could kill us all."

"See?" Bec's triumphant voice implied her opinion had carried the day. "They agree with me, too."

"But wild mushrooms are amazing." Jeffrey's voice was something between a whine and indignation. "Chefs all over the world use them, and they're so good in soup. Just imagine the soup I could make!"

They continued to bicker amicably as Imogen took in the trees, the ever scarcer colored leaves painted scarlet and yellow. It really was beautiful, though somewhat hard to enjoy. Listening for zombie moans took half of Imogen's attention no matter what she was doing. The sparse population in this part of Pennsylvania meant the chances of running into zombies were slimmer than in the cities. Her rational mind knew this, but her lizard brain wasn't listening.

She'd expected there would be more people in the park, even though it was remote. After all, it had been a gorgeous weekend when the zombies first appeared. If she'd been here, she would have stayed put. Then she realized that wasn't true. At the start, no one knew what the problem was—not the little people anyway. The speed with which the turnpike had been closed, and the number of Army, National Guard, and state trooper vehicles they'd seen, led her to believe the authorities had known the situation was more serious. Most people would have enjoyed their day at the park or their weekend camping trip, perhaps hearing something on the radio, but would still have packed up and headed for home.

"Amy is getting on my last nerve," Bec said, pulling Imogen from her private ruminations. "She's still taking showers every day, like the fuel that's heating the water is limitless."

Jeffrey snickered. "The Queen feels entitled to be clean."

Imogen frowned. "I thought we agreed we'd only use the shower every three or four days." Her skin began to itch as soon as the words left her mouth. She tried to ignore it but couldn't help scratching at her neck.

"That *is* the agreement," Jeffrey said. "But with no one really in charge, it's not getting enforced for the people who need it."

"Mike seems to think he's in charge," Zach muttered under his breath.

Imogen groaned. "Will you give it up already?"

"Give up what?" Jeffrey asked.

"Nothing," Imogen said, giving Zach a pointed side-eye. "I don't want to be in charge but you're right. We need to figure out something. It will cause problems down the line."

"It already is," Bec said. "Shower Queen is a perfect example. I swear, if she's gotten another shower when we get back, I'm gonna smack her."

Everyone laughed, except for Zach. "Mike's always telling people what to do... be careful with the propane, go collect kindling or split wood. I'm sure he'd jump at a chance to put Amy in her place."

Imogen gritted her teeth. Zach's bad attitude about Mike had crossed the line from concern to an annoying fixation. It didn't matter what she said or how she said it. He had convinced himself that Mike was abusive or had the potential to be abusive. She'd told him he should talk to Mike if he felt so strongly about it. So far he hadn't, seeming to prefer nursing his grudge.

"I think he's been kind of heavy-handed, especially with Amy," Zach continued. "I know she can be annoying, but maybe people should cut her a break."

Imogen gaped at him, thunderstruck. She couldn't believe Zach was defending the woman who'd been ready to fire her. "Why are you defending her?"

"I'm not defending her," Zach said. "She's just been through a lot."

"Not sure if you've noticed, but so have the rest of us. We just don't complain incessantly," Jeffrey said, sarcasm sharpening his tone. "Why should she get a pass?"

"I just mean she isn't adjusting to the new normal very well," Zach said, looking flustered.

The vein in Imogen's temple thumped. She stared at Zach open-mouthed. "You *are* defending her. She was going to fire me!"

Zach blinked. "Since when?"

"Since when? I told you all about it."

Zach shook his head, his eyebrows knitting together. "I have no idea what you're talking about."

Everyone was looking at her. Zach with confusion, even hurt, perhaps. Bec and Jeffrey both looked curious. Imogen felt… betrayed. How could her best friend defend that woman? Then she raised her hand to her mouth as it all came back in a rush. "Oh, Zach, you're right. I didn't tell you."

Amy had blindsided her the day she and Zach met at Six at Sylvie's, where she'd met Doug and Bec. By the time Zach arrived, she'd had a few drinks, Doug was making her laugh, and Bec was regaling them with her story of the troublesome client. Then they had joined Bec and Doug for dinner and then drinks, and then more and more drinks. Zach had even asked her as they left Six at Sylvie's if anything was wrong, but she'd brushed him off, not wanting to think about how Jay had double-crossed her and how readily Amy believed him. It would have ruined their evening.

A hot blush spread over Imogen's face. Even if the others couldn't see it, she was still embarrassed. "It was the same day when we met at Six at Sylvie's. By the time you arrived, I'd met Bec and Doug, and then you told us about getting the post-doc. I didn't want to think about it."

Jeffrey leaned forward, his eyes alight. "So what happened?"

Imogen opened her mouth to answer, then stopped. Almost everyone living at the lodge hadn't known one another before everything went crazy. Now, they were stuck with each other. If she told them how Jay had double-crossed her and Amy had taken his word for it, it would only cause dissension. Amy and Jay were already unpopular; how they'd treated her before all of this would only make it worse.

Imogen shook her head. "You know what? It doesn't matter anymore."

"Imogen!" Bec cried. "I can tell this is el primo dirt, and you're holding out on us?"

"Yes," she said.

"Really?" Jeffrey said. "We're in the middle of nowhere, have no contact with anyone, and you won't tell us? What are we supposed to gossip about?"

Imogen gave him a wry smile. "I'm sure you'll figure out something." Then she said, "I'm sorry, Zach. I know you're always on my side." Sometimes a little too much, she thought, but didn't say.

"I should hope so," he grumbled. "I'm a better friend than that."

Despite his grouchy chastisement, he had a glint in his eye. She knew he expected her to fill him in later. He was going to be disappointed.

CHAPTER 10
MIKE

Mike squinted, peering through the trees ahead. Zach had outstripped him while they climbed the ridge behind the lodge. Clyde had said the terrain was steep, but Mike hadn't appreciated what Clyde meant by that, for he'd failed to mention the need to climb the occasional boulder or outcropping of rock. Mike had hoisted himself up almost vertically a few times, and while Zach moved with the confidence and grace of a billy goat, he was less nimble. If Zach was Imogen's age, it meant he had fifteen years on him. Mike knew he wasn't that old really, and he'd always stayed in shape, but there was a big difference between forty-eight and early thirties.

Clyde hasn't climbed this ridge in a while, Mike grumbled to himself.

Still, it was nice to be out in the woods and not feel paranoid about whether there were zombies nearby. The terrain made him feel a lot better about the security of the lodge. If zombies were to come down from above, they'd have time to get out. The forest was dense enough to be a serious barrier, especially for creatures that ran into things and often found their way around obstacles by bouncing around them like pinballs. Sunshine illuminated the thinning but still brilliant fall leaves, casting everything below in jewel tones. The air had that crisp snap of fall that Mike had always loved.

He saw a break in the trees ahead. Zach was already out of sight. A few minutes later, Mike reached the tree line. Just as Clyde and Betty had said, a large meadow opened before him. Mike wasn't much for judging acreage, having grown up in the city. The meadow seemed about a football field in width and twice as long. The ground was more or less even, though the forest continued upward a bit more on the far side. He wondered how such an open space had formed in the middle of a forest, but he would not argue a good thing. They needed to supplement their food supply. In the long run, that meant growing it. Mike hadn't expected to find anywhere this close to the lodge that was suitable for a garden.

He caught up with Zach, who had stopped to take in their surroundings. "What do you think?"

"Looks pretty good. I think we can use it to grow crops, assuming any of us know how. Do you?"

"I had a garden in my yard," Mike said, shrugging. "You know… Tomatoes, green beans, peppers, that kind of stuff. And an herb garden."

"We'll figure it out, I guess."

"Bec should know something. Didn't she do something with plants?"

"Yeah." Zach turned to look at Mike. "Why didn't she come with us?"

"I asked her if she'd give the root cellar a second look. I don't trust that inventory from Amy and Jay. They seemed more inter-ested in bitching than working."

"Oh, right," Zach said, a bristle in his voice.

Mike wandered a bit, walking in a loopy circle and thinking as he studied the area. They might need to irrigate to deal with extended dry spells, which meant they'd need to get water up here. Ideally in a way that didn't involve lugging it up in buckets. "Maybe we can set up a hand pump of some kind at the springhouse in case there are dry spells."

Zach grunted, giving Mike the distinct impression that he had a low opinion of the idea.

"We'll need a deer fence, too," Mike added. "Getting it up here is going to be a pain in the butt."

"Yeah."

"Do you want to come with us tomorrow, when we go to the home improvement place?"

Zach shook his head. "I told Imogen I'd go with her to look for supplies at the other cottages."

"That might be a better use of your time," Mike said, feeling the niggle of worry about that outing recede. "I was concerned about them splitting up to cover more ground if it was just Imogen, Bec, and Clyde. You can do pairs with four."

"Pretty sure we'd have figured that out on our own. We all know how to count."

Mike cocked his head, appraising the younger man with a more critical eye. Zach seemed aggravated, but he wasn't sure why.

"Is everything okay, Zach?"

Zach turned around so fast it felt like he had been waiting for an opportunity to pounce. His mouth formed a line as straight as a ruler and just as unyielding. Furrowed eyebrows above his flashing eyes resembled dark thunderheads. "Why do you ask?"

"You seem kind of aggravated."

Zach's eyes narrowed. "Well, maybe I don't like men who beat up women."

"What?" Mike said, so surprised it sounded like a gasp. "This is about Imogen?"

"Give the genius a point. Yeah, it's about Imogen. I don't like men who hit women, especially when they're my friend."

Mike's hand tingled like it did whenever he thought about slapping Imogen before pushing her into the truck as they fled from the zoo. It felt like it had been branded with a scarlet letter *A*… Asshole. Abuser. Take your pick. Slapping Imogen, and what it had done to her, felt like a contamination he couldn't wash off.

"I've never hit a woman before, and I never will again, especially not like you're talking about. I feel terrible about hitting Imogen."

"You didn't have to hit her," Zach said, closing the distance between them. "You could have pulled her into the truck. All she's done since we got here is wince and pretend she's fine. She looks like she came up against the wrong side of a baseball bat."

"Look— Zach—" Mike sputtered. He hadn't expected this, though he should have seen it coming. He couldn't disagree with Zach because he was right. If Imogen's face was what one slap could do, he never wanted to see what an intentional beating from someone—from him—would do to a woman. Mike stared at him. He knew they didn't know one another well, but he couldn't believe Zach thought he was abusive. Now that he wasn't trying to hide his anger, fury pulsated from Zach like the heavy beat of a bass drum. His hands had balled into fists and his mouth puckered in an ugly sneer, baring his teeth.

The scorn in Zach's voice snapped like a whip. "Yeah, that's right, just stand there and play dumb. She might say it's okay, but I won't."

"All I was trying to do was get her in the truck," Mike said, trying to keep the defensiveness he felt out of his voice. "She was jumping out. There were zombies everywhere and she was fighting me. There was no time. You were there; you know what it was like. So yeah, I hit her to keep her in the truck, harder than I realized, and I feel terrible about it. You think I don't want to crawl under a rock every time I look at her? It was the best I could do, and I'm not saying it was the right thing. Maybe if you'd been driving I could have—"

"Don't," Zach said, jabbing him hard in the chest with his finger. "Don't you put this on me. Don't you dare."

Mike took a step back. "That's not what I meant," he said,

holding his hands up as he retreated. "I didn't— All I was trying to say was that I didn't have time to pull her in and drive. If someone else had been behind the wheel, ready to drive away, I could have jumped in the back and held on to her, but that's not what happened."

"I would have never hit her," Zach insisted.

"You weren't the one trying to stop her, Zach," Mike said, unable to keep the irritation out of his voice. "You don't know how hard she was fighting me. I did the best I could, and the way she looks was the price. At least she's alive for you to be angry with me."

Zach advanced, his face flushing a darker shade of red, his hands fisted at his sides. That had been the wrong thing to say.

"I don't know what else I could have done in that moment," Mike said. "But it will never happen again. I'm not a dirtbag who thinks women are punching bags."

Zach's anger flared even more, as brilliant as the autumn sunshine. It didn't matter what he said. Nothing was going to assuage Zach's anger. "Just steer clear of her," he growled through his gritted teeth.

Mike's surprised laugh came out like bark. "How do you expect me to do that, even if I wanted to? We're all on top of one another." He threw up his hands, a mixture of culpability and exasperation thrumming in his veins. "I've apologized to Imogen and she accepted it, which— I wouldn't have in her shoes. I can see I need to earn your trust, and I'll do whatever it takes, but if you've already decided I'm a scumbag, it won't matter what I do."

"Of course Imogen said everything's fine," Zach spat. "That's what she does! She smooths things over, gives everybody the benefit of the doubt even when they've shown they don't deserve it."

Mike took another step back. He didn't like retreating. It felt like an admission of guilt. He *was* guilty—of using a poor tactic under duress—but not of what Zach was accusing him of. He wanted to keep defending himself but Zach didn't want to hear it. If he put more space between them, at least he wasn't escalating the situation. Zach seemed to have already decided, but Mike knew he still had to try. They were too small a group to let something like this fester.

He took a deep breath and looked Zach in the eye. "I'm not going to stand here and tell you I'm not something that you clearly think I am. All I can do is show you. I've apologized to Imogen and I still feel awful. I've never been more ashamed. That is not how I was raised. Even if it was, it's not who *I* am."

Zach stared at him, his eyes cold.

"I understand that you're looking out for her, and I respect that. You wouldn't be a good friend if you didn't. But if you've made up your mind, it won't matter what I do to prove myself."

"Prove it how?"

"Every damn day," Mike said. "I should have been the one to start this conversation, and I'm sorry for that. If you give me a chance, I'll prove I'm not that guy."

Zach continued to shoot daggers with his eyes. Then he groaned, the vehemence behind it making it seem like an epithet.

"Ugh! I told Imogen I'd reserve judgment, but... She's the only person I'd even *try* to do it for because I don't want to." He gritted his teeth, then pinned Mike in place with the force of his glare. "If you ever raise a hand to her again, I'll kill you. I'm not screwing around."

"I know you're not," Mike said, and he meant it. The man standing in front of him looked entirely capable of premeditated homicide. Zach glared at him for another few seconds, then turned on his heel and marched toward where they'd emerged from the forest. Mike blew out his breath, puffing his cheeks. Why hadn't he thought to talk to Zach first?

Maybe because I've been too busy trying to keep everyone alive.

Still, it bothered him more than he wanted to admit. Usually, he was better at people than this. This was a rookie mistake, perhaps not avoidable, but he might have mitigated the fall out.

Then he shook his head. Like there was ever going to be a way to mitigate the fall out of hitting Imogen so hard that he had, for all intents and purposes, battered her.

"Well, shit," he said softly.

There was at least one good thing to come out of this. He knew Imogen had a fierce defender, which made him like and respect Zach more. His job now was to see if he could make the feeling mutual.

Earning Zach's respect was going to be a marathon, and he'd just discovered he still needed a pair of shoes.

CHAPTER 11
MIKE

Mike checked his weapons one last time. The hunting knife he'd found packed in a storage locker in the shed was in its sheath on his belt. The grip of his brother-in-law's gun, which he'd learned was a nine millimeter Glock 19, was snapped securely in the holster around his hips. His knowledge of how to use it came from tutorials given by Imogen and Sandy. The take-away, since they couldn't practice because of the noise, had been to point, shoot, and try to hit something. It felt substantial under his palm, but it also freaked him out. Guns had never interested Mike; they kind of scared him. One mistake and you might kill someone. He had never wanted to wield that sort of power. There was a second knife on his other hip, as well as a claw tooth hammer and a flat bar. The last was for prying things open when Kevin's Halligan might be overkill, or if they weren't together.

As satisfied as he'd be for now, he looked up to the lodge from where he stood in the parking area. The sun had risen behind the lodge only minutes ago, lightening the sky to a delicate seashell pink. He, Jeffrey, Kevin, and Sandy had slunk around while getting ready, trying not to wake the others. Mike hadn't wanted a big production made of their departure. He didn't want to see the faces of his friends pinched with anxiety and worry, and he wanted the group scavenging the cabins nearby later today to be as well rested as they could be.

He hated the idea of not going with them. He trusted Imogen, Bec, Zach, and Clyde to take care of one another. To a person, they were smart, and Clyde and Imogen were cautious. He'd never seen Bec or Clyde fight, but he knew Zach and Imogen were competent fighters. He'd seen Imogen prove herself repeatedly. Zach had been fierce—formidable, even—when they'd gone to get Imogen and escape the zoo. He'd keep Imogen safe, whatever it took.

Including putting me on notice.

Mike's cheeks burned, and he was glad the others weren't out here yet. It had been four days since Zach confronted him about how he'd gotten Imogen to stay in the truck—how he'd hit her—when they escaped from the zoo. Sometimes, the day they'd fled Pittsburgh felt like two years ago instead of two weeks. Other times, it seemed like only yesterday. The shame he felt, despite Imogen's protestations that he'd saved her life, felt like it had been there forever.

Zach's accusation had caught him flat-footed. He should have seen it coming. Peter had threatened to beat him through the pavement if he ever lay a hand on Imogen—or any other woman—when they'd caught up with the others on the turnpike. Peter had also told Mike he didn't think he'd ever need to make good on his threat, that he didn't think Mike was the type, but Mike took it seriously. It didn't matter that Peter wasn't here. One way or another, Peter would make good on it if necessary. He took what Zach had said seriously, too. It hadn't felt like a threat but a promise when Zach had said he'd kill him if he ever raised a hand to Imogen again.

Zach's aloofness since they got here made sense now. Mike had been too tired to notice at first, then too distracted. There were so many things he needed to do, needed to have, if he was going to keep everyone safe. The enormity of the task made his head swim. He hadn't been paying enough attention.

On the one hand, what had happened with Zach was a good thing. Mike felt better knowing Imogen had such a fierce ally. He'd known her for all of two weeks and felt the same way. He'd kill anyone foolish enough to even think of hurting her. But *he* had hurt her, even if it was to protect her, and he struggled to reconcile these two truths. What was he capable of when it came down to it? Just how ruthless of a person was he? He had the uneasy feeling that the answer was one he wouldn't be comfortable with, one that didn't fit his self-concept of who Mike Wójcik was.

Far worse, though, was the fracture in their group that hadn't been there before. Zach didn't trust him anymore. Didn't seem to like him much, either. He saw the way Zach flinched whenever Imogen winced or showed signs of pain or discomfort, for he did, too. But where Zach could draw upon protectiveness and righteous indignation, all Mike had was a mire of shame and self-loathing. Imogen looked and said she felt so much better. He could almost look at her and not cringe inside, now that her face didn't look so battered.

All I can do is what I'm doing. Face it head-on and show them every day that I'm not that guy.

Maybe, if he was very lucky, he could repair the broken trust.

The scuffle of feet on the stairs pulled him from his thoughts. Instead of Jeffrey, Kevin, or Sandy coming down the stairs, he saw Betty. Boo, one of the cats Bec was feeding, followed Betty like a white shadow whenever she was outside. Bec might consider Boo her cat, but Boo seemed to have chosen Betty to be his person.

The wood planks of the bridge clunked underneath Betty's feet as she crossed it. "Mike," she said, pushing her brown hair out of her eyes. "I was hoping to catch you before you leave."

"You found me," he said. "What's up?"

"I'm hoping you can help me."

She didn't continue. Her body rocked as she shifted her weight from one foot to the other and back again. She flitted her fingers, tangling them up in one another. She was nervous, Mike realized, but he couldn't think why she should be. He'd never been told he was unapproachable, but maybe the stress of the last few weeks had put him more on edge than he realized.

When she didn't continue, he prompted her, "So, what do you want to talk about?"

"We've got a leadership problem. Imogen talked to me about it and so did Amy," she said, rolling her eyes. "But Clyde and I think so, too."

Mike's brow furrowed; he was a little confused where she was going with this. "How do you think I can help?"

"I'm hoping that you'll consider teaming up with me."

Mike took a halting half step back, his belly clenching with apprehension. "Like being in charge and making all the decisions?"

He didn't like the idea, if that was what she had in mind. The lodge wasn't his place... It wasn't even his friend's place. He didn't know anyone especially well. He'd known Sandy, Imogen, and Kevin the longest—for about two weeks? And Jay too, he supposed, but Jay kept to himself more than the others. He was a dick, in Mike's opinion. He pitched in to get things done, but only when someone supervised him like a child. It was annoying, but in the end the work got done. Mostly. Mike figured that was more important than whether he liked the guy.

"Oh, no, no, no," Betty said. "Nothing like that. What I was thinking is we should have quick check-ins in the morning about daily tasks, or maybe a weekly meeting?" Her voice lilted higher at the end, making it a question. "I'm not sure what's too much, we'll have to figure that out. We should make big decisions as a group. Like your trip today, for instance. We won't agree all the time, even if we put it to a vote or we have a tie."

Mike did a quick head count, even though he knew there were ten people in their group—for now.

Betty said, "I'd like to propose that you and I make those decisions."

Mike took his time to digest what Betty was suggesting. When he spoke, he said, "You want you or Clyde because of the direct connection to the guy who owns the lodge, right?"

Betty nodded. "Yes. We're the closest thing to anyone who has a claim, so to speak." She grimaced, as if she were uncomfortable with the idea. If he was in her shoes, Mike might feel the same.

"And you want me because I'm from the new group."

Again, Betty nodded, a glimmer of cautious optimism flickering in her eyes.

"Why not Sandy?" Mike asked her. "She's a police officer. She's trained to assess situations and resolve them. I've read articles about how female officers are better than male officers at de-escalation, and I've seen her do it."

"I thought about Sandy," Betty said. "But it might be a good idea if we had a man and a woman. There are things a man feels more comfortable telling a man and vice versa."

Mike bit his lip as he nodded. "Yeah, I can see that."

"Besides," Betty said, looking him in the eye. "You're already doing it."

"What are you talking about?" he said, surprised.

Betty smiled. "You really don't know, do you?" When he didn't answer, she said, "You're always checking in with people about what might need done. You ask people what they think and talk to them about it."

He shrugged. "I was shop steward for my union local. I picked up a few things about how to talk to people, but what I do isn't anything special."

Betty shook her head. "That's what a good leader does— reaches out to people, actually listens to what they have to say and takes it into account before deciding. Most of the time, anyway." A look of exasperation flitted over Betty's face and Mike had a sneaking suspicion she was thinking of Amy. "You see what needs doing and make sure it gets done, just like me, but not everybody does that. Most people need a leader. We're going to have to make some really hard decisions at some point. If I'm going to step up and do this, then I want to be working with someone who can make hard decisions and stick with them."

Everything Betty had said was true. She was right about the listening and finding out what people needed, what they wanted; he'd done it as shop steward. No one had ever shown him how... It was just what he'd always done. He never had problems making decisions. If anything, he made them a little too fast. After his parents died, so many decisions were thrust upon him. He'd had to grow up and take charge, ready or not. The alternative would have been foster care for Faith—seventeen at the time—and Beth and Jonah, who were even younger. Mike and Faith had been determined that wouldn't happen, so they did the only thing they could—stepped up and fought tooth and nail.

"When do you want to talk to people about this?" he asked Betty.

A flush of pleasure, mixed with relief, suffused Betty's soft face. He hadn't said, 'Yes, I'll do it,' but he'd agreed all the same. The soft chatter of Sandy, Jeffrey, and Kevin's voices floated down from above as they made their way down the windy stairs. Betty glanced over her shoulder to them, then back to Mike.

"Let's do it this evening, after you get back. With the others checking out the cabins nearby, we'll have a better idea of where we stand with supplies and food." Her mouth settled in a hard line, and her eyes pinched at the corners. "We've got so much, thanks to Bob, but we're going to need more."

Mike nodded. "I know."

"Sorry we took so long to get here, Mike," Sandy said as they crossed the bridge. "Someone had trouble finding his boots."

"It was me," Jeffrey said. "I'll own it."

Kevin elbowed him. "Own it by keeping better track of them. If we need to run from zombies—"

"I know, I know," Jeffrey said, but good-naturedly. "And if I didn't, you've given me such an earful that I know it now."

Kevin chuckled, and Betty said, "Good luck. And don't do anything silly, okay? If it's too dangerous, just leave it. There's nothing out there that's worth your lives."

Sandy raised her eyebrows. "If not being dangerous is the baseline for our decision-making, we can't do anything."

"You know what I mean," Betty said. "Quit being a smart-ass."

"Let's go," Mike said, giving Betty a smile. "We've got over thirty miles to cover before we reach Wellsboro. Who's riding with me?"

"I am," Kevin said. "Sandy and Jeffrey have been singing. I'm not up for that."

"Baby," Jeffrey teased.

Sandy leveled a steely gaze at Kevin, but a smile hovered in one raised end of her lips. "I dare you to ride with us."

Kevin shook his head and joined Mike in the zoo pickup. Betty gave them one last wave, then started back over the bridge.

"What was that about?" Kevin asked. "You and Betty had your heads together like you were doing a drug deal."

Mike's laughter filled the cab of the truck. "She just wanted to talk about having a group meeting tonight. I haven't been involved in a drug deal since I bought weed in college."

Kevin chuckled, then said, "I thought you were an electrician. How'd your parents take you doing that after going to college?"

"Didn't finish. My folks—" He hesitated for a moment, but if his mom or dad had been in his shoes—parents dead and needing to keep the family together—they'd have done the same. "My folks were fine with it."

CHAPTER 12
MIKE

Kevin's comment echoed Mike's thoughts. He raised up on tiptoes, as if it would make a difference.

"That's not gonna change the view. Already tried," Sandy said.

She stood beside Mike in the bed of Clyde's truck. Kevin and Jeffrey were on her other side, and all of them were looking down at Berrigan's Home Improvement. The home improvement center was like a Home Depot but a smaller, local business. There was a garden center on one end and the loading area by a roll-up door on the other. It even had a glassed-in entrance area for shopping carts. Mike hoped the layout was similar, too. He went to Home Depot a lot and was familiar with where things were.

Berrigan's was the first building at the near end of a commercial strip about a thousand feet beyond the crest of a hill. It sat apart from the others, perhaps so delivery trucks had more room to maneuver around the building from either side. The road curved left, away from the building, before it straightened and flattened out for about a mile. From where they'd stopped, they could see the front parking lot, but not what might be behind the building.

"What do you think?" Jeffrey said. "Go for it or try somewhere else?"

Mike's dark eyes swept the parking lot. The weather had gotten cool enough that he'd had to scrounge up a hoodie to wear under his leather jacket. The heavy air and cloudy sky seemed to leach everything around them of color. At least it's not raining, he thought, though he could tell from the cloud cover that would change at some point. There weren't that many cars in the lot. Zombies wandered the large patch of gray asphalt, aimless as autumn leaves in the wind; fifty by Mike's count and all slow movers.

"We could try moving them," he said.

Sandy looked at the parking lot, her eyes narrowed. "You think?"

"Won't we have to make noise to do that?" Jeffrey said.

"Not if they just see us," Sandy said. "If we pulled one truck right up by the exit, we could—"

"That's a terrible idea," Kevin said.

Mike only half listened to the ensuing back and forth. An anger that was beginning to feel familiar coiled in his belly. Just when you thought you might catch a break, zombies came along to ruin your day. The drive from Cady's Run State Park had been relatively easy. Folks must have battened down the hatches early on out here, because all they'd seen were three abandoned cars and a dozen zombies they'd been able to drive around. For a thirty-mile trip, Mike counted that as a win, even if it begged the question of where those people had gone.

That win would be hollow if they didn't get inside the store. They needed plywood to make shutters for the lodge's windows, and hand tools and hardware. Insulation, two-by-fours, and drywall to insulate the sleeping area of the Twig. And a wood-burning stove, Mike thought, but that wasn't their task today. Kevin wanted copper tubing for a project he was tight-lipped about in case it didn't work. If they didn't get inside Berrigan's, they'd go home empty-handed, having wasted a lot of fuel.

Resolve settled over Mike like a weight on his shoulders. They hadn't traveled this far to fail. "Here's what we're going to do," he said. "It looks like they have a few rental or maybe delivery trucks parked up front there. See?" He pointed at three white pickup trucks with the store's logo on the doors that were parked outside the large roll-up door at one end of the cinderblock building. "We leave Clyde's truck alongside the building, by the garden center at the other end. Then we drive around back to the loading docks in the zoo pickup. If it looks okay behind the building, that's where we go in."

"Which is a big assumption," Jeffrey said, the rise and fall of his shrugging shoulders showing just how much of an 'if' the scenario Mike was laying out was. "We can't see that lot."

Mike nodded. "Right… But assuming we get inside, we just need to find the keys to those rental trucks and stage as much as we can by that front roll-up door."

"Then we make a commotion to draw the zombies away from the trucks if we need to," Sandy said, picking up the thread of Mike's plan. "Load up as much as we can and get the hell out of here."

Kevin's brow furrowed. "You want to leave our trucks?"

Mike frowned. He hadn't thought that bit through. "Does it really matter? We leave some trucks here, take others back. I don't see what the difference is as long as they run."

"And we aren't coming out short on fuel," Sandy said.

"I think Clyde will disagree with you, Mike," Kevin said. "He was telling me about his truck the other night. He loves it. I kind of love it, too."

"Then we'll figure out a way to bring it back while we're moving everything into position," Mike said.

"Will the rental trucks have enough gas to get back?" Sandy said.

"If this place is anything like Home Depot or Lowe's, yes," Jeffrey said. "My ex-boyfriend rented one when he moved out. Things weren't hostile, so I gave him my credit card because I didn't think he'd be a jerk and not fill the tank. There was a big penalty that he didn't bother to mention."

Mike hadn't realized Jeffrey was gay, which mattered not a whit. In Mike's experience, a person's sexual orientation was never the most interesting thing about them—unless it was someone you were hoping to sleep with. "Is this doable, or am I talking out my ass? Don't be polite if you think it sucks."

"It could work. Let's try it," Jeffrey said.

Kevin nodded, Sandy too, adding, "It's not the worst thing I've heard by a long shot."

"Let's be smart about it, though," Mike said. "No taking chances when you don't have to."

Sandy laughed. "You sound like Betty. Are you even old enough to play dad?" She bit her lip and narrowed her eyes, appraising him, and grinned. "Maybe an older FILF…"

Kevin barely suppressed a bray with laughter. "As in Mother I'd Like to…?"

"Yeah," Sandy said. "He's got the smoldering bedroom eyes. The dimples add just enough boyish charm to pull off the salt-and-pepper—"

"Oh my God, stop!" Mike said, a blush making his face hot, but by now all three of them were snickering.

"She's right about the dimples," Jeffrey said, setting off another round of laughter.

"You're gonna pay for this," Mike said, pointing at Sandy.

She smirked. "Promises, promises."

"Seriously though," Mike said, grinning despite his embarrassment. Sandy was dishing it out in a way that had taken the edge off his nervousness. "Let's be smart about this. Our situation isn't desperate enough to get killed for plywood and screws."

CHAPTER 13
IMOGEN

Imogen looked out the window of the cottage they were searching, waving goodbye to Zach and Clyde, then said to Bec, "I never thought we were going to get rid of them."

Bec laughed, and Imogen smiled, too. Bec's laugh seemed to require her entire body's participation. Being around her lifted Imogen's spirits. Admittedly, their situation felt a little less dire since they'd arrived at the lodge, but she felt almost… happy. Bec was as fun as Imogen remembered her being when they'd met at Six at Sylvie's.

"Don't be too tough on Zach," Bec said. "He's just worried about you. It's sweet."

Imogen had to work hard to keep her mouth from falling open. "What about your lecture the other day about smashing the patriarchy?"

Bec's brow furrowed. "What about it?"

"Zach isn't listening to me. He's hovering all the time, like I need to be defended and can't manage if he isn't by my side every minute. If he doesn't stop trying to dictate how I should feel about Mike slapping me so he can beat his chest and growl, I'm going to smack him. Mike saved my life, which is the end of the story for me."

Bec stared at Imogen, her lips pulled back in a grimace, and groaned. "That's some hard-core feminist critique... I can't believe I was falling into the 'but he's a nice guy' trap." She whimpered. "My brain hurts."

Imogen laughed, because Bec couldn't look more stricken if she'd kicked Boo or Buttercup, the cats she was trying to befriend using their tinned tuna. "We've been brainwashed our entire lives, Bec. It's bound to sneak up on you sometimes. There's been a lot going on, what with zombies and all. It's bad enough that we're living almost on top of one another. I'm not complaining, really," she hastened to add. "I'm so grateful Clyde and Betty asked us to come with them, and I can't believe my luck that Zach is here, but the way he's carrying on is wearing on me."

Bec scowled for another moment. She looked like she was resolving to do better deconstructing dominant paradigms going forward. "You're not half as grateful as me and Jeffrey. We'd been walking for two days when you found us after..."

Her voice trailed, then she visibly shook herself. This was the most Bec had said about their journey out of Pittsburgh. Jeffrey had mentioned they left the city with four other friends. It was just the two of them now. Like so many others, their escape from the city had been filled with tragedy.

The cottage they were busy ripping apart was a mile up the road from the lodge. After making the mistake of opening the fridge, they'd slammed it shut and opened every window. There was no power here. The lack of it underscored how different one's circumstances could be, even a short distance away. A mile wasn't far, and they still had heat, lights, and hot water because they had power.

"Ooh, lookee," Bec said. She held up an evening gown secured to the hanger by lingerie straps. It had lots of ruffles and lace and was a satiny mint green. The puffed sleeves were meant to be worn off the shoulder, and it looked to be tea length for someone much taller than either she or Bec. On either of them, it would brush the floor.

"I'm guessing a nineteen eighties bridesmaid dress," Bec said, wrinkling her nose, the smattering of freckles over it distinct against her pale skin.

"It has that look, but it's not the worst. The bridesmaid dresses for my parents' wedding were orange and hideous. You should bring it back."

"What for—punishment?" Her eyes filled with a manic gleam. "Can you picture Amy in this?"

The laugh that burbled up took Imogen by surprise. If Amy's puss was sour now, she could only imagine what she'd look like if they forced her to wear that dress.

Bec snorted as she laughed. "I ought to make her wear it as payback for being such a pain in the butt about the cats. Who did Buttercup and Boo ever hurt? They won't give us bubonic plague."

"You're going to win eventually, Bec. Even Amy is calling them by the names you gave them."

Bec seemed to consider this, then looked at the dress again. "This thing would be cruel and unusual punishment, even for Amy. It's a fashion crime if ever there was one."

Bec returned the dress to the closet. Together, she and Imogen stuffed the clothes they'd thrown on the bed, as well as the winter jumpers, socks, and underwear from the dresser that Imogen had added to the pile, into trash bags. They'd found several boxes of the extra-thick black contractor's bags at the lodge. They were perfect for collecting clothes and food.

I hope Mike and the others are okay.

Imogen squelched the thought, but not quick enough to forestall the stab of anxiety that felt like a spike to her chest. She enjoyed Bec's company, but that wasn't the only reason she was grateful they were together. Bec was good at distracting her, which helped keep her anxiety about the trip to the home improvement center in check. She, Bec, Zach, and Clyde were just going up the road, while the others were traveling thirty miles, and if all went well, another thirty to get back.

Imogen pushed the drawer of the dresser shut, using the scrape of the wood to hide the deep inhale/exhale she employed to calm herself. "I know we need clothes and food, but I feel like a thief. I know most of these people won't need them anymore, but..."

Bec stuffed the last pair of socks into the bag and tied it off. "It's better to use things than waste them. I'm going to check the bathroom. Do you mind taking this to the door?"

Imogen walked through the little cottage and dropped the bag at the front door. This cottage was truly a cottage; it was easy to see it had originally been one room and the bedroom and bathroom added later. The front door opened into the small kitchen along the front wall that was lined with windows over a farmhouse sink and butcher-block counter. Someone had remodeled the cottage at some point, keeping the rustic style but adding improvements like newer windows. A white porcelain sink and homey braided rugs made the cottage feel snug and welcoming. The stove and oven, enameled in white, looked straight out of a nineteen fifties film. It was a kitchen Imogen could picture herself in.

The rest of the little building was the main living area, with lots of windows to let in light and a woodburning stove. There had been heavy green velvet curtains, but they'd pulled them down to use at the lodge. Imogen walked to the kitchen, peering into cupboards to make sure they had missed no food. She noticed the cleaning supplies under the sink. Might as well take them, too.

Bec joined her a moment later, the small bag she'd used for the bathroom clinking softly. "There were tampons, shampoo, and a lot of moisturizer," she said. "We'll want the moisturizer once it gets cold."

"I like this place," Imogen said. "I love the lodge, but this is the place I'd pick for myself."

"It's still creepy, all this scrounging and skulking and taking people's stuff, but I guess that's the way things are now." Bec frowned, looking unhappy, then said, "I know we told Zach and Clyde we'd wait for them to come back, but why don't we walk? We can leave everything here and get it on the way back. I don't think we're going to run into any zombies out here and I could really use some exercise."

Imogen wasn't sure deviating from the plan was the best idea, but agreed. They'd been here several days and had seen nothing but animals. That might not be the best barometer of their safety, since zombies didn't bother animals, but it still reassured her. They crossed the bridge over the creek and emerged by the road. There was a sign near the road that said Trout Cabin with a jumping fish painted on it.

"I'm glad we're at the lodge," Bec said. "I wouldn't want to be down here by the road."

"Me neither."

Clyde had said the next cabin he knew of was about two miles away, a distance they could cover in a short time. It had surprised Imogen how quickly the bluff veered away from the creek, widening the bank on the far side enough for cabins. Trout Cabin was on the same side of the creek as the lodge, but at the foot of the bluff. The creek bank beside it was only ten feet high.

"The cabins down here must be at more risk from flooding if the creek gets high enough," Imogen said.

"Clyde said a few years back there was a flood, and it got so high it washed away a few planks from our bridge, and others were totally washed out."

Imogen's eyes widened in surprise. "This cabin must have flooded. Why even build here?"

Bec shrugged. "Maybe it didn't flood as much when it was built."

It wasn't until they crossed the bridge to this cottage that Imogen understood the lodge's unique location. Clyde had said all the cabins on this side of the road were at road level. That meant they were more visible and easier to reach despite the creek.

"So, are you and Zach a thing?"

"What?" Imogen said. She'd been in the United States for three years, but the bluntness of Americans still surprised her. "No. He's my friend."

Bec shrugged. "Just wondered. I don't think he's got a thing for you. I'm usually pretty good at seeing that. Or if he did, he's over it now."

"I don't think Zach ever found me attractive," Imogen said, shaking her head.

Bec's laugh erupted fully formed, as startling as a sudden rain shower. "Imogen," she said, snorting with laughter. "He'd have to be blind to not find you attractive. You're gorgeous."

Imogen's face warmed as she blushed. She wasn't used to fielding such compliments. "Well, I—"

"Just take the compliment, hon. You look like a model, but shorter."

Secretly, Imogen was pleased. *Bec* was gorgeous, with her startling blue eyes and wide pixie grin. More than that, Bec had attitude. She was sassy in a way that Imogen would never be.

"Imogen," Bec whispered. "Look."

She followed the line of Bec's pointing finger, and the road lurched under her feet. Her heart thumped triple-time and a swarm of angry wasps rumbled in her stomach. An animal—a cat—stood in the road a few hundred feet away. A sudden, irrational hope soared in her heart. Her lynxes were alive! And somehow, they'd found her…

"Oh my God," she said, her voice strangled.

"It's a bobcat, right?"

She stared at Bec, jarred by her words, then back at the wildcat in the road. The line of its back was straight, lacking an upward curve at the rump and shoulders. It had spots, but she had to squint to make them out, for they blended almost invisibly in the cat's silvery coat. Its front and back legs were almost the same size and its tail was longer than either Ferdinand's or Isabella's. The cat had noticed them and turned its head, posture tense and gaze steady. As the rush of elation drained away, Imogen realized the points of its ears lacked the extra long, distinctive black tufts of fur. The fur color was wrong, too. Iberian lynxes were browner, not the silver of this cat that going into winter would serve as better camouflage. This cat was smaller, too.

She stood frozen, mouth open, the tears of joy welling in her eyes cooling to those of crushing disappointment. The bobcat looked away and scampered across the road, disappearing into the forest.

"That was amazing," Bec said, turning to her. The wide smile died on lips and her eyes rounded in alarm. "Imogen, what's wrong? Are you okay?"

Imogen felt her face screw up. Her mouth puckered, eyebrows contracting. Her heart, which just a moment ago had burst with expansive joy, crumbled in on itself like a papery husk. She swayed slightly on her feet, then pressed her hand against her mouth.

"You're scaring me," Bec said, taking her by the shoulders. "What's wrong?"

"I thought," she said, her shoulder hitching as she started to cry. "I thought it was one of my lynxes."

"Oh, Imogen," Bec sighed, then pulled her close.

As Bec's arms closed around her shoulders, the grief welled up and burst free. Imogen sagged against Bec, sobbing into her shoulder, her gasping breaths as jagged as shards of glass. She'd had one job to do—one—that she'd embraced like a sacred vow. Keep her lynxes safe, care for and protect them, provide for the beautiful animals she loved. They had been robbed of their birthright to wildness. The least she could do was take care of them. It was the only thing she'd needed to do, and she'd failed.

Then a rush of homesickness struck like a rogue wave. Despite the cool air, moist with the promise of rain, the dusty earth of the Serengeti plain filled her nose. A puff of hot air brushed her face like a hummingbird's wing. The distant bugling of elephants, and the rumble of Mcheshi's and Matumaini's purring—a sound she associated with her childhood and the cheetahs she had so loved—overwhelmed her. And faintly, almost too soft to hear, Araminta's laughter glittered like stardust.

"I don't know where they are," she mumbled into Bec's shoulder a minute or two later. She stepped back and swiped at her face, only to see Bec was crying, too. "My lynxes, my sister, my parents…"

"I know," Bec said, her blue eyes stricken with grief. She took a shuddering breath. "I was out with my friends. When I finally got hold of my parents, they told me to get out of the city. I didn't want to, but they freaked out when I said I was coming home. My dad started crying. I could hear it over the phone, and he never cries. He's such a macho dork. So I finally agreed but…"

Imogen rubbed Bec's shoulders while she gulped deep breaths, trying to get herself under control. She hadn't meant to break down like this, nor mire Bec alongside her. "I'm sorry, Bec. I didn't mean—"

"Oh, please," Bec whimpered. She sounded like a child learning her longed-for outing had been canceled. "You think this is the first time I've cried like a baby? I can't believe I'm not doing it twenty-four seven."

Imogen's chuff of laughter was laced with miserable solidarity. She tugged the sleeve of her shirt from under the cuff of her jacket and wiped her eyes. "I got a text from my sister the day we left the zoo."

Bec sniffed and wiped at her nose with her jacket sleeve. "You mean the day we met up?" When Imogen nodded, she said, "But the phones were all down."

Imogen raised her hands in front of her, helpless to offer an explanation. "I know, but I got a signal. It didn't last long, but loads of texts downloaded."

"Was she somewhere safe?"

Imogen pressed her lips together, trying not to cry, though her eyes already welled with tears. She shook her head. "She was at Heathrow, about to get on a plane to come see me."

Bec stared at Imogen, her expression pained enough that they could have been talking about a member of Bec's family instead of Imogen's. "Where was her connection?"

"JFK."

Bec grimaced and groaned, air puffing her cheeks like a chipmunk. "When USAir quit using Pittsburgh as a hub, most of the nonstops from Europe went with it. Oh, man…"

"I'm not sure a nonstop would have helped her."

"It might not have hurt."

They stood in silence for a long time, listening to the birdsong and the creak of tree branches. Bec sniffed again. "I should've brought a roll of toilet paper from that cabin."

Imogen smiled, a tremulous thing, more reflex than anything else. "Do you think they're all right?"

"Clyde and Zach? There's nothing out here."

Imogen shook her head. "Mike and the others."

"Yes," Bec said firmly. "I don't think they'll do anything too stupid with Sandy along."

"I wish they weren't going so far," Imogen said pensively, biting her lip. She could feel the vein in her temple gearing up to thump. She breathed deep, imagining the air expanding to the very bottom of her lungs, and the vein settled down.

"Besides," Bec continued. "I can't keep crying like this without something to blow my nose, so they have to be okay."

Imogen chuckled, this time for real. "I guess that's one way to do it."

"How bad do I look?" Bec asked.

"Like you've been crying," Imogen answered. "No modeling contracts for us today."

Bec smiled, but she looked tired in a way she hadn't before.

"Half of them are anorexic and the rest make us feel fat. Fashion can suck it."

"But what about that dress we found?"

Bec's laughter sounded more genuine when she said, "We'll make an exception, but only because it's so awful."

CHAPTER 14
MIKE

As soon as they reached the back of the building, where they hoped to enter via the loading dock, Mike's enthusiasm for his plan curdled in his stomach. What they couldn't see from where they'd scoped out Berrigan's from the road was that the back parking lot abutted a shopping mall. Not the older type of mall where the shops were inside one structure, but the kind with shops sprawled over half an acre and parking near every store. That parking lot, unlike the Berrigan's lot, was almost full. Many of the vehicles had doors ajar and Mike could see bodies on the ground.

"That doesn't look good," Sandy said.

"Let's check out the loading dock," Jeffrey said. "It might be sheltered from view."

But when they reached the loading dock, they were still in full view of the mall parking lot. "I say we call it," Mike said. "I don't think it's worth the risk of what might come at us."

Kevin's brow had furrowed. He squinted his eyes, like he was trying to solve a problem. "I don't understand why there's such a big shopping center out here."

"I don't know, but I think it's too dangerous," Mike said. "We could have runners on us in minutes."

"We're here. Let's at least try," Kevin said. "If we leave now, that's a sixty-mile trip with nothing to show for it."

Jeffrey and Sandy agreed, which left Mike in the awkward position of being the only one who didn't want to continue. "If it gets bad, we leave. Okay?" Sandy said.

"Okay," Mike said reluctantly, and only because he'd been outvoted.

They got out of the truck and climbed the concrete stairs to the loading dock. The door was—predictably—locked; so was the roll-up door.

Sandy poked her chin at the person-sized door. "Will your Halligan work on that?"

"Maybe the rolling door will be easier. Let's see if anyone's home," Kevin said. He thumped on it a few times with his fist— hard enough to get the attention of anyone or thing inside. Half a minute later, something thumped against the other side of the door. "That answers that."

Mike's full attention wasn't on the conversation. He looked toward the parking lot of the mall. He saw movement among the cars, but it wasn't close. The volume of the moans on the other side of the door grew, but only by a few voices.

"We should open the regular door and use it to meter them out," Jeffrey said.

Mike turned around at that. "Like a traffic meter?"

Jeffrey nodded. "I know Kevin said the roll-up door will be easier to force open, but this door swings out. We could hold the door and let them out a few at a time. It'll be safer."

"Unless the noise we make killing them attracts runners," said Sandy.

Kevin looked at Mike. "What do you think?"

What I think is that we need to get the hell out of here, he thought, but didn't say. He kept thinking about the things inside they needed, and a sixty-mile drive with nothing to show for it. "Let's do it."

Kevin stuck the thin end of the Halligan—the adze—into the

space between the door and the jamb, right by the lock, and pulled. The steel door creaked, and the thumping and moans got a little louder.

"Help me with this," Kevin said, grunting. "Push from the other side."

Jeffrey stood opposite Kevin, gripped the handle of the Halligan just below where Kevin did, and pushed while Kevin pulled. Mike unsheathed his knife. Together with Sandy, he stood about ten feet back from the door, still scanning the mall parking lot.

"Be ready to hold that door," Kevin said.

"Don't worry… about me," Jeffrey grunted with effort, but then a loud crack and a shriek of metal rent the air, drowning him out.

The door flew open with a bang, knocking Jeffrey off his feet. Kevin stumbled backward from the sudden give, but stayed upright. Three zombies staggered out the door before Jeffrey scrambled up to slam it shut.

Sandy stepped forward to take care of a young woman. Her filthy blond hair was still in a ponytail, though it had pulled loose around her bloodied face. An old man staggered toward Mike, his once trim figure now gaunt. Goose pimples rippled up Mike's arms and over the back of his neck when he let the zombie grab his arm before he stepped in close and stabbed it through the eye. The old man's wasted body fell at his feet. He pulled the knife free, grimacing, ready to get the last zombie, but it was already down.

"Ready?" Sandy said, glancing at Mike and Kevin.

When they nodded, Jeffrey pulled the door open, bracing it against one foot. More hapless shoppers from Berrigan's Home Improvement now intent on eating them tumbled out. The stench made Mike's eyes water as he stabbed a man in the eye, then pushed him aside.

A low, erratic *thump, thump, thump, thump, thump* carried on the breeze. Runners, their footsteps muddled together, were crossing into the back parking lot. Terror welled up in Mike's throat, robbing him of breath. Sandy, Kevin, and Jeffery focused on the door and the zombies from inside. They hadn't noticed the runners.

"We've got runners! We need to leave or get inside."

The door shoved into Jeffrey. He cried out in surprise, not quite able to keep the door in place. A large man—a runner—dressed in stained gray sweatpants and a jersey shirt barreled out the door. The runner lunged for Sandy, but she ducked, tripping it. The air split with a *zing* as Kevin's Halligan smashed into the zombie's face.

Two more zombies walked out the door, moving more smoothly than the rest. If he hadn't known better, Mike almost could have mistaken them for living people.

The runners from the mall were closing in on the loading dock, so close Mike could see faces: glazed eyes, teeth knocked crooked, gnarled and grasping fingers that looked like talons, brown from dried blood.

Jeffrey stabbed a woman in the eye. Mike ripped his attention away from the oncoming mob, so close he could pick out individual hisses and grunts. He hit the last zombie in the chest, shoving it out of the way. He couldn't tell if it had been a man or a woman… its body and face were a mangled tangle of blackened flesh and gristle.

The gorge rising in Mike's throat tried to explode out of his mouth, but Kevin's rough hand on his shoulder cut it short. He pulled Mike into the warehouse's murky interior, the door slamming shut behind them.

CHAPTER 15
MIKE

MIKE COULDN'T SEE ANYTHING IN THE DARKENED WAREHOUSE. HE pressed his back against the wall beside the door, the rush of blood in his ears and harsh breaths of he and his companions so loud that the crash of the zombies outside seemed far away. They waited for the telltale echo of feet striking concrete. The seconds dragged, the silence thickening. After half a minute that felt like an hour, Sandy said, "If there were runners in here, we'd hear them by now."

Mike let go of the breath tightening his chest. "Everyone okay?"

"Yeah," Jeffrey said, his voice breathier than usual and filled with relief. Then he started giggling. Mike heard the clap of a hand over Jeffrey's mouth. In the vast nothingness of the warehouse, Jeffrey's reaction grated against Mike's brain with the sharpness of a knuckle cut while grating carrots. Mike knew he wasn't laughing because he found this funny—quite the opposite. It was nerves after their close shave.

They could have stumbled inside trying to escape those runners only to encounter more, instead of the silence of this tomb-like building. They wouldn't have been able to see until their eyes adjusted, and in the time required for that to happen could've already been dead. That was how thin the margin for error was now. Coming up against it left Mike's body chilled by the sweat slicking him from head to toe. His stomach ached, having tied itself into knots so tight if they were made of yarn they'd have to be cut out. Tiny tremors made the muscles of his arms and legs twitch.

Stop it. We're all right.

Mike pushed off the wall and took some deep breaths, attempting to shake off the brush with death. He didn't feel like he was taking these 'new normal' experiences in stride like the others seemed to. He wasn't sure he ever would.

"You were right about attracting runners, Mike," Kevin said. "We should have listened."

By now his eyes had adjusted, so the light from the skylights seemed brighter. Tall industrial shelving towered over them, packed with shadowy merchandise. He almost didn't need to squint to make out the sign at the end of the aisle across from him. "Let's get started."

"Are you guys okay breaking up in teams?" Sandy asked. "I think we should. We can cover more ground."

"What if we run into a bunch of them, the slow ones?" Jeffrey said. "Four people together have a better chance than two."

Kevin looked to Mike, a question in his raised eyebrows. Mike felt torn. He didn't know how long it would take for them to get the supplies they needed. They had a long drive back to the lodge, even if it went as smooth as the drive here. He wanted to get in and out of this place as quickly as he could while getting the supplies that they needed safely.

"Sandy's right. Let's split up."

Sandy squinted into the murky warehouse. "How about Kevin and I take it from this side over, you guys take the other. But first we've gotta see if there are any truck keys. If not, we'll have to change our plan."

Flashlights in hand, they crept down the aisle in front of them. Their footsteps echoed in the silence, giving the seemingly deserted warehouse an eerie feel. Mike expected the beams of light to reveal smears of blood and mangled corpses reaching for them at any moment.

"This is creeping me out," Kevin whispered.

No one answered. When they reached the end of the aisle, Mike's eyes swept across the cash registers. Both doors at the entrance—the outer leading to the glassed-in shoebox where shopping carts waited for customers, and the interior leading into the store—were locked and the glass unbroken. The roll-up door was at the other end of the row of registers. Just as it had seemed when they looked from the parking lot, this door, too, was intact. Whatever had happened here hadn't been as gruesome as Mike had expected, apart from getting inside.

"You think we're the first people inside since they locked up?" Jeffrey said.

Sandy shrugged, as close to an answer as anyone managed.

"The keys for the rentals will be at the service desk or the office," Kevin said. He shifted his Halligan from one shoulder to the other. "I think that's our best bet."

A minute later they were at the service desk, peeking over the counters. A rotten scent hit Mike in the face, causing him to gag. "Ugh. Got something here."

He shone his flashlight along the counter as he rounded the corner. A man and a woman lay crumpled behind it. Mike moved closer, the flashlights of his companions bouncing off the ceiling, housewares at the front of the store, tools, and service desk drawers. Bins were lined up behind the counter full of smaller items that people had returned, back when that had still been a thing.

"Oh, man," Jeffrey said. From the nasal tone of his voice, Mike could tell he was trying to breathe through his mouth. "That's rank."

As he got closer, Mike could see that the people on the floor had turned into zombies. There were bites on their hands and arms. Spidery black veins disappeared under the short-sleeved shirts both wore from what had once been festering bite wounds.

Now the wounds looked shriveled, the edges rimmed with blackened flesh. The woman's eyes were open, the whites shot through with black veins. Her open mouth displayed blood dried to brown on her teeth. The man's face had been bitten in several places, and the sides of both of their heads were bashed in.

"Maybe this happened and they shut the store but didn't know what the bites meant till later," Sandy said.

Moans started up from the side of the store toward the garden center, followed by thumps on glass. Everyone pointed the beams of their flashlights that direction. One of the industrial shelving units was on its side and pushed against the sliding glass doors to the outdoor section of the garden center. Scattered plants that had been on the overturned shelves were strewn across the floor, making starbursts of dirt across the polished concrete.

Through the barricade, figures were visible on the other side of the glass. They were too far and the view too obstructed to be more than indistinct shadows, but Mike could see hands slapping the glass, which was streaked with ragged drip patterns Mike didn't want to think about. Even though they moaned and pounded the glass doors, the noise wasn't too bad.

"Let's get the keys and our stuff and get out of here," Sandy said.

"I'll start on this side," Mike said, grimacing as he stepped over the grisly remains of what had been people not so long ago, people with lives and families and everything that went along with it: worries about their kids, bills, and people they'd enjoyed and looked forward to being with.

He looked at the many drawers and hooks on the walls, realizing this might take a while. They set to work, silent but for the pull of drawers and the rustling of the items inside that followed, and sometimes the soft jangle of metal. Mike searched drawer after drawer, becoming more frustrated.

"Found them," Sandy said, brandishing the keys. "All three

sets of keys are here if the license plate numbers match the ones on these tags."

"We'll check the trucks?" Kevin asked Sandy, who nodded. "And you guys get started on the list."

"I think we should stack smaller stuff in the center of the aisles. Then we can load it on those flat carts all at once," Jeffrey said. He paused, then added, "Anyone know how to drive the forklifts?"

"I used to drive a Bobcat at my grandpap's farm," Kevin said. "Let me see if I can figure it out. They should still have a charge."

Sandy and Kevin headed for the large roll-up door to confirm they had the right keys for the trucks. Enough light shone through the roll-up door's windows that Mike could read the Contractor Checkout sign above the last two registers. Mike said a silent prayer that they had the right keys. He could hot-wire the trucks if necessary, but it would be nice to have ignitions that weren't tampered with.

He and Jeffrey pulled boxes from shelves, conferring about what items on their list they should prioritize. "I wish we could get into that garden center and get some seed," Jeffrey sighed. "I know it's the wrong time of year, but we need to grow food next spring."

Mike grunted as he pulled a small pallet of nails from the shelf. "You're right, but we need to shore up the lodge first. I'm not as worried about seeds just yet."

"Why?"

"We need to get through the winter first." When Jeffrey frowned, looking more worried than before, he added, "We'll check the nearest town… Swedenport, right? We'll find seedlings in vegetable gardens from fruits and vegetables that fell and rotted in the soil."

Volunteers, Steph had called them, as she'd plucked out tiny forests of tomato plants. He could see her tanned skin, smell its scent after being warmed by the sun. How many times had he watched her crouched in the garden with her brown hair pulled back in a ponytail and dirt smudged on her face? He'd always wanted to let the seedlings grow tall and bear fruits, even though he knew that wasn't how it worked. If the plants weren't thinned out, none would grow well, but it had always bummed him out a little.

The memory tore his heart, leaving jagged edges that cut the inside of his chest. Tears sprang to his eyes. He'd never see her again, never watch her murder all those tomato seedlings she tossed in a pile to wilt in the sun. The tiny memories of the mundane things he'd taken for granted were some of one of the worst. The deaths of so many people were horrifying, but the scale so vast that most of the time his brain tuned it out like it had old-world disasters. But these tiny memories of people and things he'd assumed would always be there… It was easy to let them slip through the protective bubble he wrapped himself in before he realized what they were, and by then grief had already ambushed him. He took a deep, painful breath, swiping at his eyes and hoping Jeffrey wouldn't notice.

"Do you think that field is big enough?" Jeffrey said a moment later.

"What field?" Mike said, confused. Thinking about Steph had pulled him so far into himself he wasn't sure if he'd missed part of the conversation.

"The one at the top of the mountain that you and Zach checked out. Do you think it'll be big enough to grow all the food we need?"

Mike paused, a hand on the nails he'd been pulling from the shelf. "I'm not sure, to be honest. I've never needed to grow food to survive."

"We should have more than one garden, anyway, in case there's a frost or something else that messes the plants up."

Mike nodded. It was a good idea. "Somewhere lower, nearer to the creek."

Jeffrey's eyes became unfocused. He bit his lip, then said, "If it wasn't right on the road, we could use that church near the park entrance. It has a big church yard, and a fence we can build up taller." Then he muttered, so low Mike almost missed it, "Better use of the space."

"A better use?" Mike asked, a little puzzled.

"Organized religion is a waste of energy."

"You don't believe in anything?"

Jeffrey shook his head. "No, it's not that. My fundie parents couldn't handle having a gay son. They tried to pray the gay away." Jeffrey met Mike's eyes and said, deadpan, "Despite their direct line to God, I still like guys."

Mike laughed without meaning to. Unsupportive parents when you were different, especially a difference that was an excuse to persecute you, was not a laughing matter. Jeffrey had delivered the line with such perfect timing that Mike couldn't help it, and Jeffrey's grin let him know laughing was all right.

"That must have been hard."

Jeffrey snorted. "I survived, which is more than some kids do, but I was so tired of hearing what Jesus would do that I wanted to scream. My mother trotted that out at least once a day. By the time I was fifteen, I was pretty sure the guy who hung out with lepers and tax collectors and hookers wouldn't care I was gay. To make it worse, I liked to cook, and I could decorate a cake like nobody's business. My dad used to make this face when he'd walk into the kitchen and I was baking something. I can still see it."

"What's wrong with that?" Mike's own dad had taught him how to bake, beginning with chocolate chip cookies.

"It didn't conform to his idea of 'appropriate gender roles,'" he said, hooking his fingers to make air quotes. "He didn't like that I never dated girls. He'd have liked it even less if I'd brought a boy home. A few months ago, my mom tried to guilt-trip me about never having grandchildren, because adoption and surrogates aren't a thing, apparently. I shouldn't have, but I asked her if it would be better if I adopted a kid or had sex with a straight woman I wasn't going to marry." For a split second he looked like he wanted to cry. Then he recovered and said breezily, "I just couldn't help myself. She sniffed at me and said, 'Jeffrey, I don't appreciate your irreverent attitude.'"

Mike hadn't spent enough time with Jeffrey to have seen his irreverent attitude, but was getting a glimpse of it now. "I didn't realize you were gay until you mentioned your ex-boyfriend earlier. Steph always said I had no gaydar."

"I bet you turned heads, though."

Mike smiled. "A bit. More when I was younger. I always took it as a compliment. Were you on speaking terms with your folks before all this?"

Jeffrey shrugged. "Ehh... In a you're-going-to-burn-in-hell-but-we're-still-praying-for-you way. I mean, I wish we'd had a better relationship, especially now," he said, his voice growing tight. "But that's hard to do with people who think there's something fundamentally wrong with you, that you can change if you just try hard enough."

"Yeah," Mike said. It felt inadequate given Jeffrey's obvious regret that he and his parents hadn't been closer, but he didn't know what else to say.

"Steph was your wife?" Jeffrey asked.

Mike could feel the muscles of his face tighten, pulling in close to the bone in retreat. "Girlfriend. She was an ER nurse in the North Hills. She was working..."

"The ERs must have been—" Jeffrey stopped, seeming to realize what he was saying and added lamely, "I'm sorry."

Mike nodded and got back to work. He didn't want to talk about Steph, not now. Sometimes, it felt like he didn't want to talk about her ever. Kevin and Sandy found them a few minutes later, confirming that two of the trucks were definitely here. They hadn't been able to see the license plates of the other because of the angle of the parking spots they occupied. They also reported that the front parking lot was almost completely empty of zombies.

"The noise we made getting inside must have been enough to attract them," Kevin said.

"We can't assume that," Mike cautioned. "We might need to cause some sort of distraction out back so we can get away."

Kevin chuckled. "You're like Han Solo."

"What does that mean?" Mike asked him. If he had to be anyone from *Star Wars*, it would be Han Solo, hands down, but he didn't know how he fit the bill.

"'I have a bad feeling about this.' He said it all the time."

"He did, didn't he?"

Kevin grinned, then followed Sandy to disappear into the shadows. Sooner than Mike expected, he heard the faint *whir* of an engine.

"You hear that?" Jeffrey asked.

Mike nodded. A yellow light began to strobe, lighting up a patch of the darkened ceiling. The forklift didn't sound as smooth as Mike remembered from the trips he'd made to Home Depot and Lowe's, but it was a damn sight better than he'd be able to manage.

He sent a silent prayer of gratitude out to the universe. They had a secure building full of supplies, more vehicles than they'd come with to get them to the lodge if they had gas, and a forklift to speed up loading. He still wasn't sure he'd been wrong about it being too risky, but he had to admit that this was one high risk venture that was paying off.

CHAPTER 16
MIKE

The piles stacked at the roll-up door included lumber, hand tools, nails, screws, insulation, caulk, paint, and more. The closer an item was to the door, the higher its importance. This included a large spool of pliable three-quarter-inch copper tubing that Kevin had snagged. Close-lipped about what it was for, Kevin said he'd tell them later, if it worked. He also said it would be worth it.

"Do you think we should take all three of the rental trucks plus Clyde's?" Sandy asked him.

Mike dropped a small roll of wire on a bag of Quikrete, dust puffing around it. "I don't like the idea of not having two people per truck if we run into trouble with a mob, but making two more trips to get the rest isn't appealing, either."

Sandy examined their haul, face alight. They'd collected far too much for two pickup trucks, maybe too much for three. "Let's load up Clyde's truck and one rental, then see where we are."

Kevin hopped from the forklift and joined them, followed by Jeffrey, who had followed Kevin's progress in case anything fell off. They walked to the roll-up door, each taking a different window. Mike scoured the parking lot, changing windows so that he could see from different vantage points. Sooty storm clouds roiled above them, pressing against the horizon and shrinking the ceiling of sky low to the ground. The front parking lot appeared empty from every angle, but his breath still quickened as he studied the brewing storm. He closed his eyes, gathering himself. The number of variables they had to anticipate and prepare for now that wouldn't have factored into a drive home before filled him with dread.

"Looks clear," Kevin said.

"Yeah," Mike agreed.

"I think I get adrenaline junkies now," Jeffrey said. "It's not like I'm enjoying this, but the feeling when you don't die is exhilarating."

Sandy's laughter pealed through the warehouse. "That is the most ridiculous thing I've heard in a while."

Jeffrey volunteered to get Clyde's truck. Mike and Sandy would move the rental trucks into position, and Kevin would drive the forklift.

The metal of the hand crank was cool through his leather gloves as Mike worked the manual apparatus on the roll-up door. In the silence, the rattle of the rising door sounded like thunder. Mike saw Sandy wince, just like he was. By the time the door was high enough, sweat trickled down his temples. He strained to hear the footsteps of zombies streaming around the building.

Mike's narrowed eyes raked across the parking lot, but it looked clear of everything but a few abandoned vehicles. He paused on the threshold for a moment, head cocked. A faint murmur of noise tickled his ear from the other side of the building. It was so soft he could almost convince himself it didn't signify danger.

"Let's go."

He crossed to the nearest rental pickup truck, climbed in, and turned the ignition. Relief relaxed the knot in his stomach a little when it started right up. He turned in his seat and backed up until the tailgate was almost under the roll-up door. Sandy did the same with the other two rental trucks.

The forklift's yellow light flashed over the walls, shelves, and registers like a lighthouse as it rotated. The *whir* of the engine sounded like a foghorn, even though in reality it wasn't that loud. It was just that everything else was so silent. Add the rev of the engine on Clyde's truck as Jeffrey backed it under the loading area awning, and all he could think was they might as well be shouting, 'Dinnertime!'

"That's loud," Jeffrey said, his eyes squinted like he was in pain as Kevin moved the first load forward.

"Just focus on getting everything loaded," Sandy said, her tone so matter-of-fact that they could have been loading groceries.

After a quick conferral, they put the plywood in one of the rental trucks since they were lower to the ground. Kevin maneuvered the plywood on the forklift, setting one end on the tailgate. Mike and Sandy caught the other end so Kevin could back up. Then they pushed the stacked layers of plywood into the bed of the truck, grunting with effort.

"You forget how heavy this five-eighths plywood is," Mike said.

Jeffrey, who was busy loading Clyde's pickup, gave him a knowing grin. "It's all heavy if you move enough."

Between the second and third round of plywood, Mike trotted to the near corner of the building, just thirty feet away. He felt his body relax for all of a second when he saw it was clear along the side of the building. Then his muscles tensed up and his jaw clenched because he knew it wouldn't last.

After the fourth round of loading plywood, Sandy said, "Let Jeffrey help you with this, Mike. It makes me feel like a wimp, but he's stronger than me. This isn't the time to indulge my ego."

Mike nodded, surprised. He hadn't noticed Sandy was flagging, much less tiring.

"Don't let me leave without the candy," she added.

"Candy?"

"There's a ton."

"We don't need candy."

Sandy fixed him with a stink-eye. "People need cheering up, Mike. It can't only be about surviving."

He didn't bother to argue. What would he say? That they had to be miserable? He trotted past Clyde's truck, closest to the near corner of the building, and looked around it. Still all clear alongside the building. He rejoined Jeffrey to continue loading lumber while Sandy took over loading the zoo pickup truck.

The loud *beep, beep, beep* from the forklift when Kevin backed up reverberated to the roots of Mike's teeth. As they got the last of the lumber onto Clyde's truck, Kevin climbed down from the forklift and joined them, pulling one of the flat, rectangular carts loaded with supplies with him.

Mike's eyes swept over the parking lot again. The zoo pickup was piled high with boxes, insulation, and more. They'd braced plywood on the long side of the truck beds so they could cram in more stuff. He'd never seen a truck so overloaded. The first of the two rental pickups were half-loaded, and there was still a massive pile stacked inside the warehouse's roll-up door. They'd have to come back another time.

"I didn't realize how loud the world was until all the noise was gone," Sandy said, her voice tight with the effort of picking up a box.

"I know," Jeffrey said.

Mike picked up a box, pausing to listen. What had been a vague murmur had grown louder. The mob that had pursued them before was closer. He said, "I'll—"

A crack of thunder rent the sky, making everyone jump. Lightning bolts crackled across the dark clouds hugging the horizon. First a patter, then a steady rain drummed the concrete. Mike looked up at the canopy over their heads. A minute out from under the cover it offered and their supplies would be soaked.

"Where are the tarps?" Sandy asked.

Jeffrey climbed into the half-full rental pickup. "I'll find them."

Sandy nodded as she rearranged some of the load. Then Kevin said, sounding calm, "They're here, by the garden center."

Stumbling figures had rounded the corner of the building at the garden center. Under the fresh smell of rain, Mike could smell the rot. He turned on his heel and sprinted for the near corner of the building that he'd checked before, drenched as soon as he stepped out from under the canopy. He poked his head around the building, breathing harder than the sprint required. His stomach bottomed out. The zombies had gone from not being visible to halfway alongside the building.

"We need to go," he said, running back to the trucks. "I'll get the door. We can deal with the tarps on the road."

Jeffrey slid behind the steering wheel of the zoo pickup. Kevin hesitated, then dropped what he'd been loading and climbed into Clyde's pickup. Sandy hopped down from the rental pickup and flipped up the tailgate. Over her shoulder, she said, "I'm riding with you. Just one last thing."

Mike heard a crack and a low thump, like something had broken or fallen, but a clap of thunder so powerful the ground seemed to shake drowned it out. He followed Sandy as far as the door, where he reached for the release mechanism on the roll-up door that would let them pull the door down once in reach. "Sandy, hurry!"

He wound the crank, lowering the door from fifteen feet to shoulder height. Sandy jogged into view, holding a box under her arm. From the corner of his eye, Mike saw a blur from one of the shadowy aisles. "Look out!"

Sandy frowned at him, incomprehension crinkling her brow. A runner barreled out from a darkened aisle, zeroing in on her as if shot from a slingshot. It had her down before Mike could take a step. Her shriek cleaved the air, almost drowned out by another roll of thunder. Mike sprinted inside the shadowy warehouse, heart thumping, the gun he didn't know how to use in his hand. Sandy and the runner thrashed on the floor. Mike heard a muffled pop, almost like a car backfiring, and the runner collapsed. Sandy had shot it point-blank. Swearing, she pushed the runner aside and yanked her leg free.

"Are you okay?"

As he pulled her up, she grimaced. Zombie muck—blood and bone and what looked like shriveled brain—was all over her. She jammed her gun into the holster on her belt and hissed with pain when she put weight on her foot. She pointed to the box she'd been carrying, which the runner had knocked from her arms. "Grab that."

Mike looked back to the roll-up door as he picked up the box, expecting to see the zombies coming around the building, but they weren't there. Where had the runner come from?

"Are you okay?" he said again as they ducked under the roll-up door.

The zombies coming from the far end of the building by the garden center had passed the main entrance, just a hundred feet away. The rain and black storm clouds were as murky as inside the warehouse. Sandy leaned bent down, checking her leg. Mike heard the hiss of breath before she stood. She stared down at her hand. The blood on her dirty fingers looked like bright-red poppies. Her jeans were torn.

Mike choked back a cry. "That's not a—"

"It is," she said.

Her voice trailed away. She looked up at Mike, her face drained of color. Then a hardness filled her eyes. Her lips flattened together, and her jaw firmed. She unbuckled her utility belt. She removed her gun from the holster and tucked it into her jeans at the small of her back. She looped the belt over the box Mike still held to his chest. "Get out of here. My gun will be right beside me. It's a good weapon. Take it with you when you come back."

"What? No," Mike said, disbelief stunning him. She wanted them to leave her behind. She was going to—

"Go!" she said, more forcefully this time, her attention shifting over his shoulder. "I need to close the door so more don't get inside."

A zombie rounded the corner on the far side of the loaded rental pickup truck. A teenage boy, his acne-marked face laced with spidery veins. Rainwater flowed over his open eyes and plastered hair to his face. He raised an arm. Then more footsteps—these much swifter—under the heavy drum of rain and over the hum of the truck engines.

"Get out of here!" Sandy shouted, shoving Mike hard and baring her teeth. He stumbled back a few steps, but she had roused him from his shock. A tear rolled down her cheek but she wasn't afraid—she was angry. She reached up, her fingertips gripping the door, and looked him in the eye. "I'm sorry, Mike. Take care of everyone."

The door rumbled down and hit the concrete with a thud. Mike stared for a second, the rain and moans and sounds of running feet ringing in his ears. Then he turned, the box and Sandy's utility belt heavy in his hands, and sprinted for the truck he was driving.

Jeffrey shouted through the half-opened window of the zoo pickup, "Where's Sandy?"

Mike looked past Jeffrey, to where Kevin sat in Clyde's truck. At the far end of the building beyond Clyde's truck, the first runner rounded the corner.

"Go!" Mike shouted.

Clyde's truck rocketed out from under the canopy into the downpour; Kevin must have seen the runner. Jeffrey's head whipped around. The runner, no longer blocked from Jeffrey's view by Clyde's truck, slammed into the rear quarter panel of the zoo pickup. Mike saw Jeffrey swallow hard. Then the truck sped away, tires squealing, sending the runner spinning to the ground.

Mike threw the box and Sandy's utility belt on the bench seat of the rental truck. He slammed the door shut. More runners followed the first. They ran right over the runner that had fallen, never breaking stride though one of them tripped. Impact rocked the truck when they hit. Wet hands and filthy, bloody faces mashed against the glass of Mike's window.

The muffled report of a gun—no louder than a firecracker under the noise of the rain and moans—made Mike flinch. Then his foot pushed the gas pedal to the floor.

He fumbled for the windshield wipers, following the two trucks racing across the parking lot. Tall fantails of rainwater squirted from under their tires. Mike's heart constricted, as if caught in a vise. He could see Sandy in his mind's eye, sprawled on the floor of the warehouse, the crimson blood that had adorned her fingers pooling on the concrete floor. He glanced in the rearview mirror. The only difference between now and when they'd arrived was the rain and the zombies chasing after them.

And Sandy not being with them.

Her words stuffed his ears like cotton candy. *It's a good weapon. Take it with you when you come back.* Because they'd have to come back. Half the stuff they'd gathered was still there just inside the roll-up door along with however many more of the monsters that had somehow gotten inside and killed her. Mike had valued Sandy's pragmatism from the start of this nightmare. She'd held on to it, right to the end.

He reached the main drag, taking the turn onto the road too hard and swaying in his seat. His stomach sloshed. The box beside him tipped onto its side. Sandy's utility belt tumbled onto the passenger side floor mat, the boxes of candy bars landing on top of it.

Tears welled in Mike's eyes that he angrily dashed away. Sandy had died for candy bars they didn't need because she had wanted to cheer everyone up. Helpless rage filled the back of

Mike's throat with the bitter taste of bile. The bright wrappers of the candy bars made his stomach heave. He choked, biting back hard against the vomit that wanted to erupt from his stomach.

"Goddammit," he shouted, banging the steering wheel so hard it hurt. "God fucking dammit!"

CHAPTER 17
IMOGEN

Imogen bore Zach's scolding with the forbearance of emotional exhaustion. He didn't seem to notice that she and Bec both had puffy, bloodshot eyes from their crying jag. Usually, he was more observant and would have noticed. But their deviation from the plan and the countless disaster scenarios that could have—but hadn't—befallen she and Bec had scared him. She'd never experienced Zach as rigid before, but the world was different now. She'd wondered how else they would change before shutting the line of thought down. If they were going to change in ways she didn't like, she wanted the bliss of ignorance a little bit longer.

The cabin that Zach and Clyde had searched had been a treasure trove of food staples: canned goods including vegetables and beans and fruits, dry staples like pasta and rice and couscous, sacks of sugar, flour, iodized salt, chicken, beef, and vegetable bouillon cubes, vegetable oils and shortening, and several gallon jugs of real maple syrup. The only thing they hadn't found were sweets, apart from the sugar and maple syrup.

"This person loved the Hundred Dollar Club," Clyde said as he shut the tailgate of the compact pickup truck from a neighboring cabin. "And God bless them for it."

They climbed into the pickup and drove several miles to the next cabin. As they walked across the bridge, Imogen heard a rattle. Her stomach roiled. The moans from inside the cabin were low but unmistakable.

"Three's a charm, I guess," Zach muttered. His shoulders had climbed to his ears, his mouth twisted by an anxious scowl.

"Let's be smart and careful and we'll have nothing to worry about," Clyde said.

Clyde stepped onto the porch, its boards creaking under his weight. He stooped to look in the front window, shading his eyes with his hands. "There's three I can see." He stepped back from the window and tried the front door, but apart from a slight click that riled up the occupants, the door didn't budge. "The dead bolt's locked. Let's look for an extra key."

After a few minutes of searching, they found a key under a flowerpot on the flagstone patio next to the house. They stood at the door once more, this time with weapons in hand.

"I'll open the door, and let them out one at a time," Clyde said. "I think all of you should take a turn. We have to get good at this."

"Then why aren't you taking a turn?" Bec asked him with a saccharine smile.

Clyde smiled. "Beauty before age. And I'm bigger than you and can hold the door."

Imogen knew Clyde was right about needing to practice killing the things. She broke out in a cold sweat. Fear fogged her brain. It made no sense. When she didn't have the luxury of thinking about what she was doing, she could kill the wretched things without a second thought. It had happened so many times when she and Mike were together that she teased him about how many times she'd saved his life. Standing on this porch, palms sweaty against the leather gloves she clutched her railroad spike in, her body trembled and her throat tightened so much she could barely breathe.

"I'll go first," Bec said. "Be ready to help me. A big one might knock me over." Then she looked at Clyde, alarmed. "There aren't any fast ones, are there?"

"Nope. They're slow." He peeked through the window again. "They all look pretty… Yeah. They look like slow ones."

Bec looked up at him, her mouth pursed in a frown. "You're not inspiring confidence Clyde." She returned her attention to the door, squaring her shoulders and positioning herself. "I'm ready."

Imogen and Zach stood on either side of Bec. "Be ready to jump in," Bec said, a slight tremor in her voice.

Clyde gave her an encouraging smile. "You'll be fine."

He eased the door open. The smell rushed out, rotten and putrified and as cloying as a humid summer night.

"Oooh… That's so foul," Bec said, wrinkling her nose and grimacing. Then she raised her voice. "Come here, zombies. We have to kill you now."

Shuffling footsteps were followed by banging furniture. A zombie bashed against the door, one arm reaching for Bec through the opened space. Clyde braced himself as he let the door swing inward enough to make a gap, but not enough to lose his grip. The man who looked out at Bec with blank eyes, reaching for her with a clawlike hand, had been handsome. Now, the flesh sagged from his jaw and spidery black veins crawled under his skin from beneath a bandage on his neck. Bec stepped forward, yelping when the man caught her shoulder, and plunged her knife into his eye.

Pulses of black and gray liquid squirted all over her. She hopped away from the door. "Oh my God… Gross!" she said, swiping at her face. "This won't get me sick, will it?"

The next zombie reached through the door. Imogen stepped forward, sweat trickling down her neck and between her breasts. *Please don't let me get sprayed.*

She distracted herself by humming a children's nursery rhyme and wondering why she chose it. A woman with a lipless snarl of exposed teeth and long stringy hair filled the door, her face painted a dark, uneven brown. Imogen grimaced and drove the spike into the woman's eye. She fell, the stringy blond hair fanning over the face of the man Bec had killed.

Imogen scurried out of the way, her heart thumping out of rhythm. The last one was a girl, maybe fourteen. She wore her hair in high pigtails on either side of her head. Jangling bangles circled her wrists like manacles. The girl leaned over the dead adults at her feet, her head sticking out as her teeth snapped. Zach grabbed a pigtail, twisted her head, and jammed his knife into her ear. He reached the porch rail in two steps, his face an unhealthy shade of green, and threw up. Imogen handed him a tissue, which he took without a word. They waited a few minutes, calling out in case there were more inside, but the cabin was quiet. Clyde stepped away from the door, letting it open wide.

"Yinz okay?" he asked.

Bec wiped the last of the goop off her face. "I smell like ass. I call dibs on the shower."

After dragging the bodies away, they went inside. This cabin had been remodeled; the ceilings were higher with recessed lights. The kitchen—filled with chrome, stainless steel, and black-and-white frosted glass—was sleek and anonymous. They cleared the house and set to work, the mood more somber than before. Imogen couldn't stop thinking about the people they'd just killed. Had they been a family or strangers who'd met on the road? She hadn't looked close enough to see if there was a resemblance, shivering at the ghoulish thought. She pulled can after can of food from the well-stocked cupboards, her heart sinking lower and lower.

It felt wrong to take it all. They were a large group, and Imogen knew they needed more food, but she couldn't help wondering about others who might come looking for a safe haven. They'd find an empty house with no food or supplies. What if they had arrived at the lodge to find it ransacked? She turned away from the counter and looked across the kitchen, where Clyde was cleaning out another of the cupboards.

"Clyde?" He turned to her, the blue eyes under his bushy eyebrows inquisitive. "Do you think we should be taking everything? What if other people come later and need a place to stay, and food and fuel and clothes? If we've taken it all, there won't be anything for them."

Clyde frowned. "We need to get ourselves situated first, I think. After that we can think about helping other people."

Imogen wondered, given the way his face turned down, if Clyde felt the same as her. She nodded, resuming her task, but the feeling persisted. With every can she stuffed into a plastic bag or paper sack, the more glum she felt. By the time they loaded the contents of the house into the truck in silence, Imogen couldn't stand it anymore. Heart pounding, she said, "I don't think we should take everything."

Zach looked up from where he'd been pushing a box into place in the back of the pickup truck. Clyde was waiting by the open tailgate to hand another box off to Zach.

"What do you mean?" Bec held a bag in both arms, looking for all the world as if she'd just returned from the grocery store.

"It's just," Imogen shrugged. "What if other people come? If we've taken everything, what are they going to do?"

Clyde handed his box off to Zach. "Still bugging you, huh?"

She nodded, searching for the right words. "I know we have to look after ourselves. I know we can't take the high road when it's our survival on the line. It's just... what if we were in their shoes?"

"I know it sucks, but we can't worry about other people right now, Imogen," Zach said, his voice laced with sympathy.

They all looked at her, their faces variations on a theme. They saw nothing wrong with what they were doing. When it came down to it, neither did she. Perhaps there weren't rules anymore. The realization was unsettling. Imogen had always followed the rules. Or perhaps, rather than none, the rules had changed and she didn't understand them yet.

"If we were in their shoes, we'd be doing what we're doing now," Zach added. "Looking for more."

"I know," she said, a familiar, cringing sensation snaking through her body that made her heart thump. She shouldn't have said anything, shouldn't have challenged what they were doing. No one wanted to hear it, and she didn't want to make waves or upset anyone. Things were different now. She had to accept it. "Forget I said anything."

Bec set the bags she'd been holding on the tailgate of the truck. "What do you think we could do differently?"

Imogen's chest tightened, heart a drumroll running on too long. "I don't know," she said, frustration turning her voice almost into a whine. "I just hate this, you know? We just killed those people. They tried to take refuge here, just like us, and now we're taking all their things."

"If we don't, someone else will," Zach said. "We have to make sure we have enough."

She forced herself to breathe, to say what she thought, even though it made her heart race. Why did saying what she felt and thought always feel so dangerous? She knew the answer: because of how she'd grown up. She should just agree with them, if only so she could make this horrible anxiety in her chest go away. Who was she kidding, anyway? She didn't have the answers, didn't know what to do, but what they were doing felt wrong.

"And after we have enough, then what? We won't just be on the lookout for those creatures," Imogen said, forcing herself to go on even though her voice shook. "We're on the lookout for other people, afraid they'll take what we have."

"Maybe we can discuss this later, with the group," Clyde said. "Because I agree with you. If everywhere is like here, then there aren't many of us left, which means there's more than enough for everyone. We might have trouble getting to it, but it's there."

Clyde smiled at her, the warmth in his eyes surprising Imogen. She'd expected the others to be angry with her, but Clyde didn't seem to be.

"We're going into Swedenport to check out the library in a day or two," Bec piped up. She looked to Clyde, then added, "And Betty and Clyde have finished that list of towns to try for grocery stores and pharmacies, so we'll be doing that, too. Once we see how we're situated after, we can figure it out." She looked at Clyde and Zach. "Right?"

Zach shrugged. "I don't see why not, if we're okay ourselves," he said with a reluctance that bordered on grudging.

"Let's get through the next few weeks," Clyde said, nodding in agreement. "Once we're more settled and have set things up so we're safer, I don't see why we can't help others who need it. We live together as brothers or perish together as fools, right?"

The fear coursing through Imogen's body while she'd made a case for something the others hadn't been on board with eased. Clyde, at least, got it. Bec, too. Zach was more hesitant, but Imogen knew the kind of person he was. Once he felt more secure about their situation, his reluctance would fade.

She smiled, the relief she felt bordering on comical. "Did you just make that up, about brothers and fools?"

"Gosh, no," Clyde said, his cheeks becoming rosy. "I'm not that smart. That was Martin Luther King."

Bec pushed between them to take another bag to the truck. Imogen stepped back but couldn't escape the stench.

"I saw that," Bec said. Under her breath, she muttered, "God, I need a shower."

CHAPTER 18
IMOGEN

AN HOUR LATER, WITH BLISTERS RINGING HER PALMS AND DOTTING her fingers, Imogen climbed into the truck. They'd carried the bodies across the bridge and into the woods on the far side of the road. It had only seemed right to bury the people they'd had to kill, the people who weren't people anymore. They discussed cremating them but that would mean using some of their limited gasoline, and the smoke might give away their location.

Picking a site while trudging through the woods with no path, and while carrying bodies, had been dreadful, but they'd finished their grim work. Near the creek, where digging was easiest, hadn't been an option; they didn't want to contaminate the water. The graves weren't as deep as they probably should have been, which Clyde had fretted over. Imogen wasn't sure how important depth was, since the bodies of the infected didn't seem to decompose. They stunk to high heaven and smelled of rot, but decomposition only seemed to go so far, then stopped.

Imogen pushed the thoughts of zombies, the people they'd once been, and decomposition away. They were just a few weeks into this and she was already sick of it. By the time they'd collected the haul from Trout Cabin, all she wanted to do was get a shower and crawl into bed.

The hollow, vaguely nauseating feeling roiling her stomach

got worse the closer they got to the lodge. The anxiety she felt for Mike had receded with a task to focus on. Lacking a task to take her mind off how he might be, Imogen worried a blister on her index finger with her thumb. The small dome of fluid gave some, displaced by the pressure. She didn't push enough to hurt, though if she kept it up, the blister would burst.

"Worried about the others?" Zach asked.

She nodded. "Do you think they'll be back yet?"

He shrugged. "They left before we got up, so maybe."

"I wouldn't be surprised if they don't get back until late," Clyde said. "There are a lot of things we need. If the place hasn't been picked clean yet, they'll probably gather too much and then have to decide what to bring and what to leave for next time."

"You think so?" Imogen asked, glancing beyond Bec to Clyde.

"Sure do," Clyde said.

As discreetly as she could, Imogen breathed through her mouth. She wanted to ask Clyde to drive faster but he was living up to the old man stereotype of being a slow driver. Even with the windows open, in the small confines of the truck's cab, the reek of the zombie guck that had splashed all over Bec made Imogen's eyes water. Away from the hordes of the city, she'd forgotten how oppressive the stench was.

"I can't wait to get a shower," Bec moaned, sounding desperate. "I smell like a zombie."

"It's not that bad," Zach offered.

Bec gave him a 'come on' side-eye. "We both know you're full of it. Do you think the smell will come out? I really like this coat."

"We need to find Vicks VapoRub," Imogen said. "Or something like it."

"Are you not feeling well?" Clyde asked, concern in his voice.

"No, it's not that. If we have something with a strong smell like camphor or menthol and rub it under our noses, it might help."

"Overwhelm the sense of smell so the really bad smells aren't so bad," Zach said, picking up her line of thought. "That's a good idea."

"I'm so sorry, you guys," Bec said. "I know I reek."

A few minutes later, while Clyde pulled the truck to the side of the road by the lodge's parking area, a white truck rounded the bend farther down the road, followed by another truck. Clyde grinned, anticipation and relief glinting in his eyes. "That's my truck."

The energy crackled between them at the confirmation that Mike, Kevin, Jeffrey, and Sandy were returning. As soon as their truck stopped, they all tumbled out. A third truck had joined the first two down the road, and Imogen's body sagged with relief.

"If they're coming back with more trucks than they took, it must have gone well," Bec said.

"I'm just glad they're back," Imogen answered, the knot in her stomach loosening. "When we were busy it wasn't so bad, but all I've done since we finished is worry." And, she silently added, try not to smell Bec.

She hadn't liked the idea of Mike, Kevin, Sandy, and Jeffrey going so far away, even though they needed supplies. But mostly, if she was honest with herself, she hadn't liked Mike going. Their time together at the zoo had been brief, but meeting as they had on the bridge had forged a bond, the kind that would never break. She couldn't explain how she knew this; she just did. She'd never connected with anyone at such a primal level—when survival was the only thing that mattered—and part of her hoped she never would again.

She glimpsed Mike's face through the windshield as he pulled the truck into the parking area. Her lungs released a pent-up breath. Once the trucks parked, Imogen rushed over, an expectant smile on her face. Mike hadn't opened the door. He stared straight ahead at the creek, hands gripping the wheel.

Imogen's brow creased as she took in boxes of candy jumbled on the seat and a utility belt on the floor by the passenger door.

That's Sandy's belt.

The sound of opening doors tore her gaze from Mike. Kevin climbed out of Clyde's truck, shoulders slumped. His eyes were puffy and red as if he'd been crying. Jeffrey walked around the front of Clyde's truck, his face drawn. He moved like he wasn't inside his body. Imogen looked for Sandy, but she wasn't there.

Fear shot through Imogen's body, her heart skipping a beat. Mike flinched when she yanked the truck door open. "What's happened?"

When Mike looked at her, she took a step back. The laugh lines around his eyes seemed deeper, but etched with pain. The infectious grin and deep dimple that should be crowing joy over how much they'd brought back with them weren't there. He looked pale and tired, and the only thing Imogen saw in his eyes, so dark and warm they looked like molasses, was pain.

"Sandy," he said, his voice raw, like sheets of sandpaper rasping together.

Afraid to ask but needing to know, Imogen said, "Where is she?"

Mike closed his eyes. "Sandy's dead."

CHAPTER 19
MIKE

Mike leaned against the uneven edge of the wood slab counter. He crossed his arms as if trying to ward off the thoughts that had plagued him since returning last night.

He looked out the windows at the end of the kitchen table, the ones that were doors set in the wall. Outside, the landscape was the same. The winch house for the gondola still hunched by the tall tree at the top of the steps, and uneven, moss-covered stone path. The blaze of color from turning leaves was also on the ground now since the leaves were falling in earnest.

Everything was the same—and nothing was the same. Mike rubbed at his eyes with the heel of his hand. Bec and Jeffrey talked softly from where they were finishing up the breakfast dishes by the kitchen sink. Clyde and Betty were upstairs, but Mike knew they'd be down any minute. Betty had planned to do this last night, but everyone had been too shell-shocked to deal with anything after learning of Sandy's death.

Mike looked around the lodge, filled with people he hadn't known before this nightmare started. How many of them were going to die? The idea of losing everyone else filled him with dread that sent a shudder rippling from head to toe. He had already lost Steph, his sisters, and nieces. He'd do whatever it took to keep everyone safe, even if that meant he might not be.

Imogen appeared at the back of the kitchen, rubbing her arms like she'd just come in from outside. She offered him a shy smile as she leaned against the counter beside him, the slender green book about plants in one hand.

"Did you find anything?" His voice felt raspy, as if he was getting a sore throat.

She shook her head. "I'm not very good at identifying anything. I need a field guide, one that has photographs. Perhaps I can find one at the library in Swedenport."

Terror flooded Mike's nervous system. The idea of Imogen going out there left him light-headed. He felt his stomach heave, now one step shy of puking up his breakfast. It must have shown on his face, for she said, "There's no hurry, though. I can't harvest much of anything now. There are plenty of drawings in here. I just need to get better at it."

A creak on the stairs snagged Mike's attention. He was glad for an excuse to look away from her. The alarm that had flashed in Imogen's eyes when she'd seen his reaction left him feeling exposed, as if she knew Sandy's death was his fault.

Betty and Clyde arrived, the former looking around expectantly. Jeffrey and Bec had settled on the other side of the table and Zach had left the couch to join them. Jay followed in his wake, looking bored.

"Where are Kevin and Amy?" Betty asked.

The back door creaked and Kevin stamped into the kitchen. Mike hadn't realized that Kevin had gone anywhere. They should have a system for keeping track of everyone.

"I think Amy's in her room," Zach said, rising from his seat. "I'll get her."

"She knows we're meeting," Jay said to Zach. "She'll be here."

Mike tuned out the chatter while they waited, making room for Zach to sidle by him and sit down in front of Imogen. He kept hearing the same sounds, his brain skipping like a record. The slam of the runners hitting the truck's rear quarter panel, the rev of the engine, the crinkle of the candy bar wrappers as they spilled onto the truck floor, and the muffled report of Sandy's gun.

If I'd refused to go in, Sandy would be alive.

"I think everyone's here, so we'll get started."

Betty's voice pulled Mike from his morbid reverie. Jay leaned against the corner of the stainless-steel kitchen counter, and Kevin had taken a seat beside Clyde on one of the long dining table benches. Betty glanced up the stairs, then turned back to the group. The chatter petered out, and Betty shifted her weight from one foot to the other. She looked nervous, standing at the head of the dining table and the focus of everyone's attention.

"I wanted to talk about this last night, but it just didn't seem — It wasn't the right time with Sandy… not being here." She twisted her fingers together, then said, "I didn't know Sandy for very long, but I think that she'd want us to—"

Amy distracted Betty when she appeared at the foot of the stairs. She looked harried, and didn't offer an apology for being late. She leaned against the corner counter by the cabinets on the other side of the table, kitty-corner from Mike.

"You could have waited," Amy said.

"We only just started." Betty's eyes narrowed. "Did you wash your hair today?"

"Yes," Amy said.

Betty's nostrils flared and her lips compressed, turning them into a colorless line. "What is wrong with you? Why are you getting showers and washing your hair every day? No one else is."

Amy looked taken aback. "Just because we're waiting until this whole thing blows over doesn't mean we have to be filthy."

"We don't know if this is going to blow over," Betty said, sounding angrier by the second. "The most important use of the propane is for cooking! We can take showers but not every day. We have to conserve the fuel we have because I don't know how to cook over a fire. Do you?"

Amy opened her mouth, ready to argue, but Imogen said, "This is what we're here to discuss, isn't it? How we're all going to get along and do things. Perhaps we can make this part of the discussion."

Amy glared at Imogen but held her tongue. Betty seemed to gather herself, taking a deep breath, but two spots of pink colored her cheeks. Mike glanced down at Imogen, impressed with how skillfully she had short-circuited the exchange. She was biting her lower lip, chewing on it. The pinch of her eyes looked painful alongside the tight jaw. She worried the edge of the spine of the medicinal plants book with her thumb. The conflict was making her anxious so she'd jumped in to keep the peace. That would fit with what she'd shared about her family, how she'd always played the peacemaker to appease her father's explosive temper. The thought depressed Mike even more.

Betty took a deep breath. "You all know that this lodge isn't mine and Clyde's. Our friend Bob owns this place. We're still hoping that he might show up, but he was in Virginia with his wife when all of this started so…" She shrugged, motioning to Clyde. "We've been reluctant to tell people what to do since this isn't our place, but I've noticed in the time we've been here that as a group we aren't on the same page about how to do things or priorities. I think the sooner we figure those things out, and agree on guidelines for how to use things we can't easily replace, the better."

There were nods around the table. Amy's shoulders hunched, almost touching her ears. If looks could kill, Betty would be lying in a pool of blood.

"I think it's fair that you and Clyde want to make some rules," Bec said.

"No," Betty said. "We all need to do it. Make it a covenant, if you will, about how we're going to live together. We can make a list and go through them and vote on them, and the same for special circumstances, too."

Jay cleared his throat. "I don't see why any of this is necessary. We're all adults. I think we can get things done without all this."

"I've come down to dirty dishes stacked in the sink twice already," Jeffrey said. "Whoever used them left them for someone else to clean, which ended up being me."

"It's better to hash this stuff out," Kevin said. "My roommates and I had a chore wheel and it worked way better than I thought it would."

"A chore wheel," Jay scoffed.

"I think that's a great idea," Zach said. "We can draw up a list of chores and make a schedule."

"I also want to propose something else," Betty said. "There are going to be times when we can't agree on what to do. When that happens, I propose the final decision be made by me and Mike."

"Why you two?" Jay said, his tone accusatory, as if Betty had just suggested she was Empress for Life.

Betty's posture stiffened, and she wrung her hands. Jay's questions, and more likely his tone, had flustered her.

"I didn't seek this out, but I think it makes sense," Mike said. "For all practical purposes, this is Betty and Clyde's place, so one of them should be involved. I was shop steward for my union local, so I'm used to solving problems. And I was part of the contract negotiation team. Betty thought those skills might come in handy."

"Mike was with all of you who were at the zoo," Betty said. "So both groups are represented."

"A lot of us have skills like Mike," Jay said. "Better ones, even."

Mike clamped down on his irritation, working hard to keep it out of his voice. Jay hadn't been chosen first and was being pissy about it, like this was a game of kickball. "If Clyde and Betty hadn't offered to bring us with them, we'd still be stuck at the zoo or worse. I don't know where the rest of you would be, but I doubt it would be in a setup like this."

"What if we don't like your decisions?" Jay said.

What is with this guy?

"Nobody's going to like every decision," Kevin said. "I haven't known Mike any longer than the rest of you, but I know he's smart, and he's fair, and he's saved my bacon more than once. If this is what Betty and Clyde want to do, I'm cool with it."

"This isn't for everyday decisions," Betty added. "Just big ones where we can't agree on what to do."

"What if you're making bad ones?" Jay persisted.

"What if what you're doing is hurting the group?" Amy added.

Betty looked flummoxed. From the corner of his eye, Mike saw Imogen gnawing on her lip again.

"Then we revisit the tiebreaker votes," Mike said. "If everyone's unhappy, or a majority are, you can pick different people to do it."

"I don't like this," Amy said. "You two went off on your own to cook up this scheme so you can be in charge."

Imogen made a small sound in her throat that reminded Mike of a whimper. "Look," he said. "This isn't about telling you what to do. It's about what's best for the group. And we didn't cook up anything. Betty—who's the reason all of us are here—asked me. And I'll only do it if it's okay with the rest of you."

Amy sniffed, dismissing his explanation. "But people will defer to you. That's how this kind of thing works. What you're proposing is a popularity contest. I already know that I'm not very popular around here."

Sandy had died yesterday. Now Jay was getting pissy because Betty hadn't picked him for this so-called honor, and Amy was complaining about not being popular? Before Mike could remind himself to not lose his temper, he said, "If that's what you think, Amy, then maybe you ought to work on becoming more likable."

Hurt flashed in Amy's eyes, almost immediately replaced by

the hostility arcing from them like sparks. The others shifted in their seats and traded furtive glances. Imogen stiffened, bracing herself against the counter.

"That's a dick thing to say," Jay said.

"It's the truth," Mike snapped. "If she doesn't want to hear what other people think, maybe she shouldn't throw accusations around."

"Next you'll be kicking people out," Amy muttered, not quite under her breath and, Mike suspected, very much on purpose.

"Oh! Oh, no, no, no," Betty said, her hands fluttering in front of her. "I want everyone who's here, here. That's the truth, it really is. I'm so grateful that all of you are here. I know we can make living together work."

Betty looked about to cry. You bitch, Mike thought, furious with Amy for being so manipulative. But now he knew what their roles would be: Betty was the approachable one; he'd be the heavy. A little voice in Mike's head told him to keep his mouth shut, but he ignored it. "Betty's right that we're all better off together, but if you're that unhappy, no one's forcing you to stay. There are other cabins up the road."

Mike saw Jeffrey's mouth fall open, his pointy chin and foxlike appearance was almost blank from surprise before a look of 'Did he really just say that?' filled his face.

Amy's eyes widened. For a moment, her jaw went slack. "You'd throw us out?"

"That's not what I said," Mike snapped, an edge to his voice even he couldn't ignore. "I'm just saying you have options if you're so unhappy. No one is forcing you to be here."

Imogen took a deep breath and stepped out from the counter, resting her hand on Zach's shoulder. "I think we've gone terribly off topic." Everyone looked to her, rapt as kittens watching a toy dangle just out of reach. "I think some of us are talking about making decisions that aren't even relevant to our situation." She looked at Amy, then Jay. "The three of us have worked together for years and got on well. We're all tired and scared and have had a terrible shock after what happened yesterday. No one's talking about anyone moving out."

"I think we all need to chill out," Kevin said, making sure he addressed everyone, not just Amy. "A new roommate can take a while to settle in, and now all of us have seven or eight new roommates. Imogen's right; no one's talking about people moving out."

Except they were, even if it was, as Imogen had pointed out, off topic. The tension in the room began to subside. Imogen leaned back against the counter beside Mike. She was close enough that he realized she was trembling. Great, that's just great, he thought. He'd taken out his foul mood on Amy, who made it easy, and he'd upset Imogen in the process.

Amy's eyes flashed. "This is a bunch of nonsense," she snapped. "I can follow rules. I'm not one of those people who needs to have everything my own way. Come up with your rules and chores and I'll follow them, whatever they are."

She turned on her heel and stomped up the stairs. A moment later, a door slammed.

"That's mature," Jeffrey muttered.

After a moment's silence, Betty said, "I think we should take a break."

CHAPTER 20
IMOGEN

IMOGEN PUSHED ON THE SHOVEL WITH HER FOOT, LEANING OVER THE half-sized staff and putting her weight behind it. It didn't budge.

"Come over here, Imogen," Kevin said. "You're getting ahead of me. I haven't pickaxed that yet."

She looked at the gravel of the lodge's parking area and realized he was right. She tried to smother a yawn but ended up opening her mouth so wide that her jaw cracked. Her exhalation frosted in the chilly air. The October weather, which was often glorious into November, had instead plunged into the low twenties with the miserable, damp cold that worked into your bones. It felt like Mother Nature's contribution to the overall state of suckitude.

The tension since the meeting about how to do things at the lodge hadn't lessened over the past week. If anything, it had gotten worse. Deciding about Betty's proposal had been put off after the contentious meeting so everyone could think about it. This left the situation aggravated rather than solved. It would have been easy to blame Jay or Amy for the situation. The collective attitude of the Crybaby Cabal hadn't improved, but it hadn't worsened that much. When Jay wasn't pouting, he sniped, his comments always just short of crossing the line into truly bad behavior he might get called on. Amy exuded an air of aggrieved persecution so strong it might as well be body odor. Imogen didn't think anyone was avoiding her on purpose, but it always seemed to happen.

But the Crybaby Cabal wasn't the real problem.

The real problem was Mike.

His mood since Sandy had died grew blacker by the day. In some ways, he did what he'd always done. He was working hard to make sure the lodge was secure, coordinating the collection of beer and pop cans they'd strung up around the lodge on wire that surrounded their new home. With a few pebbles in each, they made noise when disturbed. The speed with which it was completed seemed, to Imogen, to have more to do with not wanting to give Mike an opportunity to become more unpleasant. He was short-tempered, hyper-vigilant, brooding, and refused to talk about Sandy.

Imogen shook her head, pushing thoughts of Mike aside. She had resolved to talk to him soon if his attitude didn't improve. It was obvious he needed to talk to someone, but that wasn't the task at hand. She corrected her position, even though it meant sidling closer to Jay. She'd given him a wide berth, afraid that if she didn't, she'd explode and hit him with a shovel. Every interaction with him only increased the anger stewing inside her. She wanted to hurt him like he'd hurt her. She wanted to kick him out of the lodge and tell him to fend for himself, like he'd done to her lynxes.

You can't let your feelings divide the group, she reminded herself for the millionth time. There was enough of that already, with Zach acting like Mike was a danger to women, and Amy and Jay's nonsense. She clenched her teeth, steeling herself for the inevitable interaction moving closer to him would involve. He always seemed to know exactly what to say to twist the knife, to needle her, but she wouldn't give him the satisfaction.

"You need to pay attention, Imogen," Jay said. He'd been in a bad mood all morning, apparently not wanting to deal with her as much as she didn't want to deal with him.

Kevin hoisted the pickaxe with a grunt. It hit the earth, digging deep into the hard-packed soil. Imogen didn't know how he managed it. Decades of cars and trucks rolling over the parking spots had compacted the soil so much it felt like cement. There'd been a week of rain to soften the earth. To Imogen at least, it still felt like rock. It had only stopped raining yesterday so Imogen had expected saturated, heavy soil, but this was far worse.

"I should have gone with the others instead of dealing with weaklings who can't even dig," Jay hissed under his breath.

The vehemence behind his words almost scorched Imogen's skin. Jay's attitude left much to be desired in general, but this white-hot hostility dialed it up a notch.

"How about we concentrate on getting some work done?" Kevin said. From the lightness of his tone it seemed that he hadn't heard what Jay had said. "They didn't need that many people to figure out a way around the washout. If the road needs fixed, it'll be a lot more work than this. There'll be plenty to go around."

Jay narrowed his eyes. "You think I'm too lazy to help?"

"I wasn't even talking about you, Jay," Kevin said, annoyed. "Believe it or not, the world doesn't revolve around you." The two men eyed one another for a moment, perhaps to see who would blink first. Jay's mouth twisted into a frown before he resumed digging.

Imogen plunged the shovel into the soil as hard as she could. She had trouble getting it to penetrate, even around the broken clumps from the pickaxe. I just want to be tired enough to sleep well, she thought. Listening to Jay whine was exhausting. Maybe the effort of trying to ignore him and physical labor would do the trick.

Since they'd arrived, dreams of Araminta and her lynxes had plagued her. Last night had been bad, dream after dream ripping her from sleep. She'd dreamed her sister and the lynxes were on a plane from London full of people turning into zombies. In the way of dreams, the passengers knew the zombies would eat the lynxes instead of them if they opened the emergency doors at thirty thousand feet and threw them out. The zombies would follow Ferdinand, Isabella, and their kittens like lemmings following the Pied Piper, and Araminta led the charge instead of protecting the defenseless cats. In another nightmare, Araminta called her on the phone, desperate, pleading with Imogen to come and find her. Then she dreamed she was in the back of pickup as they fled the zoo, Mike wresting the rifle away from her. One by one, he shot every one of her lynxes.

After that, she hadn't bothered trying to sleep.

"Do you think we'll ever get this finished?" Imogen said, grunting as she tried to drive the shovel into the ground.

Kevin laughed. He let the pickaxe clunk to the earth, keeping hold of the end of the handle with one hand. "Yeah, but it'll be a while before this doesn't look like it's been a parking space the last fifty years."

"If we get a fallen tree or two across it perhaps that will help?" Imogen asked him.

Jay snorted. "This is a waste of time. Anyone who sees the bridge will see the house. We're only doing this because Mike thinks it's a good idea."

"That's not true," Kevin said.

Imogen leaned her shovel against a tree and walked into the road, trying to ignore her quivering insides. Almost everyone had been restless since the rain had curtailed time outside, but Jay had been the worst by far. The discord he seemed hell-bent on sowing grated on Imogen, tugging at her need to smooth things over and make everyone happy. She felt Jay's glare before his shovel sank into the ground. He bent over a little, hands tight on the long handle of the shovel, and tipped out a hunk of earth so large Imogen felt a flash of envy.

"How do you think your lynxes are doing?"

Imogen took a step back, feeling as unbalanced by the comment as she would if Jay had pushed her. For an irrational moment she wondered how he'd known about her dreams. "What?"

"Are you sure you shot the lock off?"

She froze. Kevin's pickaxe pierced the ground with a hissing cut of metal into dirt. The scrape of being pulled free did not follow.

"Yes, I know I did," she said, her voice shaking with anger she could barely disguise.

Except now, he'd sown a seed of doubt. She had to run through the scene in her mind. Had the door flown open? Yes, it had. She'd only glimpsed it, but it had happened. It was real. Jay's jaw hardened and his nostrils flared. She didn't think he was giving up on this... whatever this was he hoped to accomplish.

"Do you think they're okay, or dying the slow death they ought to be?"

She gaped at him, her heart in her throat. Why was he doing this? Why was he tormenting her and intent on picking a fight? She was forcing herself to ignore him and pretend she didn't want to scratch his eyes out, and he was doing this? Only sheer will stopped her from taking another step back. He'd see it as weakness. She knew he expected her to fold, to apologize, to do what she always did: smooth things over. The glint of anger in his eyes flashed, her refusal to play her part in this script seeming to anger him more. She clamped her jaw shut, grabbed her shovel, and started digging again, jabbing the shovel into the ground like a knife. She saw him scowl from the corner of her eye. Even if she hadn't seen it, anger rolled off him like waves crashing against rocks.

"Knock it—" Kevin started, but Jay talked over him.

"You think you're so smart because you went to Oxford and wrestled with cheetahs, like you're some sort of mystical big cat expert, when you're nothing but a hack."

Imogen's heart thundered in her chest. Her arms shook as she bit her lip. She wanted to scream at him, but not because she was angry. She just wanted this to stop. As his anger grew, it seemed to siphon hers away, making her feel like she always did in the face of a man's anger: small and weak and scared. And especially now because there was no appeasing him, she could tell. He'd crossed that line she'd seen crossed so many times. Her efforts to drive the shovel into the ground grew more feeble. Tears flooded her eyes. Through a strangled throat, she tried to say, 'Mind your own business,' but nothing came out. Even if it had, she wouldn't sound strong. She wouldn't sound sure of herself, like Bec would. She'd sound like a bullied child.

"Hey," Kevin said. Pink spots of color stood out on his cheeks, and not from the cold. "Knock it off."

"Knock off what?" Jay snarled at Kevin. A sneer curled his lip when he said, "What's wrong, Imogen? Cat got your tongue?"

Imogen stared at him, the vein in her temple thumping almost painfully. She stood furious, but also frozen and helpless. She had to neutralize his anger now, to get them back on an even keel before this got worse. "I don't know why you're so angry with me," she whispered. "But whatever it is, I'm sorry."

Kevin's face flushed red. Outrage flashed in his eyes. "Why are you apologizing to him?" He gripped his pickaxe, then closed in on Jay until they were only inches apart. He jabbed his finger at Jay, stopping a hair's breadth from hitting him in the chest. "If anyone owes an apology, it's you."

Imogen watched the escalating confrontation with horror, the chill in her gut unrelated to the weather. Jay's grip on his shovel had whitened his knuckles. He held it in both hands, ready to swing. He'd been spoiling for a fight all morning. The worst thing Kevin could do was give it to him, especially when they were both hefting lethal weapons. She let her shovel fall to the ground.

"Please, stop it," she cried out, putting herself between them. Her tears left cold tracks on her face. "Please, it's not worth this! I've already said I'm sorry!"

Kevin's eyes widened with incredulity. He didn't understand

why she was trying to appease Jay, and he never would. Kevin wasn't weak and cringing, he didn't feel responsible for making sure everyone was happy. He wasn't that kind of person, but in the face of anger like this, she was.

Vibrating with the energy of a lioness about to break cover and leap on her prey, Kevin took a step back. Rage radiated from Jay like heat from an oven. She wanted to flee, but she couldn't do that until she was sure Jay and Kevin would not come to blows. Her heartbeat abandoned its steady *ba-dum, ba-dum* for a tempo that defied human physiology. If she didn't know better, she'd think she was having a heart attack. She didn't want to vent her anger with Jay anymore. It had fled, leaving nothing but fear in its wake.

Then Jay said, his voice sulky, "You're going to punish me forever, aren't you? You're going to punish me for doing something I didn't do."

She stared at him like he was speaking a foreign language. Jay had almost cost Imogen her job when that sort of thing mattered. Her job was irrelevant now but the betrayal still stung. She knew he'd tampered with the hasp on the hitch of the transport crate. She'd seen the flash of truth in his eyes when she'd been angry enough to express her own. But this turnabout from attacker to injured party? She was so taken aback she couldn't have formulated a coherent response if her life had hung in the balance.

Below all the fear, all the cringing appeasement, a spark of anger flared like a sparkler, bright and beautiful as a star. An anger that wanted to scream, 'How dare you?' How dare he make what he'd done into something she used to unfairly persecute him? But she couldn't say that, she just couldn't, not with her skin crawling with desperation to make this go away that felt like a thousand spiders. She cast about for something that might put an end to this when she noticed how glassy Jay's eyes were.

"Oh my God," she said, shock making her voice loud. "You're drunk."

Kevin's sharp inhale behind her felt like validation. Jay was drunk. She was sure of it. His derisive peal of laughter was so sudden it made her jump.

"That's right, make it my fault," he scoffed, but he took a step back as if in retreat. He hadn't expected her to say that.

She took a step toward him, catching a whiff of alcohol. It was subtle but it was there. Now that she'd seen how glassy his eyes were, she didn't know how she'd missed it.

Vodka? Has to be.

Jay had been useless until about an hour ago, when his effort improved marginally, but his mood had worsened. How early had he started drinking? Had he started last night and had another to take the edge off his hangover?

"Where did you get it?" Kevin said, sidling around her, his voice shaking with anger. "What if a pack of runners came along? What if someone got injured and needed you?"

"So what if I've had a little something?" Jay countered, but now he was on the defensive. His angry posture melted away in the face of Kevin's anger.

"It's not even noon," Kevin almost shouted. "Even if you didn't drink your breakfast, we need to be sharp. We can't afford to miss a thing because it might kill us."

Jay's lip curled, marring his baby-faced good looks. "I don't need this crap, especially from you."

The handle of his shovel hit the ground with a hollow thud. He turned on his heel and stomped over the bridge.

Kevin turned back to her, looking thunderstruck. "What the actual fuck?"

"The cabins," she said. "He must have gotten it there when we were gathering supplies. Or maybe the cabinet above the fridge. I saw some liquor and wine bottles up there but never thought to keep track of it."

"You can't even reach that cabinet without a stool, Imogen. Not that I thought to look." Kevin laughed without mirth. "Great... This is all we need."

Imogen nodded, biting her lower lip. The discovery was unwelcome, and of course she had to be the one to make it. Now Jay would really hate her.

"We need to tell the others," Kevin said.

"I know," she said, a sinking feeling making her feel like she was being sucked under the broken up earth. "But I think we should wait. We still haven't hammered out how to do things, and Mike's been so angry since Sandy died."

Kevin's face clouded over. "I don't like the idea of holding out on everyone."

She shrugged. "I don't either. Let's speak with Jay this evening, or tomorrow, find out what's going on before we tell anyone else."

"What's going on is he's a lazy pouter who needs a kick in the ass," Kevin bit his lip, then said to her. "I'll do it on one condition."

"What is it?"

"Quit letting him push you around."

"Kevin," she started, feeling exasperated, because she wasn't like him. "I don't—"

"I'm serious." His blue eyes were earnest. "He's treating you like crap, and that's after screwing you over at work. He is the one, right?"

"How do you know about that?"

Kevin shrugged. "I don't remember who told me... Mike, maybe Betty." He paused, then said, "I wonder if Peter got to Somerset with that elephant."

They fell silent. They hadn't heard from Peter after they'd parted, and hadn't expected to. Had he made it there with Cammy, the family of cheetahs, the leopards, and red pandas?

"Jay's a bully, Imogen. You have to stand up to him or he'll keep pushing you around. If you won't talk to him, I'll talk to him—"

"No!" she cried. "Please don't, Kevin. It will only make it worse."

"Do you want me to tell Mike?"

Imogen could feel the blood draining from her face. If Mike knew, he'd fly off the handle, especially now. "You can't do that," she gasped. "You can't, he'll go mad. And you can't tell Zach, either. It will only cause more problems. *Please* don't tell him."

Kevin's lips pinched together. He stared at her intently, looking frustrated. "I won't say anything." Imogen sighed in relief, the knots in her stomach untwisting. But then he added, "This time. But we have to tell everyone about Jay's drinking. They need to know."

The twist in her belly started again, but not as bad as before. "That's fair."

"I've seen you stand up for others, Imogen. For the animals. Stand up for yourself."

She could see that Kevin believed what he was saying. And maybe he was even right, but he didn't understand why it was so hard for her. Even if she told him, he'd just tell her she had to try, and she wasn't sure how she'd do that. But she didn't want to disappoint him, either. "I'll try."

Kevin smiled. "Good."

He seemed willing to let the matter drop, and Imogen breathed a sigh of relief. The idea of Zach or Mike finding out about what had just happened made her entire body quiver. Singly or collectively, they'd flip out. The last thing they needed were the fireworks that would result if Kevin told them about this. There was more than enough on their plate right now. She had to get along—or at least not be enemies—with Jay, but if he was unwilling, she wasn't sure how.

"We might as well break for lunch," Kevin said. "Let's get the tools in the gondola and get it up over the creek."

"Why, if we're just coming back down?"

"Someone might see them."

She laughed, needing the release of tension. She motioned at the half-ripped up parking spots. "Anyone who comes along is going to know something's going on here."

Kevin shrugged. "I guess it's my training. You drill, drill, drill, and then drill some more until whatever you're doing becomes second nature."

They put the tools into the gondola. When they reached the winch house, Kevin went inside to fetch the keys. Imogen tried not to think about Jay. Anyone with the slightest bit of backbone would stand up to him, but she was spineless in the face of his anger. She was pathetic.

She also tried not to think about Jay being drunk. There was nothing wrong with drinking, but not first thing in the morning. That kind of thing might be all right once in a while when one was at university. In one's twenties, that kind of behavior that could be put down to high spirits. When it persisted into later decades, it was alcoholic, especially when one was hiding it.

The first of the door-sized windows along the kitchen wall opened. Kevin leaned out. "Here you go," he said, tossing her the keys.

She caught the keys, unlocked the winch house, and flicked the power switch. The lightbulb above the winch didn't illuminate. She turned the switches off and on again, but still no light from the lightbulb. She pushed the button for the winch anyway, thinking the bulb had burned out. Nothing happened.

"It's not working," she said to Kevin.

"Really?" Kevin said. He stepped back from the open window and began flicking switches. Once again, nothing happened.

Dread crept its way up Imogen's spine, snaking through her body to coil around her organs. She crossed her arms, hugging herself, as if it might offer some protection, only now noticing that the lodge was dark. With the tall trees surrounding it on all sides, the lodge wasn't especially bright, even in the daytime and despite the many windows, unless it was very sunny. On an overcast day like today, the lights should be on.

Imogen had known they'd lose power, but that knowledge had been theoretical, an event that would happen in the future. Now the future was here. They'd need to eat the food in the fridge. Going forward they'd eat less fresh food, which was already happening. There'd be no fresh meat unless they hunted for it themselves. They'd need to use the candles and lanterns everyone collected wherever they went. At least they had seasoned firewood and plentiful potable water, which gave them an enormous survival advantage, and the cooktop would work until the propane ran out as long as they could light the burners. Their situation hadn't, in any fundamental sense, changed.

Yet everything had changed. Everything that had been possible with a flick of a switch no longer was. The world they had always known continued its fitful march, inexorable and unapologetic, into a past they didn't know enough about. A nasty shiver flickered down Imogen's spine, making her shoulders twitch. With the flick of a switch, electricity—a cornerstone of modernity—was gone, and in its place the slow, unstoppable slide toward a future where their survival was anything but assured.

CHAPTER 21
IMOGEN

Imogen rubbed at her eyes as she pulled the bedroom door closed behind her. She pulled the long cardigan sweater around herself and stepped into the dark hallway. The second floor of the lodge had always been cooler than downstairs. Now, with no heat from the radiators, the chill had a bite.

Slap.

What is that, she wondered, walking to the railing over the stairs. Firelight flickered in the opening over the stairs, brighter than she'd have expected for the early hour.

Slap.

What was that sound? She could hear someone stirring in the bedroom across the hall from her room. That was a familiar sound, unlike the slapping. Nothing seemed to be amiss. She felt confident she could take the time to go to the toilet before investigating.

She tapped the bucket of water next to the toilet with her foot, the slipper on her foot loose. The oversized slippers kept her feet warm, which was all that mattered. The heavy weight against the side of her foot showed the bucket was full, which meant she didn't have to run out to the springhouse to fill it before using the toilet. She'd have to refill the bucket so the next person could flush; without power, the pump no longer worked, so the tank didn't refill on its own. Water still flowed to the kitchen sinks but lacked the water pressure they were used to, and it was never hot. Water still flowed in the shower, too, but dribbled down the face of the mortared rocks. She reckoned that they'd start using the outhouse at some point. If only the power had stayed on through the winter.

She entered the kitchen a few minutes later, after refilling the bucket and returning it to the bathroom. Mike stood at the kitchen counter. A battery operated camping lantern provided light. A disposable, aluminum foil pie pan was attached on one side to act as a reflector and worked better than Imogen would have predicted. The kitchen wasn't bright, but it was light enough for her to see the bag of flour, salt, a torn yeast packet wrapper, and a large mixing bowl off to the side while Mike kneaded dough in front of him with flour-dusted hands. Imogen watched him slap the dough down. He shoved the heels of callused hands into the dough, then folded and turned it. Then he picked up the dough and smacked it on the counter again.

Mike knew how to bake bread, which was news to her.

Outside, the birds had just started singing while the sky lightened to a dusky blue. She was hoping for a clear day. It had been so gloomy the last few days, Mother Nature's offerings reflecting the low spirits since the power had gone out and Sandy's death.

"Good morning."

Mike glanced at her, then back to the dough in front of him. "Morning."

He continued kneading and slapping the dough, adding a little flour to the board. Imogen had never baked bread in her life, but was pretty sure Mike didn't need to use the force he was presently applying.

"Are you angry with it?"

He didn't answer, just picked up the dough and slapped it down again. The planes of his face looked sharp, and she realized Mike had lost weight. His mouth turned down in a frown, his eyebrows knitting together like angry caterpillars over his squinting eyes. "Angry with what?"

"That bread you're making. Whatever it's done, I don't think it deserves to be beaten."

His scowl deepened. He glanced over, brow lowered. Irritation flashed in his dark-brown eyes. "Will you get me one of those big mixing bowls? And the vegetable oil?"

"Sure."

She washed her hands in the dribble of water they now got from the taps before selecting a large stainless-steel mixing bowl from the cart by the cooktop and wiping it out with a clean tea towel. Then she opened the tall pantry cupboard near the back door. There was just enough light to make out the bottle of cooking oil on the top shelf. She stretched, standing on tiptoes to slide it forward until she could get a good grip. She took the mixing bowl and oil back to Mike. He had quit pounding on the dough in favor of shaping it into a ball.

"Here you go."

"Thanks," he said, his acknowledgment so clipped it sounded like she'd annoyed him rather than helping.

"How are you going to bake it?"

The oven, unlike the cooktop, was electric. Storage was all it was good for now. Mike jutted his chin at the shiny Dutch oven on the cooktop, a camp-style one with little legs. "In the fire. You put coals below it and more on the lid, and change them out as they cool. Steph used to make blueberry pies on camping trips that way."

"It won't burn?" she asked, her mouth watering as she envisioned scoops of steaming hot fruit pie.

He shrugged. "Maybe. I don't have the guide for how many coals equal different temperatures. Just going from memory."

When he didn't say more, she asked, "Would you like some tea or coffee?"

"Coffee, if it's not the Starbucks. Otherwise I'll have tea."

She looked down to hide her smile. Had he not been so grumpy, she might have teased him. Workers banding together to organize unions, and the companies that fought them, were things of the past. Mike didn't let that interfere with his loyalty to his union brothers and sisters. Imogen reckoned he never would.

She added a little more water to the already warm kettle and set it on the cooktop, striking a match to light the burner, while Mike greased the mixing bowl. He set the formed dough in the bowl, turning it over to coat with oil. He covered it with a tea towel and put the bowl at the back of the cooker.

"The dough needs to rise," he said, almost defensively. "The cooktop's a little warmer because of the pilot lights, and I'll start the oatmeal in a couple minutes. That's why the cooktop's lit."

She nodded. "That makes sense. It's lovely coming down to breakfast every day."

"Even if it's oatmeal," she heard him mutter under his breath, like the effort went unappreciated. Surely he knew that wasn't the case. She'd just told him how much she appreciated that he made breakfast. She might have said so, but wasn't sure it would be welcome just now.

The open bag of coffee was indeed from Starbucks, so she fetched two teabags and poured the boiled water into mugs while Mike washed his hands. Again, he attacked the task with a ferocity it didn't warrant. She knew he was upset about the trip to the home improvement center. Sandy's death had come as a shock to everyone, but Mike was taking it especially hard. He seemed to avoid dealing with it by throwing himself into work: making shutters for the windows, stringing up the tin can trip wire, and now baking bread. He wouldn't talk about it, and left the room when they talked about Sandy. Betty had confided she was afraid he'd start an argument if they tried once more to settle on a decision-making method.

Imogen gathered mugs, sugar, spoons, and the last of the milk from the spring house, while Mike cleaned up the mess he'd made. He joined her at the table but didn't sit down. He sipped his tea while looking out the windows facing the winch house and stairs. The atmosphere was so stifling that Imogen sighed with relief when she heard voices at the top of the stairs, followed moments later by Kevin and Bec.

"What are you doing up so early?" Bec asked.

"I just woke up." Imogen didn't mention the noise from Mike's furious dough kneading had woken her. She didn't want him to take it the wrong way.

"We're going on a hike," Kevin said as he slipped into his coat.

"This early?" Imogen asked.

"Yep," Kevin said. His blond hair looked like he'd stuck his finger in an electrical socket, and he was far too cheerful for this hour of the morning. Maybe he was used to early hours from the time he'd spent at the fire station waiting to fight fires. "I'll be ready in a sec, Bec," he added, and crossed over to the library.

Bec pulled a knit cap over her head and pulled on her jacket. "There's a fox den near the waterfall. I thought if we get there early, we might see them. Foxes are crepuscular, you know. It means—"

"I know what it means," Imogen said. "They're most active at dawn and dusk. Cheetahs are the same." She glanced out the window. The faintest hint of pink tinged the edge of the dark-purple dawn sky. "You might have a bit of a wait."

"I know," Bec said. "I can't sleep, anyway. I got my period and I feel like crap."

"Have you taken—" Imogen started, but Bec interrupted her.

"I just have shitty periods. Besides, if we don't go now, we'll be too tired to later." Bec grinned at Mike. "Mike's been working us to the bone."

Mike grunted. Bec raised her eyebrows at Imogen, her eyes questioning. Imogen shrugged, not knowing what to tell her.

"You have weapons, right?" Mike said, sounding aggravated that he had to ask.

Kevin emerged from the small library room with a rifle slung over his shoulder. They'd found two rifles and a shotgun in an old-fashioned gun case in the library. The bulge of his pocket suggested he'd also grabbed a box of ammunition. He adjusted the strap over his shoulder. "Yeah, of course."

Mike inhaled, nostrils flaring. "That's what you're taking?"

Kevin halted mid-stride. "My Halligan's on the porch. I'm taking it, too."

"What the hell are you thinking?" Mike demanded. "Gunfire will pull in every zombie within five miles."

Imogen and Bec traded a wary sidelong glance. Then Bec said, "I won't let him do anything dumb, Mike. There's nothing out here, anyway."

Bec might as well have lit a fuse. It was exactly the wrong thing to say.

"You don't know what's out there," Mike said, his tone scathing. "If that's your attitude, you have no business going outside." They must have been staring at him, because then he said, "What are you looking at?"

They all traded a glance. Mike never acted like this. It wasn't just that his voice brooked no argument; it promised violence.

"I'll put the rifle back," Kevin said, his tone careful.

Mike snorted, as if Kevin was a particularly slow pupil who had finally figured out his ABC's years after everyone else. He turned back to the window, broody as a hen.

Bec mouthed, 'What the fuck?' at Imogen, who shrugged. After Kevin returned the rifle and ammunition, he and Bec left. The lodge grew quiet apart from the occasional crack and hiss from the fire. The air felt charged, as if lightning might strike.

Imogen bit her lip while she debated what to do. Part of her wanted to go back to bed, but she hated to leave Mike like this. She knew why he was acting out. "What kind of bread are you making?"

He turned to her, finishing a sip of tea. "Wheat."

"I didn't know you knew how to bake bread."

He jammed his free hand into his jeans front pocket, his thumb rubbing the watch pocket. The dark circles that wreathed his eyes made him look like Father Time at year's end. "Haven't in a while. Thought I better get back into practice."

"I'm sure it will be wonderful."

Mike didn't reply. She sipped her tea. She took a deep breath, figuring she might as well try. "You're upset about Sandy."

Everything about him seemed to withdraw. His eyes shuttered closed, the features of his face retreating as if he were pulling windows tight against a storm.

Undeterred, Imogen persisted. "I didn't know her very long, but I liked her."

Mike didn't answer. He knocked back the rest of his tea and took the cup to the sink. Imogen sighed, hating to see him hurting like this. She knew he needed to talk about what had happened, but for whatever reason, he wouldn't. He'll just murder bread dough and act like an ogre, she thought, a tiny wisp of irritation hissing at the back of her mind.

"Mike, are you okay?"

He looked up, startled. "Of course I'm okay."

"You seem unhappy."

"I'm not unhappy," he snapped. "I'm… I'm fine."

She stood to go back upstairs. Talking to him right now was pointless but she couldn't resist making a final offer. "If you'd like to talk, I'm here."

He stiffened like someone had applied an electric shock, the set of his jaw mutinous. "You don't need to babysit me, Imogen. It's the world we live in now. Get used to losing people."

She flinched at the flare of temper, shocked by the coldness in his voice. "Get used to losing people? You don't believe that."

"How would you know what I believe? You barely know me."

The venomous disdain in his voice, the anger flaring in his usually warm eyes, set the room swimming around her. She was a child again in the path of one of her father's rages as it barreled down like an air strike. Her stomach roiled as it plummeted to her feet. Her heart beat so fast it would keep time with a hummingbird's wings. The urge to placate Mike, to soothe and appease, to please him welled up inside her, as needful as a newborn baby. She trembled, knowing she was a hair's breadth from licking the soles of his boots if it would make him happy.

I'm not a child anymore. I don't have to do what I did then.

Voice shaking, she said, "I don't think you can just get used to losing people. That's… no way to live."

His upper lip peeled away from his teeth to form an ugly sneer. "Tell yourself what you need to, but it's how we live now."

She blinked and took a step back. His refusal to give even a centimeter made her want to crawl under the floor. Mike turned on his heel and stomped to the front door. "Where are you going?"

He snatched his leather jacket from the coat-tree and yanked the door open. "Out."

Imogen watched him stalk across the porch and disappear into the woods in a state of disbelief. The only thing he hadn't done as he stormed away was slam the door behind him.

She didn't think he believed a word of what he'd just said. Mike took everything to heart. He didn't wait to be told what to do. He saw what needed doing and did it. He took it on himself to ensure they had what they needed: food and shelter, safety, even some joy, but Sandy's death had shaken him more than she'd realized. Losing Sandy was a stark reminder that try as he might, he couldn't control everything. That sometimes, just like with his family, he couldn't keep the people he cared about safe.

Imogen's lips formed a pouty frown as she thought, furrowing her brow. Then her forehead smoothed. Her lips parted as she inhaled. She held the breath suspended in her lungs as the realization hit her. She had stood her ground. Instead of trying to please and appease Mike, she'd pushed back, disagreed, and it hadn't killed her. It hadn't even hurt her. The sky hadn't fallen. She reached for the table, still trembling from the confrontation. She had told someone she cared about what she truly thought, despite his disapproval and anger, instead of what she thought he wanted to hear.

"Jiminy Crickets," she whispered and almost smiled, for that was something only Mike would say.

CHAPTER 22
MIKE

Within thirty seconds of storming out of the lodge, Mike felt like a jagoff.

He sighed, following the trail that turned right when he reached the waterfall. It was the loop that he liked the best of the several trails in the lodge's immediate vicinity. The last quarter of the trail was treacherous, littered with rocks and boulders. Every time he took this trail, he'd think maybe he shouldn't. He'd be no good to anyone if he tripped and broke his ankle. He never turned around, though. Either he was sure of his balance or he was an overconfident idiot.

He'd feel better after an hour or two in the woods. Then he'd go back to check on the rising dough. And he'd apologize to Imogen.

He still couldn't believe how quickly things had changed. He expected Sandy to walk down the stairs. That never happened, what with her being dead. Imogen thought it was Sandy's death that had him in such a black mood, and she was right, but that wasn't all it was. Every night since Sandy had died, he'd dreamed of Steph. It was as if Sandy's death was also a key—one that slipped into his psyche to unlock Steph. And that would have been great, except the dreams were more like nightmares.

Last night, he had dreamed about getting home to find the moving truck outside the house.

Huh, Mike had thought.

He was sure the moving truck was scheduled for next week. They were still only half-finished with the packing. Despite his confusion, a zing of excitement ran through him. It was happening. He was finally following his dream to move to the Outer Banks, to lead the life he wanted. Three months ago, he'd closed on the house—a tiny, old shack of a place at the end of Old Lighthouse Road in Buxton, right on the beach. A friend had told him about the place. The old-timer selling didn't want the house that had been in his family for generations ripped down and replaced by a rental that slept fifteen for five grand a week. Given the condition of the house, the price had been high but still fair for an oceanfront property. The old man's happiness that he was selling to someone who planned to live there year-round had taken away some of the price tag's sting.

Steph stood behind the truck, handing off a box. "This is the last one," she said.

"Hey, hon," Mike said.

She whirled around, eyes wide, like she hadn't expected him. "Oh, hi. Why are you here?"

"Nice to see you, too." He leaned in to give her a peck on the cheek.

Steph ducked away from him. "I thought you were going to Deep Creek with Faith."

"I told you this morning," Mike said. "Maddy's sick, so the trip's canceled."

Steph's eyes slid away to the back of the moving truck. Mike followed her line of sight. Javier, one of the docs from the hospital, a surgeon, looked down at him.

"Mike," he said. He jumped down and extended his hand, which Mike shook. "I didn't expect to see you. How are you?"

Something was off. The set of Steph's shoulders, the way she hunched in on herself without moving, and how she'd ducked away from him telegraphed discomfort. He'd seen Javier a few times when he'd run whatever Steph had forgotten to the hospital, but they weren't friends. Not the kind who helps pack a moving truck.

"Why's the moving truck here?" Mike said to Steph. "It's not due till next week."

Steph took a deep breath. "I'm moving in with Javier. We're getting married."

It took a moment for her words to compute. The enormous diamond ring twinkling on Steph's finger—so big it made the three carats in Mike's pocket look puny—kicked his brain into gear. "What are you talking about?"

"Oh, please," Steph said, irritated now. "You didn't think I was moving to the Outer Banks, did you?"

"Yeah, I— I did," Mike stammered. "We were talking about it this morning!"

Javier stepped close to Steph and put his arm around her shoulders. Mike could barely believe what he was seeing. Javier was touching his girlfriend, like he had some kind of claim on her, and she wasn't stepping away.

"Mike, be reasonable," Javier said. "Steph's been unhappy with you for so long. Did you really think she would marry someone like you? I can give her the life she deserves."

The lilt of Javier's Argentinian accent, filled with an easy confidence that fit him like the expensive-looking clothes he wore, made Mike aware of his own—old jeans, work boots, a flannel shirt over an old, grubby tee shirt. Before he knew it was happening, Mike had Javier by the throat and shoved him against the truck.

"Don't you dare touch her!" he shouted.

"Mike, stop it!" Steph cried, shoving her way between them. "Go away! It's over! I already bought a dress, for Christ's sake!"

"What are you talking about?"

But she had turned away, her hands caressing Javier's cheek. "Are you okay, baby? I'm so sorry. I knew he'd act like this…"

That was when Mike had woken up.

He was feeling the chill because he didn't have the hoodie he'd taken to wearing under the leather jacket. He gritted his teeth, the same stunned anger he'd felt in the dream rising to the surface. In real life, there was no Javier. The guy in his dream reminded Mike of an actor from that show on Netflix about drug cartels in South America.

"But there was something," he muttered, the bitterness of betrayal like glass in his throat. Steph hadn't been honest with him about what she wanted. Was it that much of a leap to think she'd also lied about loving him?

When he reached the enormous boulder at the bend in the trail, he took a running jump, gripping the cold granite as he scrambled up. On the side facing the woods, hidden from the path, was a crescent moon-shaped depression. Mike nestled into it, always surprised at how well the stone fit under his rear end, like he'd carved it himself. He inhaled the clean scent of decomposing leaves and damp air. The anger that remembering the dream had worsened subsided. The chilled stone sent a shiver up his spine. His ears were cold, as was his nose. He should have grabbed a hat.

That's what I get for storming off like an idiot.

He leaned back, now hidden from the trail, and rested his head. He'd sit for a while, watch the lightening sky, and listen to the sounds of the forest. Then he would go back, get on with things, and not think about Steph. Try to ignore the hollow ache in his chest, the itch of his fingers when he thought about holding her. Try not to ask himself pointless questions that would never be answered, like what happened? Had she really changed her mind or was it just a case of the jitters? Had she still loved him like he loved her?

Mike took a deep breath and blew it out. Imogen's startled face—eyes wide and alarmed—filled his mind's eye. *I can't believe I yelled at her. Christ, I'm an idiot.*

Mike shook his head, feeling three inches tall. Of course, it had to be her. Almost everyone was dead, their survival hung by a thread, his fiancée had been working up to dumping him, so of course he'd unloaded on the one person who always had his back. He'd been serious about going to look for Beth and Katie, Steph, too, after killing the monster his sister had become. It was beyond stupid—Imogen had been right—but he'd have done it. It hadn't been about finding them, but punishing himself. What better punishment than to become the very thing he'd failed to save his family from? Imogen was the only reason he hadn't done it.

After she'd told him about her family, how the trauma of the genocide they'd fled had changed it forever, he had remembered that glimpse of recognition he'd seen in Imogen's eyes when he'd called Steph. When he'd failed to make her understand the danger she was in. The well of knowing in Imogen's amber eyes was so deep Mike had known it had no bottom. If he'd let himself fall into it, like he might do now that he knew her better, he'd still be falling. If he told Imogen how Sandy had died, he could. An expectant ache hummed inside him when he thought about how much he wanted to.

Quit being so pathetic.

He tried again to think of nothing, to just listen to the sounds of the forest. His brain refused to settle down, Steph and Imogen always hovering around the edges. He had a zillion things to do today to get ready for winter. He needed to finish the shutters for the first-floor windows and hadn't even made the oatmeal for breakfast. If he apologized to Imogen, he could pretend this morning hadn't happened. He could keep telling himself she was wrong. He could pretend he didn't need to talk about what had happened to Sandy and that Imogen wasn't becoming—

"I don't know what to do."

Kevin's voice intruded on his unsettling train of thought. Mike sat up straighter. Then Bec said, "Do what she asked."

They were approaching from the other direction. Perhaps the foxes had been a no-show, so they'd opted for a hike. It would be nice to see them—if a little awkward—now that he wasn't having a tantrum. Maybe he could ease back into being a tolerable human being before he apologized to Imogen if they didn't mind his joining them. He leaned forward to push out of the crescent-shaped divot when Kevin said, "Yeah, I know, but you weren't there, Bec. The things he said to Imogen were vicious."

Mike froze.

"I still say you let her handle it," Bec said, sounding like her mind was made up.

They were walking past the boulder now. Stop, please stop, Mike thought, his silent prayer straining for purchase in the cosmic mix of hopes and dreams that had been dashed by the billions the day zombies appeared. He offered this one with such urgency that it felt like he could fly if he jumped off the boulder.

"But he's a bully. He won't stop—"

"It doesn't matter what he is," Bec said, cutting him off. "It's what Imogen…"

They kept walking. He couldn't hear the rest. Mike's mind raced. Who were they talking about? Not Clyde. He was as gentle as they come. Not Zach, either; they were friends. He couldn't imagine Jeffrey being vicious about anything, and it obviously wasn't Kevin.

Which left Jay.

The anger rushed back, so strong his teeth ached. Jay had done nothing but harass and harangue Imogen almost since he'd met the guy, and she just took it. He understood better than the others why Imogen shrank in the face of his anger. Why she made excuses and smoothed things over, and why standing up for herself must feel impossible. His hands fisted. Someone had to defend her if she wouldn't—if she couldn't—defend herself. She was pretty formidable against zombies. Living, breathing people were her kryptonite.

Then a terrible thought occurred to Mike, especially considering how he'd just behaved. What if they were talking about him?

He slid down the side of the boulder, branches snapping under his feet. Bec and Kevin, now thirty feet up the trail, stopped and turned. Guilt crept into their faces… Bec's in eyes that widened in surprise, while Kevin flashed a nervous smile.

"Wait!" Mike called out, jogging to catch up.

"Mike," Bec said, giving him her usual bright smile. "Where did you come from?"

"I was on the boulder, cooling off," he said, pointing over his shoulder with his thumb. "I was a jerk— It doesn't matter. Who are you talking about? Who's bullying Imogen?"

They traded a glance, unease plain in their downturned heads. Heart in his throat, he said, "It's not me, is it?"

Bec's surprised, "What?" jumbled with Kevin's emphatic, "Hell no."

Mike's body lightened like a helium balloon rising to the ceiling. He couldn't think of anything he'd said to Imogen that was vicious, that Kevin thought crossed a line, apart from just now. Even so, confirmation that they hadn't been talking about him still felt like a vindication. "Then who?"

Kevin shifted his weight and looked down at the trail before meeting Mike's eyes. "I said I wouldn't say anything."

"Who is it?"

Kevin glanced at Bec, an appeal in his eyes. She held up her hands. "Don't look at me for permission. You know what I think. She asked you to keep your mouth shut."

"It's Jay, isn't it?" Mike said.

Kevin sighed. After a long moment, he said, "It's Jay."

Of course it was. Mike's hands fisted, the anger he'd been pushing down detonating like a thousand megaton warhead. "What did he say?"

Kevin looked at Mike, but his eyes slid away almost immediately. He scratched his ear. "I've already said more than I should have."

Mike opened his mouth to press Kevin because Bec wasn't giving it up, when he realized it didn't matter. Bec stepped in front of him, her eyes wide with alarm. "Don't do anything stupid. Don't go running— Mike!"

But he'd already shaken her off, his feet eating up the distance to the fork at the waterfall.

"Mike!" Bec called from behind him, sounding a little breathless.

"Mike, wait," Kevin shouted.

He ignored them, opening up his lead as he rounded the bend at the waterfall. He could see the white and green paint of the lodge through the almost bare trees, but a haze of red colored his vision. He hopped the small dip at the tiny stream, never breaking stride. As he came around the springhouse, Jay opened the back door holding the water bucket from the bathroom. Mike changed direction, closing in on Jay like a missile. When Jay saw him, he took a step back, his face slack with alarm. "What's wrong?"

Mike grabbed Jay by the collar and dragged him down the stone steps. The bucket bounced away, clanging as it rolled on its side. Mike strong-armed Jay around the corner of the springhouse so anyone awake inside wouldn't be able to see them.

"What the hell, man? Let go of me!"

He slammed Jay against the springhouse. Jay's eyes were wide and his mouth open, intensifying the impression that he was nothing more than a spoiled teenager. Mike took a step closer until their noses almost touched. "Leave Imogen alone," he snarled, jabbing Jay in the chest.

Jay pushed Mike on both shoulders, surprising him and forcing him back a few steps. "Get off me!"

Blood rushed in Mike's ears, drowning out everything but the sound of Jay's indignation. An inferno of rage over everything that had happened, everything he'd done, exploded. Madison's tiny foot poking out from under that blanket. Putting Faith down like a dog. Beth and Katie missing. His brother-in-law dead in a bathroom that Imogen hadn't let him set foot inside, afraid it would traumatize him more. How Imogen had taken care of him at Faith's because he'd broken down so much he'd been useless, and the shame of seeing what he'd done to her face, of crossing a line he would never have crossed in his old life. Steph's unexplained change of heart, his failure to protect her, and his dreadful choice to save himself and the people at the zoo instead of looking for her. How he'd been only steps away, but helpless to save Sandy. And his terror underlying it all—always gnawing at the back of his brain—that he couldn't keep everyone safe. And now Jay, whom he'd never liked, who did nothing but bitch and whine and complain, was bullying Imogen.

Everything he'd been feeling, every scrap of pain, every frustration he'd pushed aside because he needed to hold it together, needed to be strong to get everyone through this nightmare, rained down on Jay like hounds baying for blood.

Jay took a step forward. Mike grabbed him by the throat with one hand and shoved him against the stone wall of the springhouse. He could feel Jay trembling, feel the convulsive bobble of his Adam's apple as Jay swallowed. Satisfaction rushed through him to see the sweat on Jay's upper lip, and the shock and fear in his shifting eyes searching for an escape.

"You will leave Imogen alone," he growled through gritted teeth, his voice snapping like a whip. "If I hear of anything that even approaches you giving her crap, if you forget to say 'God bless you' when she sneezes, zombies will be the least of your problems. Do you understand me, or do I need to beat you senseless until you do?"

Jay nodded. Mike stepped back, releasing his neck, and Jay streaked around the corner of the springhouse like a jackrabbit.

Mike's body thrummed with the pent-up anger of not kicking Jay in the ass so hard he wouldn't catch up with himself till next year. His hands trembled as he fisted them over and over. He knew the heat broiling his face meant he was a deep shade of scarlet. He'd been a jerk this morning, he knew that, but he'd never bully anyone, especially Imogen. She just wanted everyone to get along. Who, besides Jay, would try to undermine that?

He took a deep breath, then another, and un-fisted his hands. When he saw Bec, Kevin, and Zach staring at him, he jumped, heart in his throat. He hadn't realized he had an audience. They looked like three little owls, their eyes as large as spotlights. From one heartbeat to the next, he went from outrage to feeling foolish. How on earth could he explain his behavior?

So he said, because he couldn't think of anything else, "I'm going to make the oatmeal."

CHAPTER 23
MIKE

Mike didn't bother to grab his jacket hanging on the coat-tree. The cold air bit at his face as he stepped onto the porch. He skirted the long table and benches where he'd envisioned everyone eating on summer evenings, the screens keeping mosquitoes at bay. At the rate things were going, they might not be here come summer.

He started toward the screen door by the winch house in front of him, then wheeled around. The other side of the porch had a door, too. He went that way instead. He knew everyone could see him walk past the bay windows on either side of the fireplace, but somehow it felt there was less chance anyone would pursue him.

Everyone knew what he'd said to Jay. The furtive glances, and conversations that screeched to a halt when he entered a room, made it obvious. He was glad to escape the eyes on him. He strode past the outhouse and into the woods. The hiking trail on this side of the house was less defined compared to the one that led to the waterfall, making it easy to stray. An enormous tree had fallen a thousand feet from the lodge and he strode toward it.

When he reached the downed tree he kicked it, his hands

prickling. The desire to throttle Jay, Amy, and every zombie on the planet made him want to scream. All the zombies did was moan and try to eat them. Amy and Jay… His insides squeezed, trying to take up more space than his body allowed, sending his blood pressure skyrocketing. They bitched about everything. Jay was lazy as sin. Amy took part in the chores but complained—loudly—that they never did them the way she had suggested. They had pitched a fit about everything just before.

A stab of guilt pierced Mike's anger. He'd been terrible to Amy because he'd been angry, implying they'd throw her out. Under normal circumstances, he would have apologized days ago. He told himself every morning that today he'd apologize, but then she'd start bitching. It had been easy to let his resolve fly out the window like a dust mote. Sandy had been the opposite of Amy and Jay. She wasn't here, and they were. His jaw clenched at the unfairness.

"Pull yourself together," he muttered when he realized he had tears in his eyes.

He dashed them away. Now wasn't the time to fall apart. He turned around, leaning against the log, and glared at the lodge. It looked idyllic in the middle of the woods, with the white clapboard siding and green trim, the many windows, and the stone chimney. The curved sliver of moon carved near the top of the outhouse door made even the outhouse charming to look at. And it would be, if it weren't for Amy, Jay, and the world being overrun by dead people. If Sandy hadn't been forced to shoot herself rather than turn into one of them. She'd died not because she was stupid or they'd run into bad guys, or even because they'd been careless, but because she'd been unlucky. If they'd left five minutes earlier, she'd still be alive. But she wasn't because he hadn't spoken up.

Buttercup, the orange and white tuxedo cat, hopped onto the downed log by his elbow with a chirp. She headbutted his arm, then looked up at him. Despite his anger, he smiled. He held out his finger so the little marmalade-colored cat could sniff.

Everyone liked Buttercup; he'd even seen Amy giving her a surreptitious pet. The little fluff ball was so friendly and never missed a chance to love on someone. She reminded Mike of a cheerleader, all enthusiasm and friendly sparkle. She rubbed her face against his hand, chirping and purring away.

The slam of a screen door sent Buttercup scurrying away. Imogen followed Zach down the stone steps from the same door Mike had just used moments ago. Imogen laughed at something Zach said, and he returned it with a pleased grin. They picked their way along the stones of the path nearer the lodge, heading his direction.

"Just go away," he muttered, glaring at them.

Either they'd settled on how to run the household or were still bickering and Betty wanted him. He cringed at the latter idea and climbed over the tree, intending to walk deeper into the woods, then stopped himself. What was the point of running away like a child? He closed his eyes and took a few deep breaths, willing himself to hold it together.

"Mike!"

He turned to see Zach's gloved hand raised in greeting. Imogen offered a half smile, her hands plunged deep in her coat pockets and a scarf wrapped around her neck. Her hair flew around her face, and Mike realized it had gotten windy and he was cold.

"Are we starting again?"

Imogen shook her head. "We voted. All in favor of you and Betty being tiebreakers when we need one."

"Except Jay," Zach added.

Mike's brow furrowed, and he couldn't keep the surprise out of his voice when he said, "Amy voted yes?"

They both smiled. Zach said, "Amy said she'd do whatever the rest of the group wanted. So we counted it as a yes."

"Oh."

"No more talking about anything serious today," Imogen said. "Kevin, Bec, and Betty are taking another go at the chore list. They'll pass it around so people can add to it and make suggestions. We thought we'd take a walk. Want to join us?"

Mike huffed out a breath, relieved they'd decided, but his hands still itched to punch something. "No, you go ahead. I'm not— I need to work on the..." His voice petered out. He couldn't think of anything he had to do right *this second.*

Imogen and Zach traded a glance, the split-second meeting of eyes an entire conversation. Grief hit him, fierce as a firestorm, with so much force he had to take a step back. There was no one left in the world who knew him well enough to share a glance like that. No one at all.

"Are you okay?" Zach asked him.

Zach's frostiness and distrust had vanished after Mike had threatened Jay. Threats of violence, directed at the right person, had convinced Zach he was okay. He blinked, surprised by the question. "Of course I'm okay."

Another traded glance, then Zach said, "You know, I think I'm going to help with the chore list. I just thought of something to add."

Imogen nodded at his obvious lie. "Okay. We'll walk later."

She scrambled onto the tree, settling in beside where Mike leaned against it, her short legs dangling like a child's. He kept his mouth shut. He wanted no part of whatever she and Zach thought they were doing. But after a few moments, Imogen broke the silence. "You aren't acting okay."

He sighed and shook his head. "I'm fine, Imogen. Okay? Just... leave it."

"What is it?" she persisted. "You've been angry and miserable since Sandy died. I'm worried about you. Everyone's worried about you."

"Bet Jay and Amy aren't."

"You know what I mean." Her voice was as soft as a summer breeze. The comfort of that softness, of her gentleness, sucked him in like a warm bed inviting him to crawl under the covers. Her concern felt like an irresistible force meeting an immoveable object, and a sudden helplessness welled in his chest. He bit his lip hard, tasting blood, clutching at the pain so he could hold it close and keep it together.

"You were cruel to Amy last week," Imogen said after it became apparent he would not speak. "I know she can be awful but that's not like you."

Mike looked away. Imogen was right. But he couldn't take seeing the disappointment on her face. Even worse, *Jay* had been right. He'd been a dick to Amy. Imogen hopped down from the tree and stood in front of him, taking his hands in hers. He looked at her then, almost startled by her touch. Her amber eyes brimmed with concern.

"Just tell me."

All at once, his resistance crumbled.

"I knew it was a bad idea," he whispered. "I knew we shouldn't go inside. When I saw the mall…" He shook his head, his voice thickening with emotion. "I should have insisted. I know they'd have gone along. They wouldn't have been happy with me, but Sandy would be alive."

"Mike," she said, giving his hands a squeeze. "It's not your fault."

"But it is," he countered, taking a shaky breath. "I had a bad feeling, and I let myself be talked out of it. She was right there, Imogen, and I couldn't do a damn thing to save her."

"It's still not your fault."

The way Imogen spoke, the way she disagreed, almost didn't sound like her. Mike looked at her, puzzled at the difference between this and her general avoidance of conflict. Whatever the difference was, it was too subtle for him to parse.

"I'm not sure I can do this." He pulled his hands free, trying to blink back tears. Why the hell was he crying?

"Can't do what?"

"Keep everyone safe. I can't— I don't know how to do it."

She huffed a breath that was almost a laugh. "It's not your job to keep everyone safe. We need to do that together."

"But… It's what I've always done, except when it mattered. I didn't keep my family safe and Steph…" He took a shuddering breath. "You know the last thing we did?" Imogen shook her head. "We argued. It was the last time I saw her and I argued with her."

"Mike," Imogen said, her gentle voice imploring him to listen. "You couldn't have known. You'd have set things right if you'd had the chance."

"We were moving to the Outer Banks. I'd just given my notice at work and paid the deposit for the movers."

Imogen's mouth sagged. "I didn't know."

"She told me she was having second thoughts, that she'd gotten into the master's program at Pitt. We were moving in six weeks and she springs it on me, and only because I pried it out of her."

He slid his finger into the watch pocket of his jeans. The platinum engagement ring felt cool between his fingers. He thrust the ring between them. An anger he hadn't known was there harshened his voice and made his body hum.

"I started paying on this ring two weeks after Steph saw it. That was three years ago, when we'd been dating three months, but I knew she was the one. I carried the damn thing in my pocket for weeks when— I was going to propose to her that night. And I find out she's not sure she wants to move, that she's been accepted to Pitt. *We lived together*, Imogen, and she never said a word. Not one. And then I said all the wrong things, and we fought, and she's gone."

He stood in front of her, the ring pinched between his thumb and forefinger, arm outstretched like he was asking Imogen to marry him. The cruel joke of Imogen being presented with the ring when Steph never would made him want to laugh, but nothing about it was funny.

"Oh, Mike," Imogen said, her voice as hushed as an empty church. "I'm so sorry."

The sympathy on her face sent the pain gushing out, hot and

sticky and vital as blood. He wanted to return to when he thought Steph loved him. To when his sisters were alive and Maddy's and Katie's shining faces made his heart soar. He wanted Jonah beside him while they drove too fast with the music too loud. He wanted his life to be how it had been, for just one more day. The beautiful, fragile life he hadn't treasured enough was gone, irretrievably lost. It was more than he could bear, but not enough to put him out of his misery.

Imogen stepped close and pulled him into her arms. Mike sagged against her, sure he'd send them tumbling to the ground because she was so tiny and all he could do was hang on. He clung to her like a child to his mother after a bad dream. A memory of his mother doing just that, holding him close when he'd skinned his knee, rushed through him while he wept for what his life had been, all the dreams unfulfilled. He wept for the people he had loved. He wept for himself, because he was forty-eight years old and he wanted his mother to tell him every-thing would be all right.

When he stepped back, breaking the embrace, he swiped at his face. He was too drained to feel embarrassed by his tears. The engagement ring had slipped onto his pinky finger. The diamonds sparkled when they caught the afternoon light filtering through the bare trees. He could still imagine the ring on Steph's slender finger. The day they'd found it, her smile had been incandescent. He'd fallen in love with her right there in the jewelry shop as he watched her glowing face. The memory cut as deep as it had once warmed him. He'd never see Steph's face when she learned the ring was hers if she wanted it. If she wanted him. The weight in his heart grew heavier because he knew she had not.

He slipped the ring from his finger, the elegance of the plat-inum filigree and diamonds out of place against his workman's hands. "I don't know what to do with this."

With a hesitant glance to make sure it was okay, Imogen took the ring from him. She slipped it back into his pocket. "Perhaps you'll give it to her someday."

He swallowed around the lump in his throat. "I'm sorry I was so awful to you the other morning."

"It's okay."

Mike shook his head. "It's not, especially after you telling me about your dad. I—"

"Mike," Imogen said, interrupting him. She smiled shyly. It made her look so young. "It's okay. I'm all right. Besides, I think you made up for it when you threatened Jay. It's not what I wanted, but it seems to have worked."

His face grew hot and he knew he was blushing. He wasn't sorry for what he'd said to Jay, but it embarrassed him that he'd lost control of himself. "I shouldn't have gone about it that way." He shrugged because there was nothing he could do about it now. "Thank you, for making me talk to you."

Imogen's smile deepened. "It's what friends are for. And no one can take another day of you being such an ogre."

The smile tugging the corners of his mouth felt fragile but genuine. A spark of delight flared in Imogen's amber eyes, setting her face aglow, soft as a pastel-colored sunset. He didn't know what had made her smile and felt too self-conscious to ask. "I should find Amy."

Imogen nodded. "I think that's a good idea."

He heard Bec, Kevin, and Betty's voices from the kitchen as he slipped through the back door. They must be at the kitchen table, heads together, working on the chores list. Jeffrey sat on the couch in the main room, his back to Mike, reading a book, while Clyde dozed in the recliner. Hoping she might be upstairs so he wouldn't come to anyone's attention by checking the library, he skulked up the stairs, stopping outside the door to Amy's room.

They'd reshuffled the bedrooms in the wake of Sandy's death. Now, Imogen and Bec shared the room at the top of the stairs. Amy had moved into Imogen's and Bec's old room, which had two twin beds. Mike, Zach, and Kevin, as well as Betty and Clyde, had stayed put in their respective rooms. That left a twin bed in Amy's room free. Jay had been sleeping on an air mattress in the library room and jumped at the opportunity to get an actual bed. Mike had thought, rather uncharitably, that if she had to share with a man, at least it was the other member of the Crybaby Cabal.

If Amy and Jay were both in their room, Jay would have a front row seat to his apology. The cherry on this craptastic cake of a day. After a moment's hesitation, Mike rapped on the door.

"Yes?"

"It's Mike, Amy. Can I talk to you?"

Silence from the other side of the door. After what felt like years, she said, "Okay."

He pushed the door open just enough to stand in the doorway. Amy was on her bed on top of the patchwork quilt, leaning against the headboard with an open book resting in her lap. Her shoulders were rigid, face shuttered like a house in the path of a hurricane. The book looked like it would be upside down if she lifted it. He wondered if she'd grabbed it from the bookshelf between the two beds, a nine-by-six-inch shield of paper and ink to hide behind. The thought made him feel worse, like an even bigger jerk than he'd already been. At least Jay wasn't here.

"I'm sorry for what I said last week, and for taking so long to apologize. I was feeling—" He stopped. How he'd felt didn't matter; he wasn't here to offer excuses. "I was out of line. I know I hurt your feelings, and I'm sorry."

She regarded him, wariness lurking behind the composed facade of her blank face.

"I want you here, and I'd like for us to get along," he continued, because she didn't seem inclined to speak. "However long this lasts, it'll take all of us to get through it."

After a long moment she nodded, the gesture so small he almost missed it. A glimmer flickered in her eyes, but he couldn't tell what it meant. She raised the book—definitely upside down —in a silent dismissal.

It was what he deserved. Mike stepped into the hall, pulling the door shut, and crossed to his room. The sleeper bed by the door was closed and stowed, making it easier to navigate the room during the day—its blankets, sheets, and pillows stacked on a trunk in the corner. He grabbed a blanket and lay down on his bed, the Murphy bed closest to the door. His body seemed to melt into the slightly lumpy mattress, exhaustion hitting him like a stone wall. How had he been standing just a moment ago when he felt like molten lead seeping into the fibers of the mattress?

He glanced at the other Murphy bed, which was closer to the windows by the far wall, his own bed between it and the door. Huh, he thought, only now realizing he'd claimed this bed because it gave him a clear path to the door in case their sanctuary needed to be defended. Unbidden, Steph's voice rang in his ears. *'Who do you think you are, Mike Wójcik? The big, bad man who protects everyone from monsters?'*

His eyes filled with tears again. He couldn't remember when or what she'd been teasing him about, but he'd always remembered it. It always made him smile because it was such a Steph thing to say. Maybe he was wrong. Perhaps there was still hope, but he didn't see how Steph could have survived. He knew what he'd heard on the phone when he'd called her, when he'd failed to make her understand the danger. He could only imagine the chaos that had engulfed the Emergency Room when all those people sick with 'salmonella,' and those they'd bitten, died and reanimated.

And knowing that, he'd left the city without trying to find her. The hospital was ten miles of densely populated suburbs away, and near two shopping malls. He'd most likely have died. But going to find the woman he loved was what a big, bad man would have done—should have done—wasn't it?

Maybe it's better this way, he thought. If Steph didn't have to live through this she'd never see the terrible things that he had. She'd never see the dawning horror on Sandy's face when she realized her card had been punched and there was nothing she could do about it. Steph wouldn't have to stand by, helpless and useless, unable to do something as basic as keep the people around her alive. How hard was it to do that—to keep them safe —when they were right beside you? When had he become so inept when the task—keep people safe—was so clear a child could understand?

So maybe it was better that Steph was spared the horrors they now lived with. He knew deep down this was a lie, a rationalization to blunt the sharp edges of his grief. Steph being dead would never be better, no matter the things it might spare her. It didn't matter if she hadn't loved him anymore. He had loved her, still loved her, and always would. His body ached to hold her close and say the right things, the things he should have said.

I love you.

I need you.

Whatever it takes to keep you, I'll do it.

But he hadn't said any of them.

CHAPTER 24
IMOGEN

Imogen heard the steady *thwack* long before the lodge came into sight. She slowed her pace to a walk, breathing hard from her run. In the clearing behind the lodge, beyond the firepit, Kevin hefted an axe overhead, then struck a crack in the log. The first strike split it in two. The two halves fell to either side of the immense tree trunk chopping block.

I wish I was that strong.

Since this whole thing started, their daily lives had taken on a physicality that most of them weren't used to. Imogen wasn't weak or unfit thanks to her years of running, but her slight frame made her feel like an insubstantial wimp compared to everyone else. Apart from Betty, but Betty was thirty years older than she. Even Bec, who was only five foot three, seemed tall compared to Imogen's five foot nothing. Bec was fit from the physical nature of her work. She exuded a confidence while they chopped, dug, and hammered that Imogen didn't have.

Yet. I don't have it yet, but I will.

She changed course to Kevin, whose cheeks were ruddy with exertion. "Did you have good run?"

She nodded. "Yes. I just need to get my wind back."

"What's that?" Kevin asked, jutting his chin at the eight inches of twig in her hand.

Imogen lifted the slender tree branch. Its oblong leaves had turned bright yellow, edged with brown. The straight veins slanted out from the central midrib toward the pointed tip. "I think I found a stand of Slippery Elms, so I cut this off to compare with the picture in my book."

"Cool."

This morning, Imogen had resumed her daily run and been surprised by how much her anxiety subsided. She wore a gun and the railroad spike on the belt slung around her hips, but this was a minor concession weighed against something from before that made life feel more like her own. Mike had paled when he'd learned of her plans but tried to put on a brave face. He hadn't quite succeeded, but he'd tried.

The corners of her mouth dragged, as if gravity exerted more pull. She was still worried about Mike, even though he seemed better after talking to her. As for the rest of their conversation about Steph, there was nothing she could do but be kind. She'd noticed the tiny bump the ring made in the watch pocket of Mike's jeans was still there. She wouldn't have blamed him if he'd put it away somewhere, given Steph's apparent change of heart about their future together. But she wasn't surprised that he hadn't. She thought the ring—hands down the most beautiful one she had ever seen—wasn't just a touchstone to the woman he loved, but a reflection of Mike's character. Even if things had changed for Steph, Mike's love for and loyalty to her had not. He wasn't ready to let go yet, and there wasn't a single reason why he should. Coming to terms with the grief and shock they'd all suffered couldn't be rushed; they'd barely started processing it. It was going to take time for Mike's heart to heal, just like hers and everyone else's.

Kevin stuck a corner of the axe blade into the chopping block and leaned on it. "Thanksgiving is coming up soon. I think we should celebrate it."

She did the math. "You're right. It's four weeks from this Thursday." She hadn't realized they'd be in November next week but now that she thought about, Halloween was in four days. "It's a miracle we're alive, and we have enough food. That's reason enough to be thankful."

"We'll need a turkey," Kevin said, enthusiasm lighting his eyes and making them sparkle. "You've hunted, right?" At her nod, he grinned. "We can do it together. I saw a flock of turkeys a few days ago. I'm sure we can get one between the two of us."

"I'm in," she said. "That's a fantastic idea. It will boost everyone's spirits."

"We'll float the idea at dinner?"

She nodded, her own spirits buoyed by Kevin's suggestion. Thanksgiving was another thing about America she loved. Even people who hated 'the holidays' loved Thanksgiving. "I'm going inside. I want to get out of these sweaty clothes."

Kevin tugged the axe free and looked at the pile of logs beside him without enthusiasm. "Guess I'll do a little more. I hate chopping wood."

"But you're so good at it," she teased.

Half a minute later, she set her shoulder against the back door and gave it a shove. The warmer air of the kitchen surrounded her, pushing back against the chill of the cooling sweat on her skin. The warmth would be short-lived, but pleasant nonetheless. Since the power had gone out, they were reliant on the fireplace for heat. There'd been talk of getting a woodburning stove. The fireplace heated the downstairs. The kitchen was chilly when the fire got low, but nothing a sweater or sweatshirt couldn't remedy. Upstairs was a different story, ranging from chilly to downright freezing, but there were lots of blankets, so it wasn't a problem so far. They performed their sponge baths at the speed of light. No matter how warm the water was at the start, it was cold by the end. Imogen wondered how cold it would get this winter.

Maybe this one will be mild.

She touched the wood of the doorframe, just in case she jinxed it, then stripped off the lightweight jacket she'd found as she pushed the door shut. Mike stood at the counter, kneading dough. He smiled, looking relieved, the dimple appearing like clockwork. "Have a good run?"

"Yes," she said, the sweat on her body skittering over her skin, the faint prelude of a shiver.

"You found something," Mike said, curiosity in his voice.

She told him about the branch and what she thought it might be. She'd worried she was hopeless identifying plants and her idea of using medicinal ones to fill the gaps they'd encounter in the future would come to nothing. "I'm hoping I'll have improved by spring."

"You'll get there," Mike said. "By the end of next summer, you'll have all of us out there helping you."

Imogen warmed, buoyed by his confidence in her. Mike jutted his chin at the cooktop. "There's hot water in the pot on the back burner, so you don't freeze when you wash up."

It took her a moment to identify the feeling percolating inside her... that of being looked after. "You shouldn't have used the propane."

His grin turned sly. "It's a cast iron soup pot, Imogen. I heated it in the fire."

"Aren't you resourceful," she said, giving him an approving nod. "Thank you."

Despite his cheerfulness, Mike was still subdued, but his easygoing nature had returned. His effort to dial back the hyper-vigilance when he'd learned she was taking a run on her own impressed her. She hadn't realized how responsible he felt for everyone's safety before they talked. Now, she didn't know how she'd missed it. He was always on the alert, always thinking of solutions to problems they hadn't encountered. He made sure everyone had at least one weapon they felt comfortable with. He'd found a chalkboard and some chalk. Now they hung on the wall by the front door with everyone's names in a tidy column. When one left the lodge, they were supposed to write in where they'd gone. It wasn't the sort of thing Mike would have organized before Sandy's death had spooked him; she didn't think it would catch on.

She crossed to the chalkboard and smudged out the square by her name, replacing 'running' with 'lodge.' Everyone but Zach and Bec were here. According to the chalkboard, they'd gone to the waterfall. A soft smile played at the corners of Imogen's lips. Bec and Zach had been spending a lot of time together and she hoped, for Zach's sake, it might go somewhere.

The crash of breaking glass, followed by a shriek that made the air vibrate, made Imogen's heart leap. Her body hummed with adrenaline. Recovering herself, she darted to the storeroom door, which had flown open so hard it was closing again after hitting the wall. Amy almost knocked her flat in her haste to get through it.

Mike had followed and took Amy by the shoulders. "What's wrong?"

Color leached from Amy's face, as if she'd seen a horde of zombies. "Mice," she gasped. "There are mice in the flour."

Imogen traded an incredulous glance with Mike. Mice getting into their stores wasn't good, but she'd thought Amy was being attacked. Imogen followed Mike into the storeroom. Two broken Mason jars lay shattered on the floor, the green beans they'd contained covered with flour like branches after a snowfall, the puddle of liquid becoming a floury slurry. One of the fifty pound sacks of flour had fallen from the shelf to the floor and flour drifted in the air like pollen falling from a flowering tree.

"Crap," Mike said. He grasped the corner of the paper sack. Something small and dusted white dashed out the opening at the top, followed by another. He jumped back with a startled yelp that surprised Imogen enough to set her heart racing again. Imogen heard the back door fly open and footsteps clomping down the stairs.

"I was getting beans," Amy said. She hung back by the door, peering into the storeroom, her lips pursed. Her eyes seemed to swallow most of her face. "I glanced at the flour sack and two beady eyes looked up at me. When I realized it was a mouse, I screamed and swatted at the sack. I wasn't thinking when I pushed it." Her voice brimmed with apology, as if she'd strewn the flour on the floor on purpose.

"It's not your fault," Imogen said, glancing over her shoulder and noticing that most everyone in the house crowded the door.

Kevin now stood next to Amy, still holding his axe. "Mice? I thought you were being attacked!"

Mike had righted the sack of flour. He ripped the intact end of the top of the sack open. "There's mouse crap in here."

"But didn't we catch a bunch in the traps?" Betty asked.

"Not all of them, apparently," Mike muttered, his mouth puckering into a frown.

Imogen stepped closer to the floury mess at Mike's feet. A thin trail of white spanned the shelf where the flour had been. She checked the bottom of the sack and saw a chewed corner. With a sinking feeling in her stomach, she said, "We have to go through everything."

Imogen watched Mike's molasses-brown eyes fill with a dread that made them look black. She opened her mouth, about to ask what else was wrong, when it hit her. They had to see what else the mice had gotten into, and how much of the food they had ruined. Food that would need to be replaced, which meant doing what now spooked Mike most.

They had to leave the safety of the lodge.

AN HOUR LATER, the extent of the devastation was clear. Between the storeroom and the root cellar, the mice had gotten into most of the dry goods that weren't in glass or metal containers. A few of the sturdy plastic containers that seemed rodent proof turned out not to be, the larger holes gnawed in them raising the specter of rats. Of the five fifty-pound sacks of flour, two were ruined. Something gnawed a hole through one of the two plastic containers that held rolled oats, but both of the containers of hundred-pound sacks of steel-cut oats were untouched, since the containers were metal. Sugar, rice, quinoa, dried beans, pasta, cake mixes, dog biscuits... The swath cut through their food stores was horrifyingly broad. Roughly half of their dry goods had been ruined. They'd gone from being well provisioned to maybe not having enough to get through the winter in the space of an hour.

"Can we skim off the top of things with holes at the bottom?" Kevin asked.

"No!" Amy cried, her voice dripping with horror.

Bec's lips pulled back in a grimace. She and Zach had returned from their walk to the waterfall soon after the mouse disaster had been discovered. She still looked nauseated. "I guess, if you want to get salmonella or leptospirosis."

"Or hantavirus and bubonic plague," Amy chimed in.

Kevin threw up his hands, as if they might deflect their scorn. "What is lepto...?"

"It's bad," Bec said. "Liver damage, kidney failure, death. I don't need that on top of these freaking cramps. I already feel bad enough."

"You don't know for sure we'll catch those diseases. Eating this might be gross, but it's better than starving," Kevin persisted.

"You eat it then," Bec said.

"We're storing what we can from the contaminated stuff," Clyde said. "We can use it if we're really hard up and hope cooking it will kill anything that might get us sick."

Clyde gave Jay, who was doing his best to go unnoticed, a pointed glare. It had been Jay's job to check the food every day, so something like this wouldn't happen. In retrospect, Imogen did not know why anyone thought that was a good idea. Maybe it was because he'd volunteered in the wake of Mike threatening to beat him silly, and they'd been foolish enough to think he would be diligent.

The amount of food they had to get rid of made Imogen's stomach churn until it ached. There were some things the mice hadn't bothered with, like the salt, baking powder, cocoa, and baking soda. Everything in metal cans or containers and glass jars was fine, apart from the green beans Amy had dropped. Mike threw out the bread dough and the three loaves he'd baked yesterday. Jay and Zach both developed stomachaches after realizing they'd eaten from contaminated stores. Imogen was pretty sure it was psychosomatic.

She stared at the segregated bags and containers in the living room. Zach, Jeffrey, and Jay were wrapping them tight in plastic wrap. Jay threw himself into the work with uncharacteristic zeal. It had only taken knowing his future here at the lodge was dangling by a strand of a spiderweb, and the specter of starvation, to affect an attitude adjustment.

Amy stood by the windows at the end of the kitchen table, wringing her hands. "I'm sorry I was against having Bec's cats inside," she said for the millionth time. "If they'd been here..." She made a sound between a whimper and a moan and looked so wretched Imogen couldn't help feeling sorry for her.

"It's not your fault, hon," Betty said as she carried a chewed box of Cream of Wheat at arm's length from the storage room, her nose crinkled with distaste. She stopped to pat Amy's shoulder and glared at Jay. "If Jay had done his job more diligently, and if we'd made getting better storage containers a higher priority, none of this would have happened."

Jay pretended not to hear, but Imogen saw his shoulders hike even closer to his ears. Amy looked like she wanted to crawl under the floor. The specter of Sandy's death, and how it had made everyone—especially Mike—reluctant to venture beyond the safety of their hideaway, hung in the air like a toxic fog.

Betty sighed. "We need to find more food right away. We shouldn't have waited, but... Oh, goodness. What a mess."

Clyde spread out a map on the kitchen table. "Let's see which towns might be the best place to start."

Mike's jaw had set like concrete, clenched so hard Imogen marveled his teeth hadn't cracked. "I'll go out for food."

"I'll come, too," Kevin said.

The creak of the front porch screen door caught Imogen's ear. Amy, whom she hadn't noticed slipping away, approached the front door with something in her arms. When the door swung open, Imogen saw she held Buttercup, the fluffy orange and white cat that Bec had been feeding. Buttercup rubbed her face along Amy's jaw, purring and contented. With a guilty look, Amy said, "It's time to bring the cats inside." She bit her lip, tears pooling in her eyes. "I'll get Boo, too."

She turned on her heel and scurried outside to look for Boo, the white cat, before anyone could answer. Sighing, Bec pushed back from the table. She got her jacket from the coat-tree, and Imogen's, too. "Let's go help her." A weary, half-hearted smile tugged one corner of her mouth. "Better late than never."

Bec didn't seem angry when by rights she well could be. She had wanted to bring the cats inside since she'd first spotted them, but Amy had objected, yet she wasn't holding a grudge. Imogen took her jacket from Bec, slipping it on as she followed. She paused beside Mike, who leaned over Clyde to see what Clyde pointed to on the map. She touched Mike's elbow and murmured, "Are you all right?"

His mouth twisted to the side. He looked... annoyed. "We talked about getting better storage containers weeks ago, then let it slide because I was too scared after Sandy to go back out. We can't afford that. I get it now."

Imogen blinked, surprised. Mike's confidence had still been rocked not long ago. Now, he seemed sure of himself. Almost too sure for the man who had wept in her arms.

"Okay," she said.

He nodded once, then resumed poring over the map with Betty and Clyde. Imogen stepped onto the porch, her puzzlement growing with every step. She studied him through the windows as she walked to the screen door. As she turned to go, she saw it. It was in the set of Mike's jaw and the focus percolating in his eyes. When he cocked his head to the side, angling his ear so he could hear Clyde more clearly, Imogen understood what had happened.

Mike had decided.

Sometime between when she'd left for her solo run—which had alarmed him even though he had tried to hide it—and now, Mike decided to meet this challenge head-on. The man standing at the table had picked up the mantle he'd almost dropped before, that of keeping them safe. But now he carried the weight of it, rather than the weight crushing him.

Imogen didn't understand how he'd done it in so short a time. Perhaps admitting the shame and self-blame and grief of not saving his loved ones—his sisters and nieces and Steph, as well as Sandy—was all he'd needed. Maybe by being there for him, Imogen helped him realize he wasn't alone. Maybe he was putting on a good show, and underneath the confident facade he was terrified out of his mind.

Whatever it was, however it had happened, Imogen felt so light she almost believed she could fly if she tried. She just needed to take one step, push up instead of out, and she would float away like a balloon with a broken ribbon, drifting higher and higher until the ground below disappeared.

They had to fix this. Their survival was on the line. If the Mike she had met on the bridge that first day was back, they just might do it.

CHAPTER 25
MIKE

Bec looked up at Mike, eyes flashing, and he said, "I know you want to come, Shorty, but you're not feeling well."

Bec tried to suppress a smile at the nickname he'd given her. She almost pulled it off. "I'm fine—"

"If you were just having cramps from your period, that'd be one thing. But you're puking and I know you're running a fever. I heard you and Betty talking."

Bec blinked. "So now you're spying on me?"

"You've been bitching and moaning for three days. No spying needed," he said. "I'm not being that guy who wants to keep the womenfolk safe. None of us has any business going out there when we're sick."

She scowled, her usually good-humored countenance twisted by a frown. Then she relented. He'd known he had her when she'd accused him of spying on her because she'd abandoned pressing her case. "I don't know why I let you get away with calling me that," she said. "I'm going next time." She held out her hand. "Let me look at that list again."

She snatched the paper he offered and studied it. "Do you have a pen?" Mike pulled the pen from his back jeans pocket and handed it over. "I'm putting stars next to the important stuff—tampons, pads, menstrual cups if you want my eternal gratitude.

I cannot stress enough how important all of this is, Mike. Do you understand?"

"I do," he said. They'd had this conversation twice already. He knew the feminine hygiene supplies were the reason Bec had fought him so hard about staying behind. "I have two sisters, I get it."

I had two sisters.

The realization hit him like a punch to the gut and brought tears to his eyes. For a moment, all he could feel was the searing pain, the world-shattering displacement of losing his family. He gripped the rail at the top of the stairwell, dizziness overtaking him while his stomach bottomed out. It didn't matter that he didn't know for sure about Beth and his niece Katie. Dead or alive, his family was gone, because the dead weren't coming back as the people he'd loved. He couldn't imagine getting lucky enough to find anyone alive.

"And you absolutely must get birth control pills," Bec continued, her eyes never straying from the list. Mike blinked to get rid of the tears, grateful that she hadn't noticed. "Right now, birth control is beside the point. My cycle gets totally out of whack without them. I know this sucks for everybody, but try throwing in periods without the right supplies into the mix."

"Don't worry, Bec. I'll get your stuff."

She nodded, then handed the list back to him, seeming somewhat mollified. The fluffy white and orange cat slipped out of Bec's bedroom and twined around her ankles.

"Little Buttercup," she crooned, plucking the cat from the floor and holding it close. The white and orange tuxedo tabby purred, nestling against Bec's neck. A white blaze between her eyes ran to the tip of her pink nose, breaking up the dark reddish-orange fur. It slipped down around her mouth, making the orange below her nose look like a mustache. Buttercup yawned, exposing her delicate pink mouth and sharp white teeth.

"She really is cute," Mike said, rubbing the side of her face with his finger.

"Boo killed three mice last night," Bec said proudly.

Mike looked through the bedroom door. The white cat lay sprawled across the bed, taking up more space than should be possible for a ten-pound cat. "How do you know it was Boo and not Buttercup?"

"I saw him catch the last one and drop it with the other two. He's declawed, but he's a little death dealer."

"He's declawed?"

Bec nodded. "If I hadn't seen it myself, I would never have believed it. I'm sure Buttercup will kill lots of vermin, too."

"Good job, cats," Mike said, giving Buttercup a final scratch under the chin. "Bec was right about you."

"Get home safe, okay?" Bec said.

"I will." He was just about to step away when he figured he had nothing to lose. "Can I ask you something?" When Bec nodded, he asked, "Are you this open about your menstrual cycle with everyone?"

Her laughter took him by surprise. "It's important to normalize women's bodies and what they do. Making it all hush-hush and something to be ashamed of is how the patriarchy keeps us down."

Despite his nervousness about so many of them going out today—and his not being with Imogen while she was out there—he chuckled. Bec was a kick in the pants. "I agree with you, Bec."

"Good. We'll keep you then." Buttercup started squirming, so Bec set her down. She put a hand on his arm. "She's going to be fine today, Mike. All of them will be."

"Am I that easy to read?" he asked. He'd thought he was doing a good job hiding his anxiety.

"Yep. Keep your mind on you today, okay? Jeffrey is planning an austerity version of cooking up a storm for dinner, so you guys better work up an appetite."

She gave him a quick hug. The press of worry, like a tingle of static electricity, but painful, skated over his skin. The power had gone out five days ago. It didn't matter that he'd known it would happen once it became clear things weren't going back to how they used to be. It felt like the death of a loved one after a long illness. You know it's coming, and you know it'll be bad, but you tell yourself you've had time to prepare. Then your loved one dies, and you find out you're not prepared at all.

Three days after losing power, they discovered the mouse infestation and that half of their dry food stores were ruined. His sister Beth had loved to quote a line from an old sci-fi show and right now it fit Mike's state of mind, for the two setbacks had severely damaged his calm. He'd fretted about getting more food before the mouse fiasco, but not enough to get him away from the lodge looking for it after Sandy died, like he should have been. It was only after discovering the infestation that he'd realized he, along with everyone else, equated spring and summer with fresh food and abundance. In reality, most of what they might grow wouldn't be ready for harvest until late summer through fall. Cold weather crops—peas and spinach and maybe some other greens—might be ready in April in a good year, but they couldn't survive on peas and greens. If they were very lucky, they might have vegetables in late June or early July, but grains and beans and squash? Not until Autumn, and late Autumn at that.

Mike had learned a painful lesson. It didn't matter what happened or who got killed or how responsible he felt for it, nor how much it scared him… Unless the options before them were more reckless or dangerous, they couldn't afford the luxury of waiting when it came to their survival.

As far as losing power went, their circumstances hadn't changed all that much. They didn't have refrigeration anymore, but between the freezing water in the springhouse—cold enough to chill a bottle of wine—and the hard turn toward unseasonably cold temperatures, he didn't think food spoilage would much of an issue for the rapidly dwindling fresh food they had. They needed to find a long-term solution for the oven, perhaps building something outdoors or a potbellied stove, but that wasn't pressing while they still had the cooktop. Mike felt sure they could get more propane in the short term if they kept looking. They had the fireplace, too, though his foray into using hot coals with the cast-iron Dutch oven had been mixed. He still hadn't figured out how many coals equaled what temperature.

But psychologically, losing power was a tremendous blow. It was one more connection to the world they'd always known, now gone. One more layer of protection from the hazards they faced had peeled away. It made Mike feel exposed, like their soft underbelly was showing without them knowing it.

"Mike! Are you coming?"

Kevin's voice snapped him back to the present. He was still standing at the top of the stairs. He hurried down to join Kevin, Clyde, and Jay, who were collecting the last of their gear. "Ready to go?"

"I think so," Kevin said.

Clyde readjusted his belt below his slowly shrinking belly, then offered a tight smile. He glanced over to Betty, who had her head together with Imogen while they pulled together their daypacks, and the tight smile turned into a grimace. Betty and Imogen were joining Zach and Amy on a run to the library in Swedenport. Mike had been against them going, Clyde too, even though going into the tiny town closest to the park was as close to a milk run as it got nowadays. The route into Swedenport was straightforward. Nestled in a shallow valley with excellent sight lines, they could see zombies approaching from every direction. There was more than one way out of the town that would get them back to Cady's Run. Besides, apart from clearing out the nearby cabins and Berrigan's home improvement, there'd been no zombies, no people, nothing at all, since they'd arrived. They'd driven through Swedenport on the way to Berrigan's and there'd been nothing, not so much as a swinging door.

Mike tried not to think about Berrigan's. The rest of the

supplies they'd gathered still languished inside, not to mention Sandy's body. He'd let his fear stop them from returning and burying her body. Sandy, of all people, deserved a proper burial. Once they had more food, it was the first thing they'd do.

Mike's fruitless attempts to persuade Imogen to not go, at least not until he could go along, had been… fruitless. "Betty and Amy aren't used to fighting zombies, Imogen," he had said to her.

She shrugged. "Zach and I *are* good at killing zombies, and they have to learn sometime. Isn't necessity the mother of invention? She's probably the mother of motivation, too—for them, and for me to get my hands on anything that will help us survive. There's got to be loads of useful books at the library. Besides, I'll go barking mad from boredom over the winter without something to do."

"You aren't taking this seriously," he huffed.

Imogen's eyebrows, along with one corner of her mouth, rose. The wry *you've-got-to-be-kidding-me* look in her amber eyes made him feel like a kid caught with his hand in the cookie jar. "I don't see Clyde giving Betty a hard time about this."

"He's not happy about it."

Imogen shrugged. "Look," she said, more seriously than before. "I understand you're worried. I know you're trying so hard to protect us—protect me—but you can't be everywhere all the time. You can't. Today won't be like when Sandy died."

"You don't know that," he said, wrapping his arms tight around his middle, as if to protect his vital organs.

"You're right," she relented, putting her hand on his arm. It surprised him how comforting her touch felt. "I don't know how today will go. Neither do you. You know better than anyone that proximity does not equal safety. Numbers help, I know, but you can't control everything, Mike. We have to take chances or we won't get through this, and part of that is you dealing with how anxious this makes you. Welcome to my anxiety-ridden world."

He knew she was right. She was. And if her hand on his arm

didn't feel so damn comforting, he might come up with a better rebuttal. He shrugged her off and stepped back. Maybe she was right, and he was wrong, but he was damned if he'd admit it. "You're not thinking about how quickly things can go wrong."

She started, of all things, to laugh, her teeth glowing against her buckeye-brown skin. "Mike, I think you're about to start mansplaining."

"No, I'm not! I'm— I'm not a mansplainer," he sputtered, giving her a smile so she'd know how ridiculous her suggestion was. But in that moment, he had known he lost the argument.

Mike could see how anxious Clyde was that Betty was going to the library, despite his attempts to put up a good front. It surprised Mike when Betty said she wanted to go. She didn't stray from the lodge. Even Mike couldn't deny how much she'd livened up at the idea of a trip to the library. Even in the zombie apocalypse, a person could get a little stir-crazy.

The big surprise had been Amy. No one thought Amy would venture beyond the immediate vicinity of the lodge. When she'd said she wanted to go, you could have heard a pin drop. Given her comments about decisions being made based on popularity, no one dared disagree. She still seemed to suffer from the delusion that there was going to be a return to normal, an 'after all this.' Losing power had only strengthened Mike's conviction that 'after all this' would never happen. They were living the new normal. No one was pleased about it; everyone but Amy seemed to realize it. Maybe she'd come around after the outing.

The end of the world was exhausting in ways Mike had never expected when he'd idly wondered what would happen if there was an EMP or some other disaster. People getting along, or not, had been something he'd thought about, but not at an interpersonal level.

Jeffrey hovered near the front door. He'd been fussing all morning while helping them get ready. He seemed relieved to not be joining them and guilty about feeling that way. "We'll have food ready for you when you get back," he said.

"We'll be hungry," Mike said.

Jay spoke with Kevin while checking his daypack and weapons again. Mike watched their exchange, his eyes dissecting Jay's every gesture. He'd been on his best behavior since Mike had confronted him about Imogen. Jay seemed all right—not drunk, anyway. Mike wanted to keep him close so he could keep an eye on him, which was why he was coming along today. That, and his knowledge of medicines. Betty had agreed they needed to have a talk with him. It was good she'd be there when they did, because Mike wasn't sure he'd hold it together without her. His actions the other day had proved that.

Imogen zipped up her daypack and came over to Mike. Her eyes were positively sparkling with excitement. She hadn't really gone anywhere since they'd arrived at the lodge, apart from the nearby cabins up the road. Going out into a world filled with zombies wasn't anyone's idea of fun, but the prospect of doing something useful was good for her spirits. Mike could see that, plain as day. Knowing that didn't tamp down the desire that rubbed insistently behind his sternum so much it hurt, the needful plea dancing on the tip of his tongue: 'Wait, just until tomorrow. Just this once, for me.'

"Are you ready?" she asked.

He nodded, waiting a moment until he was sure he wouldn't annoy her by begging. "As I'll ever be."

"It's killing you, isn't it?"

He huffed out a breath. "Yes," he admitted. "It is."

She took his hand, her chin tipping up at him. The excitement was still there, sparkling away in the amber depths of her eyes, but a hint of sobriety tempered it. "Everything's going to be fine," she said, giving his hand a squeeze. "We'll compare notes at dinner. And since we'll beat you home, I'll have a book about how things work for you, all ready to go."

"Be careful, okay?" he asked her, unable to keep a slight wobble out of his voice. "Don't take any chances."

"I promise. And you'll do the same?"

He nodded. "I'll do the same."

She smiled at him, gave his hand one last squeeze, then turned away at the sound of Zach's voice behind her. Mike watched the two of them, heads together while they talked. He dragged his eyes away with an effort, taking in everyone as they prepared to leave or as they hovered anxiously at the periphery of the preparations. Bec had come down to say goodbye, Buttercup in her arms. Jeffrey stood beside her, chewing on his lip. Clyde looked grimly determined as Betty kissed him on the cheek. Kevin lounged almost lazily at the door with his Halligan over his shoulder beside Jay, who tried his best to look bored. Amy sat at the kitchen table, watching the others and looking like the new kid on the playground, not sure where she fit in.

Mike wanted every single one of them here, even Amy. Jay, well... He couldn't let fantasies of kicking him to the curb run away with him, because he just might do it. He wanted, more than almost anything else, for Imogen and the others to be here when he got back. For there to be no holes, no gaps where someone should be but wasn't. He offered a silent prayer, asking the Universe to grant his simple yet complex request, and hoping while he did so that he wasn't dooming them all by having the nerve to ask in the first place.

Imogen had been right, after all. Getting used to losing people was no way to live. Mike knew he could never get the hang of it, and that he never wanted to try.

CHAPTER 26
MIKE

Choosing Peterman's Run was a gamble since it was near St. Marys. St. Marys' population had been over twelve thousand people—a smaller city, but big for this part of the state. Located thirty miles southeast of St. Marys, Peterman's Run had a decent-sized grocery store with a pharmacy and a farm supply, without the risk St. Marys' population presented. As with everything now, these factors in its favor were also drawbacks. If it was attractive enough for them to check out, it might be for others, too. And they could go to all this trouble and still come up empty-handed.

"'Welcome to Peterman's Run, Population 879,'" Mike said. Then he winced. "Aw, man…"

A zombie stumbled out from the front door of a tidy little house—a chubby old lady in a housecoat with her hair in rollers. Her face was smeared with blood but the front of her housecoat was surprisingly clean. She'd been bitten on the back, judging by the blood stains.

"They even got grandma?" Kevin said, his voice plaintive.

Granny zombie sprinted toward them, hitting the four-foot-high picket fence around her yard with a thump that Mike could hear through his closed window. Her flabby but somehow scrawny-looking arms reached over the pointy pickets as she tried in vain to reach them.

"She doesn't look heavy enough to be a runner," Kevin said. "She's swimming in that housecoat."

They were four weeks into this thing and Mike was so tired of it his bone marrow felt swapped out for stone. "I can't leave her like that."

He stopped the truck and climbed out. His knees creaked, which they hadn't been doing as much a year ago. He wasn't crippled or anything, but he found it alarming since running for his life was more than a euphemism now. He pulled the knife he'd added to the utility belt that Sandy had insisted he take and approached the old woman. Her sunken eyes and protruding cheekbones made her look like the puppets from the old-fashioned *Punch & Judy* plays. That made him feel old, too. The younger members of their party might never have heard of *Punch & Judy*. Then the stench hit him, driving thoughts of anything else away. He grimaced, wrinkling his nose. Granny zombie smelled like a meat locker left to rot in the tropical sun. Granny hissed, getting more agitated the closer Mike got.

"I'm sorry, granny."

He was beyond her reach, but close enough to see she had no teeth. Visions of her dentures stuck in some poor sap's arm or leg sprang to life in Mike's imagination like a Technicolor film. He batted her arms away and caught her scrawny neck in his hand, then plunged the knife in her eye. He winced at the squish. She sagged as black liquid dripped from the eye socket, and he let her fall to the ground. Her curlers were still in place, her thin gray hair wrapped tightly around them.

Mike couldn't summon the energy to swear. This wasn't the last—or even the worst—thing he'd see before he died, but it was one of the more dispiriting. He wiped his knife on the grass and trudged to the truck.

"Bad?" Kevin said when he reached the truck.

"Depressing."

A few minutes later, buildings appeared—several blocks of one- and two-story brick buildings that could have been anywhere in small-town America. Clyde and Jay had stopped ahead of them. Mike pulled alongside so they could lower the windows and talk. Clyde climbed from the truck he and Jay shared and walked around to Mike's door.

Clyde squinted into the sun, pointing down the road as he turned his head to speak to them. "The farm supply is on the right. The grocery is about half a mile farther. We'll go on ahead and see you when we see you."

Mike shook his head. "Not happening. We'll clear both buildings together."

Clyde frowned. "It'll cut into our time."

"Clyde," Kevin said, leaning over Mike to speak through the window. "Not happening."

"I agree with them," Jay said from the other truck. Clyde scowled, shooting an annoyed glare over his shoulder.

Mike wondered if the scowl meant they'd talked about this in the truck and Jay had agreed to back Clyde, knowing Mike and Kevin would never go for it. He wanted to bristle at anything Jay said, even though the jerk had been behaving himself since he'd threatened to kick his ass into next year. He'd have preferred Jay with him, but Kevin had asked for his help at the farm supply store, and Clyde had assured Mike he could keep Jay in line.

"Get the stuff Bec starred," Mike said to Clyde. "I'll never hear the end of it if we fall down on the feminine hygiene."

Clyde's eyes twinkled. "I've been married almost forty years, Mike. I've learned a thing or two."

AN HOUR LATER, Mike and Kevin pulled the truck around to the back gate of the farm supply yard. Through the chain-link, Mike could see equipment stacked along the fence and back wall of the building. Kevin got out of the truck and worked on the knotted rope they'd tied to the gate earlier, after all four men had cleared the farm supply yard. Mike pulled the truck through the open gate and got out, metal, machine grease, and animal feed scenting the air, and waited for Kevin to pull the gate shut. As they walked through the yard, Kevin pointed out various types of farming equipment.

"How do you know all this stuff? Did you grow up in the country or do scouting?" Mike asked him. As soon as he said scouting, he felt stupid. He'd only been a Cub Scout, but he knew they didn't do farming.

Kevin held his hand up, the middle three fingers straight with his thumb and pinky touching. "I *was* an Eagle Scout, but I spent most summers on my grandpa's farm in Iowa." Kevin must have seen Mike's eyes flare with excitement, for he added, "A dairy farm. If we find some cows, I'm your man."

"I guess we'll take what we can get," Mike said, but he added finding cows to the mile-long list he kept in his head. "Do you still have family in Iowa?"

Kevin nodded. "Aunts and uncles and cousins. My folks were in Hershey. I moved to Pittsburgh for the job." He shrugged, then added, "My little sister's in Texas..."

Hearing the pain in Kevin's voice made Mike sorry he'd asked. It was such a normal thing to do that everyone did it without thought, but their situation was not normal anymore. Now, Mike always cringed when he asked such questions without thinking, when he dragged the conversation into the emotional minefield of grief and loss. But maybe it wasn't bad, just difficult. His attempt to bury his grief over Sandy's death—and everything else—had shown him that.

Kevin said, "Her name's Taylor. She's a senior at Texas A&M. I was supposed to go see her for Thanksgiving since our parents were taking a cruise." He glanced at Mike, his expression bleak. "She almost went to Penn State, main campus."

State College, the town where Penn State's main campus was located, was roughly two hours away. Penn State was a huge school with almost a hundred thousand students, half of them on the main campus, but it was a heck of a lot closer than Texas.

"Oh, man, I'm sorry," Mike said. The sentiment was so inadequate. That didn't stop it being true.

"Yeah. Me, too. We texted through that second day at the zoo. She said she was somewhere safe. I have to believe she still is."

Mike nodded. After talking to Imogen the other day, he'd made the same decision about Beth and Katie. Really made it, not like with Steph, which depended on how discouraged he felt.

"Anyway," Kevin said. He gestured to the dizzying array of stock tanks before them. "This is what we want. We just need the right sizes."

Mike followed him from one galvanized steel stock tank to the next. "What about those plastic ones?" he said, pointing to another section of stock tanks. "They're lighter."

"I've only ever seen this done with metal tanks." Kevin stopped in front of an oblong tank. The label on the side showed it was four feet long and two feet wide by two feet high. "This is what we need." He patted the tank, looking pleased. "We'll need a smaller one, too, for washing and cooking."

"How can we use these to heat water?"

Kevin had fessed up to his scheme on the way here. Mike wanted to know how it worked.

"I've never done it myself," Kevin said. "Just watched YouTube videos. If you help me, I'll share the glory."

"Don't want to take all the blame, huh?"

Kevin laughed. "The way it works is you shape the copper coil so it looks like a bedspring, about eighteen inches high and as wide. Then you build a small small fire inside it, and attach the coil at the top and the bottom of the tank. When you fill it with water—"

"The fire heats the water in the coil and convection kicks in," Mike said, finishing his sentence.

"Convection moves the water?" Kevin asked, eyebrows raised. "I thought that was just ovens."

Mike sighed. *Ah, to be young and clueless.* Aloud, he said, "Hot water is less dense—it's lighter—than cold water, so it rises to the surface. When it cools off, it gets heavier again and sinks below the water that's warmer. With this setup, the fire heats the water in the coil and gets lighter, so it rises through the coil and out into the tub at the top. Since the fire is always heating the water in the coil, it's always rising. When the water in the tank cools off, it sinks. The heated water in the coil is still rising, which pulls in the cooler water, and that keeps it circulating."

"Huh." Kevin's brow crinkled as he digested the explanation. "I knew it worked but not why. How do you know that? I thought you were an electrician."

"I know a lot of things," Mike said. "When the weather's nice we can set this up outside. When it's cold, we can use it inside with the fireplace. Have a bath day."

"We'll have to make the connections so we can disconnect the coil if we're moving it." Kevin pursed his lips, then added, "We'll have to share bathwater, maybe two or three people per bath, or it'll take days for everyone to bathe. Unless we want a tub in front of the fire all the time."

"That's not gonna go over well," Mike said, thinking of Amy's reaction at sharing bathwater. "We can figure it out after we have it working. I'll get the truck so we can load the tanks." He gripped the edge of the stock tank and pulled it up, testing its weight. It was lighter than he'd expected, and a thought occurred to him. "There must be something here we can use to convert the winch for the gondola so we can crank it."

Kevin's mouth twisted to the side as he thought. "The problem will be the weight. The strength of whatever's powering it will limit capacity. Can we do a water wheel at the top of the bluff with just the springhouse?"

"No idea," Mike said.

"We'll figure something out."

"You sound pretty confident."

"You like figuring out how things work, so figure it out. How hard can it be?"

Kevin was kind of right that the mechanics of a water wheel and a winch weren't that complicated, from what Mike knew of them. Then he thought of every home improvement project he'd done that would 'just take an hour,' and said, "It'll be harder than you think."

CHAPTER 27
IMOGEN

So far, they'd been lucky. They'd encountered abandoned cars the closer they got to the library in Swedenport. The vehicles looked forlorn with the open doors and bloodstained upholstery, the only clues to what had happened to their occupants. At least there were no undead. They must have moved off in pursuit of people long gone. They'd needed to move one of the cars and discovered it was still running, with half a tank of gas, so they brought it along.

The one-story library was L-shaped, with the short end truncated, as if a child had drawn it. The short end of the L faced the town square, while the long end stretched the length of the block to the first street beyond the town square. A sidewalk ran between the library's short end and the building next to it, and also to the far side of the block. The library's entrance was nestled in the ninety-degree corner on the inside of the L, the truncated short wing affording a reasonable view of the town square, even from the door that led from the lobby to the vestibule.

Imogen and Zach walked almost noiselessly over the carpeted floor, past a row of computers and tables with book displays. On their left were the stacks, the shelves perpendicular to the front of the building. This part of the library also proved to be zombie free. A few minutes later, they were unlocking the deadbolts on the lobby doors. When they reached the outer set of doors in the short vestibule, they paused and looked at the town square.

"It must have been charming," Zach said, and Imogen nodded.

The park at the center of the 'square' was actually an oval. Restaurants and shops lined the one-way, one-lane road around it. Bricked sidewalks bisected the grassy lawn of the oval like the arms and post of a cross, meeting at a grandstand gazebo in the center. The side streets to the oval extended from the brick side-walks, so that the buildings surrounding the oval were on the squared corners of the blocks. The gazebo's fanciful, onion-shaped roof and graceful columned sides gave the square an old-fashioned feel, if you overlooked the bodies on its steps and hanging over the rails.

There was heavy equipment on the far side of the oval, and a tarp that flapped in the wind. The oval's sidewalks were unworn, the bricks smooth and unblemished, suggesting the town square had been renovated recently. Papers and plastic shopping bags lay scattered in the street, flitting from place to place in the wind. The trees planted on the lawn areas at the oval's corners had lost most of their leaves, and the hedges and flower beds looked scraggly.

"I know plants always look half-dead this time of year, but it makes me sad," Imogen said. "It feels like a preview of what we can expect."

"Aren't you the cheery one. Those plants are still here and so are we. How's that for reframing?"

"Not bad," she said. "Let's get Betty and Amy."

"I WAS GETTING WORRIED," Betty said, sounding a little breathless. The corners of her eyes were pinched, and a hard line had formed between her eyebrows. Betty looked older than when Imogen had met her. Perhaps she did, too.

Imogen ushered Betty and Amy inside, Zach locking the door after them. "The building is clear," he said. "Three hours is what we agreed on. Let's not waste time."

Amy said, "Books that we think will be helpful for our survival first, right?"

Zach nodded. "We'll stack them at the circulation desk and sort through them to decide what to bring. Then we can move on to fiction, get the truck loaded, maybe the car, too, and get out of here."

"Be sure to pay attention to the windows," Imogen said. "If the zombies we saw on the side streets at the edge of town follow us, we need to be ready to go."

"I can keep watch," Betty volunteered, though she frowned as she looked at the entrance. "There's not much cover here."

Imogen shook her head as she looked around the library. "Look for books. There's better cover in the stacks."

The long end of the building had tables and chairs for twenty feet, and a bank of computer workstations along an inside wall. The front wall had several windows, most on this end near the tables and chairs. Imogen could see the far end of this longer wing was wider than where they stood in the lobby. The far end was darker, and the tall shelves of the library stacks looked like smudges rather than furniture and books. Since the computers were set up on an interior wall, Imogen reckoned the opposite side from them was either the stacks curling back around the wall on the other side, or an interior room. The circulation desk was across the lobby from where they stood, by a wide arch that opened to the shorter, truncated 'bottom' line of the L shape.

They scattered through the non-fiction section—poorly lit, because of course it would be. Everyone kept their torches on as agreed, even when they were close enough to see one another.

Almost three hours later, Imogen was deep into the alternative medicine section, making a last pass before they left. She pulled another book from the shelf, shining her torch over the cover to read the title: *The Modern Herbal Dispensatory: A Medicine-Making Guide*. She riffled through the pages. It was one of those books with beautiful photography, but unlike a few others she'd returned to the shelves, there were illustrations and charts, like a proper textbook. She set it on the book cart and saw Zach coming her way.

"How's it going?"

"Well enough," she said. "I think I have enough of these medicinal plants and field guides. How's sorting going?"

"Amy's almost done with the last batch. I just came to get you. She found a lot of good ones about medicines, and a Physician's Desk Reference. Betty got a bunch of homesteading and womanly arts books." He held up his hands to forestall her protest. "That's what she called them, not me."

Imogen smiled. "You're off the hook this time."

"Most of the books are loaded in the truck and car. That Physician's Desk Reference is heavy. I wish we'd had it before the others went to that pharmacy." He shrugged. "Maybe they'll find something like it for pharmacists."

"I'll just put these in my rucksack." Imogen shrugged out of her rucksack and set her torch on the shelf. Dropping to her knees, she stuffed the books inside. She wanted to keep the herbs book with her in case something happened, like needing to abandon a vehicle. It would be a shame to lose such a useful book.

"I've got room in my backpack for some of them," Zach said, taking a book. "You should see how many mysteries Betty got."

"Cozies?"

"If you mean the light, fluffy ones, then yeah."

"I'm still surprised Mike agreed to us doing this without him," Imogen said. "He was dead set against it at first."

Zach snorted. "You pulled a charm offensive."

Imogen looked up at him. "What are you talking about?"

"You nodded a lot, cocked your head to the side, and gave that little smile, and he was saying yes before he knew it."

"I think it had more to do with agreeing with my reasoning," she said, feeling a little offended. "He can't be part of every single outing and we can take care of ourselves. Well, you and I can," she added at his raised eyebrows. "I don't think charm had anything to do with it."

"Uh-huh," Zach said, sounding unconvinced.

Annoyed, she said, "I only told him he couldn't be everywhere at once, and that he was verging on mansplaining if he kept talking." She chuckled, remembering how she'd known she had him when he smiled and that dimple appeared.

"I think it had more to do with you than anything else."

Imogen stopped zipping her rucksack. She squinted up at Zach. "What's that supposed to mean?"

"He likes you, Imogen."

She stood and slipped the rucksack over her shoulders. "I like Mike, too."

A grin stretched across Zach's face, reminding her of a satisfied cat. Then he puckered his lips and kissed at the air. "*That* kind of likes you."

A happy little zing of excitement took her by surprise. "Oh, honestly…" Imogen said, feeling nonplussed. "This is the apocalypse, Zach. Not grammar school."

"Apocalypse shmapocalypse… Still likes you."

"Not long ago you thought he was abusive."

Zach shrugged. "I can admit I was wrong about that."

"You're not serious about this, are you?"

Even as she asked the question, the idea that Zach wasn't serious made her feel a little… sad? But that feeling flitted away under the weight of her dawning horror that he *was* serious. There was no question Mike was handsome—tall, dark, and rugged. And handy too… it was almost a cliché. His smile was the most outrageously appealing smile she'd ever seen. Not just because of the dimple, though the dimple was enough on its own. It was the way his smile arced to his eyes, with a suffused sort of glow that lit up his face, like a pearl with a tiny light at its center. His eyes were such a deep brown they verged on black, and so warm she always thought of molasses. She'd never seen a shade of brown darker.

Good Lord, she thought, her cheeks beginning to burn. She'd put a lot of thought into how handsome Mike was without knowing it.

A sudden, sinking feeling dragged her stomach to her feet. She stared at Zach in open-mouthed dread. "Have you been gossiping with Bec and Jeffrey?"

"Of course not," he said, the sly grin creeping over his face meaning he most definitely had been. "I might have overheard them. They're very observant."

"They're very— I can't believe this!" she sputtered. "You've all been discussing me and Mike?"

"You have to admit our entertainment options are pretty limited."

"Zach!" She protested. "Do you know how wrong this is? Mike just lost his girlfriend. He was crazy about her and misses her terribly."

"How do you know that?"

"Don't be thick, Zach. He told me."

Zach's eyes narrowed. "He told you?"

"Who should he have told?"

Zach shrugged. "I don't know, but guys don't usually talk about stuff like that with a woman they like."

"Apparently, Mike does," she said, trying to impress upon him that whatever he thought was going on, he was wrong. When Zach laughed, she snapped, "You know what I meant! Not that he likes— He was going to propose that day, when all this started."

Zach's eyebrows climbed his forehead over eyes that glowed, as if she'd just told him the juiciest piece of gossip ever. Which, she realized belatedly, she had, feeling like she'd lost the tactical advantage in a game she hadn't known she was playing.

Voice flat, Zach said, "He was going to propose to her?"

"Yes."

"Like, he had a ring all ready to go?"

Imogen gritted her teeth, exasperated. "Yes. He showed it to me."

"He showed you the ring?" Zach barked, his voice rising.

"Good Lord, Zach! Be quiet!" She looked down the aisle of the book stacks, paranoia taking hold. "Are you a parrot?"

"So how did that happen?" he asked, his desire for details no doubt visible from outer space. "Did he just start telling you he had a ring, or did he say he had something to show you?"

"It was in his pocket!" Imogen cried. "Why are you making such a big deal of this? We were just *talking*. It was the day we had the vote, when he finally opened up about Sandy's death. The rest of it just came up."

Zach nodded once, like he was considering the secrets of the universe. Then, sounding smug, he said, "He hasn't told anyone else or showed us a ring." His voice became singsong as he said, "You're the one he confides in."

The vein in her temple started to thump. Imogen closed her eyes and tried to count to ten, but questions pinged inside her brain like an overactive chinchilla. There was no way Mike liked her. None. Was there? Even if he did, she didn't like him, not that way. Zach still looked far too pleased with himself when she opened her eyes again. Then her stomach bottomed out a second time. "Don't you dare tell Bec and Jeffrey about this! I mean it, Zach. Quit. Gossiping. What if this gets back to Mike?"

"Now you don't want him to know?"

"You're giving me a headache," she growled, rubbing the thumping vein at her temple. "The three of you are going to make everything awkward."

"I don't think so," Zach said, pursing his lips, his eyes going unfocused in an exaggerated display of pretending to contemplate possibilities. "In fact—"

"You're impossible," she huffed. "Mike loves his girlfriend, and he's grieving. Loving someone doesn't change in a month."

"I'm not saying you're wrong, Imogen," he relented. "Of course he loves his girlfriend and he's grieving. That doesn't mean he can't like you, too. Until Bec pointed it out, I hadn't noticed, to be honest. I'm not even sure he knows it himself, but he likes you."

"This is the stupidest conversation we've ever had."

Imogen turned on her heel and stalked down the row ahead of him. She could hear Zach chuckling behind her, which only irritated her more. So what if she'd been the one to speak with Mike when he'd been so out of sorts after Sandy had died? Everyone had seemed to expect it would be her, herself included. It made sense since she'd known Mike the longest. Except that wasn't true, she realized. Sandy and Kevin had known him just as long.

They weren't with us on the bridge.

But now that she thought of it, why had the others assumed she'd be the one to approach him? Betty could have spoken with him, or Bec, or even Clyde. Again, she came back to them being on the bridge together. Yet she bristled at that. It wasn't only that they'd been on the bridge. It was more than that, but not Mike liking her. They'd been through a lot together, what with going to his sister's. She'd been there at one of the worst moments in his life, when he'd needed a friend. Everyone knew that, so of course they all thought she should be the one. She and Mike had grown close, so much so that Imogen had told him about her family. Given the circumstances, it would happen with anyone, wouldn't it?

Would I mind if it hadn't?

A really unpleasant feeling took hold in her middle at the idea of losing the closeness she had with Mike.

That doesn't mean I like him, just... that I value our friendship.

But if that was so, why had it been so important to her that Zach not only give Mike a chance to redeem himself, but that they be friends? She bristled, more irritated than Zach's teasing deserved.

Good Lord… why am I letting Zach's nonsense get inside my head? He has no idea what he's talking about. Mike's not interested in me… of all the ridiculous things to suggest. Even if he was, I'm not interested with the world going to pieces. Mike is great, obviously, but me and him?

"Whoa!"

Imogen jerked to a halt, having almost run straight into Amy. "Sorry," she said, taking in Amy's wide eyes and upraised hand. "I wasn't paying attention."

"It's time to go," Amy said. "We finished the last sorting."

Imogen nodded. Zach reached them and said, "Did you find what you wanted, Amy?"

Amy nodded and readjusted the books she held in her arm. "Yes. Betty's eager to get going, and so am I."

Imogen glimpsed the title on the spine of one book before Amy shoved it into the crook of her elbow: *How to Win Friends and Influence People.* Inwardly, she winced. Her former boss was already making progress getting along, which had thawed some of the generalized frostiness. The book was further evidence that she wanted to be a part of the group. Perhaps she was wrong to pity Amy and should take it as a good sign. Imogen fell in alongside Amy and Zach. It had surprised her when Amy said she wanted to come with them but also secretly pleased her. They were all stuck with one another. They had to get along. Today, apart from Zach's annoying nonsense, everyone had.

Betty relaxed when they came into sight, giving them a smile from where she stood near the entrance. Everyone picked up something—bag or box or rucksack—as they readied to leave. I better make sure I have everything, Imogen thought, not sure why since she'd just zipped the rucksack, but it never hurt to look. She dropped the rucksack to the floor and dug through the books inside.

"What wrong?" Zach asked her.

"I don't have my torch," she said, squinting up at Zach.

"You had it in the stacks."

"I must have left it."

"What's wrong?" Betty asked, sounding anxious.

Imogen smiled to reassure her. "Nothing, I just realized I left my torch." She zipped the rucksack half-closed and hoisted it onto her shoulder. "It's a good one; I don't want to leave it. I'll just be a minute."

CHAPTER 28
MIKE

Two stock tanks, a plow winch, seeds, feed for chickens, irrigation tubing, and probably a hundred smaller items later, Mike leaned against the pickup truck, panting. "I am too old for this shit."

Kevin gave Mike a baleful stare from the other side of the truck bed. "My grandpa was farming dairy cows into his eighties. How old are you anyway?"

"Forty-eight."

Kevin's laughter rang across the parking lot.

"I'm still too old for this crap," Mike said. "Steph used to tease me about calling her brother, who lived in Chicago, to help move furniture. I know I'm not decrepit, but you don't feel it as much at your age if you strain something."

Kevin rolled his eyes again and tossed a rope to Mike over the top of the supplies. "Whatever, old man."

Mike caught the rope and threaded it through the tie-down loop before he realized that he'd mentioned Steph without thinking about it. And at least this time, without the bright flare of grief that left him stumbling over his words. The pain welled up, making his throat tight and his chest ache and feel hollow. It still hurt. It hurt like hell to think of her. He didn't remember losing his parents making him feel as exhausted as when he thought of Steph.

But the grief didn't feel as sharp today, and that stung in a different way. It would be better if he could remember her without feeling paralyzed by loss, but it felt disloyal. Just a few days ago he'd felt like the grief would crush him. How could he feel so differently today? Maybe because he'd talked about how his and Steph's last conversation had ended with Imogen. It wasn't that she had anything to say, but telling her had gotten it out of his head, just a little.

He threaded the rope through the next tie-down loop and tossed it back to Kevin. "If Clyde and Jay are doing half as well at the grocery store and pharmacy as we have here, this is going to be—"

He stopped mid-sentence. Something wasn't right. He turned around, scanning the area for zombies.

"Do you hear that?" Kevin said.

"Yeah, I do."

The rumble of an engine got louder, then a blue Ford F-350 cruised into the parking lot. Two men were in it, and a gun rack with three rifles was mounted on the back window. Instinctively, Mike's hand settled on the gun on his hip. For all the good it'll do me, he thought, deciding not to pull it from the holster. Imogen and Sandy had given him the basics: how to load the magazine with bullets and seat it in the weapon, how to sight up, a proper firing stance, but he'd had no actual practice. The sound would carry and their ammunition was limited. It wasn't worth the risk.

Kevin swallowed hard. "I guess we're gonna meet the neighbors."

Mike nodded, tension gripping him. These were the first people they'd run into since they'd arrived at the park. It surprised him, how anxious seeing people made him feel. It had only been four weeks since they'd fled Pittsburgh but the paranoia that had developed, the urgent need he had to keep everyone safe—from zombies and, apparently, people—felt like it had been there his whole life.

The truck came to a halt and doors clunked open. The man who exited the passenger side was tall, about six feet, with dark-brown hair cropped close. He had one of those pleasantly anonymous faces with a straight nose, square jaw, light-brown eyes, and an open expression. Handsome, but not too handsome, and not the kind that stuck in your mind. The man raised a hand. "Hello."

The man who'd been driving the truck was much shorter, about five foot eight, and lean as a whippet. He had a restless energy that made him seem on the edge of fidgeting. Mike met the shorter man's eyes and could tell at a glance he was smart. "Hello," the short guy said. "Good to meet you."

"Hi," Mike said, with Kevin's greeting echoing his own. They all looked at one another. Then Mike said, "I'm Mike. This is Kevin."

The big guy said, "I'm Jim."

"Anthony," the short guy volunteered.

Again, they all looked at one another. Finally, Anthony said, "So are we gonna dance or stand here and look at each other?"

The tension broke. Mike stepped forward because Anthony was right. Standing there looking at each other felt like a junior high dance. After they'd traded handshakes, Anthony said, "Where are you guys from?"

"Pittsburgh," Mike said.

"What was it like there?" Jim said. "We're from Scranton. It went from normal to disaster movie overnight."

Mike nodded. "It got bad fast in Pittsburgh, too."

"What are you planning to do with those stock tanks?" Anthony asked, jutting his chin at the pickup truck.

"Collect water," Kevin answered.

Mike had to stop himself from smiling. Kevin was playing things close to the vest, not exactly dishonest, but not completely honest, either.

"Was that your truck and people at the grocery store up the way?" Jim asked.

Mike's heart ramped up so fast and hard he has trouble hearing what Jim was saying. His grip on Sandy's gun tightened. He wanted to leave, find out what they'd done to Clyde and Jay.

"…get twitchy when food's involved. We didn't stop or mess with them," Jim said, trying to sound reassuring.

"They're our people," Mike said, his voice hard.

He glanced at Kevin. He'd picked up his Halligan, which had been leaning against the truck. "What did you do—"

"Nothing! Not a thing!" Jim said, flustered, holding his hands up in front of him, and Mike realized the man didn't have a gun. Even so, sweat gathered on Mike's upper lip, hidden by the mustache he kept closely trimmed.

"We didn't stop," Anthony added, making a show of holding his hands out in front of him. "We're at the Safe Zone at the high school in Farwell, just past Renovo if you're heading east on Route 120. The National Guard is in charge."

Anthony wasn't armed either, Mike realized. Were the rifles on the truck rack all they had with them? He'd seen the signs for Renovo, but it was beyond where they turned off 120 to get to Cady's Run. Anthony rattled the information off quickly. A person could come up with a practiced lie, but his voice had the ring of truth to it.

"How many people?" Kevin asked.

Anthony said, "About eight hundred now."

"Eight hundred?" Mike blurted out, surprise winning out over wariness. The last time he'd seen that many people in one place had probably been at the outdoor concert at Hartwood Acres the symphony did every year. But it would account for the overall lack of people in the area, even if just half the population of the smaller towns had gone there.

Jim nodded. "I take it your group's a lot smaller?"

Neither Mike nor Kevin answered. Anthony and Jim waited for more, but that was all they got.

"Was that you guys who cleared out the grocery store in Wellsboro?" Kevin finally asked. "By the time we got there, nothing was left."

Anthony and Jim traded a glance. "Yeah... Are you set okay for food?"

Kevin looked at Mike, a question in his eyes: do you believe them? Mike looked at the two men. Even though his senses were on high alert, he believed them enough. He gave Kevin a subtle nod.

"We're getting there," Kevin said, setting his Halligan on the ground to lean against his leg. "The grocery store will help."

Despite his wariness, and obvious willingness to mix things up, Kevin still managed to project an easy confidence, an 'I'm just one of the guys' vibe that Mike hadn't seen before. Even the way he stood was different, his bulk somehow diminished, making him less of a threat. Like a chameleon, he'd changed his colors to match the wallpaper. They didn't want a fight with these men unless it was absolutely necessary, and they needed the food in that grocery store.

Anthony and Jim both relaxed. Anthony said, "We've been out seven days now, scouting the area for supplies and people. You got here first. It's all yours."

Jim nodded. "I wouldn't feel right taking food out of your mouths. It sounds like you might need it more, and the Safe Zone has a lot. Just trying to be like the ant, not the grasshopper."

Both Mike and Kevin nodded.

Jim said, "Where are you guys set up?"

"We're off State Road Six, more or less," Mike said.

"Okay," Jim said, the friendliness in his voice undiminished. "You don't know us and want to play it safe. I get it."

Mike shrugged. "No offense intended. You're the first people we've seen in a while. It's good to know there are more of us."

Jim brushed Mike's explanation away. "No offense taken."

He paused, then said, "Do you need help getting anything else loaded up here or at the grocery?"

"I think we've got it covered, but thanks for asking," Kevin said.

"Okay, then," Jim said. "You're welcome to join us at the Safe Zone if you don't want to go it alone. The National Guard commander is really on the ball. It's a good group, and we're still taking people in."

"Are you going to turn people away?" Mike asked, taken aback.

Anthony shook his head emphatically, while Jim said, "No! Of course not! I just meant you'll be welcome."

Mike narrowed his eyes, studying the men. Jim's alarm that Mike might have misunderstood him seemed sincere. I hate this, he thought, feeling like he was turning into a paranoid nutcase. Finally, he said, "Thanks, we'll think about it."

Jim nodded and offered a tentative smile. "Well, stay safe. A lot of people had camps up here, and there are campsites and cabins in the parks and state forests. We checked out Cady's Run a little, and that other one…"

His brow furrowed, and he bit his lip as he tried to remember. Mike's eyes darted to Kevin surreptitiously. Kevin's face had blanched but he tried to cover it with a cough. Mike's hollowed-out stomach tightened around a trapped, sinking feeling that hadn't been there a moment ago. These men had been to Cady's Run.

"Susquehannock," Anthony supplied. "Not much there besides trees and creeks, though I bet the hunting's good. Wouldn't be surprised if some folks are there but I think the Safe Zone's a better bet."

"Thanks for the heads-up," Mike said. "We haven't been out that way."

Anthony nodded. "We've seen more of those, you know, crazy people down this way. Still not a lot, but be careful."

"Thanks," Kevin said. "We've only seen a few zombies today but they're like cockroaches, always more around."

Anthony's eyebrows shot up. He looked as if Kevin had just told him that leprechauns were real and he had proof. "Zombies?"

Kevin glanced at Mike, a half grimace on his face that let Mike know Kevin was dropping this in his lap. With an embarrassed reluctance, he said, "They're dead but they're walking around and all they seem to want is to eat us. We know for a fact people get that way from their bites, and destroying the brain kills them. Sounds like zombies to me."

"They said it was that salmonella," Jim said. "If you believe what they told us."

"Doesn't really matter anymore, does it?" Kevin said.

They all deflated at that, which made Mike feel—not relaxed—but less wary.

"I guess we'll get to it," Jim said. "The invitation stands for your group… safety in numbers. Never thought I'd be part of an endangered species, but I think that's what we are."

An endangered species. Mike hadn't thought of it that way, but Jim was right. Jim and Anthony wrote directions to the Safe Zone on the back of a paper bag from the farm supply checkout. Mike and Kevin shook hands with the men and watched them disappear into the store.

Mike studied the directions, then shoved them in his pocket. He and Kevin didn't speak as they finished tying down the load on the pickup with a mounting sense of urgency. Minutes later they pulled out of the parking lot, and Kevin said, "What do you think?"

"They might be trouble."

Voice uneasy, Kevin said, "We pulled Clyde and Jay's truck around the back of the grocery store to the loading dock. Are we supposed to believe that those two went around the back, saw the truck, and just drove away?"

"They might have," Mike said. "Like he said, people are

probably getting twitchy about food. Hell, look at us. If they've got enough food, it wouldn't be worth it."

"They didn't seem worried about who we might be."

Kevin's voice trailed away but he might as well have shouted it. Jim and Anthony hadn't been wary. They'd been confident and relaxed, as if they weren't here on their own.

CHAPTER 29
IMOGEN

IMOGEN KNEW SOMETHING WAS WRONG AS SOON AS SHE SAW AMY standing at the inner door to the vestibule. Amy held the door ajar, her rigid shoulders making her look like she'd been hung on a hook. Amy's eyes darted to her, so quickly Imogen wasn't sure it had happened. Then, almost imperceptibly, Amy shook her head 'No.'

Imogen's reptilian brain uncoiled, its cool scales rubbing the knobby bones of her spine. The sharp bite of its fangs sunk into her heart. Its venom flooded her body. Amy's refusal to look at her set free a raging torrent of fear. What was happening to scare Amy so?

Imogen crept closer to Amy, sidling along the wall, and stopping just short of the floor-to-ceiling window by the door. Amy's white-knuckled, trembling hand gripped the open door. Her mouth twisted to one side. A slight echo distorted Betty's voice. Imogen's heart raced, the palms of her hands sweaty and cold.

"We're hanging on so far," Zach said, his voice louder than Betty's.

"We saw all the books in the truck and car. Thought we'd come and see who was here."

Imogen's breath caught in her throat. A man's voice, one she didn't know.

"We'd have done the same," Zach said. He almost sounded relaxed, but she could tell he wasn't. An undertone, tight as high-tension wire, hummed below the surface.

"Is it just the three of you?"

A woman's voice, the consonants harsh. A survivor's voice, the kind who discarded whatever slowed her down, people included.

"Oh no, thank goodness," Betty said, breathless. "It's just the three of us here. Our group is larger."

"Are you here in town?" the woman said.

"A bit farther away, toward Mina," Zach answered.

"With my cousin and her neighbors," Betty said. "She called me when all of this started. She was on her own, and I was too. I was lucky to get out of Pittsburgh."

"What's it like there?" It was the man again, sounding genuinely curious, his voice warmer than his counterpart's. "I lived here in town. My name's Ben, and this is Gillian."

Imogen couldn't see anything from where she stood. Betty had said it was just the three of them here at the library, so she couldn't reveal herself but she needed more information. She looked around, trying to figure out how she could get a look at these people. She didn't know how many there were, or if they had weapons...

Of course they have weapons, idiot. Why else would Amy be warning me off?

Imogen knew she had to calm down. She couldn't reveal herself, but needed to get a better sense of the situation, which meant getting a look at the strangers. She had to move. The computer stations against the opposite wall were the closest place on this side of the library with a view of the door. The cover they offered was almost nonexistent. There were chairs for patrons pushed under computer stations, but the kind with spindly metal legs. The circulation desk on the lobby's other side would be better, but she couldn't get there without being seen.

I could crawl through those chairs.

At least she'd be at floor level, and she doubted they'd be looking at the floor. She would be terribly exposed but it was all she had. She hesitated a moment. Were their positions reversed, Imogen wouldn't want her friends risking their safety. She'd want them to hide if she knew whatever it was about these strangers that had spooked them so. The sensible thing to do was stay hidden and make sure she wasn't seen.

She scuttled across the room, ducked low, then dropped to her hands and knees, waiting a moment to make sure no one had seen her. Then she lay on the floor and belly crawled, the carpet scratchy against her trembling hands. Dust tickled her nose. Gratitude for her tiny frame bubbled up, but it didn't last. As she crawled below the second chair, she belatedly realized they wouldn't offer a quick escape. "This is madness," she whispered under her breath. "Absolute madness."

Between the second and third chair, she could see as high as Amy's back and through the glass door into the vestibule as high as Zach's waist. He'd pulled his jacket back. His hand rested lightly on his gun. Bloody hell, she thought, her brain strobing faster, as if she'd seen a saber-toothed tiger. And, more importantly, that the tiger had seen her. The instinct to back up and flee reared up, so strong she almost gave in to it. Instead, trembling, she crawled forward.

When Imogen reached the last chair, she pressed her head against the floor and craned her neck. A strange feeling of exhilaration swirled into the fear like a raspberry ripple in vanilla ice cream. Through the panes of glass in the door she saw the woman. She was average height, Imogen thought, but from this angle it was hard to tell. Her blond hair was pulled back tight from her face, which was severely thin, to the point of looking emaciated. The woman's lips were wreathed with so many wrinkles that Imogen guessed she was a smoker. She seemed to be in her fifties, but might be younger. Nothing about her suggested warmth or friendliness. She was the last person Imogen would have on her welcoming committee. Zach blocked the man, who was at least trying to make up for his companion's deficits. Imogen couldn't see Betty. She must be standing to Zach's right.

"...about a hundred strong," the man—Ben—was saying. "Do you know where the Berrigan's Home Improvement is?"

"I think I passed it once," Zach said.

"We're north of it a ways. You should come with us," the woman said, sounding as if a little of the frost had been chipped away. Her voice still had an edge, an insistence that made the back of Imogen's neck prickle.

"That's generous of you, Gillian," Betty said. "But my cousin will worry."

"We can get the rest of your people," the man added.

Maybe Betty shook her head, for the woman frowned.

Zach said, "We really do need to get on the road."

A long pause followed. Imogen's pulse thumped in her ears, making her feel half-deaf. It was a wonder they couldn't hear it. What on Earth would she do if they forced Zach, Betty, and Amy to go with them?

You'll hide, get back to the lodge, and go find them.

But if the strangers came into the library, what then? I'll hide, she thought. But the library wasn't large. If she was discovered, then this Gillian and the man would know the others had lied to them.

"It's really been wonderful talking to you," Betty said. "Knowing there are more survivors makes me feel a little better, but I told my cousin that we'd be back before dark."

Then Amy said, "Get out of our way."

Imogen blinked, so surprised she stifled a gasp. Amy hadn't spoken until now. She wasn't bothering with politeness, but sounded like a badass who'd show them what for if they didn't do as she said. They were done with these people—she was making sure they knew it.

"Sure, sure," the man said. "We didn't mean to hold you up."

Imogen got a sense of motion beyond Zach when he stepped forward. The man must be shaking hands with them.

"If you change your mind, you know where to find us," the man said.

"No, we don't," Amy said.

"I'm sorry?" the man said.

"You never told us where you are," Amy said. She sounded as hostile as a wife confronting her husband's mistress. "Just that your group is north of Berrigan's."

Another silence. Imogen held her breath. When the woman—Gillian—spoke, her voice was more hostile than Amy's. "We're careful about our exact location. We put up a sign and meet people at Berrigan's."

None of their group who had gone to Berrigan's had mentioned any sign. It had either been put up later, or Gillian was lying. Either way, Gillian had not appreciated Amy's question. Things back at the lodge might be improving in the Amy department, but she'd just made an enemy of Gillian. Gillian's stare was the same as Imogen had seen countless times as a child in the eyes of lions and leopards, cheetahs and hyenas—a predator's.

"We're leaving now," Amy said.

A charged silence fell. Finally, Zach said, "It's been good meeting you."

Imogen heard the shuffling of feet, then Betty added, "Be safe."

A clatter, then movement, ripped Imogen's attention from the increasingly terrifying Gillian. Amy had dropped her flashlight. She crouched in the doorway to pick it up. Shielded behind the solid lower half of the inner door, her eyes flicked into the library. She found Imogen immediately, proving just how poor her hiding place was, and mouthed one word: 'Run.'

Imogen pressed her hands over her mouth to stifle the cry shoving its way up her throat. Sweat trickled down her sides. Her limbs shook. Amy had only mouthed one word, but it cut Imogen to the core.

Amy shoved something flat under the closed door, then bent

up the part sticking out. She stood up and walked through, the hydraulic dampers sighing before the door hit the tiny obstacle, keeping the door cracked open a quarter of an inch at most. Perhaps Amy thought Ben and Gillian wouldn't leave right away. Maybe she was trying to help Imogen hear what they said if they lingered. Or maybe she was buying time for Imogen to get out of sight.

Silence settled over the library.

Whatever Amy's reason for propping the door, Imogen wasn't sticking around. She had to find a place to hide. Ben, if that was even his real name, said he used to live here in town. What would happen if she chose the wrong direction and ran into him? Where would she say she was from? In such a rural area in Pennsylvania, Imogen would stick out like a sore thumb. There were not a lot of Black people out here, especially with skin as dark as hers. If she ran into these people after they'd met the others, it would be too strange to write off as coincidence.

She lay frozen, mind racing, willing herself to move. Would Gillian and Ben follow her friends? Were they really bad people, or had Amy mistaken desperation for ill intent? Imogen had always known Amy was smart. No one survived the cutthroat world of nonprofit executives without being able to read people. Gillian was abrasive, but Imogen couldn't set any store by that. Until recently, Amy had been as cuddly as a porcupine.

She tried to remember every word of the strained conversation with the strangers as she backed out from under the chairs. Any small detail might make a difference. Was she blowing a stilted conversation out of proportion? What if she hadn't understood Amy correctly? Even as she tried to convince herself of this, she knew she hadn't.

Then it hit her, so hard her bones ached.

Her friends would take both vehicles. They'd have to. Ben had said they'd seen books in both the car and truck. There was no plausible reason to leave a vehicle behind if Betty, Zach, and Amy were the only members of their party. The tears welling in

Imogen's eyes dripped to the carpet. She pressed her hand over her mouth as her shoulders quaked. A frenzied terror gripped her, making everything before seem trivial. How far was she from Cady's Run—ten miles? Fifteen? And then another five miles beyond the border of the park to the lodge? On foot, she'd be lucky to make it there by nightfall.

Mike will come.

She latched on to the absolute truth of it, as if she'd been buried alive and Mike had the last shovel on Earth. If they didn't return, Mike would come for them. All she had to do was hold on until he did.

CHAPTER 30
MIKE

Heart pounding, Mike stepped inside from the loading dock.
"Clyde, Jay… You guys in here?"

"In here!"

Clyde sounded relaxed, even excited. A rush of relief hit Mike so hard he could have melted into a puddle.

"Thank God," Kevin whispered.

The grip of Sandy's gun felt slick in Mike's hand. Kevin held the Halligan in two hands, ready to use it. Mike re-holstered the gun and followed Kevin deeper into the back of the store. Many of the high shelves were almost empty of goods. The flicker of a headlamp led them to Clyde, who was putting a last box on an overloaded dolly.

"How's it going over there?" Clyde asked. "I'm just finishing up the groceries. I cleaned out spices like Betty said, and Jay's doing the toiletries and pharmacy. How'd yinz do?"

Skipping a greeting, Mike said, "We met some people."

Clyde stopped pushing the box into place but kept a hand on it so it didn't fall. "What kind of people?"

"Two guys," Mike said. "Driving a Ford F-350. They said there's a National Guard Safe Zone in Farwell with eight hundred people."

"Farwell?" Clyde said, his eyebrows rising above his glasses. "That's just past Renovo."

"What's just past Renovo?" Jay asked, walking into the back of the store from the retail area. He held a large box in his hands. The box couldn't be heavy because he wasn't straining to hold it.

They told Clyde and Jay about meeting the men, and shared their impressions and uneasiness, especially that they had known they were at the grocery store. Mike tried to be even-handed in his retelling and not give in to the temptation to indulge his paranoia.

"So you're not feeling really terrible about them, but not great, either," Clyde said when they had finished.

"We don't know if they were alone," Mike said. "We need to get going, and be careful on the way back."

Jay frowned. "Maybe we should split up and take different routes. The only thing we know for sure is there are two guys in one vehicle. If it's just them and they do try to follow, they won't be able to follow us both."

Mike nodded to cover his surprise. For the first time since they'd arrived at the lodge, Jay seemed engaged in the group's welfare rather than thinking only of himself. Then again, personal danger seemed to have that effect on him.

Clyde's bushy eyebrows wriggled together like caterpillars. "I hate to waste the gas, but that's not a bad idea. If you don't have a good feeling about this, Mike, I think we should."

"I'm done in the pharmacy," Jay said. "Once we get these last things loaded, we're ready to go."

"There's some room in our truck," Kevin said. "We didn't quite finish up because we wanted to make sure you were okay." He looked at Mike. "I think we're okay with what we got."

Mike nodded. "Let's finish and get out of here."

MIKE COULDN'T KEEP STILL, jitters of energy making his muscles twitch. He checked his watch again. At Clyde's suggestion, they'd agreed to stagger their departures. It made Mike feel better about how paranoid he felt.

"It's five minutes since Clyde and Jay left. Let's go."

His hand already gripped the handle of the truck door when Kevin turned toward the loading dock. Over his shoulder, Kevin said, "I'm checking the pharmacy. I want to make sure Jay got everything."

"Now?" Mike said impatiently, but Kevin had already disappeared inside.

He followed, trying to quash his annoyance as he turned on his flashlight. There were two skylights in the pharmacy's ceiling. The light wasn't bright, but better than the rest of the store. The hollow rustling of Kevin picking up and setting down bottles sounded noisy in the deserted store. It gave Mike the creeps.

"Kevin, we need to go."

"Clyde said he left the pharmacy to Jay, since he knows the drugs. We didn't ask him if he checked Jay's work. When has Jay ever done what we've asked him to do?"

Mike pinched his lips tight. He wanted to argue the point, but couldn't. "I'll take this end," he said. "You start down there."

A few moments later Kevin said, "Everything's labeled by the drug name, not what it does. I fight fires and flunked Chemistry. How am I supposed to know what these are?"

"Look at the manufacturers? You might recognize something you've taken. There must be a Physician's Desk Reference or something like it."

Mike's impatience grew as Kevin rifled the shelves. Then Kevin hissed, "That lazy son of a bitch." He stepped out from the shelf he'd been searching, holding up a box. "Birth control pills. There are nine of these on the shelf. Bec put them at the top of the list."

Mike's body started to hum, with anger or anxiety he couldn't tell—maybe both. All he wanted to do was get out of here. "It might have been a mistake. I have a copy of the list. Let's check."

They both studied the list, then Mike started at the A end of the shelves, Kevin the Z.

"There are Z-Paks on the shelf," Kevin said.

Mike's heart sank as he checked the shelves. There were three medicines in the letter A alone that Jay hadn't collected. "Let's check the storeroom. Jay might have taken the meds from there and left these for other people."

Kevin snorted, stepping out from the shelves to dump cartons and bottles on the pharmacist's counter. "You really believe that?"

"No," Mike said through gritted teeth. Clyde had said he left the toiletries and pharmacy to Jay, since he had a medical background. Clyde clearly hadn't checked, but he'd had work of his own to do. Now they had to do it.

"I'm going to punch Jay when we get back," Kevin muttered, more venom in his voice than Mike would have ever thought Kevin possessed. "First, he's a jagoff, then he's drinking, the mice, and now this. He probably brought a flask and sat on his ass, having happy hour."

Mike pivoted to the door with a red and gold sign that said, Pharmacy Storage – Authorized Personnel Only. He turned the knob, expecting it to give way. When it didn't budge, he knew Kevin was right.

Mike slammed his hand on the locked door. He'd given that creep a limited benefit of the doubt and even that had been a mistake. He spun on his heel toward Kevin and said, "Where's your Halligan?"

Forty-five minutes later, Mike and Kevin were still fuming over the half-assed job Jay had done in the pharmacy. They had four large boxes filled with medications, plus a copy of The Pharmacists Drug Handbook. Not only was the book thick enough to inflict a concussion if used as a weapon, it had helped them choose other drugs they might need. There were over thirty boxes of tampons on the shelves and they'd found three cartons more in the storeroom; the same went for sanitary pads. There were four additional cartons of birth control pills in the pharmacy's storeroom that Jay hadn't bothered with. He had, Mike noticed, managed to clean out the condom display. He'd done a better job with toiletries, but there were still many things he'd skipped. They were taking a last pass through the feminine hygiene section. Mike hadn't been able to find the last of the items Bec had said was a high priority.

"There are still a few boxes for treating yeast infections. Should I get them or leave them for someone else?" Kevin asked.

"Get everything."

Mike kept searching the shelves, and Kevin kept asking him questions. They decided to make an exception to 'Get everything' for the Summer's Eve disposable douches. Their function did not meet Bec's criteria of normalizing women's bodies. A thrill of triumph rushed through him with an electric tingle. In the beam of his flashlight was the last triple-starred feminine hygiene item. "Ha! Found ya, you little bugger."

"Hidden treasure?" Kevin asked.

Mike held up a handful of boxes. "Near enough. Bec was almost as insistent about these as she was about the birth control pills. They're menstrual cups."

Kevin snickered. "You look like you're holding a winning lottery ticket."

Mike shrugged. Under Kevin's amused gaze, his face grew hot. "I never thought I'd be this excited about feminine hygiene supplies, but do you want to deal with Bec being pissed off?"

Kevin grimaced. "Yeah, no… That's a hard pass."

"If I get to Jay first, I'm not waiting for you, Kevin. I'm beating him senseless."

Mike ripped open the packaging, removed the menstrual cups, and shoved them into his shopping bag. He winced when he looked down the aisle at the cardboard and plastic packaging littering the floor. Leaving all this mess on the floor made his fingers itch to pick it up and throw it away. Uncertain what to believe about the men they'd met earlier, they didn't have time to be tidy. Also, Kevin would razz him about it forever.

"First, he has a bad attitude, then he starts day drinking, and now he's not even pretending to pull his weight?" Kevin shook his head, picking up a variation on the mantra he'd muttered since they started scavenging.

"Jay's going to have a come to Jesus moment as soon as we get back," Mike agreed. "Do we have enough? I want to get out of here." He had wanted to leave since Kevin first went back inside. Jim and Anthony had said they'd leave the grocery store alone. That they hadn't shown up should have made Mike feel better, but it didn't. His brain had taken the bait of schemes and disaster scenarios and wasn't giving it up.

"Let's get out of here," Kevin said. "I feel like Jim and Anthony are going to show up with a squad of goons any minute."

They headed for the truck, the creepy crawly feeling that had been percolating at the back of Mike's mind since they'd encountered the two men boiling over. Worry for the safety of Imogen and the others slithered out from where he'd banished it earlier and poured itself into the mix. He knew they'd play it safe going to the library. Imogen was smart and cautious. Betty wasn't a risk taker and neither was Zach. Amy was a pain but she wasn't stupid. If any of them thought things weren't as safe as they could be, they'd turn around and go back to the lodge.

They made room for the additional cargo, cramming the smaller items between the farm supply haul. Mike squinted as he climbed into the truck, the late afternoon sun at just the right position that it hit him in the eyes just below the visor. He leaned back against the truck's bench seat, grateful it was Kevin's turn to drive.

"I owe you one, man."

"How's that?" Kevin said. The truck's engine turned over and purred like a kitten.

"I promised Bec I'd get everything she wanted. If you hadn't double-checked..." He shivered, not wanting to think about the grief she'd have given him.

They drove in the opposite direction from the one they'd taken into town—no passing Zombie Grandma this time. The map Clyde had marked their route on lay across Mike's knee. The stew of anxiety and anger of the last hour, plus the physical exertion of the day, was making itself known. He pulled Sandy's gun from the utility belt and set it on the dashboard.

Kevin cocked an eyebrow. "You really think you'll need it?"

Mike stifled a yawn, then said, "I just want to be ready."

CHAPTER 31
IMOGEN

"You have *got* to settle down," Imogen whispered under her breath, her voice so cruel it sounded like her father when he raged at his frightened daughters and angry wife. "You don't have time to keep leaping to the worst possible conclusion in a single bound."

She forced herself to calm—to breathe. After a minute that felt like a lifetime, she slipped on her rucksack and crept along the wall, heart thundering in her chest, heading for the stacks. At least she hadn't been in the short wing of the library on the other side of the lobby, where there were lots of windows. When she reached the cover of the stacks, she leaned against the wall, feeling as tired as if she'd just run a marathon. Dim afternoon light filtered through the windows at the far side of building, where the emergency exit was located. Since there was no power, at least she didn't have to worry about an alarm going off.

The pull to walk through the stacks straight toward the windows and the emergency exit vibrated in her bones, but she'd risk being seen from those windows. If she approached from the side, she'd have better cover. Decision made, she removed the handgun from its holster, the weight unfamiliar in her hand. She was competent with firearms but she'd never fired this one. In her current predicament, she didn't care how much noise the gun would make.

Imogen slipped further into the dark stacks, keeping a hand on the wall. She wanted to run but didn't want to risk tripping on books that hadn't been reshelved, and she didn't dare use her torch. She reached the first corner, huffing out a sigh of relief, when she heard the noise. She froze, the vein in her temple throbbing, blood singing in her ears, every sense stretched to the breaking point.

There it was again, ahead of her but muffled. She cocked her head, trying to identify it. It didn't sound like a zombie. Besides, there was no smell. Perhaps it was an animal, a mouse or a rat. Stepping with care, she continued, pausing after each step. When her hand hit a protrusion on the wall, she almost cried out, leaping backward, before she realized it was trim around a door. She remembered standing in the open door, covering Zach while he checked the small storeroom.

"You're fine," she whispered, taking a glacial step forward, for part of her just wanted to hide.

Her stomach dropped when she heard the noise again. Imogen leaned closer, putting her ear to the door, not sure she'd be able to hear anything over the *whoosh* of blood in her ears, but she did. She frowned, listening. It sounded like someone… crying?

The noise stopped, then started, then stopped again. Imogen pulled away and stared into the darkness, indecision wrapping her straitjacket tight. She should leave, get out of here and not look back. Whatever was happening on the other side of that door wasn't her problem. But what if someone needed help? What if whoever was crying in there needed medical attention? Could she live with herself knowing she hadn't bothered to slow down, that she might have treated a human being like roadkill?

Shit, shit, shit.

She put her hand on the doorknob, thought better of it, and

got her torch from where she'd stuck it in the front of her jeans. She clicked it on, training the light on the floor. Holding her gun in her other hand, she twisted the knob with the hand holding the torch, and pushed the door ajar. A startled cry followed, then shushing and rustling in quick succession.

"Hello?" Imogen whispered, barely able to catch her breath around the boulder in her throat. She swept the torch's beam across the room crammed full of books and book return carts.

Another cry, high and thin—the cry of a child—stopped as if smothered. Imogen stepped further into the room, jerking the light in that direction. Two small children cowered behind one of the book return carts. Both had filthy dark hair and were pale with fright under the dirt. Their dark eyes seemed to swallow half of their faces. A young girl had her hand over the mouth of a boy, who looked a few years younger. She had the look of a trapped animal, a wild terror that the boy's eyes shone with, too. She couldn't be over ten, the boy maybe seven.

"Hello," Imogen said, her voice shaking. She lowered the gun and pointed the torch at the ceiling, so the light reflected down. That way, they could see her, too. "My name's Imogen."

When she took a cautious step forward, the boy flailed against the girl's tight grip. The girl looked around, the terror in eyes and on her face threatening to explode. "I'm stopping," Imogen said. "I'm sorry. I won't come any closer."

She looked at the children, flummoxed, and so filled with adrenaline it felt like she was hovering above the floor. Now she couldn't go. From the state of them, the children had to be on their own. She bit her lip, then remembered the chocolate bar in her breast pocket.

"Are you hungry?"

The girl sat forward at that, loosening her hold on the boy, then seemed to realize showing interest might have been a mistake. She pulled back but let her hand fall from the boy's mouth.

"I'm going to reach into my pocket, inside the front of my coat. I've got a chocolate bar. Would you like some?"

"Yes," the boy said, his voice so loud Imogen cringed.

The girl said nothing, but she nodded and licked her lips. Imogen holstered her handgun. She unzipped her coat and reached inside, the wrapper of the Twix bar crinkling against her gloved fingers. She pulled it out and held it up, then tossed it to them.

The girl scrambled to snatch up the candy. She ripped the wrapper open. For a terrible moment, Imogen thought she might eat the whole thing, but she handed one stick of the chocolate bar to the boy. They gobbled up the sweets. Imogen strained to hear anything beyond the room that might be happening in the library. She needed to get out of here.

"Thank you," the girl whispered.

"Do you have anything to eat?" Imogen already knew the answer and wasn't surprised when the girl shook her head. "Is there anyone looking after you?"

The girl's mouth quirked down, but only for a moment before she shook her head. The boy's bottom lip puckered but he didn't cry.

"I live in a nice place, in the woods," Imogen said. "My friends live there, too. Mike and Kevin, Betty and Clyde, Jeffrey and Rebecca, who's ever so nice. Would you like to come with me? You could have something to eat, and a bath, and sit by the fire to get warm. You wouldn't have to be here on your own." She paused, almost saying 'we could look after you' but that might be too much.

The girl stared at her. After a long moment, she said, "Do we have to stay?"

Imogen blinked, so shocked she had trouble getting her head right to answer. "Of course not, unless you want to."

The girl looked at the boy. He whispered in her ear, then she said, "Okay."

How was she going to get them out of here and avoid the people outside? Imogen hesitated, then decided she'd have to tell them.

"That's wonderful," she said, offering a smile. "Here's the thing, and I don't mean to frighten you." Both children stiffened. "There are people outside who I don't know."

The girl's pupils blew out like inflating balloons. "Are they back?"

Oh God, Imogen thought. What had these children seen? "I don't know who they are," she said. "I'm afraid of them, to be honest. If you come with me, we must steal away, quiet as mice. I don't want them to see me or see where I live. We'll have to sneak. Can you do that?"

The fear on their small faces flayed Imogen's heart. What had they been through? Would she be able to get them away with her? Would she have to leave them?

No. That's not happening.

The girl whispered, "We're good at sneaking."

Imogen nodded. "Get your things, then."

They came out from behind the cart with nothing, just the clothes they wore. Imogen dropped to her knees as they approached. "My name's Imogen. Can you tell me yours?"

"Carolyn," the girl said. "My brother is Billy."

Carolyn sounded so small and looked so vulnerable. Now that they were closer, she could see the pinch of hunger on their faces. The weight of the responsibility she was taking on hit Imogen like a twenty-ton weight. She breathed in, then blew out in a long, steady stream.

"All right, Carolyn and Billy. I need you to listen to me carefully. The people outside don't know we're here. We need to keep it that way. There's a door by the windows at the back." Both children nodded, and Imogen wondered how long they'd been hiding here. "We're going out that door, and then we're going to hide. Once those people have gone, my friends will come find us."

Carolyn nodded. Billy didn't, but his attention on Imogen was total. She hoped it meant he understood. She led the children from their hiding place and over to the door. She squinted out the window, momentarily thrown by the next building just feet away from the door. She'd thought the door opened onto a street, not a narrow walkway between the library and another building. The relief of knowing they had some cover was a tiny thing, but it was something. Imogen held fast to this kernel of knowledge like it was the secret to life. She knelt down in front of Billy and Carolyn. "You must do exactly as I say. Okay?" Carolyn nodded. "Say it out loud."

Her parents had done a lot of things wrong, but this wasn't one of them. When it was important—when they'd wanted to drive a point home—they'd made her and Araminta say they understood out loud. Having to say it had always made it more real.

"We do what you say," Carolyn said, her voice trembling.

"We listen," Billy whispered, so low it almost seemed he was pouting.

"Okay," Imogen said with a nod of her head. "I'm going to hold your hands once we're outside. Whatever happens, don't let go unless I tell you to."

Imogen stood, taking a deep breath. Steeling herself. Then she pushed the door open two inches. The cold bit at her face and frosted her breath. The temperature had dropped while she'd been indoors. She looked both ways. Seeing nothing, she slipped into the alley, beckoning the children to her. She took their small hands in hers, Carolyn on her right, Billy the left. This was bad enough on her own, but now she had these children. What if—

Not now.

Her breath rasped in her throat, too shallow to catch a real breath, as she looked down the narrow walkway between the library and the next building. The truck was gone; the car, too. She didn't see anyone, but who knew how many there were?

"Come on."

The children held her hands like starfish. She half expected them to bolt away. They didn't know her, had no reason to trust her. She'd offered them candy, employing the oldest kidnapper trick in the book to get them to let down their guard. All she lacked was a windowless white van.

Like cat burglars, they slunk to the corner at the back of the building. Imogen poked her head out, heart thundering in her chest, then jerked back, her brain lighting up like she'd just seen an entire pride of saber-toothed tigers. Two men stood on the sidewalk, facing the other direction. It had been Ben and Gillian before, at the library entrance. Now she knew there were more of them.

"Stay back," she whispered, disengaging her hands. She crouched low, her head almost at ground level. The rucksack shifted on her back, wanting to unbalance her as she peeked around the corner. One man was tall, blond hair sticking out from beneath his knit hat. His build was hard to distinguish because of his bulky coat. The other man didn't have a hat, his dark hair blowing to the side in the breeze. He was heavier set, and when he looked toward the town square, she could see his nose was askew, even in profile.

Imogen hadn't seen the face of Ben, the man with Gillian. She'd only heard his voice. One of these men might be him. Her face chilled from the sudden sweat that bathed her body. She clamped down on the fear mushrooming inside her that told her to run and not look back, ever. Not knowing how many of these people she faced didn't matter. The only thing that did was Amy had told her to run from them. She'd do just that and bring these children with her, but she had to be smart about it.

Imogen flinched when a shout rang out, even though it was clearly beyond where the men stood. They turned toward the town square, then jogged out of sight. She looked up and down the street again, then pushed back to a crouch. She held her hands out to the children, looking into their solemn faces.

"We're running straight across the street to the next block. No matter what happens, don't stop. Are you ready?"

At their mute nods, she tightened her grip on their hands. Imogen took a deep breath. Then they broke cover and ran.

CHAPTER 32
MIKE

The muscles of his legs ached, wanting to stretch. He'd glimpsed the truck Clyde and Jay had been driving parked under the cover of the rhododendrons a few thousand feet before the lodge. If he hadn't known where to look, he'd have missed it, which made him feel better about how their hideaway was coming along. The heavy tap of the rain against the windshield was too loud to be white noise, but the swish of the wipers had lulled him almost to sleep. The route Clyde mapped out for them had been circuitous, and now the early November darkness had them in its grip. He'd been in the truck far longer than he liked, but gratitude filled him as Kevin steered the truck around the last bend before the lodge.

"I'm glad we're back," Kevin sighed.

"Me too."

The partially torn-up parking area by the bridge had turned into a mud pit. Large rocks, fuzzy with green moss, had been placed among the turned-over earth like marbles. A decaying, fallen tree lay along the roots of the rhododendrons surrounding the parking area, to be placed later. Mike was unsure about this plan. When finished, it would make loading supplies on the gondola more difficult. Since the gondola wasn't working because of the power failure, it didn't matter right now. He still wanted to get it operational somehow. There were so many supplies to gather. It would take years for this area to grow in enough to hide its original purpose, anyway. Kevin backed the truck in on the undisturbed side of the gravel surface, put the gearshift into Park, and turned off the ignition. "I'm not looking forward to schlepping all this stuff up the steps."

"No rest for the wicked, I guess."

Mike stretched his arms high over his head once out of the truck, his breath frosting as he zipped up his leather jacket. He hadn't noticed that the rain had turned to sleet until now. He tugged at the first tie that held their load of supplies.

Bobbing lights accompanied Clyde and Jeffrey's voices as they made their way down the steps. "How's it going?" Kevin called to them.

They didn't answer until they reached the bridge. Clyde said, his voice tight, "We thought you were the others."

Mike stilled. "They're not back yet?"

"No," Jeffrey said. He pushed the swoop of his brown hair behind his ear. "We thought you were them."

"When did they leave for the library?" Kevin asked.

"About an hour after you did. They should be back by now."

Dread welled up in Mike's throat, choking him. The library was closer than the stores he'd visited today by twenty miles. He said, "No one went to look for them?" Clyde and Jeffrey shared a miserable glance, and Mike regretted his words. "I'm sorry. I didn't mean it like that."

"There's something else," Clyde said. The borderline panic in his eyes chilled Mike to the core. Clyde looked like a worried walrus, his mustache bobbing over his puckering mouth. "On the way back, I realized Jay was drunk. I had to take over driving."

"What?" Kevin barked.

"He was—"

Kevin waved Clyde's answer away. "I heard you, I just—" To

Mike, he said, "I can't believe the balls on that guy. It explains the half-assed job" Mike scrubbed the back of his neck, the urge to find Jay and beat him senseless making his hands shake.

Clyde and Jeffrey looked at them, confused.

Mike forced his fists to unclench. "We went back inside before we left. Kevin had a feeling. There was a lot Jay didn't collect, like most of what Bec had starred as important. It was..." Mike searched for the right word. "Ridiculous. He left cartons of birth control pills and tampons behind, but he cleaned out the condoms."

Clyde looked horrified. "I— he— He said he got everything," Clyde sputtered. "I— We divided up the work at first. Jay said he'd get the meds and other stuff. It made sense he should do the pharmacy since he's a vet." Clyde's eyes begged them to believe him. "When he came and helped me with the food, I thought he'd finished kind of quick, but he's a lot younger than me."

"It's not your fault, Clyde," Mike assured him. "We'll clear this up as soon as I get back from town."

"I'll come with you," Kevin said. "This thing with Jay can wait. I'll get the keys for the other truck since it's already unloaded." He paused, then said to Clyde and Jeffrey, "It is unloaded, right?"

"Wait a minute," Jeffrey said, halting both Mike and Kevin mid-stride. "It's already dark. If you look for them, we have two groups to worry about. What if they're on their way back and you miss them somehow?"

Reluctantly, Clyde said, "I think Jeffrey's right. Bec is in an absolute state. She'll freak out if there are more of you out there. Betty wouldn't want anyone putting themselves in danger."

Clyde looked about to cry. Mike clamped down on his tongue so hard he could taste blood. Trouble was the only reason he could think of that explained why Imogen and the others were still gone. As much as it chafed against every instinct, he knew running off half-cocked was a bad idea.

Mike patted Clyde on the shoulder, knowing it wouldn't be much comfort. Clyde sniffed and swiped at his eyes.

"Let's unload the truck then," Mike said, relenting. "We'll see where things stand then."

AN HOUR LATER, all but the heaviest of the contents in the truck were unloaded. Boxes and bags were stacked in the main room to be sorted and put away or put into storage. Camping lanterns glowed on the kitchen table and the wood slab counter beside it, where Jeffrey and Bec sorted supplies.

Mike glanced up at footsteps on the stairs. Jay stepped into the light cast by the fire and lanterns. Mike could tell at a glance Jay was drunk; his eyes were glassed and droopy, and he walked with exaggerated care. The smile he offered was out of place in the tense atmosphere. "Hello there, all," he said, over-enunciating his words.

"Kevin," Mike said. "You ready to go?"

"Are you sure about this?" Clyde said, but his heart wasn't in it. "If they're stuck, I'm sure they've found a place to hole up."

"Holing up?" Jay said, sounding bewildered, a hint of a slur at the edge of his words. "Where're you going?"

"To find Imogen, Zach, and Betty," Kevin said, shooting Jay a venomous glare. "Something you could have done hours ago if you weren't so goddamned useless."

"What do you mean by that?" Jay said.

Bec stood up from where she'd been sitting beside Jeffrey, her hands balled into fists. Spots of pink appeared on her cheeks, and her mouth worked as if she were trying to bite back a torrent of abuse. She turned on her heel and stormed upstairs.

"I mean you're drunk." Kevin advanced on Jay and jabbed his chest with his index finger. "We spent an hour doing your job instead of being here looking for the others." With a sneer, he added, "You didn't even help Clyde unload the truck."

Jay's face flushed red. "Back off, man," he said, giving Kevin a shove.

To his credit, Kevin didn't shove Jay back. "What if something had happened to you and Clyde?" he demanded. "What if you ran into those guys again and they weren't friendly? You were sitting on your ass getting loaded while the rest of us were working. And when you got back, it never occurred to you to look for Betty and the others. You just kept on drinking."

"I got the things I was supposed to," Jay said, pushing back against Kevin's tirade.

"No, you didn't," Mike said. When Jay opened his mouth, he cut him off. "Don't. Just don't. We don't have time right now. Kevin, let's go."

Clyde looked out the window, anxiety weighing his features down. "That sleet will suck the light from the headlights," he said, mostly to himself.

"All the more reason to go now," Mike said, noting Clyde's wringing hands and the way Jeffrey gnawed his pinky finger.

"I want to find them as much as you do," Clyde said. "But Betty wouldn't want you out in weather like this."

Kevin said, "Let's—"

Bec's heavy footsteps stomped down the stairs. Kevin caught one look at her and stopped talking, which made Mike look, too.

"Jay," she said through gritted teeth.

When he turned her direction, she hurled a small white box at him. He raised his hand to protect his face, but one of its sharp corners hit his brow line with a hard snap.

"Ow! What the hell?" Jay rubbed at his face. Tiny beads of blood speckled a scratch above his eyebrow. A box of o.b. tampons lay on the floor at his feet. Bec stalked toward him like Mike had seen Imogen's lynxes do to one another at the zoo, but they'd been playing. Bec was not.

"First you leave most everything I asked for behind, and then what you do bring is this?"

"What?" Jay said, bewildered.

She put her hands on her hips. "Scented tampons? Really?" Jay looked at her, uncomprehending. Given that they'd just been discussing going into Swedenport to look for the others, Bec's outburst was coming out of left field. "Have you ever smelled these things?" she demanded.

"Of course not," Jay said, looking at her like she'd lost her mind.

Bec scowled at him. She stooped to pick up the box and pulled out a tampon before ripping the wrapper and shoving it in Jay's face. Glaring at him, she said, "Sniff."

Jay flinched away. "I'm not sniffing a tampon."

Bec snorted. "It hasn't been used."

Jay searched the room, the desperation in his eyes begging someone to intervene. Mike was so angry with Jay for not doing his job today that he wasn't sure he'd intervene if a zombie was after him.

"Did you know scented tampons are a thing?" Jeffrey murmured.

Mike, Kevin, and Clyde, all watching the confusing confrontation unfold, subtly shook their heads.

"Who scents a tampon?" Kevin whispered.

Jay sniffed, then scrunched his face as if he'd smelled a skunk.

"Yeah," Bec said, tears pooling in her eyes. "That's what you brought back for us."

Oh, Mike thought, getting it. Bec wasn't upset about tampons. She was, but that wasn't what this was about. She was afraid for their missing friends. By so blatantly ignoring hers and Amy's and Imogen's needs, Jay had made himself an easy target to dump that fear on as anger.

Jay stared at Bec, his eyes comically wide. He blinked like he'd stumbled out of a dark cave into sunshine. Bec's rigid posture softened. Her mouth twisted down, and she bit her lip. Mike could see she was already sorry for her outburst. Bec wasn't fundamentally mean or unreasonable, just upset and hormonal.

"It's just flowery," Jay said, defensive. "It's not, you know… It's just flowery."

The way Bec reared up was like watching one of those blown air dancing tube people used for roadside advertisements. "It's potpourri," she growled. *"Pot-freaking-pourri.* This smells like a funeral parlor on a toxic waste dump."

"You said— You said to get tampons," Jay stammered.

"Which you barely did! And I didn't say *scented.*" Jay looked like a trapped animal searching for a way to flee, but that would mean admitting he was wrong. Bec glowered at him as if he'd farted at an introductory dinner with her parents. "God only knows what crap they used to make them stink to high heaven, and I'm supposed to put them up my hoo-ha for a week? This is what I'm supposed to give to Imogen when she gets back?"

Her voice broke, and she burst into tears. She turned and ran up the stairs, dropping the tampon to the floor. The room fell silent in her wake. Then Jay said, "What a b—"

"Don't you dare," Jeffrey said, advancing on Jay. "Not after what you pulled today, and not about Bec—ever."

The room fell silent again. Mike already liked Jeffrey, but the way he'd just defended his friend raised Mike's opinion of him several notches. Jeffrey shook his head, the disgust on his face absolute, then said, "I want to check on Bec. Are you going or not? If you are, I want to come."

The pounding behind Mike's eyes, which he hadn't noticed so much while Bec was reading Jay the riot act, felt like hammer blows. He knew Clyde was right. It was dark, and the sleeting rain was coming down harder than ever. A section of road leaving the park was washed out, but he couldn't do nothing. "How about we drive to the park entrance?" he said to Kevin and Jeffrey. "If they're coming, we'll see them."

It was a pointless exercise, and he knew it, but he hated feeling so powerless.

"Maybe you should stay here, Jeffrey," Kevin said. "Make

sure no one gets hurt." He jutted his chin at the little library room, where Jay had retreated.

Jeffrey's eyes flashed. He opened his mouth to disagree, Mike was sure, then deflated. "Fine," he said, then added, muttering, "I'll just stress cook."

"Let's go, Mike," Kevin said. He snatched the truck keys from the table by the front door before hoisting his Halligan to his shoulder. Kevin had opened the door before his words registered through the pounding in Mike's head.

"Be careful," Clyde said, the relief in his voice belying his earlier caution.

Mike grabbed his leather jacket and followed Kevin. Anger at Jay roiled just beneath his worry. He couldn't believe how selfish Jay was, and he was not putting up with the crap he'd pulled today. He'd made a promise to himself; he wouldn't break it. Now, more than ever, being surrounded by dependable people mattered. Alcoholics, if that's what Jay was, were unreliable—unless it came to drinking. They'd prioritize drinking over everything else, no matter how well meaning they might be when sober.

The truck rumbled to life as Mike climbed in. Neither man spoke, the tension in the cab feeding off itself. Mike realized he was clenching his fists so hard he had indentations from his fingernails on his palms. He shook them out, only to find them fisted tight a minute later. The grind of his teeth put his nerves on edge, but he couldn't stop. He peered into the darkness, not able to see more than shapes. As Clyde had predicted, the sleeting downpour sucked the light from the headlights. If the temperature dropped much more, the sleet would turn to snow.

"I can't see anything," Kevin growled.

Sleet struck the windshield like bullets. Mike pinched the bridge of his nose, a jab of pain beginning to throb under his eyebrows. He hoped they'd found shelter and were able to stay dry, instead of trudging through the vicious weather, getting colder and wetter by the minute.

"The sign's ahead," Kevin said. His voice was almost flat—resigned. The truck slowed to a halt by the sign welcoming visitors to Cady's Run State Park. Then Kevin said, "Screw it."

He drove past the sign and turned onto the two-lane state highway, picking up speed. Energy that coiled in Mike's body seemed to burst open. They were doing what he'd wanted to do from the start.

Brakes squealed. The truck swerved around a woman in the road. The back end fishtailed, making Mike's head swim.

"Jesus," Kevin cried, fighting for control of the truck.

Finally, the truck stopped. Mike looked out the back window. The woman was running toward them. His eyes widened. "It's Amy." He pushed the door open and almost wiped out on the slick asphalt.

"Mike?" Amy said, fear and hope in her voice. She stopped a step short of him, red-washed in the taillights. "Oh, thank God. Thank God…"

Mike took off his coat and wrapped it around Amy's shivering body. Her teeth chattered like maracas, and mud splattered her drenched clothes from the knees down. Angry, red furrows scratched her face. "Amy, what happened? Where's everyone else?"

Amy's face went slack. "They're not back?"

"No," Kevin said. Mike hadn't even noticed Kevin beside him. "What happened? Why aren't you with them?"

A sob burst from Amy's mouth. "Oh, no… Oh, no!"

Mike placed the back of his hand on Amy's cheek. He'd felt slabs of meat right out of the fridge that were warmer.

"She's freezing," he said to Kevin. "Let's get her back to the lodge and warmed up. She can tell us what happened."

CHAPTER 33
MIKE

They got Amy in the truck, her teeth chattering in counterpoint to her shivering body. She couldn't stop crying. This was not the officious, know-it-all busybody Mike had met at the zoo; her distress was a feast for his fear.

Mike drove this time. It wasn't until the third time the truck almost slid off the slick road that he finally slowed down. By the time they thumped to a halt by the gondola, his hands hurt from his death grip on the steering wheel. Amy could barely walk, so Mike picked her up.

Kevin took off, disappearing into the sleeting darkness. The only light came from cracks in the curtains, and a small square of flickering gold in the door. Amy's shivering body felt like a series of tiny earthquakes against Mike's chest. The steps felt steeper than ever and he forced himself not to rush. Many were uneven, some precarious even when dry. Now slick from the icy rain, he couldn't afford to rush. At the top of the stairs, Amy said, "Put me down. I can make it."

Clyde waited on the porch with a lantern, holding the screen door open. Bec was ready when they got inside, her anger forgotten. She blanched as she took in Amy's appearance, then said, "Come on, Amy. The guys will bring hot water to your room. Let's get you washed up and into dry clothes."

Amy took the arm Bec offered for support. Jeffrey bustled after them with a steaming pot of water. Ten agonizing minutes later, Amy and Bec returned. Tension had tightened the muscles of Mike's shoulders and neck to stone. The pain behind his eyes had gotten worse, a steady *pum pum, pum pum* that got louder the longer the brutal suspense continued.

Amy slumped to the couch, the firelight flickering off her pale skin and blue lips. For a brief second, Mike wondered if they shouldn't let her rest a little. Clyde wrapped a blanket around her shoulders, and Jeffrey pressed a steaming mug of tea into her hands. The tips of her fingers were blue. She must have lost her gloves. Then silence, apart from the hiss and crack of the fire. She gulped the tea, too much at once to judge from the wince before she swallowed.

"We ran into some people as we were leaving, just Betty, Zach, and me," she said, clearing her throat before drinking her tea again. "Imogen had gone back inside. She'd forgotten her flashlight. I warned her to stay out of sight."

Mike's stomach raged like the muddy water overspilling the banks of the swollen creek below. He wasn't sure if this made the situation better or worse.

"I got a bad feeling about them, right from the start." Amy shuddered. "The woman—she said her name was Gillian—was like a shark, and the guy was too friendly, you know? I just— There was something off about how they showed up right when we were leaving."

Mike traded a glance with Kevin, who looked just as unnerved as Mike felt. The men they'd met, Anthony and Jim, had shown up right as they were finishing loading the truck outside the farm supply—as they were leaving.

"I could tell that Zach and Betty felt it, too," she continued. "They started asking where we'd come from and where were we staying, were we nearby? They must have asked four different ways where we were set up."

"Did they say where they came from?" Jeffrey asked.

"They said they were north of Berrigan's Home Improvement."

Mike's breath caught in his throat. Was this a different group from the Safe Zone, or had Jim and Anthony lied to them about where it was, if it existed at all? Was the promise of safety something they used to lure people in? But lure them into what?

"When I pressed them about their location, Gillian said we should just go to Berrigan's," she said, looking from Mike and Kevin. She took another sip of her drink, her hands still shaking. Mike didn't know if it was from cold or shock—probably both. "They said there was a sign, and they checked for people. Maybe they do," she said, shrugging. "But they never answered the question."

"Did they take Betty and the others?" Clyde asked, his voice shaking with anger.

Amy shook her head. "No. I mean, I don't think so. I don't know what happened to Imogen. We had to leave her. Betty told them we were staying with her cousin, near Mina."

Clyde almost moaned. "That's the opposite direction."

Amy nodded. "She didn't want to give away our location. I got pushy about leaving, to get them away from Imogen, so we had to go." Amy looked from one person to another, her eyes beseeching them to understand. "They'd seen books in the truck and car, so we had to take both." At the confused questions, Amy explained about the car they had picked up. "If we left one behind, it would have been suspicious. We were trying to protect Imogen because they didn't know she was there."

Bec took the now empty mug from Amy and took her hands in her own. "We know you were trying to keep Imogen safe."

"A truck started following us about a mile out of town. Betty and Zach were in the truck and they sped up and the truck fell behind. I followed in the car. I don't know the area, and we turned onto this road and stopped. And that's when—" Her voice broke, getting high and squeaky. "That's when Betty told us to leave and go a different way. She said it would get us back here without having to go through town and she would keep going where she'd told them. But that we should… we should go the other way and let you know what had happened."

She started crying, great hiccuping sobs that distorted her speech. "I didn't want to leave them. You have to believe me. Zach said no, he wouldn't leave her. When I said I wouldn't either, Betty shoved me against the car and told me I had to leave before the truck caught up." She rocked back and forth, trembling, holding on to Bec's hands like a lifeline. "So I did."

Clyde patted Amy's shoulder, the room silent but for her weeping and crackling of the fire. "She's a spitfire when she's angry. I know you wouldn't leave them on purpose, hon. We all know that."

Clyde's kindness only made Amy cry harder. Mike clamped down on the scream coiling in this throat. He didn't want her to cry. He wanted her to tell him what had happened.

With an effort, Amy pulled herself together. Bleakly, she said, "I got a flat. I tried to change the tire, but I think the bolts were stripped, so I started walking. I walked for hours. I don't know what happened to them."

"Do you think Imogen is still in town?" Mike asked.

Amy nodded. "She'll find a place to hide. She's smart and good under pressure. I know she doesn't like me and thinks I don't recognize her strengths, but I do. She'll hunker down and wait for help if she can."

"Imogen doesn't dislike you," Bec said, squeezing Amy's hand. "I know she doesn't."

The room went silent once more, except for the crackle and pop of the fire and Amy's sniffles.

Clyde cleared his throat. "Amy needs some food." He looked at Jeffrey, who had become the unofficial chef.

"Crap! I put soup on. I hope it hasn't scorched," he said, hurrying to the kitchen.

Kevin stood up, his shoulders squared. "We have to go look for them."

"No," Mike said, the words slicing his throat like shards of glass. "We need to wait."

"Mike—" Kevin said.

Mike shook his head. "Clyde's right. It's dark and sleeting. If it gets much colder, it'll turn to snow. I want to go as much as you do, but we need to be smart about this. We need a plan."

Kevin frowned, almost quivering from the effort of heeding Mike's advice. "Do you think the guys we met earlier are from the same group?"

"You met people today and didn't tell us?"

It was Jay who'd spoken from the archway of the library. Mike had forgotten he was here. "We told you already, when we came to get you after we ran into those guys who said they were from a Safe Zone. Maybe if you hadn't been drunk, you'd remember."

Mike felt the fight drain out of him and puddle around his feet. Clyde's mustache twitched as his mouth puckered and relaxed in a stutter-stop loop, the tears gleaming in his eyes magnified by his glasses. Jeffrey came back with a bowl of soup. Amy took it from him, balancing the bowl on her knee, but didn't eat. Bec walked to Jeffrey, slipping her arm around his waist and laying her head on his shoulder.

"I didn't want to leave them. You have to believe me," Amy whispered, a quaver in her voice that veered dangerously close to tears. "I swear, I didn't." When she wiped her nose with the back of her hand, Clyde fished in his pocket and gave her a handkerchief.

Mike crouched in front of Amy and looked her in the eye. "I believe you. You did the only thing you could—get back here and let us know what was happening. You couldn't have done any more."

Amy's eyes filled with tears. The pain and gratitude Mike saw in them was almost pathetic, and he wondered what else had happened to her that no one had believed when she'd told them.

"Can you show us the route you took on a map?" Mike asked her. Amy nodded. "We need to decide who's going to town tomorrow and come up with a plan. We—"

Mike's throat closed up, and he turned to the fireplace, gripping the bark of the half-log mantlepiece. It felt like ten years since he'd met Jim and Anthony at the farm supply earlier today. Were they a part of this, or was it just a coincidence? A coincidence seemed impossible—meeting people from two different groups on the same day after seeing no one for so long?—but he couldn't rule it out. Amy said she'd gotten a bad vibe from the people she'd met immediately. That hadn't exactly been the case when he met Jim and Anthony earlier. He'd wondered if they'd been watching them, but the more he thought about it, the more far-fetched that seemed.

Mike's heart raced, refusing to settle down. He had to find Imogen and bring her back. When they'd fled the bridge together, a bond had been forged without him knowing it. Imogen would laugh at him if he told her, but part of saving her then meant keeping her safe now. All he'd had to do was say no, insist that the outings be done one at a time with larger groups of people. But just like the outing when Sandy had been killed, he hadn't.

His chest ached, the pain sharp and bright. What if she was gone? What then? His throat felt so tight he could barely breathe. First Steph and his family, now Imogen. What would he do if he never saw her again? He could slip out after everyone was asleep. He could go into town on his own. He wouldn't be risking anyone else's life and he could—

No, I can't.

Just like he'd told Kevin, he couldn't run off on his own without a plan. There was no margin for error. If they didn't do this right, they might never see Imogen, Betty, or Zach again.

He'd have to wait, feel the dread, and then let it go so it didn't cloud his judgment. He could do that. He *would* do that. He would find Imogen and Betty and Zach. He'd bring them home, where the odds of keeping them safe were in his favor, and he'd never screw up like this again.

CHAPTER 34
IMOGEN

IMOGEN BOLTED UPRIGHT, UNSURE WHERE SHE WAS BEFORE everything flooded back: the library, the strangers, Amy telling her to run, her friends being forced to leave her behind, and finding Billy and Carolyn while fleeing from the library. She looked around the murky storeroom above the yarn shop, crammed with boxes of yarn, knitting needles, and other items the shop sold. Carolyn and Billy lay beside her, curled together in a ball under an afghan that had been on display.

Imogen lay her hand on Carolyn's head. The girl twitched in her sleep, her eyebrows drawing together. "Shhh," Imogen whispered. "It's all right, shhh…"

Carolyn settled back into peaceful oblivion. Imogen eased out from between the children. The building was freezing, so cold she could see her breath. She crossed her arms over herself, already shivering. The floor creaked three steps into crossing to the window. She stopped, wincing, then crept to the front of the building to look out at the street below.

The buildings of town spread out from the town square in tidy blocks at first, then the orderly grid faltered where the terrain became hilly. The buildings looked just as they had yesterday. Apart from being a little neglected—and if you ignored the odd body or abandoned car—she could almost believe it was the early morning hours of a regular day in the world before. The sky was just beginning to lighten, enough that Imogen could see that heavy clouds crowded the horizon.

Imogen sighed, unsure what she should do and having no one to talk it over with. "I bet you're sorry you agreed to this, Mike."

She could only imagine his distress when the others had returned to the lodge without her. There'd be no dimples for days, of that she was sure. She cast aside the drama playing out in her head with a shake. Where she found herself now, and what she was going to do next, needed to be her focus.

Imogen looked out the window in the other direction, away from the town proper. After escaping the library yesterday afternoon, Imogen, Carolyn, and Billy had crept house by house, street by street, until they reached the two-lane state highway that ran along the town's edge. A creek ran alongside the highway. There were bridges across it but Imogen wasn't sure how far away the next one was. There were a few shops in this area— a gas station, an ice cream parlor, a mom and pop diner, and this yarn shop.

The red brick building was two stories, a small house from the late 1800s converted to retail space with a shop on the first floor, an office, storeroom, and a bathroom on the second. The water was off, but they'd still used the toilet. It beat squatting over a bucket or bowl.

Movement farther down the road caught her eye. Hope surged in her breast… It was her friends come to find her, she knew it. She sagged with relief, almost laughing aloud. Then she realized that wasn't it. The way the figures moved was all wrong —the uneven, stutter-stop progress, the way they bumped into one another with little if any reaction. Zombies, perhaps twenty-five.

It was good that they were slow zombies, but it was unnerving that they were so close. They had seen so few zombies since they'd arrived at the lodge, apart from those in the cabins where they'd collected supplies. Now there were zombies coming near, and from the direction she needed to go. She didn't dare walk along the highway. If the people she and her friends had run afoul of yesterday were still around, she couldn't afford to be so exposed.

Maybe I should just wait, she thought.

The little shop seemed safe, unless someone came along. She knew her friends would come looking. What they'd think when they saw she had two children in tow, well... It didn't matter. She had two children in tow and they'd make it work. She just needed to sit tight and stay out of sight and try not to think about the people from the library. Did she remember how to hot-wire a car? She pictured the ignition wires that Mike had touched together to start the cars they'd used in Pittsburgh. She thought so. She'd make it so. She'd need to see if she had a screwdriver in her rucksack and pray that some cars still had batteries with a charge.

"Good Lord, it's always something."

Imogen heard a *thump* below. She froze—not breathing, not moving. She had checked the entire downstairs yesterday, holding her railroad spike at the ready. Nothing had been there —no zombies, no people, no bodies.

Her senses were on high alert and warring with each other. Her instincts told her to hide, to run, but also to investigate. She needed more information. She was up here wondering what had made the noise and jumping to the worst-case scenario. It might just be a box too close to the edge of a display table that had lost its battle with gravity. Whatever it was, she had to go see.

She crept past Carolyn and Billy and into the hallway.

"Hello?"

Imogen froze in place, still as the air after a tempest. Her heart raced, zooming from one side of her rib cage to the other. The muffled voice was downstairs. She backed up when she heard heavy tread on the stairs. The voice called out again, "Hello?"

Was it one of them—the people from yesterday? She strained to hear, to see if she recognized the voice, but they didn't call out again. Her stomach did flip-flops, beating on her insides, insisting they had to run far away—now.

Once through the door to the storeroom, she crouched beside Carolyn and Billy. She put her hand over Carolyn's mouth, then shook her with the other. "Carolyn, wake up."

Carolyn woke with a start, her eyes opening wide and filling with terror. Imogen held her finger to her mouth to show the need for silence, but Carolyn's sudden movement had woken Billy, who cried out.

"Shh, someone's here. We need to be quiet."

Carolyn scrambled to her feet, yanking her brother upright. He blinked, still groggy, but stayed silent as the grave when Imogen explained the situation. She took each child's hand. They'd slip down the hallway to the office at the back, where there was a fire escape. They made it two steps before a man appeared in the door, snow dusting his shoulders and encrusting his boots.

Imogen shoved the children behind her as she backed up. The man's eyebrows shot up in surprise. He held his hands up to show they were empty. "Whoa… We didn't know anybody was here. We don't want any trouble."

Imogen stared at him. It wasn't the voice of the man that she had heard yesterday. That didn't mean he wasn't one of them.

"Jim?" another voice called. "You okay?"

More footsteps on the stairs, then another man appeared. He was shorter than the first man, Jim. When he saw Imogen, all he said was, "Oh."

Imogen didn't know what to do. She'd been prepared to run, but now the only route of escape was blocked.

"Who's this?" the second man said.

"Don't know," the first man said. "I'm Jim," he continued, looking straight at Imogen. "This is Anthony."

Jim was tall and broad, his blond looks All-American—or

Dane. One never knew. "It doesn't matter who I am," Imogen said, her voice shaking. She wished she sounded badass, but she didn't. She sounded frightened. "We were just leaving."

"You're English," Jim said. When she didn't answer, he looked around the room. "You're on your own?" Again, she didn't answer. He shrugged, almost smiling. "Right, none of my business."

He looked to his companion in silent appeal. Anthony said, "We've been scouting around the last week. Shoulda been home yesterday but we ran late after meeting some people and I don't like to drive at night. You can run into a mob of them real easy in the dark." His eyes became vacant, perhaps remembering the day he'd learned that lesson. Then he added, "We saw the yarn shop and thought we'd stop. Our wives knit, you see."

Imogen stayed silent. The men exchanged glances. "Do you need anything?" Jim—the big man—asked.

"I need you to get out of our way. We're leaving," Imogen said, remembering how Amy's rudeness yesterday had worked. Normally, being rude made Imogen's insides crawl, but nothing about this situation was normal.

Instead of scaring the men off, Jim said, "We can give you a ride if you need one. Which direction are you headed?"

Imogen shook her head. She could feel Carolyn trembling behind her. She was trembling, too. Billy whimpered like a frightened puppy. If they wouldn't let her pass, there wasn't much she could do. She had a gun, but drawing it didn't seem like a good option, especially with the children beside her, and either man could overpower her before she could stab them with her railroad spike or knife.

Jim said, "There's a group of them, the creatures, coming down the road if you're going east. Have you seen them? You don't want to be on foot if you're going that way."

Imogen snorted. He had a firm grasp on the obvious. Carolyn tried to shush her brother, to no effect. Imogen glanced over her shoulder and said, "It's all right."

From the corner of her eye, she saw Jim nudge his friend with his elbow. "Maybe we should go. We can try to hit Berrigan's before going home."

Imogen's head snapped up. Her heart raced. The people from the library had talked about Berrigan's. "What do you want there?"

Jim shrugged. "Whatever we can find."

"You're not meeting anyone there?"

The men looked at each other, then Anthony said, "No."

He was lying. She could see it in his eyes. "You're with them, aren't you? Or are you just meeting them?"

"Lady, I've no idea what you're talking about," Jim said.

He sounded genuinely bewildered, but Anthony studied her intently. A heavy ball of anger lodged in Imogen's throat. These men were part of what had happened yesterday. Before she thought better of it, she said, "What did you do to my friends?"

Again, they traded glances. "I don't know what you're talking about," Anthony said.

The metal clang of trash cans being kicked over made Imogen jump. Carolyn cried out in fright, latching her arms tighter around Imogen's waist. Billy's whimpers graduated to crying. The three adults looked to the windows over the street. Anthony took two steps into the room. Imogen pulled her railroad spike from its sheath on her belt.

"Whoa," he said, holding his hands up in front of him. "Easy now. I just want to go look out the window. I won't touch you."

"Damn right, you won't."

"May I?" he said, indicating a path past her.

Imogen kept the railroad spike aloft in front of her. Anthony slipped by, making no attempt to grab them. When he got to the window, he said, "There's one down there, flopping around on the street." He crouched lower. "There are more coming…" He turned to Jim. "Do you think there are any near the Safe Zone?"

"Safe Zone?" Imogen said, then wished she hadn't. The only

Safe Zones she'd heard about had been very early on, and they'd dropped from the grid soon after.

Jim said, "We're from the Safe Zone at the high school in Farwell." Almost under his breath, he added, "Should have started with that."

Could they be from a Safe Zone? "Where's that?" Imogen asked him.

"It's out past Cady's Run State Park," Jim said. "Do you know where that is?"

"I know where it is," she said, trying to keep her voice from trembling. Did the people in this Safe Zone know she and her friends were hiding in the park? "How big is this Safe Zone?"

Anthony said, "Jim, we need to go. It's not too many to get by in the truck but more are behind them. If we need to back-track to get around a larger pack, that could be a long drive." Then to Imogen, he said, "Are you sure you don't want to come with us? It's a good place. The National Guard is in charge. They know what they're doing."

Imogen shook her head. "I'm not going anywhere with you."

Anthony continued to study her, as if troubled by the idea of leaving a woman and children behind. "I'm gonna walk back past you to the door. You won't stab me, right?"

Imogen jutted her chin at the door. "Go on."

"You better look for yourself," Anthony said as he walked by her. "I don't know what direction you're going, but if you're on foot, stay put until they pass." He left the next part—if they passed, not when—unsaid.

Imogen pulled the whimpering children to the window. The zombies she'd seen before were greater in number and closer. Snow fell from the dark clouds now, obscuring her view, leaving her with no idea how many might be out there. The two-lane state highway had no center divider; in a city, it would just be a regular, if wide, street. If she left with the children on foot, they would need to go a few blocks toward the town square to skirt the zombies. That meant venturing closer to the library and anyone who might be lingering there.

Frustration overwhelmed her. She didn't know who these men were. She didn't know if they'd been at the library yesterday or if they didn't know what she was talking about. Was there really a Safe Zone in the area? She bit the inside of her mouth to stop from screaming, because she didn't know anything: who to trust, who to fear, where to go.

No, she realized. She knew one thing. Whether zombies or the people from yesterday, she and the children were not safe here. She just didn't know what the right decision was to *keep* them safe.

Then Jim said, "Are you sure you won't let us at least give you a ride? You don't have to come with us to the Safe Zone but..." He paused, seeming to cast about for the right words. "You seem really scared."

Tears flooded Imogen's eyes, and for a horrified moment she thought she would bawl.

Then Jim added, "I don't feel right just leaving you here, especially with little kids. I have kids, too. If they were out here, I'd want somebody to help them."

Imogen looked at him, searching his face. She saw sincerity in his brown eyes. They were a light brown, almost hazel—nothing like the dark molasses color of Mike's. A wave of want battered her from all sides. She wished Mike were here, more than anything in the world. He'd know what to do. He'd keep her and the children safe, no matter the cost. It was what he did, who he was.

"Jim, we need to go," Anthony said.

Jim nodded. "We're going south till we hit 120. We can drop you anywhere you want, or you can come with us. It's up to you."

Moans drifted down the street from the approaching group of zombies. Indecision crushed Imogen in its unforgiving grip. Should she stay and wait for her friends, knowing there were zombies coming and maybe more on the way? Or should she throw in with these strangers and hope they weren't bad people? She'd always thought that people were good, but now she looked at these men—and the aid they seemed to offer—with suspicion. She would never have looked twice at either of them if she'd run into them at the gas station or the grocery store before this calamity, except to say hello. They would have wished her a nice day, like Americans always did, and gone on their way.

Imogen felt a tug on her jacket. Carolyn looked up at her with frightened eyes. "I want to go."

"I want to go somewhere safe, too," Imogen whispered.

Carolyn shook her head. "I want to go with them. I'm scared here."

Anthony said, "I'm sorry, but we're leaving. If you want to come, you need to decide now."

Imogen looked at Anthony, then out the window. She knew her friends would find them if they could, but what if they couldn't? What if something had happened to them and she and the children were on their own? If she didn't take the help Jim and Anthony offered, it might be a death sentence.

Imogen didn't know what to do, only that she was in over her head. She might as well be at the bottom of the Mariana Trench. But Carolyn wanted to go with them, so…

Am I going to defer to a child?

A burst of protectiveness swelled in Imogen's chest. She couldn't let anything happen to Carolyn and Billy. They had no one. If keeping them safe meant taking a chance with these men, she had to do it.

"We'll take a ride," she said. "I'll tell you when we want to get out."

Anthony smiled, his relief palpable. "Okay. Let's go."

CHAPTER 35
MIKE

Despite the snow that began soon after they set out, Mike had been encouraged by their progress.

Then they reached Route 120.

Zombies roamed the road and the woods. Runners had burst out from a mob wandering across a field with a split-rail fence a mile outside of Swedenport. They'd had to get out fast. Nothing was ever straightforward, however. They couldn't backtrack because they had to stay away from the route to Cady's Run. They didn't want to risk blocking their return. That alone had taken an hour. Mike felt overwound, like he'd run ten miles the day before without bothering to stretch afterward. The pickup truck Kevin drove pulled alongside the curb at the outskirts of Swedenport's residential area and Bec climbed out. Jeffrey got out immediately, but Mike sat for a moment, white knuckles gripping the steering wheel. Everything would be okay, he'd told himself over and over. They would find Imogen here in town, then they'd find Betty and Zach. And then they'd figure out how to deal with the people who'd set this in motion.

He joined the others at the truck's open tailgate. When he looked at Kevin, Mike felt like he was looking in a mirror. Kevin had the same dark smudges below his eyes, the same haggard paleness and exhaustion. But he also had the same grim determination. Bec held the map flat against the uneven metal. Snowflakes dusted the still warm map before melting and dampening the paper.

"The library is a quarter mile ahead, on the left-hand corner." She pointed ahead of them. "I think that building there is the municipal building Clyde told us about. It's yellow brick and three stories, just like he said."

Jeffrey adjusted the rifle over his shoulder and took the lead. Mike turned up the collar of his coat against the cold. The temperature had plunged overnight, frosting everything with a subtle, diamond-like sheen in areas sheltered from snowfall. The rest had a frosting of white already several inches deep. Even wearing an extra sweater, scarf, and a dark knit cap, the cold seeped into the marrow of Mike's bones.

Two minutes later, they were well into the town proper. It didn't look that bad. Fading evacuation notices promising shelter in a Safe Zone were stapled to telephone poles. They buttressed the story Jim and Anthony had told yesterday, but Mike was unswayed; he knew they were mixed up in this somehow. Plastic bags littered the gutters, weighed down by the snow, and were tangled in the spiny limbs of jagger bushes. Mike's agitation was so great he barely noticed the litter. The houses in the town's center were built between the early eighteen hundreds and the late nineteen thirties. They ranged from the spare lines of Federalist farmhouses to Sears Craftman kits. The older homes were right on the street. The newer homes were set back to accommodate small porches, from a time when people used them to socialize with their neighbors.

Jeffrey picked up a crinkled flyer from the gutter. "These evacuation flyers for a Safe Zone are everywhere. It backs up what those guys said."

"Yeah, maybe," Kevin said, but he sounded reluctant to agree.

"Maybe that's why we've seen hardly anyone," Bec said. "If rural areas had more time to evacuate."

"Maybe we keep our minds on what we're doing," Mike said, more sharply than he meant to, but it stopped the speculation. He didn't care what had happened here before yesterday. All he cared about was finding Imogen and the others.

They slowed as they approached the square. Mike searched for anything that might indicate Imogen was hiding in one of the buildings they passed—a broken window or lock, snow brushed out of the way in front of a closed cellar window. The only broken doors he saw were still ajar. Imogen would have closed an open door to keep zombies out.

They skirted the wide steps that led to the imposing brass and glass front doors of the municipal building, opting to search along the side for a less conspicuous entrance. Kevin stopped at a side door and looked it over. Then he slipped the adze of his Halligan between the door and the jamb and pulled. A loud crack followed five seconds later, a smile lightening the exhaustion on Kevin's face.

"That was fast," Bec said.

Kevin nodded. "Can't be slow when you're fighting a fire."

Bec and Jeffrey followed Kevin, lights glowing from their headlamps. Mike stepped into the darkness after them, his breath frosting more heavily than outside before swirling away into the dark. Their footsteps echoed off the wide hall and high ceiling. Mike shivered, but not from the cold. All night he'd been plagued by scenarios of what had happened to everyone. Entering this dark, abandoned building felt like crossing a tripwire and setting in motion an inevitable and terrible outcome. What fate had Betty and Zach driven into? Had they continued to be followed after Betty made Amy leave? Had they been taken captive, or something worse? He shuddered with an involuntary hiccup of his shoulders. Clyde had looked ten years older this morning, frail and diminished. He put up a good front, but Mike could see his advocacy for a cautious response weighed on him. It weighed on Mike, too.

A feeling of inevitability—of doom—flared for a moment,

like a flame when logs in a fire are stirred. Mike second-guessed everything he'd done the past twenty-four hours. Why had he agreed to Imogen going to the library when he couldn't go with her? It wasn't like he was her dad, or even her boyfriend, but what the hell had he been thinking? She was a grown woman who could make her own decisions, but he should have tried harder to persuade her to wait for him. So what if the apocalypse was turning him into a mansplainer? It was better than Imogen going missing, or worse. He should have tried to… He didn't know what, but he should have tried.

"Stairs ahead," Kevin said, speaking softly.

Mike's scalp prickled under his knitted hat when they entered the stairwell, which was even more frigid than the hallway.

"I'm going to freeze to death before a zombie gets me," Bec muttered.

They paused at the bottom of the stairs, waiting for any sound or movement that might indicate zombies. Soon, all that echoed off the walls were their footsteps and the bobbing lights of their headlamps. The dark, quiet building felt like a sepulcher, a repository for things long dead. Just like their friends, the world this building had been built for was gone.

When they reached the roof, Kevin tried the door with a push from his Halligan. But it wasn't locked, as they'd expected, and instead flew open, sending him stumbling forward. A second later, a blur of motion swept him from view like a leaf on the wind. Bec and Jeffrey bolted after him, Mike on their heels. As he stepped over the threshold, a zombie's cold grip closed around his shoulder. Instinctively, he pulled away, slamming against the open door. It didn't budge; it must have hit a back stop. Mike ducked toward the stairs, trying to break free. The zombie followed. It caught his collar at the same moment his toe caught on the threshold. With the zombie at his back, still clutching his collar, they fell through the doorway.

Mike threw out his arms, flailing to stop the fall. Gravity

pulled and panic exploded, engulfing all rational thought, because if he fell, that was it. He'd break the zombie's fall on the stairs, where it would kill him if the fall didn't. Darkness, the damp smell of concrete, rot and snarls, and clutching fingers surrounded him like the maelstrom of a tornado. His knee hit metal, cold steel fire exploding the joint. But it slowed his fall just enough that he caught the rail. He felt a yank on his wrist as the zombie sailed over him. He slammed face-first into the concrete wall as he half fell, half slid onto the stairs. The muddy taste of blood filled his mouth, his bottom teeth rubbing on the cut they'd just made on the inside of his lip. He pushed off the wall, a lower tooth wiggling when he spat out blood.

On the landing, the zombie growled. Its headfirst fall hadn't done the job. Mike pulled upright, using the handrail. Limping on his throbbing knee, he reached for the zombie. He didn't turn it over to see who it had been—a mother, a father, a young person just starting out on life's journey. Instead, he shoved the knife in the space between the last spinal vertebrae and skull.

Mike squinted as he emerged from the stairwell, scanning the roof. Several zombies were down, and his friends were up. "You okay?" Bec asked, trotting over to him.

Mike nodded and shook out his arm. A gob of something he'd rather not think about from inside the zombie's skull flew off the end of his knife.

"What were they doing on the roof?" Jeffrey said, then asked, "Is everyone okay?"

Mike didn't answer as he wiped his knife with a rag he kept in a pocket. His attention was on the town as he walked to the edge of the roof. The snow continued to fall, thick, heavy flakes in a race to the bottom, coming down much heavier than when they'd entered the building minutes ago. His knee throbbed, but not as much as he'd expected.

The library was in the lower left corner of the town square, with a church on the next corner. The rest of the buildings around the square were shops and restaurants, a post office. The park in the center looked like the set for a holiday romance. Mike didn't care about any of that. There was nothing around the library that indicated anyone was there. Any clues were being buried under the snow. He ground his teeth, an impotent fury building inside him, its low hum vibrating as it grew.

"Stupid snow," Bec said, sounding peevish. Mike knew she still wasn't feeling well, but she'd been determined to join them. "Let's split up the square and go building to building. We're wasting time here."

Kevin said, "Me and you, Jeffrey and Mike?"

Bec and Jeffrey agreed, but Mike was too preoccupied to answer. He studied the street beyond the library where Amy said they'd parked the pickup and car. That was the direction they'd go if they couldn't find Imogen.

No. That's where we'll go after we find her.

"Bec and Kevin take this side of the square. We'll take the other," Jeffrey said. He turned toward the stairs, then stopped. "Crap."

Mike turned from the square. Zombies stumbled down the two-lane highway that ran alongside Cady's Run, the same creek that ran below the lodge.

"Where are they coming from?" Kevin said.

Mike looked farther up the highway, squinting to see through the heavy snow. Farther down the road, a slow-moving mass crawled over a two-lane bridge spanning the creek. There were too many trees, the falling snow too heavy, to see beyond the bridge except the zombies being funneled over it.

"We should move the trucks to the other side of the square," Kevin said.

Jeffrey groaned. "We won't have enough time to search the square. We'll get cut off."

Mike could feel the tension crackling from one person to the next, their collective fear feeding off itself. "We can't leave her," Mike snapped, more hostile than he'd intended. He took a deep breath, trying for a more even tone. "If you guys want to go, I understand, but I'm not leaving until I find Imogen."

"I'll check the square again," Bec said, as moans reached them, the sound drifting through the velvety snowflakes. Not ten seconds later, Bec cried, "I think I see her!"

Mike reached her almost instantly, following the line of her pointing hand. Along the two-lane state highway, five figures walked quickly to a dark pickup truck. The leader was large—a man—followed by a woman and two children holding hands. A shorter man brought up the rear. A faint bleep just loud enough to hear, followed by the lights of the pickup glowing to life. The woman turned her head. Mike's breath caught in his throat when he saw the buckeye-brown oval of Imogen's face.

"It's those guys," Kevin said, turning to Mike. "In the F-350."

Mike couldn't tell the truck's color, because everything he saw looked red. Rage erupted from deep in his belly, engulfing him, as it all clicked into place. The men from the farm supply were part of the group from the library and now they had Imogen. If Jim and Anthony had kids with them, Imogen would be more likely to trust them. How long had these people known they were in the area? Did they know where the lodge was? Had they been stalking them all this time?

Mike yanked the door to the stairs open, barely feeling its weight, and plunged into the darkness. The sons of bitches were not spiriting Imogen away right in front of him. She was not disappearing into the swirling snow, her smile slowly fading from memory. Mike hadn't come to find her, only to lose her.

Not today.

Not ever.

CHAPTER 36
IMOGEN

The tongue of the seat belt over Imogen's lap slid into the buckle with a *click*. Billy scrambled onto the back seat of the truck's club cab and sat in the middle, followed by his sister. Imogen fastened Billy's seat belt, then reached over and squeezed Carolyn's knee. She smiled at the girl, who had managed her own seat belt with the quiet competence of an older sibling. She glanced at Jim, who was driving. This truck was much bigger than the two pickups from the zoo and the home improvement center, and even Clyde's. Imogen had needed the handhold to hoist herself up, while Anthony gave the children a boost.

Heat blasted from the vents. The warm air on her face was the best thing Imogen had experienced in the last twelve hours. Anthony pulled his door shut and the truck pulled onto the highway, away from the mob of zombies coming over the bridge. Snow swirled, falling fast and heavy, the mob behind them soon an indistinct smudge.

Jim and Anthony were doing their best to make her and the children feel comfortable. Imogen had noticed the rifle butt resting on the console between the front seats. The end of the barrel pointed down, under the dashboard. It made her uneasy, but they'd made no move to disarm her. Maybe all of this was a trick, an elaborate ruse to lull her into thinking she was safe, but she couldn't worry about that right now. She'd made her decision. If it turned out to be the wrong one, she would deal with it.

"I don't like this snow," Jim said. He paused, then caught her eye in the mirror. "Are you comfortable back there? I can turn up the heat. You must be cold after spending the night in that building."

Imogen tightened her arm around Billy. She hoped it made him feel secure because she felt anything but. "We're fine, thank you."

Oh God, what have I done? Then she scolded herself. *You've made your decision. Trust that it will be okay.*

Soon Billy slumped against her, the heat and relative safety of the truck allowing sleep to pull him under. The snow spiraled down, white fluff tumbling from the sky as if shaken from a box of feathers. Jim turned the windshield wipers to high but they were not quite up to the task. No sooner would they clear the windshield than snow blanketed it with white again. He switched on the headlights and used the brakes to slow down.

"Don't want to slide off the road. Then we'll be in it," he said, more to himself than her or Anthony. He looked straight ahead, his eyes squinting as he concentrated on the road ahead of him. "I know you don't want to say where you're from, and that's fine. I know there are cabins in the state park."

Imogen's stomach lurched. A bolt of fear tensed her body. Jim glanced at her in the mirror, perhaps hoping to see if she'd reacted, but she kept her face impassive. At least, she hoped so.

"We were coming from Scranton and Heather, that's my wife, she had friends when she was a girl who had a place in the park, built before it became state land. Anyway, we decided we try for a cabin but then we ran into people headed for the Safe Zone. That sounded better to us, so that's what we did."

"If you and your family are safe, it sounds like you made the right decision," Imogen said, noncommittal. She thought Jim was talking so much because he was nervous.

"I still can't believe this is happening sometimes, you know?"

Imogen did. That feeling of stunned dislocation, as if she were dazed from a car crash, was tangled up in anxiety, too, for she'd backed herself into a corner. Jim lapsed into silence, apparently needing all his concentration to drive. Anthony said little. He trained his attention on the road, pointing out potential hazards to Jim. Carolyn had fallen asleep, too, in the warmth of the truck's efficient heating. The small furrow in her brow had smoothed out. Noticing the small change sent a flood of tenderness spilling over the edges of Imogen's heart, one she knew would always be particular to these children she barely knew.

Jim began to talk again, about his wife and children, about life in Scranton. He'd driven a truck, making deliveries for United Parcel Service. His wife had been the receptionist at a dentist's office. "It wasn't anything fancy, but it was enough. We were happy."

His voice broke on the last—on happy—and Imogen couldn't help but feel for the man. If he had ulterior motives, he was putting on one hell of a performance. The more he talked to her, the more she felt that wasn't the case.

Anthony twisted in his seat toward Imogen. "Are you sure you won't come with us? You shouldn't go out in this storm, especially with little ones."

There was genuine concern in his eyes. She wanted to take him up on his offer, but what if she never saw her friends again? Imogen looked at the sleeping children. Should she let them take Billy and Carolyn? Did she trust them enough to let the children go with them?

"What the..." Jim's eyebrows were drawn close in the reflection of the rearview mirror. "Someone's following us. Or behind us, anyway."

Imogen twisted in her seat, trying not to jostle Billy, and looked out the truck's back window. The vehicle was a ways behind them, the twin pinpricks of its headlights struggling to pierce the falling snow.

"That's got to be my friends," Imogen said, elation and relief surging through her. She felt light-headed. It had to be them, because who else would be out in this weather? Mike had come looking for her, maybe with Kevin and Bec. That meant the others had made it back safely to tell what had happened at the library. The knot of worry in her gut since Zach, Betty, and Amy had left yesterday loosened and unwound. "Pull over so they can catch up."

Jim didn't speed up, but the truck didn't slow down. "I don't know. You thought we were with the people you had a run-in with yesterday. What if it's them?"

Her relief and elation fizzled. In her excitement, she hadn't been thinking clearly. Whoever was in that vehicle could be the people she'd encountered yesterday. But what if Jim and Anthony were those people, sowing doubt in her mind to fool her?

Anthony gripped the butt of the rifle between them. "Stop the truck. I'll get in the back."

"No!" Imogen cried. "They might be my friends."

But the truck was slowing down, stopping a moment later. Anthony grabbed the rifle as he opened his door. He was out of the cab and jumping into the bed before she could say more, the truck resuming course.

The cab had become very warm, but the sweat that coated Imogen's body had nothing to do with the heat. She twisted in her seat again. The truck following them was gaining ground while dread and hope fought a pitched battle in her heart. Then her breath hitched. An untethered feeling of drift from the rear of the truck made her stomach clench.

"Whoa, it's getting slippy." Jim said. He turned the steering wheel into the slide. The unmoored feeling ceased as the tires found purchase again on the snowy road.

Imogen wiped condensation from the window, the glass cold under her fingertips, for she'd taken off her gloves. She squinted, trying to see the side mirror. A second set of headlights appeared, making two vehicles following them, the closer still gaining ground. Jim checked his rearview mirror, his brow furrowed and eyes pinched with anxiety. The engine revved and they picked up speed.

"What's happening?"

Carolyn's voice was heavy with sleep but tinged with anxiety. She'd already picked up on the tension. Imogen reached over Billy to touch the girl's cheek. "Everything's okay."

Carolyn looked at her, disbelieving. Imogen wanted to say more, but she didn't believe what she'd said. What was the point of telling the child more lies that wouldn't comfort her?

Headlights flicked on and off behind them, like wintry, earthbound fireflies. The truck again started sliding. Carolyn cried out in fright and Jim said, "It's okay, honey. It's just a little slippy sometimes."

"My mom went slow in the snow," Carolyn whispered.

Jim traded a glance with Imogen in the mirror, one that said, *I want to go slower, but I'm afraid.* Did that mean Jim and Anthony were not part of the group that they'd encountered yesterday? Or were they afraid of dealing with her people?

Anthony thumped on the window. Snow clung to his knitted hat, a heavy accumulation on his shoulders. "They're gaining," he shouted. His voice sounded like it was at the bottom of a well. "Keep going or stop?"

Jim pointed forward. Anthony nodded. The truck's engine revved, centrifugal force shifting them from side to side with every bend. Imogen held her breath on the next gentle bend in the road. She realized she didn't know where they were or how far they'd gone. Everything looked so different blanketed in snow, and it was snowing so hard it was difficult to see. Had they passed where she'd planned to ask them to let her out? How crazy was she for wanting them to in this weather with two small children?

Imogen watched the speedometer creep up: thirty-five, forty,

forty-five. "You're going far too fast. We'll slide off the road if you don't slow down!"

A crack penetrated the sound-dampening effects of the swirling snow, loud enough to make everyone jump. "Did they just shoot at us?" Jim said.

Imogen's heart pounded as adrenaline spiked her pulse. "It will be all right," she whispered, reaching for the children, but her voice was shaking. "Slow down," she said to Jim.

"They're shooting at us," he countered.

From the corner of her eye, Imogen saw movement. Anthony, moving in the truck bed. She twisted around to get a better look, wanting to reach through the glass to push the swirling snow out of the way. Anthony had the rifle in one hand. He braced himself against the tailgate on one knee. He was going to shoot at the truck behind them.

Imogen pounded on the window. "No! Stop it! No!" The sharp report of Anthony's rifle cracked the hush of the snowy landscape. "Stop! They might be my friends. Jim, you've got to stop this. Someone's going to get hurt."

The trucks behind them had pulled abreast of one another. Even though Jim had slowed down a little, the truck slid again. The children cried out as the truck swerved, its mass carrying them without direction from the driver, before Jim got it under control.

"Dammit," Jim said, his voice shaking, sweat beading on his forehead and trickling down his temple. Six inches of snow had fallen in the last twenty minutes. What had begun as a storm was turning into a blizzard.

"Jim, you've got to stop."

The headlights reflected off a bright-yellow sign with a thick line that seemed to turn ninety-degrees to the left. Imogen couldn't be sure, for the right side of the sign was snow-covered from an off-kilter post, but she still said, "Jim, please slow down. There's a turn ahead."

He didn't. Imogen tensed, reaching over for the children as

they slalomed through the turn. She braced herself for the feeling of weightlessness that would mean they were sliding, but it didn't happen.

Jim sighed and turned the wheel straight. The truck didn't follow. A blur of snow was followed by another flare of bright yellow before the truck careened off the road. It listed down and left, thumping over the berm. They kept sliding, jerking and jostling, until the truck stopped with a sharp, sudden jerk and a hollow grind of metal.

"Imogen?" Carolyn said, tears in her voice over Billy's howl of fear.

"Are you okay?" Jim said, sounding shaken.

Imogen squeezed Carolyn's shoulder. "I'm here, Carolyn. Billy, it's okay. Are you all right?"

"I don't know," he whimpered.

"Oh, God, Anthony," Jim said, sounding dazed. He pushed on his door. It resisted, then opened with a groan. "Don't get out of the truck," he said. "I'll deal with whoever they are."

"Wait!" Imogen cried, but he was already lost to the raging storm.

She was finished deferring to Jim. If it was her friends following them, they'd never shoot at people they didn't know, not without provocation. Maybe it hadn't been a gunshot; maybe the crack had been something else. Whatever the case, she wouldn't leave Jim to handle the situation. He was armed—she'd seen his pistol. She didn't want anyone else to be hurt.

"I have to go," she said to the children. Their pinched faces begged her not to leave them. "Stay here. I'll be right back."

"No!" Billy clutched Imogen's arm. She pulled, but his grip was like Super Glue.

"I'm scared," Carolyn wailed.

"Stop it!" Imogen felt as heartless as her parents had once seemed to her. Tears streaked Billy's and Carolyn's faces, their terrified eyes twisting her heart. "It might be my friends. I have to make sure no one gets hurt. I'll be right back. I *promise.*"

She wrenched her arm from Billy's grip and opened the door. Wind swirled the snow around her, sending plump, heavy snowflakes into the truck. Imogen stepped out and tumbled to the ground, unprepared for how high the truck now sat. She slid a few feet down the side of the ditch, scrabbling in the snow to stop herself. For a fleeting moment, she wondered if she was more shaken from the crash than she'd thought.

Snow slid down the collar of her coat, the icy crystals melting on her neck and sliding down her back. She got to her feet, trying to get her bearings in the riot of swirling white. She climbed back to the truck, jumping to push the door shut, and struggled through the deepening snow.

CHAPTER 37
MIKE

"I'll murder the sons of bitches."

Mike's teeth ground so hard his jaw ached while the snow sheeted down like rain. He gripped the steering wheel like a lifeline. Bec sat beside him, tension filling the space between them.

He fought to keep his mind on driving. By the time they'd run to their trucks to make chase, Imogen had been forced into the F-350 and it was long gone. He hadn't counted on so much snow, though he should have. The clouds had hung low and dark in the sky since he'd woken. By the time they caught up enough to see the glow of the red taillights ahead of them, the storm had almost whipped into a whiteout. The wind howled. Gusts rocked the truck. At least ten inches of snow blanketed the ground with last night's snowfall. The road was getting more slippy, but Mike didn't slow down. He was too afraid they might disappear into the storm. The engine responded to the press of his foot on the accelerator, cranking out more horses.

"Mike, you're going too fast."

He didn't bother to glance at Bec, despite the tension in her voice. She was right but that wasn't why he didn't look. He couldn't stand to see her pursed mouth, knitted eyebrows, and the steely determination in her blue eyes—every one of them reminders of how badly he'd screwed up.

"We can't let them get away."

"They won't, unless we slide off the road and get stuck."

"I'm not slowing down." Instead, he pressed the pedal harder.

Bec snorted, exasperated. "You can't save them by being stupid!"

She was right. If the truck ahead of them hadn't turned on its headlights in an almost vain attempt to see through the falling snow, they wouldn't even know where they were. But rationality had taken a back seat to the desperate anger coursing through Mike's veins that filled him with volcanic heat. All he could think about was what might be happening to Imogen and how he'd let her down. What if they tied her up and a bunch of zombies came along? She'd be dead, worse than dead... she'd be—

Stop it.

"Stop what?"

"Nothing," he said, realizing he'd spoken aloud.

The windshield wipers swished back and forth like a metronome set to double allegro. The squeak grated his nerves like a cheese grater slicing knuckles. He glanced in the rearview mirror. Kevin was keeping up, though he and Jeffrey were probably cursing him. The taillights of their quarry glowed brighter as they closed in. Mike squinted. They had been gaining on the truck, but now they weren't.

"He's going faster," Mike growled.

"Of course he is. You're chasing him." The steering wheel didn't respond when Mike adjusted direction for the gentle curve. The helpless sensation of drift replaced the grip of the tires. "We're sliding, Mike!"

He resisted the temptation to jam on the brakes, instead turning the steering wheel into the swerve and gently depressing the brake. The pulse of the antilock braking traveled through the pedal to his foot.

"We're going off the road," Bec cried.

Mike gritted his teeth, adrenaline thrumming. The truck wasn't responding. They were already in the oncoming lane and heading for the ditch. Panic flooded his brain, tightening his throat and making him dizzy. He'd blown their only chance to save Imogen.

Then the wheels caught and the truck corrected.

"For Christ's sake, slow down!" Bec implored. "Flash the lights on and off at them. They must think we're going to hurt them if we catch up."

He didn't see how flashing the lights would make them more amenable to slowing down or stopping but he did as she asked. Anything that might help, he would try. He twisted the turn signal indicator and the lights strobed into the storm. They were gaining on the truck again. The skidding back end of the truck behind them pulled his attention to the rearview mirror, but it recovered almost immediately. Maybe Bec was right and they should keep following at the same pace, keeping the truck in sight without trying to overtake it.

The headlights behind them flashed.

"What are they doing?" Mike said, more to himself than Bec.

Bec twisted around to look through the back window but Kevin and Jeffrey had pulled around them into the oncoming lane; the two trucks were almost abreast. She rolled the window halfway down. Kevin's voice reached them, muffled, like he had three scarves wrapped around his mouth. "Slow down or pull over."

"He won't stop," Bec shouted back.

A sharp crack split the blinding storm. Mike startled, jerking the steering wheel, almost sending the truck into a slide. A massive branch at the side of the road had split away from a tree, thumping into the snow. Then another, much sharper crack followed. A hollow, metallic *ping* above Mike's head raised the hair on his neck. "Did they just shoot at us?"

Bec had ducked, and now raised her head to peek over the dashboard. "I don't know," she said, sounding shaken. Kevin and Jeffrey had fallen back. Mike pressed harder on the gas. "Mike, will you stop? If they're shooting at us, we don't want to get closer!"

The truck ahead took the next curve far too fast. Mike's heart felt like it was collapsing in on itself like a dying star. The F-350 slid, turning sideways, heading for the ditch like the driver meant to go that way. Time slowed. Mike watched the F-350 slide. The brake lights flared to no effect. Then it almost seemed to fly, like a skier over a jump, before pitching off the road sideways into the ditch.

"No," Bec cried, her voice tight with fear.

Mike hit the brakes, the antilock braking—and luck—all that kept them from sliding, too. The wind howled like a banshee, snow blowing in all directions. Mike's heart thundered, almost pounding its way through his rib cage. If they didn't have their seat belts on—

Their own truck slid.

"Crap," Mike said, fighting with the steering wheel to keep them on the road. They skidded to a halt thirty feet behind the crashed truck, their front left tire slipping off the edge of the pavement.

The back right tire of the truck that had crashed spun in the air like a top. Mike shoved the door open and ran into the white-out. He shouted for Imogen, but the storm drowned out his cries. The snow gave underfoot, yielding to his weight. The wind took a breath, while the sheeting snow fell from the sky like a conquering army. Mike heard the faint *ding* of an open door indicator chime.

"Imogen!"

A shape approached him, appearing like an apparition made solid. "Mike?"

Relief flooded through him when he heard the clipped British accent. Nothing had ever sounded so good. He slid to a stop, almost knocking Imogen over before pulling her close. "Are you okay?"

He needed to let her go, to see if she'd been hurt, but his body wouldn't comply. He was surprised again at how small she was as he held her against him. Connection to the people he cared for was so fragile, especially now. If he let go of her, it might break.

"Thank goodness you're here," she said. "I was so frightened."

He wanted to ask her more so she'd answer, so he could hear her voice and know this was real. Mike forced himself to let her go, a pitched battle raging between his arms and his brain. The contrast of the falling snow's only purpose seemed to be directing his attention to Imogen's face. Snowflakes balanced on her eyelashes and frosted her long hair peeking out from under her knitted cap. Mike stared at her, almost stunned. Then he came back to himself, to the cold, the danger, their adversaries. "Are you okay? Did they hurt you?"

"No, nothing like that," she said.

Bec reached them, crying out in relief. "Imogen!"

"We have to get the children," Imogen said. "And see if Jim and Anthony are okay."

"Children?" Bec asked, her confusion plain as Kevin's and Jeffrey's voices neared.

All Mike heard were the names.

Jim and Anthony.

Shock waves rolled through his body. His blood pressure skyrocketed, temples pounding in time to the hammer of his pulse. He'd known. He'd known it as soon as Kevin pointed out the truck. It was the men they'd met earlier. The men he'd been suspicious of, but not enough. He hadn't recognized the threat, and he'd almost lost Imogen because of it.

"Help!"

The voice came from the crashed truck, desperation palpable. A heavy hand landed on Mike's shoulder. He jerked around, alarmed. Kevin glared at him, his eyes narrowed. He looked like a Viking who wanted Mike's head on a pike. "Don't be stupid. I mean it."

Mike nodded. When Kevin let go, he charged, floundering and stumbling, slipping down the slope of the ditch toward the voice. A figure materialized in the swirling snow, as if from the ether—a man, bending over another man crumpled on the ground. He looked up, his eyes meeting Mike's. His knitted hat was pulled low on his head, but Mike recognized the light-brown eyes and the blond scruff of beard.

It was the big guy, Jim.

Mike vaulted forward, the fear and helplessness of the endless night of waiting fueling his wrath. He barreled into Jim, hitting him square in the chest like a linebacker intent on murdering his opponent. They tumbled over the man on the ground, landing with a muffled *whump*. Mike cocked his arm back, acting on instinct. His fist connected with Jim's face, though his gloved hand softened the blow.

"I'll kill you," he shouted, unable to land the blows fast enough. Then hands were on him, and people between them. He struck out, only registering Imogen in front of him at the last moment. He barely pulled the punch short.

"Stop it," Imogen cried. "They were helping us. Stop this, Mike. Stop it right now."

A tremendous gust of wind howled into the ditch, pushing against his back so hard Mike stumbled. Jeffrey grabbed his elbow to help him regain his balance. "We saw them force you into the truck."

"They were helping us, giving us a ride!" Imogen glared up at him, the freezing wind and icy snow flakes no match for the heat in her voice.

"Us?" Kevin asked.

"I found some children."

Jeffrey gave Jim a hand up. Kevin dropped to his knees beside the man in the snow, who almost looked like a snow-covered log.

Kevin removed his glove and pressed his fingers to the man's throat, then pulled back the man's eyelid. "His pulse is strong but he's out. And he's freezing. We need to warm him up." He squinted up at Imogen and Jim. "Was he in the back of the truck?"

Imogen nodded. "Yes. I'll leave him to you? I need to collect Carolyn and Billy."

"Let's get him to the truck," Bec said. "If we can find the truck."

Mike tried to catch up, thrown by the turn of events. He'd been sure they had kidnapped Imogen, but she said that wasn't the case. Was it possible to get Stockholm syndrome overnight? Who were these kids, and where had they come from?

Get a grip and help her.

Imogen disappeared into the swirl of snow at the crashed truck's tailgate. Kevin and Jeffrey were lifting the injured guy.

"Jeffrey," Bec shouted from the crest of the slope beside the road, almost invisible. "This way."

And then she was gone, spirited away in a blur of motion.

CHAPTER 38
MIKE

Mike heard Bec's yelp, shot through with fear. She hadn't been spirited away but knocked down. Bec rolled on the ground, snow flying around her as she struggled with—

Zombies, he realized. Runners. Somehow the mob they'd seen in town had caught up with them despite the storm. Mike ran up the slope, but Jeffrey had a head start. Jeffrey reached the road and dove for Bec, who thrashed under the creature upon her.

Another blur raced by. Behind him, Imogen shrieked. Mike floundered through the deep snow to find Imogen pinned against the truck, her face pressed against the glass of the passenger door window. Terrorized screams from the children inside the truck were muffled by the closed door and howling wind. He fumbled under his heavy coat for his belt and the knife sheathed on it. The runner—three times her size—pressed Imogen against the window while trying to bite her neck. Mike lunged, sliding, his gorge rising with fear of seeing blood blooming bright red against the snow. He grabbed the runner's long hair in his hand and yanked it away, but Imogen was pulled along with it, the collar of her coat between its teeth. The runner barely noticed Mike. He stepped in close and drove the knife deep at the base of its skull.

Then he was on the ground, the air knocked out of him. Snow filled his nose and mouth and stung his skin. A runner lay atop him, two hundred pounds if it was an ounce. The reek and rot assaulted his nose, even through the snow stuffing his nostrils.

The sharp snap of teeth at his ear sent Mike thrashing. But his fingers closed on nothing. His knife had been knocked from his grasp. The runner shifted position and lunged. It saved Mike's life, for he managed to scramble out from under it. He burrowed his hand through the snow, searching until his fingers brushed something solid—the hilt of the knife. He clutched it and lurched to his feet, turning to face the zombie. It reared onto its knees and vaulted, knocking Mike flat on his back. The knife slipped, but his icy grip managed to hang on. As the zombie fell upon him, Mike jammed his knife into its eye.

Gray, viscous liquid and black zombie blood poured from the zombie's ruined eye. Mike turned his head to the side and felt the splatter against his neck and hat. He squirmed free, pushing the zombie away. Imogen grappled with another runner. Through the howl of the wind, he heard shouts and screams.

Mike could hear but not see his friends fighting the runners on the road. Then another came at him, so fast he couldn't get out of the way. It knocked him to the ground. A thunder bolt of pain shot up his spine. He scuttled away again, scrambling to his feet, and caught the runner from behind to deliver the killing blow. But the runner lurched back and stood up, dragging Mike along. He let go and shoved. The soft flab under his hands felt like jelly. The runner tumbled away, deeper into the ditch, landing against something hard with a sickening thud. It didn't get back up.

He found Imogen at the truck. She jumped, trying to reach the back door of the club cab from the passenger side. This side of the truck was on the high side of the ditch, the door at an awkward angle. As Mike took a step toward her, he hesitated, looking back at the runner. It wasn't wearing a coat, nor any clothing that would keep it warm outdoors. The person this runner used to be had been inside, in a place he thought was safe.

The truck door opened with a metallic creak. Jarring screams of small children filled the air. Mike turned from the runner for the truck. A small child huddled in the snow by the back tire. Imogen had climbed onto the running board, leaning inside the cab from her waist.

His stomach clenched when he reached her. Imogen had a second child by the shoulders of his jacket. A runner climbing through the open back door below had the child by the ankle. He shrieked and twisted, his terrified screams filling the cab.

Mike sidled inside the door around Imogen. Leaning inside, he caught the child's right forearm in his left hand.

"Billy, I've got you," Imogen cried, but desperation muddled her voice.

The boy thrashed and Mike almost lost his grip. Foot on the running board, he climbed into the truck. He held the boy's arm so tight he feared he'd break a bone. The runner's hissing mouth snapped at the boy's leg. He wore boots but it still might bite through. "Get him under his arms," he said to Imogen. "I can get that thing off, but I have to let go to do it."

Her eyes flashed at him, frightened. Then a brutal determination supplanted the fear. She let go of the boy's jacket, trusting Mike's grip, and hoisted herself further over the lip of the seat. She slid her hands beneath the screaming boy's shoulders, wrapping them under his arms like fishhooks.

Mike let go. He wrapped his left hand in the seat belt and gripped the front seat headrest in his right. Then he hoisted himself into the truck, legs first. As soon as his butt hit the edge of the seat, he kicked. The flat of his left boot hit the runner's head, snapping it back. The runner's grunts turned to agitated hisses as it turned its attention to Mike.

"That's right," he grunted. "Look at me."

Mike kicked again, the bottom of his boot hitting the runner full in the face. Its grip loosened, and the child flew by at the edge of Mike's vision. The runner growled in fury at the loss of its prey. Mike kicked again, with both legs now that the boy was out of the way. Bones crunched and the runner's head lolled sharply toward its shoulder, then slid out of the truck.

Mike twisted and jumped out. By the time he righted himself, the runner reappeared. Head slumped against its shoulder, it vaulted across the seat. Mike slammed the door shut. The zombie hit the window, cracks spiderwebbing across the glass.

Imogen was halfway up the steep side of the ditch, dragging the children through the snow. Mike swooped up the little girl. Imogen hoisted the boy up without breaking stride. The shouting had died down. They crested the top of the ditch, where downed forms littered the ground. Mike couldn't tell if they were his friends or runners. He gripped Imogen's upper arm, dragging her and the boy through the raging storm. The glow of the truck's headlights beckoned him like a moth to a porch light. When they reached the truck, he yanked the driver's door open. He thrust the girl he carried inside. Imogen handed off the boy, who Mike slid across the seat beside the girl. Imogen was turning away when he caught her arm. Even with the bulky coat, she was tiny.

"Get in."

Imogen resisted, fighting his grip. "I have to help."

"You have to keep them safe."

Through the swirling snow her eyes met his with a fierce desperation. "I can do both!"

"But I can't!" he said, strong-arming her into the truck. He didn't care what she wanted. He needed steel and glass between Imogen and the threat.

"Stop it," she cried, fighting him while he shoved her behind the wheel.

Their eyes locked, the amber irises of Imogen's eyes a pale

mirror of his own. Her lips parted, a soundless protest hovering between them. In the glow of the dome light, the tears in her eyes glittered. Mike saw, as if for the first time, how beautiful Imogen was. He'd never seen her—truly seen her—like he did in this moment. He hadn't let himself see her like he did now—through the eyes of a man who might want her—until he might never see her again. He memorized her face... the almond-shaped eyes, the button nose, cupid's bow lips, and the deep buckeye-brown skin that had caught his eye that first day on the bridge.

"If you need to leave, you leave."

Then he slammed the door shut.

He struggled through the still falling snow toward a shout. The big guy, Jim, thrashed with a runner. It wasn't as tall but had knocked him back. He raised his hand and a shot rang out, a bullet piercing the runner's eye. It crumpled to the ground and Jim fell to his knees. "No... Oh, no! Heather... I didn't mean it. I didn't mean it..."

Jim knew the woman this zombie had been. He wasn't getting up but leaning over her, pushing the wet hair out of her face. Bec and Kevin, with Jeffrey between them, stumbled over. Mike almost passed out with relief.

"Where's the other guy?"

"In our truck," Kevin said.

"Go, I'll get him," Mike said, gesturing to Jim, though a smaller, harder part of him wanted to leave Jim there. This chase Jim had led them on had put almost everyone he cared about in danger. He watched Jim for a moment, on his knees in the snow, the storm howling around them as he wept over a woman he'd cared about. But instead of hating him, Mike's heart ached.

He pulled Jim from the runner that had been someone he'd loved, Jim too dazed to resist. Mike turned him around and shoved him hard toward the truck. "Get in!"

Abruptly, the wind died down. For a moment the world became silent and white, the heavy snow falling straight down.

Underneath the silence, a buzz hummed from farther down the road. Then the wind returned, taking the buzz with it, but Mike knew what he'd heard and what it was.

He followed Jim, making sure all his friends were in the other truck before opening the passenger door of his own. The smell of wet leather and denim, of terror and sweat, hit him like an ocean wave that knocks you so hard you don't know what's up and what's down. He got Jim seated beside the children. A moment later he thumped into his own seat behind the steering wheel, Imogen beside him with the boy on her lap.

Mike turned the key, wincing at the grating, mechanical shriek, since the truck was still running. The little boy's hair was wet from melting snow. If he'd had a hat, he didn't now. The girl had spilled over onto Jim's lap. On autopilot, Jim patted her shoulder. Imogen's shoulders slumped, her coat askew. She looked up at him, her pupils so dilated only a sliver of the amber iris remained, and a fierce protectiveness surged in Mike's chest.

Something banged on the truck and everyone yelped, the children crying out. Mike squinted in the side mirror. A runner had reached the tailgate and was working its way around the truck's rear quarter panel. He hit the gas too hard, sending the tires spinning. Tearing his eyes from the mirror, he eased up on the gas. The truck moved forward and the runner, arm outstretched, missed catching hold of the slick metal.

The truck inched forward and the other followed. They outpaced the runner quickly as it floundered through the snow. Mike focused his attention on the road he could barely see. Before, he'd driven far too fast. Now, he was afraid to, terrified of sliding off the road and getting stuck. There were zombies after them and the howling snowstorm bearing down. He couldn't afford another mistake.

Mike pressed on the accelerator, the speedometer inching up to fifteen miles per hour; still too fast but nothing like the earlier reckless pursuit. He would slow down when they outpaced the runners some more. Gripping the steering wheel tight, he started to shake, the far side of the adrenaline rush hitting him hard.

Imogen melted against him, her head heavy on his shoulder. He tried to speak but his throat wouldn't work. Finally, voice hoarse with emotion, Mike said, "Let's go home."

CHAPTER 39
IMOGEN

THE PEALS OF LAUGHTER WERE LIKE THE AIR—BRIGHT AND SHARP. Billy flew through the air in a soft arc, landing on his back and disappearing into the white fluff of snow. Mike waded to him through drifts deep enough to cover his knees, Carolyn following in his wake. Imogen could hear the girl's muffled but excited chatter and suspected she was begging Mike to throw her again. Billy struggled like an overturned tortoise, a glimpse of hand or foot peeking into view. Mike bent down and extended a hand, pulling the snow-covered boy to his feet. Then he plucked Carolyn up by an arm and a leg. Squeals of delight filled the air as he spun around once and sent her flying.

Imogen smiled, but underneath the pleasure of watching the children play, a deep ache percolated. She'd had the first snowball fight of her life with Zach, on the grounds of the Cathedral of Learning on the University of Pittsburgh campus. Even after living in England and seeing the real thing, the forty-two-story gothic-style building had left Imogen's jaw scraping the ground. Zach had been the instigator of that afternoon's adventure. Remembering it now, she could feel the icy snow trickling down her neck where it had gotten past her scarf. Afterward, they'd tucked themselves away in one of the cathedral's many alcoves ringing the edge of the ground floor's Great Hall, eating Suzy

Q's and drinking vending machine cocoa, while they waited for their shoes, hats, and gloves to dry on the scalding radiators.

She was miles from the places she'd gone with her friend. That didn't stop everything around her trigging an avalanche of memories she treasured that now hurt. She smiled as she watched Mike and the children. The blizzard, and the frigid temperatures that followed, had turned out to be good for more than thwarting zombies.

Imogen straightened from the library window, wincing as she did. She rubbed her lower back with her hand, the sore spot still tweaking a week after the truck slid into the ditch. The storm had raged for three days, leaving four feet of snow in its wake. They hadn't been able to look for Betty and Zach, nor travel to the Safe Zone where Jim and Anthony had lived with their families.

But today that would change. Once the storm passed, Mike, Kevin, and Jim—one of the men who'd tried to help Imogen, Carolyn, and Billy that first day of the storm—had made their way to a cabin two miles distant. Not long after they arrived at the lodge, they'd found snowmobiles there. In retrospect, everyone wished they'd brought the snowmobiles to the lodge, but no one had known how to drive one, and they didn't seem well maintained. Getting them into good repair hadn't been important compared to the more pressing task of gathering supplies. But Jim could operate a snowmobile, so he and Mike had worked to get them running. They weren't going out ill-equipped and unprepared, but Imogen wasn't happy about Mike going along. She'd said nothing, of course. She knew Mike didn't *want* to go, but he had the most experience working with engines. Snowmobiles weren't the same as cars but close enough that his skills could make or break the trip to the Safe Zone.

Imogen looked up at the games on top of the bookshelf in the library. The lodge hadn't been built with short people in mind. Normally, she'd get a chair to stand on, but her wrenched back wouldn't like that.

"Want me to get that for you, hon?"

Clyde was already rising from the rocker that he'd pulled over to the bay window beside the fireplace. He'd spent a lot of time there, staring into space. Clyde had been the one to suggest they take the snowmobiles to the Safe Zone before looking for Betty and Zach, who by this time could be anywhere. Everyone could see how much the ruthless pragmatism had cost him. His jolly demeanor had become somber, and the twinkle in his eyes, which Imogen had thought was Clyde's baseline, was absent.

"Thank you," she said, stepping out of his way. "Maybe we can get in a game after the children come in."

Clyde retrieved the game and set it on the little green desk tucked in the corner. The Tiffany-style lamp on the desk didn't work anymore but the charm remained. "Playing in the snow tires them out, all right. Our girls were the same."

A sheen of tears filled his eyes, magnified by his glasses. Imogen took his hand and squeezed. Clyde squeezed back, his eyes fixed on nothing as he blinked the tears away. Zach wasn't Imogen's partner of forty years, but she knew something of Clyde's pain. The agony of not knowing what had happened to Zach and Betty only compounded their absence.

She left Clyde to himself—he didn't seem to want to talk about Betty yet—and walked through the main room to the kitchen. Bec and Jeffrey were finishing up their breakfast at the kitchen table. Amy stood at the first of the three sinks, washing dishes. Kevin and Jim had gone outside earlier to get the snowmobiles ready. At the top of the stairs, she saw a figure from the corner of her eye. She turned her head in time to see Jay disappearing into the upstairs hall. He'd been keeping to himself, solitary to the point of being reclusive. The dynamic—most everyone angry at him and he so defensive it bordered on hostile —couldn't go on. Everyone knew it, but no one seemed to know how to fix it.

She lowered herself to the bench across the table from Bec

and Jeffrey, trying to hide a wince. Bec jumped to her feet. "I'll get you a chair. Benches are terrible when you have a bad back."

Bec pulled a heavy oak chair over. The dark-brown wood was polished smooth, with rounded arms and thick spindles in the back. They reminded Imogen of old-fashioned library or train station chairs. Barring a disaster, the chairs would outlast them all.

"Thank you, Bec," she said, more comfortable than she'd ever be on the bench. She should have just asked someone to pull the chair over but hated to appear as if she couldn't take care of herself.

"They'll be leaving soon," Jeffrey said, polishing off the last bite of his oatmeal.

Imogen nodded. "It was kind of Kevin to help prep the snow-mobiles so Mike can spend time with Carolyn and Billy."

Jeffrey elbowed Bec in the ribs, his eyebrows raised, as if he expected her to say something. She rolled her eyes, dismissing him with a snort. Mike and the children had become fast friends. Maybe it was because his nieces had been around the same age. Maybe Mike reminded them of their father. Maybe he was just good with children. Whatever the reason, watching him with Carolyn and Billy gave Imogen's heart a squeeze.

Amy set the last plate on the dish rack and joined them at the table. "Is Anthony still upstairs resting?"

Bec nodded. "He had a headache so he went to lie down." She lowered her voice. "He's so upset that he can't go to the Safe Zone."

"Maybe he'll join us for the story this evening," Amy said. "It might take his mind off things."

They had finished *The Golden Compass* again, rereading it for Carolyn's and Billy's benefit, and moved on to the *The Subtle Knife*, the second book in the series. Amy took part in the house-hold more than she had before the library. She had a knack for doing different voices for the characters and had become every-one's favorite reader. She'd even offered to make some proper curtains, rather than the makeshift assortment they'd pulled together. The back door opened, followed by a vigorous stomping of boots. They could hear Mike's mutters from the kitchen table while he wrested his boots from his feet. He padded into the kitchen, coat over his arm. Snowflakes melted in his hair and still clung to his coat despite obvious attempts to dust them off. He beamed, his cheeks flushed crimson.

"Those two are little nutcases."

Bec grinned. "Says the man throwing them around like sacks of flour."

Mike squeezed Imogen's shoulder as he walked past her on his way to the front door to hang up his coat. He had to detour two steps to do it. It was a small thing, but made her feel looked after. She was sure everyone noticed. After her conversation with Zach, she felt self-conscious. They'd all fussed over her since the harrowing encounter with the runners. She didn't know if she'd wrenched her back in the crash or fighting the runners. In the end, it didn't matter. The result was the same.

Bec tortured Imogen with trigger point massages, the technique picked up from a friend who'd been a massage therapist. Everyone had been brilliant about packing snow into plastic bags or getting ice from the creek, so she could ice her back. Mike wasn't doing anything different than the others, but the way he looked after her was different. He was unobtrusive but always seemed to be around when she needed something—an arm to lean on or a drink or food before she knew she wanted it. Every small gesture, no different than what the others did, felt loaded in a way it hadn't before.

I'm not even sure he knows it himself, but he likes you, Zach's voice echoed at the back of her brain.

Mike joined them, leaning against the wood slab counter below the windows that looked over the porch. "I don't think I've ever seen snow like this. It's worse than Snowmageddon in… Was it '93?"

He looked to the other Pittsburghers for confirmation. Amy,

who was a few years older than Mike so old enough to remember the famed snowstorm, nodded. "It was '93."

"That closed down the city for a week."

"Snow is always the best when you're a kid," Bec said. "I prayed for snow days."

The others agreed. Imogen couldn't relate. She hadn't grown up with snow. Icy conditions sometimes occurred in the south of England, but snow was rare. There was also the minor detail of attending boarding school. Even if there had been lots of snow, snow days wouldn't have been a thing.

"I packed up some food for your journey, Mike," Jeffrey said. "It's in your backpacks."

Mike nodded, but his and everyone else's attention was drawn to the front porch. Jim and Kevin walked across it with heavy stomps to shake loose the snow. A gust of frigid air accompanied them through the door.

Mike said, "Are we ready to go?" Jim nodded. "I'll go change into that snowsuit. Be back in a minute."

A flurry of activity erupted with their departure now imminent. Jeffrey ran down the list of food he had put in their packs with Jim, and Amy reminded Jim about the thermoses of hot tea. Jim shifted uncomfortably under the attention. The past week had been an agony for him and Anthony. They hadn't been able to go back and check to see if more of the runners they'd killed on the road that night were people from the Safe Zone. They could find the truck more easily, but the bodies buried under the snow would be another thing altogether.

Jim knew his wife had been one of them, however. Imogen didn't know him well, but she could tell he was affected by having to kill the zombie she'd become. Given that, and the runners not being dressed for the weather, the likelihood that their Safe Zone had been compromised, if not overrun, was never in doubt.

Imogen caught Bec's hand after she'd stacked some dishes

out of the way on the counter. In a low voice, she said, "Will you help me with my boots?"

"You can't walk them down, Imogen."

"I know that," she answered. "I'll just go to the top of the stairs."

Mike returned, and he and Jim collected last-minute items. He raised an eyebrow at Imogen when he saw she wore boots and a coat. "Where do you think you're going?"

"I'm walking you out. I have a wrenched back, not a broken leg."

He looked like he wanted to protest but didn't. "Okay. Let's go out the back door so I can say bye to the kids."

The air bit her face and ears so she pulled up the hood of her coat. She let Mike help her down the steps. The children waded over when they saw them, their faces flushed but now pinched with anxiety.

"I'll be back in a couple of days," Mike said. "You'll be good for Imogen, right?"

They both nodded, so grave it made Imogen's heart ache. Mike dropped to his knees and pulled them both to him. They looked small in his arms as she watched their three heads put together.

"You're coming back?" Billy whispered. His mouth had turned down. The uncertainty—the dashed hope in his voice— painful to hear.

"You bet I'll be back," Mike said breezily. "We have a snow fort to build. And Thanksgiving is coming up, even if it feels like Christmas."

The boy almost grinned, reassured by Mike's confidence. Carolyn hugged him again, not letting go until he threatened to throw her in the snow.

"That wasn't much of a threat," Imogen said, after he had tossed both children into the frozen, fluffy flakes.

He flashed her a grin. "I know, but it makes them so happy."

Imogen looked down to hide her smile. Carolyn and Billy

weren't the only ones the snowy aeronautics made happy. She followed Mike through the shoveled snow, its height on either side of the path comical, to the top of the winding stairs. Jim was already down at the partially torn-apart parking area, its purpose more skillfully obscured by the snow than anything they'd done. Anxiety coursed through her, making her stomach churn. What if Mike was hurt miles from help in the cold and snow? Billy wasn't the only one fearful about whether or not Mike would return.

"If we can't make it, we'll turn around," he said, reading her face at a glance when they reached the top of the steps. "Jim said there's plenty of food at the Safe Zone and God knows we need it—gasoline, too. We won't get stuck there."

Imogen nodded, trying to make the motion smooth and easy because she felt like a puppet on strings being pulled by a last-minute replacement for the puppet master.

"I'll be back before you know it," he said, more gently now. "I'm not missing Thanksgiving, especially not this year."

He pulled her close, enveloping her in his arms. She held on, relaxing into his embrace, into the solidity of his body. Even through the thick layers of the snowsuit, his lean frame against hers made Imogen feel like she had something real to hold on to in this changed world, that their friendship was corporeal instead of an intangible sentiment. The air cooled her neck when Mike pushed back the hood of her coat. His lips brushed the crown of her head, there and gone in a moment, so soft and light she could have mistaken the kiss for a breeze.

A soft laugh of surprise escaped her, loosening a jumble of emotions that pulled her into a whirlwind, into a life that she somehow knew would be changed even more when she broke free of it. The feelings were out of place, out of order, mixed up in a way she didn't understand. Comfort. Worry for his safety. Grief for everything and everyone they'd lost. Gratitude that Mike saw himself as a partner in all of this—these children they'd taken in, this place, this group of people who were becoming a family. And something else, too. Something small and tentative that felt muddled up, both part of and separate from everything else. It was all too much to bear on her own. Mike made it feel manageable.

He let her go, but slowly, as if he had nowhere to be nor miles to travel. She squinted up at him as she broke the embrace, swatting at her hair which had blown across her face. Mike tucked it behind her ear, the leather of his glove cool, the look in his eyes one she didn't want to parse.

"I hope you're not getting sentimental on me," she said, a note of tartness in her voice. She took a deep breath, trying to get back on an even keel after the unexpected rush of emotions.

He smiled, the curve of his lips and that dimple that went on for days so damn appealing she almost couldn't stand it. His molasses-brown eyes twinkled. "Maybe just a little." Then he sobered. The dimple vanished. "Everything will be all right, Imogen. I know you're worried, but trust me, okay?"

She took a deep breath, afraid that if she spoke he'd hear her fears and worries. Normally, she was better at this. She should tell him she had all the confidence in the world that this trip was no big deal. She should make him feel at ease, assuring him that everything at the lodge was okay and would be until he returned —that she was okay—so he could concentrate on the task ahead. It was what he wanted to hear.

"I'm not worried, not really."

Mike's head cocked to one side. He looked at her like he'd always done, and not. Something was different. *Mike* was different since they'd returned to the lodge. He seemed cautious, almost reserved, with a kind of watchfulness that hadn't been there before. And because of Zach being such an absolute prat she was reading into every look and gesture. It was driving her mad.

"Is that true or what you think I want to hear?" Imogen blinked at him, surprised, and opened her mouth to deny it. Mike touched his gloved index finger to her lips, her breath frosting around it like smoke. "It's okay if you feel differently, Imogen. I'll believe enough for both of us."

Jim's snowmobile rumbled to life. Mike glanced over his shoulder, then said, "I better go."

"Please be careful. Try not to crash," she said as he went down the stairs.

He stopped and looked back when he reached the first landing where the stairs turned left at ninety degrees. "I'll drive fast and take chances."

His bark of laughter let her know she'd made a face, giving him the reaction he'd been looking for. Just as he turned to continue down the stairs, an unguarded fondness filled his glinting eyes. His smile—which she'd always thought handsome —lightened, becoming carefree. Her breath caught when she realized she was glimpsing the young man Mike had been before his parents died, before the responsibilities of adulthood were thrust upon him far too early. She'd never thought of Mike as somber. Now, she could see how that life he hadn't wanted nor been ready for had sobered him, had crowded out the fanciful to make room for the pragmatic. How cruel, to have been on the verge of following his long-deferred dreams... Marrying the woman he loved, living the life he'd always longed for, his familial duties faithfully discharged, only to have it snatched away. The younger Mike she'd glimpsed hadn't adapted to the changes, and the responsibilities that came along with them, with the quiet competence of the Mike she'd come to know. How he must have raged at the unfairness of his life being turned upside down, never knowing that crucible would forge him into someone they all counted on now.

She watched him finish the stairs and cross the bridge. He joined Jim and they spoke for a moment while Mike shrugged his backpack over his shoulders. Then he grabbed the helmet on the seat of the snowmobile, pulled it over his head, securing the strap under his chin, and mounted the machine. The engine rumbled to life. Jim gave Mike a thumbs-up, which Mike returned. Engines revving, they pulled onto the ribbon of snowed-in road, disappearing from sight long before the sound faded.

Imogen stood at the top of the stairs long after her feet had gone cold. *I'll drive fast and take chances… Smart-ass.* But a smile curled the corners of her mouth, making the Cupid's bow of her upper lip deepen.

Billy and Carolyn's chatter from behind the lodge had an argumentative quality now. Time to take them inside, warm them up, and fix something to eat, then play a game of Sorry. She looked through the barren trees laden with snow and the ice-rimmed creek splashing below. The snow brightened everything, banishing the gray-brown drab of the Western Pennsylvania winter. From the corner of her eye, she spied a bobcat bounding through the snow at the edge of the road that lay snug beneath the icy frosting. Like a porpoise it hopped high, skimming the top, before plunging again into the deep drifts. The cat's coat was tawny, spotted white and black and tan, much browner than the more common silvery-gray. Long black tufts sprouted from the tips of its pointed ears like flags.

"No," she breathed, light-headed.

That wasn't a bobcat. She was looking at an Iberian lynx.

Imogen sagged against the tree at the top of the stairs, the release of anxiety so deep she'd mistaken it for bone melting away. A smile spread across her face and she laughed, the warmth spreading through her chest as shiny as a new button.

"Freddy…" she whispered, awe unfurling inside her.

The lynx stopped. As if he'd heard her, he looked up the bluff, right at the lodge. He cocked his head, snow frosting his thick fur. Imogen waved her arms above her head, ignoring the discomfort it caused.

"Freddy! I'm here!"

He looked at her a moment longer, then resumed bounding alongside the road before veering back into the forest. She watched him navigate the snow and fallen logs, blending with the gray of boulders and brown of tree trunks until he vanished.

Freddy was here. Were Isabella and their kittens with him? "They have to be," she whispered. "They must be with him, surely."

Her lynxes were *alive*… By some miracle they had survived and somehow, against every conceivable odd, they had followed her.

"I have to tell Mike."

The crush of disappointment when she remembered he was gone felt like the twist of a knife. Things were better when Mike was here—*she* was better. The laughter felt more genuine, the work less arduous, her anxiety easier to bear. The quiet moments, too, were more. What that more was she couldn't say, but she felt it all the same.

The wind picked up, blowing snow into the snowmobile tracks and filling them in like they'd never been there at all. As if the men who had made them were never coming back. Imogen felt a flutter in her chest and a hard clench in her stomach that hit like a punch.

"You better come back," she whispered. Now that Mike was gone, she could say what she hadn't before because he might not agree. Because he'd try to talk her out of it. Because she didn't understand what she was feeling herself. "I don't want to do this without you."

She took a deep breath, blinking back tears. Then she turned away from the road below and all it represented in this moment —Mike and her lynxes and her hopes and fears for them both— to follow the sound of Billy's and Carolyn's voices.

THE END

———

Pre-order Undead Impact

(Steel City Apocalypse, Book 3)
For more information: www.amgeever.com

Sign up for my Stories from the Edge newsletter at http://bit.ly/ newsamgeev. Newsletter subscribers enjoy exclusive pre-sales from my online store. You can also find out where you can see me at live events, get advance notice of new releases, and find other special goodies just for newsletter subscribers.

Keep reading for the Sneak Peek first chapter of Undead Impact, Book 3 of the Steel City Apocalypse, at the end of this book!

ACKNOWLEDGMENTS

Thanks to my readers, who make all the tears and grind worth it. I hope you enjoyed reading about 'Our Gang' as much as I enjoyed writing their adventures.

Alpha & Beta Readers: *Sarah Lyons Fleming, Rhonna Woodie, & Roseann Powell*, for helping make this book the best it can be. **Editing:** *Kimberly at Kimberly Dawn Editing*; **Creatives:** *Molly Phipps of We Got You Covered Book Design* for the great covers.

Very Special Thanks: *Arthur Crivella* for your generous loan of 'The Lodge.' My Apocalyptic (and Romance) Babes, *Lindsey Pogue and Camille Picott*, for just being you. *Rachel McNorton*, for being ***the best*** Comic Con wingwoman in the world, and one of the best nieces in the world, too ('one of' because all of my nieces —Jodi, Carolyn, Rachel, Maxine, and Lorelei—are in a dead heat tie).

As always, *my wonderful family*, whether by birth, marriage, or honorary association. I'm writing these acknowledgments on my dad's 89th birthday, so Happy Birthday, Daddy! I love you so much!!!

And Drew, who I'd follow to the ends of the earth (and soon will).

. . .

— MARCH 2, 2023

SNEAK PEEK: UNDEAD IMPACT - UNPROOFED & UNEDITED

CHAPTER ONE

ARAMINTA

As Araminta tugged her carry on bag over a bump, the small suitcase twisted, turning sideways and forcing her to stop.

"Bloody hell," she said, so frustrated she wanted to scream. She pressed the button on the grip and slammed the pull handle down, then picked her bag up by the top handle and continued her headlong dash.

"I'm going to miss my flight," she muttered under her breath. If only she could travel by Floo Network, like Harry Potter and his friends. She didn't have a fireplace in her flat, but she'd move if it meant she could use that magical travel apparatus.

In the press of the crowded airport, a creepy crawly feeling made her skin prickle. She hated the tight confines of crowds, and wasn't looking forward to being packed into the plane like cattle in a cattle car. But if she wanted to see Imogen, she had to do it. She wormed her way through the other travelers, trying not to bump into anyone while leaving a string of 'Pardon me' and 'Excuse me' and 'So sorry,' in her wake. As of a minute ago she'd tacked 'I'm going to miss my flight' at the end.

"This is the final boarding call for Delta flight 5993, now boarding in terminal three," the overhead speakers announced.

Araminta picked up the pace, pushing her tired body to comply. She caught a glimpse of herself in a shop's plate glass window and grimaced.

I look a fright.

A wild cloud of dark curls bobbed around her head as she ran. Her eyes were still bloodshot despite the drops she'd used, and she would probably be charged a fee for the bags under her eyes. Between scouring hers and Graham's laptops and back up drives for the missing report, then packing and scrambling to get to Heathrow, she'd never gone to bed. But she'd found the bloody report Graham had accidentally erased on a backup drive, which meant she had just enough time to catch her flight. Maybe.

Her anxiety had only worsened at the Delta ticket counter, where it had taken an ice age to rebook the ticket. She'd tried to rebook over the phone in the taxi, and then while on the train from Euston station to Heathrow, but she kept getting the 'All circuits are busy' recording. The change fee and the fare difference ended up being over a thousand pounds. She'd taken the hit and would think about her ever growing credit card balance later. She still hadn't let Imogen know that she would be arriving tomorrow.

"This is the final boarding call for Delta flight 5993 to New York. I repeat, this is the final boarding call for Delta flight 5993. All passengers report to the gate for immediate boarding."

She stumbled, almost falling, when she hit a stationary object. No, not a stationary object, but a small child. The announcement echoed in her ears as she stooped to pick the child up. The little girl's blue eyes had gone wide. Her lips were pursed, as if she were weighing whether or not this merited crying.

"Oh, God! I'm so sorry," Araminta said "Are you all right?"

Settling on not crying, the child nodded. Araminta grabbed her bag and sprinted away.

"Hey! Stop! You knocked my child over!"

Araminta ignored the angry voice. She had checked on the child, who was fine, and she was going to miss her plane for her trouble. She saw the gate ahead and poured on a burst of speed. Imogen was right; she really should take on an exercise regime. Her heart sank when she saw the gate agents looking pleased with themselves, as if they'd just finished up a job well done.

"Has the plane left?" Araminta cried.

The female gate agent pick up the phone, asking if the door could still be held. The male agent, so tall and gaunt he looked unwell, reached for her boarding pass. "Run," he said.

Araminta waved the boarding pass over the scanner, ignoring the man's outstretched hand. She thundered down the gangway. When she saw the half-closed door she shouted, "Wait! Wait!"

The door pushed open enough for a flight attendant to lean out. She said, "Hurry up! We were just closing the door."

"Oh, thank you! Thank you so much," Araminta said, breathless, as she squeezed past the flight attendant. "Thank you so much."

She stopped at the head of the near aisle, gasping for breath. She dropped her carry on case and extended the handle so she could pull the bag behind her. The flight attendant looked at her boarding pass and frowned.

"You're going to have to check that. The overhead bins in coach are full and this is a bulkhead seat. There's no under seat storage there."

"Just let me check, please."

Not waiting for an answer, Araminta started down spacious aisle of First Class. The individual seats that turned into lie flat beds, each angled away from the one beside it and with screens along the top to ensure privacy, looked like self-contained capsules of luxury. The overhead announcement informing passengers of their imminent departure buzzed in the background.

Araminta looked at her ticket to find her seat number: 20-B. The extra thousand pounds had bought her a bulkhead seat in the first row of what passed for a slightly better version of cattle car, which the airline euphemistically called Premium Coach. Apart from the seat reclining three centimeters more, and seats that almost made one not feel squished like a sardine in a tin, there wasn't much difference between premium and regular coach. You did disembark the plane sooner. You were also close enough to glimpse into First Class and see just how crappy your overpriced ticket was.

At least we won't have to cancel our trip.

She smiled at a woman's upturned face in the middle section of luxury capsules, surprise making her take a second glance. The woman was quite large, very high-end fashionably dressed, and looked unwell. Sweat beaded her brow. She breathed through her mouth just shy of panting, and her face was flushed crimson.

"Are you all right?"

The woman looked up. Her brown, piggy eyes narrowed as she inspected Araminta. Araminta could see the moment the woman decided she was beneath her notice. Then she looked away, not bothering to reply.

Have a dreadful flight, Araminta thought, annoyance getting the better of her. A dreadful flight would match the woman's attitude, but she knew she shouldn't wish such things upon anyone. She tugged on her bag, the first aisle of Premium Coach just beyond the toilets. She stopped, waiting almost a full minute for the man two luxury capsules behind the rude woman to close the overhead bin. When he turned to take his seat, he said, "Oh, pardon me. I didn't see you there."

He was tall, with sandy blond hair and a smile with teeth so white they could trigger a migraine. Araminta's perfunctory smile in return was just polite enough. She was exhausted, winded, and tired of dealing with crowds of people she didn't know. She reached 20-B, pleased to see it was not only a bulkhead seat but on the aisle. A bulkhead seat saved her from crawling over people when she had to go to the toilet—which she loathed—and was why she preferred sitting on the aisle. She dropped her purse in her seat, opened the overhead bin, and groaned.

"Bloody hell."

The flight attendant had been right. There was no room. She wrestled the door of the overstuffed bin closed, no mean feat given how short she was, and turned to the center section of seats. She tried two more overhead bins. In both she was confronted with a row of wheels from the bottom of other people's carry on suitcases with jackets and purses stuffed between them.

She sighed, resigning herself to checking the bag and missing her connection in New York. She rifled through her purse to find her phone, water bottle, and lip balm, and then somehow crammed the purse into the overhead bin. She flopped into her seat, leaving her carry on suitcase in the aisle beside her so the flight attendant could check it. Another £40 charge for that, but at least the scolding from the flight attendant would be free. She looked at the first aid kit attached to the bulkhead wall. Did they charge for using that too, she wondered.

"Excuse me." She looked up, expecting to see a flight attendant, but it was the man from the last row of First Class peeking over the privacy screen of his capsule. "There's room in my bin, if you'd like to put your bag there."

"Really? You'd do that?"

"No problem at all," he said, smiling as he steeped into the aisle.

Araminta sprang to her feet when she realized he was coming to fetch the bag himself. "No, no, I'll get it." He backed up and opened the bin for her. "This is so kind of you. I might just make my connection in New York now."

"The overhead bins are awful when you're in coach," he said.

He extended his hand. "Thomas Blackwell, pleased to meet you."

Araminta took in his bespoke suit trousers, thousand pound shoes, buttery silk shirt and conservative tie as she shook hands and introduced herself. She was pretty sure Thomas Blackwell hadn't flown coach in years, if ever. She pegged him as an investment banker who worked in 'The City,' aware that she was guilty of stereotyping, but he had that look. She'd gone on a date with an investment banker once, and they were not her type. He's probably going to want my number, she thought, gripping the bag to lift and stow.

"Ma'am, you can't do that."

A male flight attendant had appeared, as if he'd materialized from thin air. A disapproving scow marred his otherwise pleasant face.

"Pardon me?" Araminta said.

"You can't use an overhead bin in a different class compartment," the man said. "I'll see if I can still check your bag, or if there's anywhere to put it. Who let you bring it aboard?"

Scarcely before Araminta's brain caught up to this development, Thomas said, "It's not a problem. We're traveling together but couldn't get both seats up here."

Araminta blinked in surprise.

"I— Well— I'm sorry," the flight attendant said. "But those are the rules." He didn't look the least bit sorry. He looked as if he was enjoying his little power trip.

"I'm sure you can make an exception, just this once," Thomas said. He oozed entitled charm like some people oozed desperation. "We'll miss our connection otherwise."

The flight attendant looked at Araminta askance. He didn't believe Thomas, that much was clear. But he couldn't really argue the point without calling Thomas a liar, and calling luxury capsule passengers liars was not the done thing. Before the flight attendant could reply, Thomas took the bag from Araminta, stowed it in the bin, and clicked it shut. Thomas expected to be deferred to and right now, Araminta was glad of it.

Then, to her utter astonishment, Thomas squeezed her shoulder and said, "Are you sure you don't want to swap seats with me, love?"

It was all she could do to keep her mouth from falling open. He was taking this charade a bit far, but she wondered what he'd do if she said yes. "No, no. Really. You're tired, and you need to be rested for your meeting when we land."

A smile curled the corner of Thomas's mouth. Then he winked and disappeared into his capsule.

That's worth giving him my number when he asks.

"Please take your seat, miss," the flight attendant said, shooting Araminta a dirty look as she sidled past him.

She dropped into her seat, relieved, and buckled her seatbelt. The young woman in the seat beside her smiled a greeting. She picked up her phone and sent a quick text to Imogen to let her know she was coming, then switched off her phone. She flipped the top of the water bottle, squeezing some into her mouth as the plane pushed away from the gate, then shoved it between her leg and the seat. Even as petite as she was, it squeezed her tighter into the seat. If this was what passed as premium economy, she didn't like to think about this long a flight in the regular one.

Weariness settled on her body as heavy as lead. Now that she'd finished her mile long obstacle course through the airport, the lack of sleep was catching up with her. She closed her eyes as the plane lifted off, hoping she might get a little sleep. Sleep usually eluded her on planes, but it never hurt to hope.

The young woman beside her nudged her elbow against Araminta's arm, impinging on the armrest between them. Araminta ignored her. If her seat mate wanted the armrest, she should have claimed it sooner. Groans and the low rustling of the passengers in the dark plane reminded Araminta of the babbling brook recording she listened to at night to fall asleep. Just as she felt herself drifting away, she heard a familiar voice.

"Excuse me."

She opened her eyes, expecting a flight attendant, but it was Thomas Blackwell from First Class. He held a cut crystal cocktail glass in his hand. A wedge of lime floated among the ice cubes.

"I thought you might like a drink."

"Oh," she said, surprised.

"I hope gin and tonic is alright. Sorry about the ice. Americans put ice in everything."

Araminta smiled, accepting the drink. The smoothed indentations of the crystal pressed against her fingers. "That's very kind of you, but you'd better take your seat before the flight attendant gives you a dressing down."

"See you later," Thomas said, the dazzling pearly whites flashing at her. He paused before disappearing through the curtain separating the peasants from the quality and added, a mischievous twinkle lighting in his eyes, "If you want to swap seats for a bit, I'm just over here."

He was definitely going to ask her for her number.

I could do worse, she thought, squeezing the lime into her drink. The faintly medicinal taste of the gin had a nice bite under the botanicals as she sipped the icy cocktail. Sometimes, cold drinks transported her back to before she left Tanzania to attend school in England. Cold drinks went hand in glove with waves of heat rippling from the ground of the wide open vistas surrounding the preserve that had also been her home. Cold drinks tasted so much better there, though this was pretty close.

Once they reached cruising altitude, the same flight attendant collected the cut crystal glass from her, his exasperation plain when Araminta explained that her friend in First Class had brought it back to her. She reclined her seat, which didn't go back very much. The additional thousand pounds had given her a bulkhead seat and three centimeters of additional pitch. Still, it probably wasn't even half of what Thomas's seat in First Class must have cost him. One day she'd fly in a luxury capsule, but that day had not yet arrived.

Araminta relaxed into the seat, weary to the marrow of her bones. The lack of sleep, discombobulation of her hectic journey to Heathrow, and steeplechase through the terminal to catch her plane receded. She relaxed into the kindness of a stranger, and the knowledge that she'd see Imogen tomorrow.

As the plane banked, the curtains separating premium economy from First Class parted enough for Araminta to glimpse a flight attendant. The woman pick up the speaker system handset on the bulkhead wall behind Thomas Black-well's seat.

"Ladies and gentleman, if there are any medical professionals flying with us today, please press the call button to summon a flight attendant. Thank you very much for your assistance."

ABOUT THE AUTHOR

A.M. Geever lives in her hometown of Pittsburgh, Pennsylvania. An avid reader of science fiction and fantasy from an early age, the only job she ever wanted—besides being a writer—was to be a Star Fleet Officer.

She is woefully unprepared for the zombie apocalypse. The idea of becoming a zombie because the car runs out of gas is the only thing that gets her to the gas station when the gauge hits a quarter of a tank; otherwise, that Subaru would be running on fumes. She loves her critters (River Song, a Queensland Red Heeler, and cats Chiana, Hitachi-san, Buttercup, and Boo), her kick ass family, movies, punk rock, traveling, family stories, political discussions over countless cups of tea, otters, unions, Ireland, tiger, sloths, cooking and baking (though the latter makes her fat anymore), and the not-so-little elf who cleans the kitchen most nights.

When not dreaming up the end of the world, she spends most of her time with her family and fur babies, and loves to travel to exotic locales.

For more information, check out her website, www. amgeever.com